Mercenary

R. J. Connor

**TOP HAT
BOOKS**

Winchester, UK
Washington, USA

First published by Top Hat Books, 2014
Top Hat Books is an imprint of John Hunt Publishing Ltd., Laurel House, Station Approach,
Alresford, Hants, SO24 9JH, UK
office1@jhpbooks.net
www.johnhuntpublishing.com

For distributor details and how to order please visit the 'Ordering' section on our website.

Text copyright: R. J. Connor 2013

ISBN: 978 1 78279 236 9

A CIP catalogue record for this book is available from the British Library.

Design: Stuart Davies

Printed and bound by CPI Group (UK) Ltd, Croydon, CR0 4YY

We operate a distinctive and ethical publishing philosophy in all
areas of our business, from our global network of authors to
production and worldwide distribution.

In memory of Stanley Balkham
Forever in our hearts

Prologue I

The Priory Inn
London, Kingdom of England.
October, 1483.

"By God's blood, thy father slew mine, and so will I do thee and all thy kin."
John Clifford

Over the course of time there have been many blood feuds; some have lasted only days, some have lasted years and others have gone on to last for generations. These bitter, twisted affairs arise from many factors, whether resentment, anger or hate. There is always a cause to these feuds if you care to peel back the surface and delve deeper into the roots of things. Yet so often these feuds spiral so far out of control and for so long that even the cause can become lost, forever in the pages of history. It makes one wonder, what on earth were they fighting for? What was it really all about? Well one thing that's certain is that whatever the cause, a feud triggers retribution and vengeance, and extreme acts of violence. At times, one is left with a powerful sense of justice.

A blood feud is not something that you volunteer for, it is something that you are born into. It's quite literally, in the blood. It's instinctive, it's overpowering and it's integrated deep into your bones. Yet not everyone is infatuated in such a way. It is possible to fight it should you choose, but a hatred so deep passed down over generations is no easy thing to rid yourself of. Quite often it is necessary to give in to the inevitability, kill or be killed. What would you do?

Now I'm sure you've heard of many feuds, both old and new. But there has never been, and nor will there ever be, one quite like that as the one of the Longswords and the Ashbournes. A feud well over three hundred years in the making, stained with blood, death and much worse. The start is hazy of course, but the feud continues on as strong as ever and this is where our story begins...

There was a hollow knock on the wooden door of the Priory Inn. The innkeeper, a balding fellow with a few wisps of white hair and a round stomach, looked up from wiping his worn tankards, something which he had attended to several times that evening already. He surveyed the door with a cautious look for a moment wondering who in their right mind would take to the streets at such an hour. Excited at the prospect of a possible customer he scuffled across the room, knocking a few of the chairs as he went.

It was in fact rare for the inn to be so empty at this time of year; it was early autumn after all. But with the war brewing and the constant downfall of rain and heavy wind that had plagued the summer, most dared not venture far from their homes and travellers were altogether scarce. It would seem that even the weather was as affected by the war as the people's spirits were; dark, foreboding and generally rather unpleasant.

Swinging the heavy oak door forward the innkeep was greeted by a strong gust of wind and a face full of whipping rain. He wiped the water from his eyes on the back of his sleeve and identified the vague outline of what looked like a scraggy hooded middle aged old man. Still squinting he could just make out a wry smile on the man's face and a glimpse of his crooked yellow teeth. The innkeep struggled to make head or tail of why the man would have any reason to smile on a night such as this, but he greeted him all the same.

"Need a room for the night?" the innkeep asked grumpily.

"No," he replied. "Ale will do." The man walked past the disgruntled innkeep and entered the inn. He took his time to glare around the square room. It was small, with only a handful of tables, but there was a roaring fire in the grate and it had a cosy feel to it. Apart from the innkeep it was practically empty except for a dark haired man sitting at a table near the open fire in the far corner alone, head down, concentrating on a hot bowl of stew. For a brief moment he watched the man as he carefully tore

2

himself a chunk of bread and dipped it into his bowl, then slowly, purposefully, walked over towards him. Sitting down opposite he spoke.

"Good evening, Robert."

The man, somewhere in his mid-forties, stopped what he was doing as if stunned. For a moment he was completely still. There was a short, awkward pause, then he regained his composure and finally looked up from his supper. He had been roused from deep thought, and the lines on his face deepened in loathing and fear.

"Grenwick," he mumbled.

Robert held his gaze, looking deep into Grenwick's eyes for a moment. He fancied he caught a glimpse of the evil that lurked there. He had to turn away. Grenwick's face broke out into a threatening smile. He had a way about him that made men feel uneasy. It was one of his best assets and it's what made him such a good interrogator. He could instil fear into you with just a simple stare.

Robert Longsword and Grenwick Ashbourne were two men that knew each other well. Their families had been at war for three centuries since the age of the crusades. Something happened back then, something terrible. But no one living, not even Robert or Grenwick, could contest to what that was. They had been lucky. They had grown up during a truce. When their longbow men fathers had been victorious at the famed Battle of Agincourt, a ceasefire was agreed between them. Thirty-eight years of peace ensued, something Robert was grateful for, but for Grenwick it was infuriating.

At the Battle of Castillon when Richard was sixteen he got his first taste of battle, and he remembered it well. The smell of it, of shit and death, so strong he could taste it and it was bitter on his tongue. He had found it was not pleasant to kill a man but had learnt that it was necessary. For Grenwick, though, it was not a necessity but an indulgence; he basked in the glory of death.

Both of their fathers were lost in that fight and when civil war broke out two years later it threatened to tear their truce apart.

Thirty years on and the Wars of the Roses still ravages the land. King Richard III and his Yorkist supporters have the ascendency. Henry Tudor the Lancastrian claimant to the throne is exiled in France and the Duke of Buckingham's rebellion has been quashed. However the King's son Edward, the Prince of Wales, lies dying in his bed and with him the Yorkists' stronghold over the throne. Now was the time to strike.

For the last few months Robert had been in London, working as a spy. He did what he must, though his heart yearned to be somewhere else entirely, somewhere very far from there. His Spanish wife, whom he had loved dearly, he could not save. There was nothing he could do to prevent her untimely death. Their son was just a boy and he had left him behind. It had cut Robert to do so but what choice did he have? He had no wife, he had no money and he was desperate. Abandoning his son, he returned to England. He was a mercenary and he would do what he did best and raise the funds to give his son a better life. He only hoped beyond all hope that he lived long enough to see him once again.

The innkeep, sensing some tension between the two men, edged his way over slowly, breaking the silence that had ensued and gently set down a clean tankard of ale on the table with a soft clunk, fresh foam dripping down the side on to the wooden surface.

"Thank you," Grenwick muttered, taking his eyes from Robert for a split second. He waited for the innkeep, who clearly wanted nothing better than to get away from the pair of them, to move back out of earshot so he could speak once again.

"I know you work for Henry, Robert," he whispered locking his gaze to the eyes of Robert once again.

"What makes you so sure?" Robert replied, fidgeting slightly in his seat.

Grenwick watched him intently.

"I have my sources, Robert. Had I not had the smallest of respect for our fathers' arrangement I would have tracked you down long ago."

"So why now?" Robert asked, knowing exactly where the conversation was leading.

Ignoring the question Grenwick carried on. "I know what you saw the other night."

"I have no idea what you mean," said Robert casually, hastily returning his gaze back to his stew.

Grenwick lowered his head. He leaned in closer and whispered, "You were seen at the Tower of London."

Robert froze with shock. Grenwick could see the fear dawning in his eyes, and Grenwick knew it to be true. Not that he doubted Tyrrell's word, the slippery slug. He had claimed to have seen Robert only days ago sneaking in the shadows of the castle. Grenwick could tell from Robert's reaction that he had no idea he'd been seen.

Robert sighed. "I am a simple man, Grenwick, earning money where I can. I care not for the goings on in the world; I care only for the money to feed me and my son. I do not get involved in your war and I certainly have no idea what goes on in that tower!"

"You lie, Robert Longsword!"

At the sound of raised voices the innkeep once again looked up from wiping his tankards. Sensing the innkeep's eyes prickling the side of his face Grenwick thought it time to leave, and he stood up tall. "Until we meet again, I'll be watching you Robert," he growled, looking down at Robert squarely. He held his gaze just a fraction longer than was comfortable. Then he spun on his heel and headed to the door of the inn, nodding curtly to the innkeep. He ignored the suspicious glare from the innkeep as he walked out into the wet, stormy night.

Once outside in the mud drenched street, Grenwick looked

across to his men lurking in the shadows. He could just make out the whites of their eyes until a sudden flash of lightning illuminated them all, five of his sworn swords. He walked through the wet mud of the narrow street to meet them. They looked uneasy about their whereabouts on such a treacherous evening but never questioned it. What must be done must be done and Longsword was their number one priority.

"The bastard's in there all right. Take him, and I want him alive. He is just one man so do not fail me. I will return with the others!"

The men nodded to show they understood the order and temporarily sneaked back into the shadows. With satisfaction Grenwick swiftly turned and raised himself up onto his horse that was tied up to a post. He glanced up at the faded wooden sign swinging in the wind outside the Priory Inn and suppressed a smile before turning his horse and riding into the night. *I've got you now, Longsword.*

Back in the inn Robert was upstairs in his room. He paced up and down, the floorboards creaking beneath him. *What shall I do? They know I was there, they know what I saw and now, they know where to find me, they're watching me!* He knew now that his life was in jeopardy. But he was so close to the end. The final pieces of information he had intended to give to Henry lay written on a piece of paper on the table in the far corner of the room. He knew that what lay written on that paper could earn him a reward big enough to set him and his son up for life. But in the wrong hands it could be his own death warrant.

Robert froze. It dawned on him he could be about to die. He had to deliver this letter at all costs. It would be his final mission. Robert gave the paper one last look of utter despair and read the words he had etched there only hours before.

Henry,
Today at the Tower of London to my disgust and disbelief I witnessed

the murder and execution of the two young princes Edward and Richard at the hands of James Tyrrell on the behest of their uncle King Richard III. How can someone do such a thing to their own flesh and blood? He was chosen as their guardian and protector. The boys as you know were declared illegitimate to the throne and it is my sincere belief that he was behind it. Even so, it appears that was not enough for Richard who knew that only on their death would his throne be secure. He has had the bodies hidden under the chapel's staircase and will hush up their disappearance by any means necessary. However this information if made public could turn the war back in your favour. The people will never stand for this and will rise against him and join forces with you. Use it and you may yet be crowned King of England.

Robert.

Robert glared out of his window. He could barely make out the street below in the darkness. He stood and listened to the sound of the rain as it came thudding down onto the thatched roof of the inn. Suddenly the street lit up as a bolt of lightning flashed across the sky, and then he saw them, five men making their way towards the inn; Grenwick's men, Robert knew. He wasn't in the least bit surprised. Grenwick was a liar, a thief and a murderer.

There was an almighty crash downstairs as the men entered the bar. Robert heard raised voices. No doubt James was taken unawares. He felt sorry for the innkeep who he had become a good friend to over the years. He had served Robert as one of his men-at-arms and fought for him at the First Battle of St Albans, but like him had gone into hiding after the defeat. James had found himself a place here in London and Robert wished the man no harm. He went to his trunk at the end of his bed and took out his sword. If this was to be his last night in this world he would go down fighting. Too long had he lived in fear, too long had it been since he had felt steel in his hand. He might not be able to kill Grenwick but he could kill some of his men, and at least that would go some way to avenging his father's death. He knew in his heart that Grenwick was responsible.

When Robert entered the bar he had to pause to discern who was fighting whom. Many times he had heard a drunken James claim to be a master with the mace, so he could only assume that the great metal-plated club that was circling the air must belong to him. Robert judged by the blood that flecked his tunic and the brain that suddenly spattered his face that the mace had been used to crush the skull of the dead man that lay sprawled on the floor. Before James could swing it round again however, one of the men darted forwards and slashed a dagger across his face, causing him to fall backwards. Robert pounced, wielding his sword high, bringing it down in a great arching motion taking the man's arm clean off at the elbow. Blood spurted from the wound and Robert could taste its iron tang upon his lips. Fumbling at the wound the man slumped to the floor screaming. He writhed in agony, as vomit cascaded down his mantle. Ignoring their comrade's pleas for help, the other three men closed in towards Robert.

"There need be no more bloodshed, Robert. Lower your sword, come with us and we will spare your friend's life," said the man closest to Robert. He had black matted hair and a small black goatee to match.

"And what of mine? Will you spare that too?" Robert spat.

"That is not for me to decide. Take the risk, Robert, or die here by my sword." The man raised his sword in preparation, waiting for an answer, the seconds ticking on.

"No Robert, don't you dare!" cried James, down on the floor, panting. "You fight!"

One of the other men turned to James and kicked out at him, saying, "Shut up you old fool!" before turning back to his comrade. "Kill him now, Michael, forget what Grenwick said."

"No!" screamed James. He wasted no time raising himself. He mustered all of his strength and swung his mace merely inches off the floor towards the shin of the man who had kicked out at him. The man yelped and tried to jump out of the way. It was too late, and the mace made contact with a sickening crunch as his ankle was smashed to pieces. Like the man with no arm he went down screaming. Michael turned to see his comrade fall, and Robert wasted no time in thrusting his sword straight into Michael's gut.

"Oh," was all he said before Robert twisted the blade. The room was filled with a putrid stench as the man's bowels emptied. Disgusted, Robert pulled the blade free. Michael's eyes rolled before he crumpled to the floor saturated in his own filth.

Robert turned to face the last man, who was barely twenty, yet with his sword raised, eager for the fight. He had been trained well. *Fool*, Robert thought. "Do you expect to take both of us?"

By now James was on his feet, his face a savage mess. Robert could see his cheek bone, yet he showed no signs of being deterred.

"There are more on the way, and you will die tonight, Longsword!" the boy shouted back at him.

"He's right, Robert, you must get out of here. Take my horse. It's out the back, go!"

"But James, what I said before-"

"I will see it done, now go; I will finish up here." James turned to the young man and edged towards him, a look of determination on his bloody face.

Robert turned and fled from the back of the inn. The last words he heard was that of the young man's ringing in his ears as he turned to James and said, "Time to die old man!"

Outside the inn Robert was already saddling James's horse. Not the finest of horses, a palfrey, auburn in colour, but she would suffice. As Robert swung himself up and put his feet in the stirrups, there was a piercing cry from inside the inn. It was the young man's voice. "Good luck, James," Robert whispered, before racing the horse off up the street.

* * *

"Sir, is that?"

Grenwick turned to see Robert fleeing from the scene. "No! After him, men!" he growled.

Grenwick watched on from the high ramparts as Robert went thundering past the tower heading along the embankment towards the church of Saint Magnus and London Bridge. Grenwick's fists balled on the stone, his knuckles white. *Damn those men! I told them to take him.* "Lee?"

"Yes, milord."

"If any of the men that went to the Priory Inn survived, hang them!"

"Yes, milord."

Grenwick made his way around the ramparts following Robert's movement as he went, while twenty of his best men emerged out through the front gate in hot pursuit. He knew Robert would not be able to outrun them for long but if he could get across the bridge before they caught up with him then it would be no easy task to find him. He could easily lose them among the narrow streets of London. *That was the problem with this city*, Grenwick thought, *too many places to run and hide for stinking cowards.* But however long it took, Grenwick knew he'd find Robert again and when he did he would enjoy extracting the information from him that he wanted and then he would kill him himself.

"Grenwick," a voice said from behind him, a slithery voice he knew well. He whipped around to see King Richard standing a few feet behind him, while several of his men, all of them archers, fanned out around the ramparts. He had shoulder length dark hair that did little to conceal the angered expression on his gaunt face. "I see you have successfully subdued the target?"

"Your Grace, I'm afraid he managed to evade capture; he is extremely cunning, but nothing that my men cannot deal with. I assure you he will be caught in due course."

But the King looked thoroughly unconvinced. "Tell me Grenwick, how do you propose to do that? From where I stand it looks an awful lot like he's about to get away."

"I have men after him, your Grace. It is only a matter of time."

"You will call them off," the King demanded.

"But your Grace...?"

The King was furious. "Silence!" he cried, his cheeks turning a deep shade of puce. "You have failed me, Grenwick and you forget yourself; you are not the King! You will never question one of my orders ever again, are we clear?"

"Yes, your Grace," Grenwick conceded.

The King turned and spoke to one of his men, who nodded and shouted out, "Archers!"

Grenwick looked around to watch King Richard's archers as they all took an arrow from their quivers and placed it on their bows before aiming them up into the sky. He looked down from the ramparts and he saw Robert on his brown mare race along the embankment heading towards the bridge. *Know this Robert, I may not have killed you, but I will kill your son.*

"Shoot!" the command was given and the arrows soared into the air.

Grenwick watched as they fell with silent speed and came hailing down around the bridge. One arrow thudded into Robert's back and as his body arched in pain another rammed into his side, puncturing his lung. For a moment he swayed there on his horse before tumbling from his saddle and within seconds he was lost to the river below.

Prologue II

Palace of Córdoba
Córdoba, Crown of Castile. January, 1492.

"Following the light of the sun, we left the Old World."
Christopher Columbus

Christopher Columbus sat, his mind a thousand miles away. It was not the first time the Spanish monarchs had kept him waiting. Several times before had he sought an audience with them and each time he felt that they were merely toying with him. But this could be his last chance and he was adamant he would gain their support. *I will be courteous and lick their arses if I must.*

The King himself had invited Christopher back on this occasion and he couldn't help but think he was getting closer to his goal. King Ferdinand II of Aragón and his wife Queen Isabella I of Castile had gone a long way to unifying their two kingdoms under one banner; España. They were swiftly rising to prominence as two of the most powerful monarchs in the world and among the richest as well. *Who better to have backing my expedition than them?*

For a long time Christopher and his brother had worked on the idea of travelling to the East Indies from Europe but via a westward voyage, something that had never been attempted before. The land route to Asia had become perilously dangerous since Constantinople's fall to the Ottoman Turks. Therefore a new route was needed and Christopher was certain he had found the answer. They already had half the financial backing they needed through Italian investors, but what they really needed was royal support. Having already been turned down by King John of Portugal who believed an eastern voyage around the southern tip of Africa was possible, Christopher sent his brother Bartholomew to Henry VII of England who also turned them down while he turned his attention to the Spanish monarchy. After many discussions with the King and Queen and their advisors and some heated debates, they had previously turned him down, not once but twice, believing his estimates of how long it would take were some way off. However here he was again at the summons of the King.

The King had always seemed quite keen on the idea, although being somewhat sceptical he did see the benefits such an expedition could bring to his country. It was the Queen however who was proving a tougher nut to crack, asking difficult questions and pointing out all the possible problems that could be faced during the voyage. It was clear who wore the hose in their relationship and it certainly wasn't the King. Christopher smiled to himself.

"My Lord, the King and Queen will see you now," spoke a familiar voice. Christopher looked up from his seat to see Davíd, one of the King's personal guards looking down at him. "I am to escort you personally."

Rising from his seat Christopher nodded and replied, "Lead the way, Davíd." He followed the guard down the long hall watching him in his yellow and red robes and linen ruff with his long spear as he tapped the butt of it on the marble floor with each step. Christopher's eyes wandered to the walls where a great array of paintings had been displayed. Past monarchs, great battles and even, he was surprised to see, the recent victory over the Moors. As they reached the great hall the doors were guarded by two more of the King's men. They tapped the butts of their spears on the floor and stood aside. Davíd pushed open the great wooden doors and Christopher followed him through.

As he made his way across the hall Christopher could see the King and Queen perched atop their thrones but they were not alone. They were in conversation with two men; one he recognised as the commander of the royal guard but the other he did not. Both wore armour. As he approached, the King broke off their conversation and gazed down upon him, his eyes flicking in nervous jumps. The Queen smiled, her spirits high. "Your royal Majesties, Christopher Columbus," Davíd called as he tapped the floor.

I wish he'd stop banging that bloody spear. Christopher bowed his head in acknowledgment.

"It is good to see you again, your Majesties, and many congratulations on the splendid victory you have achieved in your Conquest of Granada."

The King waved Davíd away with his finger but it was the Queen who replied first. "Thank you, your kind words are most welcome. Finally the Reconquista is over; however it was not us that fought so valiantly on the battlefield. Reserve your praise for the newly appointed General Córdoba here," she said as she gave the older of the two men an admiring look. He was middle aged and had slightly greying hair but was handsome none the less. The General smiled back at her.

"Your Grace exaggerates," he replied.

Christopher looked up at the King, whose face was stern. The dark hair that flowed down over his chubby cheeks did little to hide his expression. His wide eyes surveyed his finger nails seemingly disinterested in the conversation. Christopher quickly turned his attention back to the General. "Señor, I have heard so much about you and your exploits in Illora. Your reputation precedes you."

"Please," the General replied, turning to face him. "The victory in Illora was as much down to my squire here." The General gave the second man a pat on the back. He was young with searching brown eyes, lightly tanned skin, shoulder length black hair and a long nose. "With some outstanding leadership and sheer bravery! Let me introduce you to-"

"Ricardo de Guadalest, our very own El Cid," the Queen

cut in.

"An honour," said Christopher, giving another bow.

"No, the honour is mine," Ricardo replied. "We have heard much about you and your proposed voyage west."

"Yes, we were just telling the King and Queen, what an excellent idea we thought it was," the General chimed in.

So that explains it. Christopher looked up at the King who was now staring blankly at the far wall. The Queen, however, still only had eyes for the General. "So modest. Did you know that it was the General himself who successfully concluded the Muslims' surrender? He is a fluent speaker in Arabic."

"Come now, enough," said the King, turning to face Christopher. "We have decided to grant you permission for your proposed voyage to the East Indies and will give you our financial support, on condition that you gain us the upper hand in the spice trade. The war has cost us dearly and we need to refill our coffers."

"I will, your Grace, thank you, your Grace."

Before the King could say anything else the Queen spoke, apparently unaware that she had been previously interrupted. "Should you be successful, we will reward you with ten per cent of all profits. You are also to be made Admiral of the Seas, to let the world know that the Spanish mean business."

The King shook his head, but the Queen seemed mightily pleased. It's true she was a beautiful woman as was sung among the peasants, sitting there in all her glory, with free flowing brown hair and small pink lips; even Christopher couldn't deny it. Yet it had always seemed on previous occasions that the King was the one showing the most support for his venture and now it appeared to be her. This was a twist in the tale. Christopher watched the Queen as her piercing dark eyes darted to the General once again. *And now I know the reason why.* Christopher smiled and bowed his head. "Your Majesties."

As Christopher turned to walk away he caught the eye of the

General. "Señor," he said. "Can I tempt you to dine with me this evening? For on the morrow I will set sail and it would be an honour to share some decent food with some decent company."

"I would be delighted," the General replied.

For over two years now Christopher Columbus had been in discussions with the Spanish monarchy and so had spent a lot of time at their court. He had lived at the Alcazar de Córdoba, the Palace of Córdoba, during that period and he was starting to think he knew it better than he knew his own home. *Oh how I miss my sweet Genoa.* Still, he could not complain. He had been given fantastic lodgings, a large rectangular room, well furnished with a large table and chairs with which to entertain guests. There was a balcony draped with luxurious red silk and a view over the fertile green palace gardens. Another smaller room just off of it which contained his grand four poster bed also boasted drapes of a deep sapphire satin. They might be an odd pair but the King and Queen had seen to his every need. The service had been thoroughly excellent and the food delightful. However, on the morrow he would be heading to a new world. It was the day that he had dreamt about for years and he wasn't going to let a little bit of home sickness spoil his moment of glory.

There was a sudden knock at the door. "Come in," Christopher called.

It was the General who entered, a little earlier than expected but Christopher admired his punctuality. It was strange not to see him fully armoured as he usually was. He thought it fascinating how a man looked so less intimidating with normal clothes on. He wore a black shirt on top of which was a splendid green tunic trimmed with gold. He also wore plain black hose and a black leather belt with a golden buckle. As always he bore a friendly smile and he waved as he entered.

"Good evening, Señor."

"Oh please, call me Gonzalo," the General replied. "All this lordship nonsense, it's enough to drive a man insane, wouldn't you agree?"

"Well, it appears we share one thing in common," Christopher said, returning the smile. "Please take a seat."

The General took a seat at the table opposite Christopher and plonked a heavy bottle down on the table. "Aye and I'm hoping we share a liking for fine wine, too?"

Christopher couldn't help but laugh. "Gonzalo my friend, as far as first impressions go, you're dazzling me. I am liking you more and more each minute."

"Let's see if you agree with what you say after the night is through." The General chuckled and helped himself to one of the goblets that sat on the table and filled it with a healthy amount of wine. He passed the goblet to Christopher before filling the other and taking a mighty swig. "So tell me, what is on the menu?"

"I have asked the servant to provide us with boiled pork and peppers, in a spiced wine sauce."

"How delightful!" cried the General.

"And that is just the first course," Christopher replied, causing both men to laugh again. "But before we eat, please, I must know more about your victory at Illora."

The General stopped laughing and his smile faded. He paused for a moment and then revealed his story...

Illora, Kingdom of Granada. January 1492.
We had just captured the town of Loxa and so advanced on the town of Illora and there we laid siege. It was a strong town, well provisioned and its illustrious fortress topped a high rock that stood defiantly in the heart of a great valley. Only four leagues were there between Illora and the Moorish capital. We knew if we took this town we would have a base with which we could launch an assault on the city of Granada itself. The tall castle had long kept a watchful eye over the wide expanse of country below. It was often called the right eye of Granada.
Whilst we descended upon Illora they made every preparation that

they possibly could to aid its defence. Of course the women and children were taken to the centre of the town to be kept as far away from the fighting as possible. In all of the suburbs, barricades had been put up to slow us down, and holes had been made in the buildings from which arrows and other missiles could be fired. Also, they had opened doors of communication from house to house. The Moorish commander that was in charge of Illora was one of their very best; he was courageous and ready to fight till the death.

When we arrived the King bade us make camp. We decided to divide our forces and made several encampments all around Illora, so it was completely surrounded. The King himself took a spot high upon the hill of Encinilla and from there gave his orders. He knew the stoutness of the Moor commander and knew his men were accomplished fighters and so had us dig trenches and put up palisades. The guards were also doubled and we had watchmen adorn the towers.

When we were ready I spoke to the King. For many years I had been captain of the royal guard but now I wanted to prove my true worth, here on the battlefield. I begged him let me lead the attack and to my surprise he granted my request and complimented me on my true spirit. More men like you are we in need of, he told me. After gaining the command it was my squire's turn to talk to me. He was fifteen, too young and this was to be his first taste of battle. He had only been my squire for less than a year, before that he had been my page. But he was full of spirit and an equally adept fighter. I had trained him well. Being his first campaign and because of his youth, many of the soldiers had questioned the hardiness of his well embroidered chivalry. He wanted to prove not only to himself, but to the King and his men that he had what it takes.

So I made a decision. I split the forces, I would lead an attack from one side of the town with the Count of Cabra and his men, and Ricardo I gave the command over the Duke Infantado and his men. The Duke, like Ricardo, was in his first campaign and so offered his men forward for the assault. When the two hosts set forth it was a sight to behold. The men that surrounded me were all war veterans whose armour was dented and chipped from years of battle. The men that surrounded Ricardo were fresh with brilliant new armour and full of colour. Some of the older men laughed. But Ricardo was not deterred.

"Men," he cried. "We have been looked down upon for our wondrous display. But I just call it jealousy. Let us show them, that though our undamaged swords may rest in decorated sheaths, we still know how to use them!" At that moment cheers erupted all around him. "Forward now, forward to the enemy and in the eyes of God we may enter this affray as unseasoned knights but we will leave it as proven cavaliers!"

The men responded with more cheers and so Ricardo led them forward into the assault. They were met with a bombardment of stones and arrows raining from above. But nothing could damage Ricardo's resolve and on they marched and into the suburb he strolled with his sword in his hand. The battle was fierce and the men fought ferociously with Ricardo's words still ringing in their ears. The harder they fought the more men were lost, for every house had been turned into a fortress. But after a tiring contest the Moors were driven into town.

I and the Count's men had just succeeded in taking over another of the town's suburbs and so met with Ricardo and the remnants of the Duke's men in the centre of the town. I gazed upon Ricardo and his men and though they were thinned in number, covered with blood, dust and many were wounded, not a single man could doubt their prowess nor sneer at their embroidery.

Having taken the suburbs, we were mightily in control and all that was left for the taking was the castle. I ordered three batteries forward, each equipped with eight giant lombards and we let loose a storm of missiles on the fortress. The castle was in no way designed to withstand such an attack from powerful siege engines and so the damage inflicted was monstrous. The walls were smashed to pieces and the towers soon came crumbling down. Many were killed as their houses were crushed to powder. I felt almost sorry for the Moors. They were terrified, amidst the dust and the noise.

As I said, their commander was ready to fight to the death, but when *he looked over his town all he saw was chaos and destruction. His people had no will to fight anymore and Granada seemed in no hurry to send them any aid. With a heavy heart he accepted defeat and surrendered.*

Having fought so bravely the King let the remaining people of the town leave, taking with them all of their possessions, except of course their weapons, and they were escorted by the Duke and the Count within two leagues of Granada to the Bridge of Pinos.

But after the battle was done, it was not the King's name on the lips of the men, for it was mine. "Gonzalo, Gonzalo, El Gran Capitán!" they cried with such passion as I have never seen. The Great Captain they called me and never have I felt as much pride as I did in that moment. In reward, the King placed the town of Illora under my command and at the Queen's wishes promoted me to rank of general. Despite my obvious joy I could not take my mind off of one thing. The bravery and courage shown by Richard and the men I placed under his command.

"A splendid victory and a most compelling tale," Christopher said when the General had finished.

"Aye that it was," the General replied. "Yet it weighs heavily on my mind."

"How so?"

"That victory didn't really belong to me, it belonged to Richard."

Christopher raised his eyebrows. That was the second time Gonzalo had referred to his squire as Richard. He had assumed the first time was a mere slip of the tongue, but to repeat it, that would suggest it was no accident. Christopher watched Gonzalo intently, whose gaze had dropped to the table, somewhat deep in thought. *Surely he knows the name of his own squire?*

"Ricardo?" Christopher suggested, somewhat interested by this.

"Sorry?" the General asked, looking up from the table.

"You called your squire Richard, but surely you meant Ricardo?"

The General looked annoyed with himself, like he had revealed something he was not supposed too. "Ah yes, well, Ricardo," he nodded in Christopher's direction to acknowledge his correction, "Was born an Englishman. It was from his mother that he inherited his Spanish appearance. He prefers to be called by his Christian name but we prefer to call him by its Spanish interpretation when in public."

"To dissociate Richard from being English?" Christopher found it easier to call the squire by his true name.

"To a degree, I suppose, yes," the General replied.

Christopher was intrigued, he could not deny it, but he did not want to push the matter. He liked the General and wasn't going to risk offending him. "Well, his exploits certainly were heroic. You hold him in high esteem, this I can see."

"Even at such a young age, he is one of the finest soldiers I have ever seen." The General let out a sigh. "He deserved a knighthood after his part in that battle, but I didn't give it to him. You see, I have come to love him like a son. If I was to knight him I fear I would lose him."

"He has ambition, that much is clear. How did you come to meet him?"

"It was not long after the death of my first wife, almost three years into the Granada conquest. I had returned home to see to her burial and was travelling back south through the Crown of Aragón on my way to Granada when I passed through a small town called Guadalest. It was there in the town market that I saw him. He was just a mere boy of nine, but I watched as he tried to fight off three older boys who had stolen fruit from a little girl. It was something of no importance yet it caught my eye nonetheless. I saw something in him, something that reminded me of myself when I was his age. I took a liking to the boy. I bid him introduce me to his parents, but they were dead. He was in the care of an elderly couple who had found him when he was just a baby. They wanted the best for the boy and when I suggested it, they were more than happy for me to take him on as my page and train him to be a knight. So there you have it, and here we sit, six years on and the boy is now a man."

"What happened to the boy's parents?"

"Oh, it is a sad tale, one that I shall not utter here. Something horrible befell that family. I spoke to the old man who cared for him and he told me all about it. He has closer ties to Richard than Richard knows. Every day I refrain myself from revealing the truth of his upbringing to him, but I fear for the repercussions of what it might bring. I fear for the boy's safety."

Sensing the anguish in the General's eyes Christopher refrained himself from asking about what the old man had said. "So what does your wife make of him?"

"She has always been jealous of our relationship. But if truth be told I have never loved her as I loved my first wife. I only married her at the Queen's behest and as of yet we have no children to speak of and one doubts if we ever will. I do have a daughter from my previous marriage but Richard is the son I always wanted."

"I know exactly what you mean. I have two sons of my own. The eldest, Diego, is twelve and I truly want the best for him. As it happens, the Queen has offered to make him a page at her court."

"The Queen is generous."

"She seems well taken with you, my friend," Christopher said, smiling, hoping to lighten the General's mood.

He half returned the smile. "My reputation among the army was rising and I think she wished to keep me close, and by marrying me to one of her ladies in waiting she would achieve that. I have served her for many years and have always been loyal. If I ever loved anyone as much as I loved my previous wife, it would be my Queen. I would die for her if I must, it is my duty. It is safe to say I have her ear, yes. My new found acclaim seems to have pleased her and she always heeds my council."

"May I ask why you supported my venture?"

At this he did smile. "You are a brave man, Christopher, such a voyage would be perilous, but you would do it, not for power or for land but because it is something that you have dreamt of doing all your life. You would do it under the banner of a foreign King or Queen even though they are not yours to serve and you do all this for the betterment of others. I find a man's true merit comes not with fine words but in his actions, and you —just like Richard — are willing to go and get it, no matter the risk. There are too few men like us. This is why I support your venture."

At the General's words Christopher was taken aback. No one had ever said such words about him and this was coming from someone he barely knew. "You speak like you know my mind, yet you do not. You are a wise man, Gonzalo, and I see why you have risen among the ranks. I thank you for your kind words and salute you for your achievements on the battlefield and wish you my best in what is to come." Christopher raised his glass in tribute.

The General followed suite and raised his glass. "And I wish you a safe and successful voyage to the East Indies and may you face a calm sea and a steady wind."

Both men drained their glasses.

"I will keep a keen ear out for any news," the General continued. "But I expect a full report on your return to Spain."

"Oh I am sure that can be arranged," Christopher replied. "As long as you bring the wine?"

At that both men broke into spurts of laughter, which eventually died down to a silence. They sat like that for some time, both trailing their own thoughts.

It was Christopher who broke it. "I am truly inspired by your relationship with your squire. The love and bond you share for one another is quite remarkable." He paused for a moment. "Can I ask you something?"

"Of course," the General replied.

"Do you know the meaning of the name *Richard*?"

The General had not anticipated such an unusual question, and he shrugged. "I confess I do not."

"Well, I shall inform you. It means powerful leader."

Understanding dawned on the General's face.

Christopher continued, saying, "You would do anything for the boy, that I can see."

"Aye, I would."

"Then I hope that you see it in your heart to do what you must and let the boy go. I am afraid you cannot hold him back forever. He is destined for great things and I for one will watch over his career with great interest."

"You are right, but I cannot. I will of course, God knows I will, just not yet."

Chapter One

Castle of Guadalest
Guadalest, Crown of Aragón. June, 1513.

"There must be a beginning of any great matter, but the continuing unto the end until it be thoroughly finished yields the true glory."
Sir Francis Drake

When you look at your life, what do you see? It's a broad question, is it not, but one that we all ask ourselves at least once in our lives. Often it's in times of crisis, sometimes it's when you feel the need for change but sometimes it's when you can't justify the things that have happened to you. It makes you question yourself, your life, even your faith. Does my happiness count for nothing? In times like this you may ask yourself, what have I accomplished? Can you honestly say you have done anything that has made it worthwhile? The truth is I believe I have, yet is that really the remedy for true happiness?

But please, you must forgive my rudeness, let me introduce myself. My people call me Señor Ricardo de Guadalest but to those who know me best, I am plain Sir Richard and I am the first Rois de Llaurí Baron of Alcalali. I am an Englishman, well, in part. My father was an English knight, if the rumours are to be believed but my mother was a Spaniard and I reside in her native homeland. Both my parents are dead, so I am told. I was raised by an elderly Spanish couple from as young an age as I can remember. They said they found me when I was just a small boy; I never felt they truly loved me but they raised me as well as can be expected. They sent me to page at the age of nine for the General Córdoba, who knighted me after the Battle of Cerignola in 1503. I am a knight, as I am certain my father was before me, and no doubt his father before him. It was my ambition to continue my family's name whatever it may be and I was to find that out along with all the horrors that came with it. My life has been an adventure, to say the least.

During my time I have witnessed many things, some wonderfully good, some terribly bad. I have experienced the intimacy of a woman's love, one wholly and entirely devoted to me. Had a child of my own and raised her to the best of my ability. I have fought in countless battles in many different places and I have served kings and honoured my vows. However despite my noble deeds and pleasantries in life, I have also lost what I held dear to me.

What does is it mean to be a just knight? Is it to be chivalrous in all that you do and be loyal to your cause, to be faithful to your brothers in arms and merciful to your enemies? To fight for a cause such as a holy crusade or to serve your king in battles abroad? Is there honour to be found fighting as a mercenary or in a special order? Is what we do all for the good and right in the eyes of God? Do we serve the weak or try to impress damsels with our shiny shields and our great war horses? There is a lot that signifies a knight. Most have wealth, power and land. Some are good and some choose to abuse their position and forsake their vows. I myself have no wealth and I have little power. I have some land, yes, but to what great purpose? It was granted to me I'll warrant from no less than the Pope himself, a barony, and I've invested all the little money I had so that the people of my land might prosper, but they have not. The heavens refuse to open and the earth is left as dry as the sand in the African desert meaning the seeds won't grow, food is scarce and the trade nearly non-existent; in fact had it not been for the local Knights of Calatrava there would have been none at all. Does this sound like the life of a great knight, one who rides to war with great prestige and prowess? Perhaps it is not. But I have done all these things that I have mentioned and dare I say it done them well, yet where has that left me? I have lost all those that I have ever loved, and more.

Yet still I stand on a field of victory and how have I come to this conclusion, I might hear you ask? Was it all worth it? The honest answer is yes. Why? Because I failed my family, no. But because despite that, I served my purpose as a true and just knight, because I took my vows and followed them accordingly and with distinction. I did what I was asked and without question. I fought with honour and did my best to protect the weak as any true knight should. So despite my own personal losses, I achieved my childhood dream, becoming the valiant knight that I was born to be. Yet something is missing, and why do I feel so hollow?

I was lucky enough to be blessed with a beautiful wife and a sparkling young daughter but they were taken from me. I remember the night it all started, like a bad dream, only one that haunts my every day thought. It was mid-June and I was on duty up at the old fort in Guadalest. It had been a wearisome day having worked the orange groves, or should I say the pathetic excuse for ones, outside the grounds of my small palace, work that had yielded no rewards and all before I started the long night shift. I had previously promised my wife I would retire from the world of war and live an honest living. I did so by trying to grow oranges, a sweet fruit that I had taken a liking to since it was introduced to me by Christopher Columbus. I had hoped they would flourish in the Spanish sun but so far the few trees that grew had withered and died. There is honour in war even more so I told my wife. But she swiftly reminded me that from a woman's perspective there is no honour in leaving a wife and child without a husband and a father, leaving them to fend for themselves in such difficult times, and perhaps she was right. My duty was to them now.

Yet my days serving the General for King Ferdinand II had not gone unnoticed. The Pope Alexander VI had purchased the title of Duke of Gandia and its occupying lands for his son Pedro Borgia. The title was passed on through two generations of Borgias to Juan Borgia, who personally requested that I command the garrison at the local fort in Guadalest. The fort itself had long been a fortification of great strategic importance in the days of the Moors, but now it stood high upon the cliff top in the centre of the Guadalest valley, derelict and uninhabited. Juan who resided in the Ducal Palace of Gandia over ten leagues away had not wanted to see the castle fall into disrepair should ever he frequent it, and so promoted me to captain of a small but elite group of warrior knights titled the Guardians of Guadalest. Our task was *simple; to guard the fort and its few possessions. It was easy money. The Borgias were rich, after all, and so it was theirs to waste and with the orange groves not producing, the gold was well needed. With that in mind and the chances of danger slim, I had no hesitation in accepting his offer. Even my wife could find no reason to object. I had good men around me, men I could trust well. I could leave the fort in their capable hands during the day and I would personally supervise at night.*

This particular night I remember I was sitting atop the Penon de la Alcala, Guadalest's famous watch tower, gazing up at the flags that fluttered above it. One was yellow and black striped and bore the red bull of the Borgia dukes and the other was a sea of blue upon which stood the Tower of Guadalest, either side of which was a key. I sat on the floor, my legs outstretched with my back to the wall and as sleep slowly seeped over me I rested my chin upon my chest and all was quiet until I heard Simon's voice...

* * *

"Calm night."

Richard rubbed sleep from his eyes before raising his head and looking over to the left to see Simon emerging from the trap door that led to the tower's top. Simon walked towards him, clad in the solid black of their order with the guardian's sigil trimmed in gold emblazoned on his chest. It was split into four quadrants, two red and two white. The red bore golden bulls and the white golden castles. It signified the bond formed between Gandia and Guadalest. It flickered in the torchlight and for a moment the bulls almost seemed alive to Richard as Simon approached him. He was a tall man with blond shoulder length hair and piercing green eyes. He was always quite the charmer.

"It is," Richard replied, placing his head back against the wall, leaving Simon to take a seat beside him.

Richard and Simon were very close friends, as close as two men could be. They were both English to a certain degree.

Richard was half Spanish, Simon on the other hand was born and bred in England, yet he had never confided in Richard how he had come to be in Spain. However, he was like a brother to him; he loved him and he trusted him and therefore did not wish to force the issue if Simon was unwilling to discuss it. They had shared this bond ever since the day Simon had been drafted in by the Duke two years ago. It was a move that came as a surprise to Richard, but he had no complaints. Since then, they had spent four nights a week together, keeping an eye out for an enemy that just didn't seem to exist.

It was a fairly warm, mild early summer evening. The absence of cloud made the stars clearly visible. There was a very faint breeze blowing in from the sea coolly lapping against their faces and for a second they just basked in this small comfort as they watched the stars blazing magnificently in the night sky. It had become a regular pastime of theirs over recent weeks.

"I have no idea why the Duke wants us to guard this place. Who, on this God forsaken earth, would want to take it?" Simon blurted out, turning his head slightly towards Richard.

"Why care? He is willing to pay us fair, besides it is not for us to question the Duke's intentions, even if they are somewhat peculiar," Richard replied.

"This is true. I can't deny it, yet it would be more fun if we were under siege, my old friend, would it not?"

"Aye, it would."

Both of them chuckled, but it was short lived.

"Argh!"

A sudden cry pierced the air taking them completely by surprise. Extremely startled, Richard's back straightened. He glanced at Simon and saw his face, lined with a mix of confusion and concern.

"What in God's name was that?" Richard asked, returning the glare, sounding just as anxious as Simon must have felt.

"It sounded like Carlos!" Simon replied.

Richard knew the moment he heard the cry who it was, but he dare not believe it. He had heard that cry several times before on the battlefield; it was the sound of sudden death.

As if in unison both of them bolted up onto their feet and ran to the edge of the balcony. From this vantage point the whole fort was visible below them. But there was no avoiding the crumpled heap that lay splayed, limbs at awkward angles, in the centre of the courtyard. To Richard's utter horror and dismay there was Carlos, a good man and worthy member of the Guardians of Guadalest, a look of shock on his face and an arrow protruding from his chest. *What the hell is going on?*

All of a sudden the night sky lit up as fiery arrows flew through the air raining down on the old fort. Richard had to squint hard but looking out over the fort ramparts beneath the orange glare he could just make out in the shadows the vague movement of several hooded figures that were rushing through the under growth leading up the hill heading towards the fort.

"Take cover!" Simon cried, pulling Richard down by his long black cloak as the arrows started to crash into the tower.

When the arrows finally stopped Richard braved a chance at crouching up slightly and lifted his head above the balcony edge to take in the damage. There were only two buildings in the fort's courtyard, the horse stables which were ablaze and the Moorish mausoleum which was made entirely of stone and so was eerily unaffected. As for the castle many of the windows in the fort had been smashed through and an orange glow came from within. Fire had started inside the castle's walls and it would surely spread. It was at this moment that he saw the ladders come hurtling up against the walls as the attackers attempted to climb in.

Never had the fort been under siege in all the time that Richard had been there. The last time it had been besieged was several hundred years ago. However, it was time that the Guardians of Guadalest were put to the test. They had already lost one man in Carlos. That put them down to only four guards, Richard and Simon and their Spanish counterparts, Raúl and Juan, who were already trying to put out the stable's fire. Richard could judge by the amount of arrows and ladders that had been raised up against the wall that there must be at least twenty attackers, a small force but one much greater than their own.

"Come on, let's go!" he called to Simon.

Simon followed him as he made a dash for the trap door that led to the tower's top. After descending the ladder they made their way through the castle. Smoke was everywhere which made the usually easy route out to the courtyard rather more difficult. Finally they emerged through the thick wooden doors at the front of the castle and rushed down the stairs to the fort's courtyard, the fresh air a relief to their parched lungs. Richard drew his sword and Simon followed suit unsheathing his own. Knowing they were fighting a losing battle with the fires, Raúl and Juan let the horses free and fell in behind them, also drawing their swords. Although considerably outnumbered the Guardians of Guadalest were well trained and would fight to the death. If this was to be their end then they would kill as many of these hooded bastards as they could.

"All right men, we wanted action, we've got it! Whatever comes over that wall, we do not back down!" Richard cried, trying to raise the morale of his men. "We are the Guardians in the Night! We will not back down!"

As he uttered the last word there was a crunch in the gravel as the first attacker landed on the courtyard surface. He wore a long black cloak and was hooded, a dark mask covered his face so he could not be seen. The only form of recognition Richard could make out was that he had a faded symbol on his chest, what appeared to be a single green leaf. He had never seen it before. *Who could they be? What did they want?* With a yell the man charged towards him just as two of his companions dropped over the wall and joined in the skirmish. Richard surged forward to greet him, ducking as the man swung, the blade missing his scalp by mere inches. He sliced his own sword across the shins of the man, sending him crashing to the ground, howling and writhing in agony. Rising, Richard sprinted on towards the next man. Simon had already embraced the other in single combat. More now were spilling over the wall, however, and Raúl and Juan too were entwined in the action.

Richard could tell from the offset that they were dealing with professionals; they were clearly trained men-at-arms, some perhaps even knights. The man he faced blocked off another of his stinging blows, but luring him into a false sense of security Richard struck down again heavily from up high knocking the man off balance. It gave him the split second he needed to strike. He did so by bringing his blade down in a diagonal cutting motion across the man's torso from shoulder to hip. Richard watched as his blade tore through skin and muscle. Blood splattered the ground and sprayed his face red. He let out a roar, a deafening sound from a man that was ready to kill. His long black hair was matted with blood and his dark brown eyes burned with a passion that he had not felt for many years. This is how it felt, the heat of battle and the lust to kill.

He turned to see Simon on the floor, his back to the ground, trying to fend off his attacker. Richard ran to his friend's aid. Coming up to the attacker from behind he sent his sword crashing straight through the man's back, hearing his ribs break as he watched it emerging through his chest.

"Are you all right, Simon? You appear to be underperforming!" Richard said, pulling him to his feet.

"Yes, fine!" he replied. "He got lucky, was all."

"Well, be careful, that was a close call, friend."

Raúl and Juan came over to join them, having successfully fended off their own foes. Raúl now sported a bloody nose where he had taken a sword hilt to the face and a deep gash could be seen on Juan's upper thigh. A wild swing had lamed him but it was not enough to stop him from smashing the man in the face with his axe.

"These are trained assassins, Ricardo," he said, wincing as he took a step on his injured leg. "We will not hold them for long."

"It is our duty to try, we must!" Richard replied. "We gave the Duke our word."

Knowing he spoke the truth, Juan nodded and they fell into formation edging their way back towards the burning castle, bracing themselves for the inevitable onslaught. They could hear the sounds of footsteps as the remaining attackers piled over the wall and closed in around them. As they neared through the smoke Richard counted at least a dozen of them, arched into a semi-circle, moving slowly. It left them with no choice but to edge back further and they found themselves at the foot of the stairs that led up to the castle's doors. There was nowhere left for them to run, to the death.

"Come on you bastards!" Richard cried. "What are you waiting for?"

There was a brief moment's pause, before being broken by a low whistling sound as something flew through the air. An arrow came shooting from one of the men surrounding them, thudding straight into the forehead of Raúl, who dropped to the floor, dead. Richard let out another ear splitting roar and flung himself forward. He barrelled into the first attacker, taking him completely by surprise, sending his sword squelching straight through the man's throat. The other hooded masked men closed in, but in his anger Richard managed to kill two more, before being forced back. The three of them left were fending off blows from all angles now and were forced to retreat back up the stairs towards the castle. The only slight advantage now was the higher ground, not that it counted for much. They were still outnumbered three to one, and they were starting to feel fatigued. Juan was struggling badly now with his severely injured leg. He slipped on the next step and crashed to the floor, his chain mail ringing upon impact. Horror twisted his face as a hooded figure swiftly approached him, slamming down his sword into Juan's stomach. Juan let out a high pitched scream as blood gurgled from his mouth.

"Run!" Richard cried to Simon as he turned and fled. He knew death was upon him but he wasn't going to give them the satisfaction.

Simon followed Richard and turned, fleeing up the staircase towards the burning building. They ran through the main doors, closing and barring them with a wooden beam. It was no easy task and for all the good that it did, they were trapped, and by now most of the castle was aflame. The heat was incredibly fierce. *So this is to be my tomb.*

"The window!" Simon cried, his breath rasping in his throat as the heat seared his flesh.

They looked to the stained glass window at the back of the main hall, but had no time to admire its beauty. Richard knew what Simon had in mind, but it was a hundred foot drop at least to the lake below and the chances of missing the rocks were highly unlikely. There was a loud thumping sound as the attackers attempted to knock down the wooden front doors. *Thump, thump, thump, thump.* It wouldn't take them too long.

"What do you want!?" Richard heard himself cry out in despair.

There was a sudden silence, and the thumping stopped. It was followed with a brief pause. All that could be heard was the crackling of flame above. He waited.

"We want the gold, Richard!" It was the voice of an Englishman.

"You know my name?" Richard looked at Simon in astonishment, but his friend just shrugged. "Then if you know me, you should know that there is no gold here!"

"We didn't come here for the gold, Richard, we came here for you!"

"But, why?"

"Come with us, Richard, show us where the gold is and we won't hurt your family!"

"I have no idea what you're talking about. Leave my family out of this!"

"We know your father left you the gold, Richard."

"What? I- I- have no idea-"

"You lie, Richard Longsword! Where is the gold? Come with us now or your family will die!"

"Longsword? Who? Did you know my father?" he screamed.

"You do not have long, Richard. Are you willing to risk your life and the lives of your family?"

"I don't know about any gold-"

"Then your family die!"

"No- you can't!"

Loud cracking noises came from above. The roof would soon give way, and there was no way out. *Thump, thump, thump, thump.* The attackers were hitting the door again. It too would soon give way. Simon and Richard did the only thing they could and edged their way further back across the hall towards the far end of the room where the fire was least fierce.

"There's no way out, Richard," Simon mumbled. "We should give in to their demands."

"No, the window, It's our only chance!" Richard replied.

"But Richard even you said- it would be ridiculous to attempt-"

"I know, but we must, think of my family, Simon!"

Simon nodded. "You're right, let's go."

Staring toward the window, his face glistening with sweat and soot amidst the orange glare, Richard stood bracing himself for the inevitable. He turned and spoke softly.

"Promise me, Simon, should I not survive, please will you save my family?"

"I will," he replied.

The doors to the hall flew open with a splintering crash as the attackers broke through.

"Now, Simon, now!" Richard cried. He just had time to grab his shield which hung on the wall before he turned back and ran with ferocious speed along what was left of the room. Just below the window was an altar of sorts and using it as a foot hold and springing off it he flung himself head first with his shield covering his face as best as he could, towards the window. He went crashing through the glass and fell, spiralling towards the dark abyss below.

Richard hit the water with an almighty splash, his hand slipping from his shield as he surged into the lake beneath him. Already he could feel the bruising pain on his back. He gasped out and as he did, water seared into his lungs. There was little he could do as he tumbled helplessly through the water, its roar ringing in his ears. The impact had not been enough to slow his descent and his momentum forced him to the lake's bottom where he felt his head make contact with hard stone. Balancing on the verge of unconsciousness, he slowly floated up towards the lake's surface where he groped for his shield. Through watery eyes he could just make out the castle ablaze way up high at the cliffs summit as the roof caved in.

"Simon," Richard muttered, as darkness closed in around him.

Chapter Two

The Blacksmith
Guadalest, Crown of Aragón. June, 1513.

*"Also say to them, that they suffer him this day to win his spurs, for
if God be pleased, I will this journey be his, and the honor thereof."*
Edward III

*If you have ever experienced the death of a close friend, you may have
some incline as to how I was feeling. And I don't mean someone you
know of in passing. But someone you were willing to tell all your
secrets to, someone you could trust, someone you loved. If this has
never happened to you then you should count yourself lucky, for I must
confess, there is nothing in this world more unbearable. It is a horrible
feeling the moment you realise they are gone, it's like a storm brewing
inside of you, frustration, anger and pain. I was at a loss, my soul
weakened and my body trembled. There was a pain aching inside of me
that I knew had nothing to do with the fall. Simon was like a brother to
me; he was the best companion a friend could ask for. His death truly
would be difficult to bear. He was so young. He had his whole life ahead
of him. But now he would never have a family of his own and feel true
love as I have or learn that there is more to life than all this folly.*

*It's true he was a knight, yes, and there is always a risk of death
when you're a knight. But still, I couldn't understand why. Why here?
There was no cause to die here, no reason, no need, a quiet village on
the coast of Spain far away from war, so why? They didn't want the
fort, they wanted me. They called me Longsword, but who was
Longsword? They said they wanted gold, but what gold? I speak the
honest truth when I say I had no idea what they were talking about.
They knew my father, that much was clear, but I knew little of him. My
knowledge of my true family was nothing but a few scraps of information and unconvincing dreams. Could these men hold the answers?*

My heart yearned to know more about my parents but there were no clues, no traces, nothing. The elderly man who found me, alone and crying, had said that there was an English knight who frequented these parts around the time I was born. But nobody knew who he was or where he came from. He disappeared after that and presumably died in battle. I wish I could tell you more, but knowledge of my early life is vague at best. Some nights I think I can picture my father's face, but it is gone as quick as it comes. The only father figure I have ever known is that of the General Córdoba. He treated me like a son and taught me my trade, to fight, with lance, shield and sword. I served with him and fought for Spain in their wars against the Moors and the French. So perhaps I had made some enemies there, but these were not French assassins, they were English...

* * *

As Richard lay waking, his father's face appeared in his mind but it was gone in a flash. The light was painful on his eyes, his vision blurry, his head hurt, his body ached, his chain mail was damaged, his clothes were soaked through and he felt cold. It was not one of his fondest memories. As his eyes regained focus, he realised that he had washed up on the shore of the lake still clinging to his shield. He pulled his arm free of it and as he did it fell in two. The damage it had suffered, he observed, was beyond repair.

As far as he could tell he was alone. It was now daylight, several hours had passed and the sun glared down on him, taunting him. He tried to sit up but he was in considerable discomfort so he lay back down. He raised his hand to where he now sported a lump the size of a large pebble and he prodded the tender spot to check for damage, causing him to wince. As he lay on the soft sand, a stiff breeze picked up and made him shiver. The hairs on the back of his neck stood on end, *strange weather for a Spanish summer*. He wrapped his wet cloak tight around himself, though it did little to console him and forced himself into a sitting position. He looked around, though what he was hoping to find he didn't think he'd ever know. What he really wanted was justice and revenge and to uncover the truth. But they were gone. Long gone. *How long have I been unconscious for?*

He looked up at what were now the ruins of the old fort. Hundreds of years had Guadalest Castle graced the cliff's summit, in the beautiful valley that swept down to the sea, with a huge lake surrounding it. It was truly a remarkable sight in all its glory. One big square keep made of solid stone. It had the small watch tower at its peak that could see for miles around. There was only one way up to the fort by a small dirt track that led up the hill. The castle backed on to the cliff edge and the only way to it was through the rectangular courtyard at the fort's front. It, too, was trimmed with tall, solid stone walls, the side ones of which were impossible to scale unless you had a wish to fall to your death. Only from a frontal assault could the courtyard be breeched and even then there was not much room to manoeuvre. It was an ideal location to defend and for hundreds of years it had stood unconquered, until now. *We were too few, too few, what could we hope to accomplish?* Richard looked on at what was once a magnificent structure, but now it was reduced to nothing more than ash and stone. Smoke could still be seen spiralling upwards from its remains. *What will the Duke say when he finds out? And what will become of the Guardians?* But they were all dead, he was no longer its captain, and he had no garrison.

"Simon," he panted again as tears welled up in his eyes and he felt no shame in it. In his distress Simon was all Richard could think of. It was only then that he realised how much of a true friend Simon really had become to him. The silent tears trickled down over his bony cheeks as sadness overwhelmed him. It was at this moment when the image of his late friend appeared in the forefront of his mind that the sudden realisation of what had just happened hit him, as hard as if someone had slapped him around the face. It was like having his head dunked in ice cold water and his wits raced back to him and it finally dawned on him the seriousness of the situation. His family were in trouble, his wife, his daughter needed him desperately and yet here he sat, on the sandy shore, full of self-pity and wasting time. *Fool!* "Oh God," he mumbled. *I must save them, I have to protect them.* "I must get to them first!"

Richard rose to his feet and scanned the surroundings. He needed to get out of there and quickly, but he was on the wrong side of the lake. He started to run and edged his way around the water as fast as his slightly battered and weary legs would allow him to. As he made his way around the shore he could feel his feet crunching in the wet sand. It was seeping between his toes, causing his feet to sink, trying to hold him back. *I have lost my boots, it would seem.* But there was no time to look for them now. Despite the setback Richard surged on and as he found his way further around the lake he could see a dark image lurking on the far shore. He strained his eyes across the lake in an attempt to make out what it was but it was far too difficult to tell. Instinct would have his initial guess believe that it was one of the attackers still lurking, trying to find out if he had survived the fall but to still be here alone, during broad daylight, seemed both unwise and highly unlikely.

Panting, he slowed down to a jog, his breath heavy. He crept closer and closer until finally to his utter astonishment he realised what it was. It was Lonzo, one of the horses from the fort stables, alone, neck bent, lapping up the water at the lake's edge. To Richard's amazement he was saddled and bridled. *God is on my side after all.* Richard had assumed the horses would be long gone by now, either dead or those that survived the fire would no doubt have broken loose and run free. But Lonzo was his horse. They shared a bond and here he was, eager and ready to serve when Richard needed him most. Lonzo was his pride and joy, costing him a small fortune back when he was squire for the General. Richard admired his skin, black as the night, smooth and shiny to the touch, like velvet. Lonzo was a grand war horse, a destrier, big and strong and despite his size as fast a horse as Richard had ever known. Lonzo never liked to be alone, preferring to find comfort and ease in the presence of his master, so Richard rushed around to meet the horse before it fled into the wilderness and was lost forever.

At first Lonzo seemed wary and backed away from him slightly. He was in no position to begrudge the horse. He too would be cautious after what had just happened. Perhaps Lonzo had suffered an injury and been hurt in the fire. But he was used to the smell of Richard and the touch of his hand on his back and he soon let Richard approach. Lonzo allowed Richard's fingers to run through his mane and stroke him gently. But time was of the utmost importance and sensing the right moment Richard swiftly climbed atop the horse. Lonzo dug his hooves into the sand and dragged them back in anticipation and neighed when Richard slapped him on his hide. Richard roared loudly, piercing the silence of the usually quiet surroundings, echoing off the mountains deep in the valley. Richard willed Lonzo on as he raced him up the bank, digging in his heels, spurring him on. Over the hill they soared and out of sight of the old fort and Richard didn't even glance back, not once.

He knew the country intimately in fact few knew it better. He was adamant he knew a quicker route back home than they did but he had no idea how long he had been unconscious for. His heart sank when he realised that something was wrong. If it wasn't bad enough that he had come across the tracks of the attackers heading in the direction of his home, the smoke lining the horizon that was no doubt gushing from the roof of his palace left him feeling somewhat queasy and nauseous. His mouth was dry and it was becoming impossible to swallow. Visions were now searing through his brain, the most unpleasant sort. He saw his wife's body, the look of fear in her eyes. He suspected the worst, he could not deny it, but he had to find out what had come of them; he had to get home.

Lonzo bounded along the dirt track that weaved down the wooded mountainside which separated the valley of Guadalest with that of Richard's own. He pushed Lonzo as hard as he dared until he reached a ford where the Xaló River emerged splashing across the track, it marked the entrance to his land and he knew the quickest route would be directly across the desolate orange groves. Tugging on the reins he urged Lonzo on towards the wooden fence that surrounded his fields. Lonzo leapt gracefully into the air and cleared it by a good foot. As they forced their way up the gentle slope his village soon bounced into view, and it was chaos. Houses were aflame, women were screaming, children were crying and the villagers were trying to put out the flames. Above his home, black smoke was billowing into the air but nothing could be done. His palace was burning to the ground just as the old fort had done. By the time he reached the path that led up to the front gate it was a blazing inferno. Richard's heart crashed into the pit of his stomach.

He leapt from the horse, making sure to tie him to a post, sensing the beast's unease, and navigated his way around the burning building, looking for any signs of his wife and daughter. He raced to the east side of the palace to the watch tower, a solid stone structure that rose near sixty feet into the air. On top of it flitting in the acrid breeze was a flag of red and gold upon which was depicted the coat of arms of Richard's house, which so happened to be a miniature version of the tower itself. It had been built before Richard's time as a defence against marauding pirates and bandits, who could be seen coming from miles away. A warning would alert the residents of the village who would take refuge in the tower for not only were the walls strong but the only way to enter it was via a drawbridge sixteen feet off the floor making it nigh on impregnable. To cross the drawbridge however they first had to enter the palace and only from there could they enter the tower. But seeing the village in such anarchy Richard could only presume the warning was never given. *What the hell are Paulo and Gringo up to?* He could only hope his wife and daughter had made it into the tower before the palace went up in flames.

But to Richard's horror there was no drawbridge; it had burnt to the ground.

"No!" Richard screamed but at that moment he saw a rope thrown from the opening of the tower where the drawbridge should have been and to Richard's slight relief out emerged Paulo and Gringo who climbed down frantically.

The two of them were twins, almost identical, and only those that knew them well could tell them apart. They were monks of the Cistercian Order but sons of a knight. Their father had been a member of the Order of Calatrava, which was set up as a military branch to the Cistercian Order. The Cistercians had been made up of knights or sons of knights that had converted to monkhood and when their father died Paulo and Gringo had done just that. But in their hearts they were not monks, they were fighting men and the Knights of Calatrava, on the contrary to the Cistercians were monks who had become knights. It was the wish of Paulo and Gringo to follow in their father's footsteps and they had begged the leader of their order to send them to a Calatrava stronghold. He agreed on the condition that they still conform to their duties as monks, to which they agreed reluctantly. They were stationed at Castell de Castells, a castle at the far end of the Xaló Valley run by Calatrava knights. They arrived with great expectations but so far they had been sneered at and found themselves to be the object of amusement to the others.

It was Richard who saw their true worth. He had a canny knack for looking into a man and summing up their virtues and qualities in a matter of seconds and he liked what he saw in Paulo and Gringo. He offered them a place in his community and when he was in Guadalest it was their responsibility to man the tower and guard the small village. They were elated to be given such an opportunity to prove themselves, and besides it got them out of their monk duties. As for the Calatrava knights they couldn't care less. It suited both parties.

"Ricardo!" Gringo gasped as he approached Richard, with Paulo hot on his heels. They were both soot faced and sweating. They wore the white mantles of the Calatrava knights despite not yet being knighted, which Richard guessed they must have stolen when they left Castells. Emblazoned on them was a red Greek cross with fleur-de-lis at its ends, which strikingly reminded Richard of the Knights Templar. That's why Richard hired them; from a distance they looked intimidating, but Richard knew they were not the sort. Both had short brown hair which was matted with sweat and they had dark expressions on their tanned faces.

"What is it?" Richard demanded, "Where are my family?"

It was Paulo who replied. "Ricardo, I am sorry. They came in the dead of night, hooded and cloaked."

"We never saw them until they were upon us," Gringo added. "We tried to lower the drawbridge but the first thing they did was set fire to it."

"There was no way for them to cross," Paulo carried on. "We tried to get to them but the fire was too fierce." He held up his hands in defence, showing they were red, raw and blistered. "Some of the men put up a fight but they were outnumbered and all we could do was watch."

"My wife and daughter, are they dead?" Richard asked, head dropping, tears welling in his eyes. All that he had built, all that he had worked for, as little as it was, had been destroyed in one foul swoop.

"Good God no, they live, they were taken," Paulo replied. "After these men sabotaged your family's escape route they broke through the palace doors and took them hostage, before setting it ablaze." Paulo's eyes averted to the palace which was already nothing more than a ruin.

Richard raised his head, hope in his eyes, the palace temporarily forgotten. "They live? Where were they taken?"

"They went north-east," Gringo answered.

"Then we must follow." Richard took a moment to assess the carnage surrounding his home. Two men had been killed, one a farmer and the other a tanner. A woman and her babe were also killed, burned alive in their home. *On my honour they will pay for this, by God they will pay.* All the horses had been let loose and most of the livestock killed. "There is little we can do here now, so let's go."

Richard turned and led them south-west back the way he had come.

"Why do we not yet pursue them?" Paulo asked, surprised.

"Because," Richard replied with a slight curving of the lips. "I need new boots."

Richard entered the village of Guadalest, trudging up the track bare footed. He was tired, panting and clutching the side of his head which still ached from the fall. In fact, now that he had calmed down somewhat it was plaguing him more than it had done before. Still fresh from the attack, he thought it best to keep a low profile for a while. He decided the best option was to leave Lonzo with Paulo and Gringo in the forest just outside the village and make his way in on foot. He was much less likely to catch anyone's attention that way. He had no idea how quickly word would have spread about what had happened at the fort but he was far from in the mood to be questioned. There was simply no time with his wife and child in grave peril. He raised his hood, wrapped his cloak about him and made his way along the village street. He suspected he would meet little resistance as he looked more like a beggar than anything else, in his soiled clothes and without any shoes. The strong aroma of beef and ale wafted up his nostrils as he passed the inn. A local was entering, no doubt to get drunk without a care in the world. What Richard would have given at that moment to be in there having a tankard of ale with Simon and perhaps something to eat. But he told himself that he mustn't dwell on the past but instead he must stay focused. He very much doubted whether the news had spread to the village, but the last thing he needed was the furore that would inevitably sweep the place if they knew he was here, and to have to recount the event to every living soul in it, would be just too difficult to bear.

The village at Guadalest was big in comparison to Alcalalí but still somewhat small and it all centred on the main square. There was one road in and out that ran along the west side of the square. Other than that it was home to a few shops and the inn. A handful lived there but it was mainly local farmers and travellers that came and went to resupply, sell or trade in the market. Making his way to the square, Richard paused to admire the familiar market. Although he had been captain of the fort's garrison for the best part of ten years, this is where he had spent a lot of his childhood and he knew every crack and crevice. It was where the elderly couple that raised him had lived and it was at this very market that he had met his wife, Louisa Rois de Llaurí. Llaurí was another town someway further north situated between Gandia and Valencia. She had been visiting with her father, the Lord of Llaurí. The recollection made Richard smile, for he had loved her the moment he laid eyes on her. She was only six at the time and she had lost her father and for a moment found herself all alone. It was not long before she was beset upon by three bully boys. It was Richard who had come to her aid. That was the very same day he met the General Córdoba.

It was fairly busy in the market, meaning it must be Saturday. Time had completely escaped Richard. He would come here often on a Saturday with the elderly man to buy vegetables if ever they needed them and other such things. He had loved it here and it was a comforting sight, with nothing seeming out of the ordinary, except suddenly, he noticed with surprise a group of soldiers congregated outside the blacksmith. The village was part of the duchy of the Duke of Gandia and these were clearly his men for they wore the yellow and black of his house, with the red bull emblazoned on their chests. They passed through every now and again to lend their custom and to check all was well. Usually Richard received advance warning of this for it was his obligation to host them at the castle, but more oft than not they refused his invitation. They preferred to spend the time drinking and whoring at the inn. This time, however, Richard had not and the soldiers were far too heavily armoured for that. Richard was keen to find out more about their purpose, so he headed to a stall not far from them and pretended to buy some fruit and leaned over to eavesdrop on their conversation.

"So run it by me again, the fort was attacked, you say?"

"No, not a single sign to suggest so, no sign of damage to the main gate, the doors were found open but undamaged."

"So what happened?"

"Must have been an inside job, after all, six guards worked there, five were found dead and one is missing. Doesn't take a genius to work out he done it!"

"The Mercenary?"

"Yeah, he was captain of the guard, and rumour has it he's the Baron of some pile of shit village too, Señor Ricardo de Guadalest he goes by, seen as some kind of saint in these parts. Anyway our orders are to find him and bring him in for questioning."

"Blind me with a hot poker, why would he risk losing all that? It doesn't make sense!" the soldier shook his head. "And you say he burnt down the castle. The Duke must be furious."

"He is. This Ricardo won't be a Baron for much longer."

"No, he'll find himself sitting in a nice cell in the Duke's dungeon."

Richard was overwhelmed with shock at how clever those men had been. Until that moment, he hadn't considered he would be marked as a suspect in what had happened. They must have made sure that the whole attack looked like he may have played a part in it, hiding their dead, unlocking the gates from the inside and leaving them open. It was now starting to make some kind of sense. By doing that, they made sure that he would have to flee and pursue them. It was why his wife and daughter were still alive. They wanted to make sure he would follow them. Well, as if kidnapping his family wasn't hard enough, now he was a wanted man as well. *Wanted for the murder of my own friends, how they could think it of me? I have always been loyal.*

"I shouldn't have come here. It was a stupid mistake, I must get out," he said aloud as his heart began to race in his chest.

"You shouldn't have what?" the fruit seller began to ask as he turned to face Richard. "Hey, get away from my stall, you beggar!" said the fruit seller when he saw the state of Richard. "Go away, thief, before I call the guards!"

Richard was more than happy to oblige, but he wasn't going to leave before he got what he came for. Moving from the stall, he slipped his way past the guards and through the door into the blacksmith's, unnoticed.

"Erm, can I help you?" asked a familiar voice.

"Joseph." Richard lowered his hood.

"Richard!"

"Joseph, I haven't got long, listen to me-"

"You're a wanted man, Richard, please, you can't be here."

"It wasn't me. We were attacked, they framed me. I don't know who they are but they said they knew my father. Joseph, they took my family, they took Louisa and Maria!"

"My God, Richard, I had no idea, I'm so sorry. I knew you couldn't have done it, after all they were your friends, our friends. I told the soldiers so, they've been asking around about you."

"They questioned you?"

"They did. I told them you were my friend and you weren't

capable of such an act, but they seem convinced. I almost believed them."

"Joseph, you shouldn't have, they will be watching you! Well, listen, I haven't got much time, I need armour, a sword and some boots!"

Joseph smiled, looking at Richard's feet. "Boots?"

"Don't ask," Richard responded.

"Well, you've come to the right place. Follow me."

He followed Joseph into a small backroom behind the counter. There were no weapons or anything of value. Joseph lifted the round carpet in the middle of the room to reveal a trap door leading down towards a secret basement. Richard was a little confused but Joseph lit a torch and handed it to him and without hesitating Richard made his way down. He entered a room as small as the one above. The light easily found all four corners of the room but to his surprise it shone back at him and for a moment he was temporarily blinded. He lowered the torch and edged forward, slowly taking his hand away from his eyes, and looked upon the source of the reflection. His mouth dropped. The light was reflecting off the most wondrous steel plate armour he had ever seen.

"Where did you-?" Richard asked, his breath taken away.

"It was my great grandfather's. He was a captain in the Spanish army, you know, before he took up being a blacksmith, but I have reshaped and redesigned it using the revolutionary ideas the great English mind my dear mother gave me, with the latest Italian and Flemish techniques. I've been working on it for months. It's one of a kind. Try it on."

It was definitely the most splendid thing Richard had ever seen. He had fought in many battles and seen many men, both his own and foreign of all sorts of rank, some rich and some poor, but never had he seen a man adorned in such armour. It was beautifully crafted steel, made ever so thin but strong as stone. The cuirasse was inlaid with gold as too were the greaves and gauntlets. It came with everything including vambraces, spaulders, sabatons and a great bacinet.

It took Richard an age to put the armour on, requiring Joseph's help. He put the steel plate on over his chain mail and when that was done he returned his black surcoat which bore the sigil of the Guardians and his cloak and last of all a pair of black boots that Joseph lent him.

"I do not have a sword or shield?" Richard protested.

"Ah, you are in luck, to some extent. Simon asked me to make him these." Joseph went across the room and opened a trunk and when he returned he had a sword in one hand and a shield in the other. "He always was a fancy lad, took me a long time mind, but he paid me well. I'm sure under the circumstances he would have wanted you to have them."

Richard took the shield on his left arm. It was black trimmed with gold and in the centre it bore the emblem of the Guardians, and was incredibly light. He held the sword aloft with his right hand. It was astonishing. The steel blade was pristine with not so much as a scratch on it and the golden hilt had black leather bound around its grip and in the pommel, delicately and beautifully crafted too, was the guardian's sigil.

"How do I look?" Richard said, lost in admiration of Joseph's work.

"Ha-ha!" Joseph replied. His laugh brought Richard back to civilisation.

"What?"

"Well, I hope you're as good a swordsman as they say, because you'll need to be to pull that off. You don't look like a baron, you look like a king!"

Even Richard suppressed a smile.

Chapter Three

Guardians of Guadalest
Guadalest, Crown of Aragón. June, 1513.

"The humblest citizen of all the land, when clad in the armour of a righteous cause, is stronger than all the hosts of terror."
William Jennings Bryan

The feel of the armour on Richard's body was almost soothing, calming the itch that had been building up for many months. Every element of his being was craving the sense of battle and his body willingly accepted its embrace. Too long had it been since he'd worn such attire but it fitted all too well. He felt like a child again, picking up that wooden broom for the first time pretending it was lance in hand, that he was some brave knight in a distant land fighting a holy crusade, spilling Saracen blood upon the sand. But it was not the Saracens that would fear his wrath on this day; it was Englishmen, his ancestral forebears. They would rue this day, that alone he could promise. *For my father they will pay. For Louisa and Maria they will pay.*

He left the shop fully armoured, a long sword at his hip and weighing considerably more than when he went in. Despite that, it was the lightest armour he had ever donned and he felt more alive now then he had in years. He felt whole again. Before, he had been like a blacksmith without his hammer or a scribe without a scroll but now, he was himself again.

Yet as soon as he laid eyes on it he knew it was priceless. *How can I afford such things?* Richard was almost embarrassed by the title he bore and ashamed to call himself a baron. His people looked up to him, but he saw himself as little more than a farmer and a poor one at that. But to Richard's disbelief Joseph gave it to him completely free of charge. The only price to pay was letting

Joseph accompany him. It was far beyond his better judgment, though Richard knew he needed all the help he could get.

"How much do you want for all of this? I don't have the coin but…" Richard had asked him, defeated, adamant he did not have the funds to consider buying the armour out right.

"Nothing," he had replied. "I am coming with you."

If there was one thing Richard had learned of Joseph over the years, it was his stubbornness. Even if he tied him to the rafters, stole his horse and left him behind, he would only find a way to escape and follow him. He was a loyal friend that Richard could never deny and despite his often clumsy nature and ability to find trouble in the most unlikely of places, he was surprised to feel comforted in the knowledge that he did not have to face this burden alone. He had his friends with him, his brothers.

They took the necessary steps in ensuring that Richard was completely covered up using his long cloak. Now that the Duke's men were after him it would be unwise to present him in such décor. Heading onto the street cautiously, Richard was followed by an enthusiastic Joseph who stopped to breathe in the sweet air of adventure.

"Wipe that bloody smile off your face, Joseph!"

"Sorry," he murmured. "I have never left the shop for anything other than supplies before."

Richard sighed at his friend's innocence. "No matter, but we must not draw any attention to ourselves under any circumstances. We need to get out of the village as quickly as possible."

"Yes, of course."

"Remember the plan? Go straight and retrieve your horse, then head to the food stalls and purchase some basic provisions. I will head back across the village to retrieve Lonzo. Meet us at the northern wall. Let's go."

They headed across the street and into the afternoon sunlight. The heat was much stronger now that he had steel encasing his body underneath his black cloak and he soon began to sweat. The village was busy as was common on a market day, which would give him ample opportunity to blend in. However, the soldiers were still situated at the nearest stall and needs would have Richard and Joseph pass them first. Heads bowed they made to pass them. *At least there is a cool breeze,* Richard observed.

No sooner had Richard thought it, there was a small gust of wind strong enough to send dust swirling into the air. Joseph just had time to cover his eyes but he got a mouthful and began to cough, drawing the attention of the soldiers and in his temporary moment of blindness he walked straight in to the nearest one.

"Hey! Watch it!" the man roared as he shoved Joseph head first hurtling towards the ground.

"I beg your pardon, Sir, my friend is clumsy," Richard said as he retrieved Joseph from the floor, lifting him from under the arms, whilst he spluttered and coughed. "An accident, I assure you."

"Well, you just make sure there are no more accidents. I won't be so forgiving next time."

Richard whisked Joseph around and swiftly ushered him away from the scene, feeling the soldier's gaze boring a hole in their backs. Joseph, still shaken up, grabbed hold of his arm for support, taking a good handful of his cloak as well, pulling down slightly. It was just enough to raise the cloak half way up his shin and reveal his new greaves. The soldier who Joseph had disgruntled was still watching them from a distance and he noticed the glint the sun made as it shone off his shin plate.

"Bit grand for a common peasant, wouldn't you say?" the soldier asked, elbowing his mate in the chest.

"What? Oh...yes," he replied as he looked to where the soldier was pointing. "Let's check it out."

"Oi, you there!"

Richard had been noticed, but with half of Gandia looking for him it was only a question of when, not if. But still, they had no idea who he was, and that at least could buy him some time.

"I'm talking to you, Señor Ricardo!" the soldier shouted, confident that he had got his man. Who else in this godforsaken village would own armour like that and take the trouble to conceal it?

Shit. Richard turned and for a split second had eye contact with the soldier. He was a brute, bigger than him by a whole head length, with thick hairy arms and a thick black beard.

"There he is, boys, get him!" he roared. The soldiers were quick to heed the bearded man's call. They leapt into action brandishing their weapons and Richard and Joseph were soon beset upon. "That one in the cloak there, take him alive!"

Richard pushed Joseph with all his strength and flung him sprawling behind a wine stall, much to the displeasure of its owner. Richard couldn't afford to be taken. There would be a trial and it would be days, perhaps weeks, before his name was cleared. Then again, he was adamant that if Juan Borgia could get his way he would be marched to the nearest tree and hung. Richard had to make a stand. In one swift movement he flung his cloak from his shoulders and watched it crumple to the ground. He took his shield from his back and unsheathed his sword arcing it in to the air.

"Come and get me, if you can."

Onlookers gave a gasp. It was quite a sight to behold. He looked every much the knight of legend. The soldiers stopped in their tracks for a moment. They were most of them novice boys and were yet to face such action. To see such a warrior in such armour was an overwhelming setback, but it was short lived.

"What are you waiting for you, useless dogs? He's only one man, so get him!" the bearded man cried.

The first soldier came at Richard rather clumsily wielding his sword. Richard brushed it aside easily with his shield and put a heavy plated boot straight into the man's stomach sending him winded to the floor with an "Oomph".

Meanwhile on the floor behind the wine stall, Joseph raised

his head to find a hand in his face.

"You English are so clumsy. Take it, I won't bite," a man said. Joseph looked up to see Gringo, a smile cracked across his face. "Hello Joseph, it has been a long time. What you doing down there? The fighting's over there."

"If you must know, Richard pushed me," he replied as Gringo lifted him from the floor before dusting himself off.

"I understand if you're scared you know- I mean-"

"I wasn't scared, I..."

"Of course you weren't, but don't worry. Reinforcements have arrived, look!"

Joseph looked over his shoulder and to his right, two stalls down, he saw Paulo, Gringo's twin brother. Paulo gave Joseph a wink and turned to the nearest fruit stall. He picked up a basket of apples and flung them straight across the street just as the rest of the soldiers surged forth to meet Richard. Not expecting the sudden landslide of rolling objects underneath their feet, the soldiers were sent crashing to the ground.

A cheer came up from the crowd that had now gathered to watch the spectacle unfold. The soldiers were clearly unpopular in the village. Paulo took a bow and they applauded him just before he ran up and booted the nearest soldier in the head, which just happened to be the rather unpleasant black-bearded man, knocking him unconscious. The rest of the soldiers found themselves under a barrage of fruit as the crowd began to hurl their shopping at them. Even the unpleasant wine merchant was involved and the fruit seller began giving out free ammunition.

"Amigo, let's go!" Richard heard Paulo call. Searching for the source of the voice he spotted him as Paulo waved his arm in gesture. Richard ran after him as he surged deeper into the market, swerving in and out of the stalls. Not before long they were joined by Joseph and Gringo.

"Let's get out of here my friends," Paulo suggested.

By now the soldiers were up on their feet and were in hot

pursuit of the four men. Paulo came to a nearby building and led them up a flight of stairs, gesturing Richard and Joseph to come inside the nearest door. Gringo, however, had turned and was hurling fruit down the stairs at the soldiers, lemons and pears crashing into their helms. He even managed a wave to the crowd before being dragged inside by his brother.

They made their way up some more flights of stairs and burst out onto the roof of the building. They barricaded the exit with whatever they could find as they had done the door downstairs.

But now they were trapped.

"What now?" Richard called out.

"Never fear, amigo!" Gringo said in response as he reached into his sack and pulled out the same rope he and his brother had used to climb out of the tower earlier.

"And you just happened to have that on you, did you?" Joseph asked.

"You never know," he said with a smile as he began to tie one end of the rope to a wooden beam before hurling the other end off the side of the building.

After escaping the village they made their way across hilly farmland, looking to put as much distance between them and the soldiers as they possibly could. The angry shouts of the now conscious bearded man could still be heard from some way off.

"We must get to the trees," Gringo called. "It will not be long before they are on our trail and we are all on foot."

The forest would provide them with cover and if the soldiers were on horseback it would certainly slow them down. As they headed towards the tree line it was clear Joseph was struggling. His breath was heavy and he was sweating fiercely.

"Come on, Joseph, we are nearly there," Richard said, trying to encourage him.

"I can make it! Don't worry about me, it has just been so long since I have run so fast!"

"You've been drinking too much wine, you mean."

"I was that wine merchant's best customer before you pushed me at him!" he snorted with laughter. "Ah, don't make me laugh, it hurts too much!"

They made it to the tree line and stopped to take a breath. Looking back towards the village there was still no sign of the soldiers. But they wouldn't be long; they were planning something, Richard felt in his gut. They needed to get as far away from Guadalest as possible and fast, but to do so they needed horses.

Lonzo! Richard had almost forgotten him amid the escape. But as luck would have it he was tied up not far from there.

"I will just take a moment. I will not be long." It took him no time at all to locate Lonzo and return to his men. The horse was glad to see him, but not Paulo and Gringo who had left him unattended. He rubbed his head on Richard's arm, until he noticed the remaining fruit in Gringo's sack, which all sins forgiven he went over to nuzzle at. This left them with a problem. There were four of them and they only had one horse. They had intended to share for the time being but that plan had been dependent on the acquisition of Joseph's horse. There was no choice but to make the journey on foot. Richard was loath to leave Lonzo behind however, as he was such a valuable horse. *No, I will take him all the same; he will come in handy*, he thought. The assailants, though, were all on horseback. *They could be miles away by now. This quest is folly.*

"I know what you are thinking, Ricardo," he heard Paulo say. "I have seen the look of defeat on many a man, but let me tell you now, hope is not lost. While we have strength, we can prevail, and the Guardians of Guadalest will serve justice."

"The Guardians?" Richard replied. "The Guardians are dead and I with it. What can we hope to accomplish? We have but one horse. We are one knight, two men-at-arms and a blacksmith and not to mention, they could be miles away from us by now."

"You lost your brothers, aye, and their deaths will be

avenged, you have my word on that. As long as the Guardians have a captain then they remain strong, and the way I see it you have some new recruits." Paulo got down on to one knee and Gringo did the same beside him. "We offer ourselves to the cause."

Richard looked over at Joseph, feeling somewhat taken aback. Joseph was at first a little hesitant. But he was a proud man who often spoke of the great deeds his great grandfather had performed. For a long time Joseph had thought of taking up the sword but it was one thing forging one, wielding one was entirely another matter. To Richard's surprise, he too walked over and got down on to one knee, saying "You have my sword too, Richard, of what little use it may be."

"You know what it is my brother and I seek," Paulo intervened. "We wish to honour our father. You are the Baron of Alcalalí. You have the power. Knight us and by God I swear it, we will forever be in your debt." Richard had never knighted a man before and he was not sure if they were yet worthy of such an accolade, but he felt a huge sense of pride in his friends and he knew better than anyone that it took more to define a knight than mere achievement. It took bravery, courage and honour, something these men had in abundance. Richard suddenly felt compelled by hope, despite their small number.

"Forgive me," he said. "For a moment I had lost faith and you have shown me the true meaning. While we have strength there is still hope." Richard withdrew his sword and there in the sanctuary of the trees he dubbed them, even Joseph. "I say to you rise, rise now as knights and Guardians of Guadalest. We will have blood for the death of our brothers!"

With that, the three men stood. Paulo and Gringo pulled off their white mantles and hurled them to the floor before embracing one another. Joseph, on the other hand, looked pale but Richard shook his hand and congratulated him nonetheless. There was the sudden sound of a horse whining deeper into the forest. Richard turned.

"Where did that come from?" Joseph asked. "It cannot be the soldiers surely. We would have seen them coming from the village."

"Joseph, bring the horse, Paulo, Gringo, follow me!" Richard headed further into the trees. As they thickened and the sky became darker he feared they might become lost, but then he heard the sound again and it was getting closer. The sound of men could be heard through the undergrowth. As they neared, they reached a ridge in the trees where it sloped down into an open clearing. He signalled for the others to get down and they studied the sight below.

There was a camp of at least thirty men judging by the horses and number of tents. At the far side was the largest. Richard's heart leapt as he thought, *I wonder if Louisa and Maria are in there.* The men that were visible and sitting round fires were clad in black, the same as the men that had attacked the fort. Most were eating, some resting and a few were entertaining woman. *Local peasant girls they have kidnapped no doubt.* But what truly puzzled Richard was why on earth they had come back here. Their tracks had led north, so why circle back?

Richard's eyes ran to the black banner next to the big tent with the green leaf embroidered upon it. *They are still here.* Richard locked his gaze on the tent, his eyes trying to envisage what was beyond the canvas. *Could my wife and daughter be in there?* A woman screamed. *Maria?*

"What should we do, Ricardo?" Gringo asked. "There are too many to assault."

"We will wait till nightfall and circle round. My family is in that tent, I know it, and we will get them out."

There was a sudden snap in the trees behind them as the unmistakable sound of a man treading on a dead twig echoed through the wood. All of the men in the clearing had heard it too, and looked up to where they lay hidden. Richard turned his head to see who was there. They were being followed.

"There they are men, get them!" the bearded man's voice rang out. The soldiers had surrounded them. "And they've brought some friends to play!" By friends Richard assumed he meant the very men they were tracking. As the shout went up so did torches all around, and it appeared they had brought reinforcements of their own. The commotion had stirred the men in the camp and they snuffed out their fires and made for their horses.

"No!" Richard cried. He was so close to his goal.

"Ricardo, there is no time. Take the horse and go with Joseph, follow them," Paulo said.

"But what about you?"

"We are Guardians now, and we will do what must be done. We will hold them, go!"

"They will show you no mercy for helping me."

"Please Ricardo, just go."

Richard took one last glimpse down at the campsite. Figures had emerged from the large tent. He saw a girl ushered out with a sack over her head surrounded by masked men, struggling as she was bundled by two men onto a horse.

"Maria!" he called. He saw her head jolt as she recognized his voice. *It's her.*

There was shouting in Richard's ear. He stood and turned to see a soldier charging towards him, torch in one hand and sword in the other. Richard drew his sword and dodged the oncomer, hitting him on the back of the head with the flat side of his blade, sending the soldier headfirst down the hill towards the campsite. Most of the camp had fled by now.

"Ricardo, go!"

Joseph was already on top of Lonzo and Richard swung his leg up.

"Thank you," he said to Paulo.

Richard charged Lonzo down the hill and into the enemies' camp, where there were still men remaining trying to find a way out. He slashed his new sword at the back of the first man he passed, hearing the sizzle as his blood spattered the embers of a nearby fire. The grotesque waft of burning blood tickled his nostrils but it did little to deter him. He hacked away, his shoulder aching, sweat running into his eyes. But still he continued to stab and cut, left and right, killing at least six men while Joseph clung to his back. They made their way up the hill on the following side. As they reached the far tree line he brought the horse about and looked back. He could see in the far torchlight Paulo and Gringo putting up a stern fight against the soldiers, some of which had now come down the hill. They were outnumbered and would not last long he knew. It was an odd sight, the Guardians of Guadalest fighting against the soldiers from Gandia and men in black alike. The men in black tried to defend themselves from the onslaught of both the Guardians and the soldiers, and the soldiers just attacked everybody within sight. It was a free-for-all.

"Richard, we must go," Joseph spoke softly in his ear.

Richard knew he spoke the truth. There was nothing he could do to help Paulo and Gringo now. He must find his wife and daughter. He whisked Lonzo around and into the dark they rode.

Richard waited behind a tree. He could hear the rustling in the leaves as someone approached. Not all of the men in black had had time to get their horses, and some were forced to flee on foot. *I will hunt them down one by one.* Joseph was holding on to Lonzo hidden as best as they could. Richard stood, sword in hand, waiting. All had been quiet in the darkness of the forest except for the odd hoot from an owl, but now he heard the crunching of the leaves, and he knew they were close. He saw the outline of their cloaks floating in the air, almost ghostly in the moonlight. Two men were all he could see.

As they made their way past him, Richard sprung out from behind the tree. In a wild reaction the closest man tried to swing his sword, but Richard brushed it away easily with his own before running it across the assailant's neck. The man slumped to the floor, blood pulsing out from the open wound, soaking into the forest floor. The second was more prepared and met his sword in a clash of steel that punctured the forest air like a cannon shot.

Richard glared at his prey as they danced, circling each other in the light of the moon that seeped through the branches of the trees. The man was strong. He met Richard's blows easily and pushed forward with stinging attacks, and it was all Richard could do to parry. His mind erupted with doubt. Suddenly he was in fear for his life. Without warning Joseph ran and tackled the man to the ground, to both his and Richard's complete surprise. Before the man had a chance to react Joseph had picked up a rock from the ground and smashed it down into the man's face. Richard heard his nose break and he saw the man's blood rush over Joseph's fingers, but he did not stop. He carried on until the man stopped moving. When it was done for a moment they stood in total silence, Joseph staring at his blood stained hands.

"That is the first man I have ever killed," he finally said, more to himself than to anybody else. Richard could see the pain in his face. He had seen it many times before upon younger men's faces in battle when they had killed for their first time. It was a horrible feeling.

Richard remembered his first time. He was squire for the General Córdoba fighting in the Granada wars. He remembered pulling a young Muslim boy from his horse and stabbing him in the stomach with his dagger. It had not been a pretty kill and the boy must have suffered immense pain. Richard always wondered if that boy had ever killed anyone prior to that point, or whether he had been just as scared as Richard had been on that day.

There was a sudden disturbance in the undergrowth as someone pushed on a branch. It was followed by a cry as a man surged towards Joseph, his sword raised. Richard pushed Joseph out of the way and threw his sword with all his might. It circled through the air and sliced through the man's rib cage with a sickening crunch.

"It appears we are even," Richard said to Joseph with a smile as the man slumped to the floor. Joseph did not return the smile but he nodded all the same, relieved to be alive. Richard went to retrieve his sword and wiped the blade on a tuft of grass.

"Hello amigo!" came a loud cry from behind Joseph. Without thinking Joseph turned and punched Gringo square on the nose.

"Oi! That hurt," he gurgled, blood pouring from his nose and into his mouth.

"Is that how you greet all your friends, Joseph?" asked Paulo, walking out from the trees to inspect his brother's face.

"Oh Gringo, I'm so sorry, I thought-"

But before Joseph could finish what he was going to say Richard burst into a fit of laughter. Even poor Gringo couldn't help but join him and before they knew it they were all at it. Even Joseph had to smile, his first kill momentarily forgotten.

"It's kill or be killed, my friend," Paulo said, slapping Joseph on the back. "You did well!"

"You saw?"

"Aye, we saw, we were tracking that man here," Paulo said, pointing to the man that Richard had just pulled his sword from. "And he just happened to stumble upon you."

"It's good to see you alive!" Richard said, embracing the twins in a bone crushing hug. "How did you get away?"

"Oh, it was easy." Gringo was still holding his swollen nose. "Nobody can track better in the dark than us. We led the soldiers away north further into the forest before circling back around."

"But they won't be fooled for long. They will be able to follow our tracks come day break; we should move," piped in Paulo.

The four of them readied themselves as best they could. Joseph retrieved Lonzo and gathered their things and they made their way east in the direction the men in black had gone. Richard had seen his daughter and so knew that she at least was still alive. That alone gave him hope. Now the pursuit was truly on.

Chapter Four

The Great Captain
Córdoba, Crown of Castile. June, 1513.

"Never attack on ground chosen by the enemy."
Gonzalo Fernandez de Córdoba

Richard had to think about it for a while but the more he thought about it the more it seemed the right way for them to proceed. The assailants' tracks were clearly visible and easy enough to follow. Yet it felt almost like they wanted to be followed. There was no caution in their flight, it was clumsy, unprofessional and extremely unusual behaviour for trained assassins. It was obvious that they were now heading north having reached the coast. Richard would almost stake his life towards Valencia. The assailants had horses and would be many leagues ahead by now. Richard and his merry band were few and had only one horse but he knew the country well and had they wanted to pursue, it may have been possible, but something just didn't feel right. *Who were they?* Well, they were English, that was for sure and so Richard could only assume that they were heading back to England. His bet was that they had a ship anchored in the harbour at Valencia. The truth was he had no idea how far behind they were and he didn't dare risk pursuing them to Valencia. If Richard got there and the men in black were gone, then all might be lost. But if they did have a ship, then to get back to England needs would have them sail south and around Gibraltar. It therefore seemed wise to turn their efforts south in the opposite direction. If Richard could not catch them then at least he might be able to head them off, if this was indeed their intentions. Besides heading south would take them past Córdoba. If there was one person in this world Richard knew he could count on for help, it would be his mentor, 'El Gran Capitán' although to Richard he was just Gonzalo Fernandez de Córdoba. Like a father and most definitely a friend and as chance would have it, if there was anyone in Spain who knew if there was a foreign ship lurking in Spanish waters, it would be him.

"The Great Captain?" Joseph asked again. "You wish for us to see the Great Captain?"

"Yes, Joseph, I do."

"Why didn't you tell me before we left? I would have brought my best shirt."

By this point Richard had to shake his head. "Honestly, Joseph, I had more pressing things on my mind than helping you pick out your clothing. Besides, Gonzalo is a retired battle commander, he is not a king at court. Your attire will be the last thing on his mind."

Joseph went to argue but Gringo cut across him. "Ricardo, is it wise to change our course? We risk losing the trail."

"I know, my friend, it is a difficult decision, but for some reason I feel we must. Gonzalo may even be able to help our cause. He has never let me down before."

That seemed enough to convince the twins, and they walked on ahead both following their own trail of thought. Joseph, on the other hand, didn't need convincing. "Did you really fight with him?" he blurted out.

"I- what- yes- how do you know these things?" Richard replied.

"Simon told me. I thought he was making it up, but you really did?"

"I fought for him during the Conquest of Granada as his personal squire and at the Battle of Cerignola as his second in command, yes."

Joseph's eyebrows rose in disbelief. "He must have thought highly of you."

"He knighted me."

"To be knighted by such a man!"

Richard looked at him somewhat offended.

"My apologies, Richard, I couldn't have wished to be knighted by a better man, but still," he carried on, "To have been knighted by the Great Captain himself! That takes some beating, and to have fought for him, too."

"Aye, but that life is behind me now. I chose to give it up."

Joseph chuckled. "My best friend was General Córdoba's greatest lieutenant." He shook his head in disbelief, and it made Richard smile. "What's he like, Richard, truly?"

"Gonzalo? A man, like any other, good natured, not as fearful as men make him out to be; still you wouldn't want to be on his bad side. He was a fearless warrior and a fierce friend."

"Tell me of Cerignola. What was the battle like?"

Richard had never been asked to recall a battle before and he was surprised by the memories that came flooding back to him and how easily the words flowed from his mouth...

Cerignola, Kingdom of Naples. April 1503.

It was mid spring, I remember, because it was not long after the trees had blossomed. We had entrenched ourselves on the hillside occupying the heights of Cerignola. Our artillery, consisting of twenty guns, was strategically placed at the very top of the hill while our infantry secured the bottom. We had taken the time to build walls and put up stakes in an attempt to slow the enemy down. Around the hill we dug a long trench, also to slow the enemy down, but we filled it with men armed with arquebuses. This was the first time any such guns had been used in large quantity during a battle. In front of our infantry I was positioned with the Jinetes, the light horse whom I had the pleasure to command. The heavy horse we kept in reserve under Prospero Colonna. Our forces numbered in the region of six thousand. We only had seven hundred men-at arms-and eight hundred horsemen.

The French, however, had a force in the region of ten thousand. They had three thousand infantry and were joined by three thousand Swiss pikemen and even had a larger contingent of mounted horse. We barely had time to dig up the trench before the French mounted horse charged our lines for the first time. Our arquebuses had previously been unproven in battle but today they would be put to the test. We had one thousand men armed with the guns and each arquebus took at least two minutes to load. However horse after horse went down under the bombardment of metal balls as the arquebuses fired at will. The few French knights that made it past the guns and through the stakes were met by sword and pike from our infantry and men-at-arms. To make matters worse for them our heavy guns were piling on the destruction.

After two unsuccessful charges the French made another attempt during which their commander the Duke of Nemours was killed. This left the French forces under the command of the Swiss commander Pierre du Terrail who led his infantry in the next attack along with what remained of the French mounted horse, but they were again forced back from arquebus fire. Pierre was also killed. The French had lost both commanding officers in less than a few hours, leaving them in a state of disarray. General Córdoba ordered a counter-attack against the disorganised enemy infantry and our heavy horse that had been left in reserve were called into action. I led the attack with our Jinetes, and the French suffered heavy casualties.

Yves d'Alegre was in command of the French rear guard and having watched the defeat of both the French and Swiss infantry called for a withdrawal and left the battlefield. I pursued him with my company. It was a total French defeat; they lost about four thousand men and we lost a hundred of our own. All of the French supplies including their wagons and all their artillery fell into our hands. After the battle was done the Great Captain Córdoba upon seeing the field strewn with French bodies who like us were all Christian, had three long tones played and we all prayed for the fallen.

For many years I was hailed as the hero of the battle but it is false. Our victory that day was down to the men who put their lives on the line to test a weapon that until that point had not been proven. I am sure that without the arquebuses we would all have died that day. Still, *that said, I was young and it was a heroic victory, one to savour.*

* * *

Other than the day Richard wed, the battle had probably been the most glorious day of his life, perhaps even more so. He had been elated, surrounded in jubilation. He had led his men to victory and they had praised him, and he remembered how they celebrated long into the night. It was not a moment one discarded lightly. It was an overwhelming experience that lived on long in the memory. Richard found it strange that he could be happy surrounded by so much death but he had been doing what he did best; fighting, killing. It was one of the greatest and most monumental moments in Spain's history and he was there and he played his part. It was a significant victory in the Italian Wars and went a long way to securing land in the name of the King. It was after this great battle that his mentor, the Great Captain Córdoba, dubbed him with the knighthood that he so desperately sought. Now he was like his father, and he only hoped he would be proud, that man he never knew, of what Richard had achieved.

So much euphoria had surrounded the battle at Cerignola. It was Richard's greatest moment as a soldier even eclipsing that of his feats in the Conquest of Granada when he was fifteen. But it would be the last time he ever took part in such a conflict and he was still trying to contemplate how he had gone from such heights to this. Then, he had had everything, all he had ever dreamed of and now he had shrunk down to nothing. Ten years had passed since that unforgettable night yet it felt more like a hundred. Despite his thirty seven years, he felt much older.

Gonzalo was like a father to Richard. He had treated him no less a son than he did a squire ever since the day he fostered him. However, it had been the best part of ten years since he last saw him but Richard knew he needed him now more than ever. After the Battle of Cerignola, Gonzalo went on to secure the Kingdom of Naples for Spain, driving out the French. He was then declared viceroy and enjoyed that honour for three years but was later recalled by King Ferdinand to enjoy a well-earned retirement. Richard had been meaning to visit him in his hometown for such a long time, but his position at the fort had prevented any such journey. Finally, he was on his way at last.

It wasn't the easiest of journeys, taking them across country, over hills and through wooded valleys. It took them the best part of ten days. Despite the relatively slow pace they were lucky enough to travel through several apple orchards and past a large stream, allowing them to break their fast and quench their thirst. On the third night of their journey they came by an inn completely by chance. It was in a small village called Arrayan and was surrounded by woodland. It was extremely remote but a haven for local farmers and men from the surrounding villages. It provided them with a decent meal, an ale or two and a woman should they wish it. Joseph blushed at the thought but Gringo took full advantage. "You never know what night is going to be your last!"

Paulo got into a friendly game of dice with four farmers, something he was particularly good at. However it ended with a few sour looking faces when he won a palfrey from each of them. Richard had to appreciate his talent. All three of his companions added a particular skill that was valuable to the group. Joseph was a blacksmith, after all. Paulo, on the other hand, was a tactician, very clever, seeing things before they happened. As for Gringo, well, he was just Gringo, and Richard wondered where would they be without his humour. He was a sly dog and equally adept at squeezing out of the tightest of corners.

They all left the inn considerably higher in spirits than when they arrived and now, thanks to Paulo, had a horse apiece and a spare to carry Richard's armour. But the horses were not the only new recruits. Richard had met a man by the name of Alexandre

Jiménez. He was a stout man, broad in the shoulders with thick arms and chest. He was red of head with a bushy red beard and had a laugh to match any man he knew. As far as Richard could gather, he was a landless lord and had lost all manner of ranks and titles, something that appeared to cause him great personal distress. He was a proud man, fuelled on by whatever demon it was that was hanging over his back. Like them, he was travelling the road with his five companions offering their swords for coin. It was only after a storm sent them into the forest for shelter that they got lost and wandered upon this place. Richard couldn't help but think it was no mere coincidence that they should cross each other's paths but for whatever reason, it was as if it was meant to be. He told Alexandre who he was. This brought a smile to Alexandre's face though Richard was pretty sure he didn't believe him.

"Señor Ricardo de Guadalest?" he asked, dumbfounded. "I thought he died during the Italian Wars, or that's how I heard it. Made his name at the Battle of Cerignola, never heard a trace of him after that."

This time it was Richard's turn to smile. He never previously thought about what others might think of his sudden disappearance off the map. *Dead, is that what they all think? Well a dead man back from the grave makes for a bad enemy I suppose.* Still, Alexandre took an avid interest in the plight of Richard's wife and daughter, so that at least he did believe.

"Aye, our loved ones are worth dying for, are they not?" he had asked Richard.

Yes they were, had been his response and if that is what it took for their safe return then he would offer his life up in a heartbeat with not a second thought. But that was not an option. The men that attacked the fort would only kill his family after his death, of that he was almost certain. *No, I will take the fight to them and then we shall see who triumphs.* "You seem an honourable man and your men loyal. If I had the finances I would hire your swords."

"Me and mine would be honoured to join your cause."

"But I have no coin to pay you; all I have has been taken from me."

"You misunderstand me. I do not want your coin. There is more to be gained by such a task than coin in my pocket. This is where a man shows his true worth. There is glory and respect to be had here. What I want is to make my name and I will have it known that Alexandre Jiménez did not turn down a man in need, but instead embraced him as a brother."

And so Richard had command of a small retinue of men which included a lord, three knights and five men-at-arms. Together they were ten strong; they had horses and they had provisions, and they were ready.

"Tell me, Alexandre, how would you like to meet the General Córdoba?"

"It would be my pleasure."

It took a further seven days traveling from Arrayan before they reached the city of Córdoba on the afternoon of the tenth day. But the going was a lot quicker and the time passed more easily in the presence of Lord Jiménez and his men. When they arrived, Córdoba was a beautiful sight to behold. It was one of the oldest cities in Spain and was once the most populous city in the world. In ancient times it has been both an Iberian and Roman city. To enter it they needed to cross the long standing Roman bridge that ran over the Guadalquivir River. As they did they got a good view of the town's cathedral with its sand coloured stone walls and its tall bell tower. Even further in the background they could see their ultimate destination, the Alcazar, which had been granted to the General on his return from Italy.

It took them almost an hour to get there, winding through the city streets. They drew the eyes of all the people they passed. Córdoba was a placid town and had not seen mounted men-at-arms for several years other than perhaps the General's men. He was well loved by his people, a decorated war hero but a man of peace nonetheless, who ruled his city well. They approached the gates, once a Visigoth fortress many centuries before it had been rebuilt, and now a palace of magnificent beauty. Like the fortress at Guadalest it had a courtyard known as the Patio Morisco. It had two towers, the Torre de los Leones, the Tower of the Lions and the Torre de Homenaje, the Tower of Homage. The stone walls were the same colour as the cathedral and inside was a series of Roman mosaics.

They passed several of them on their way to the General's audience chamber led by one of his guards. When they arrived the guards on the gate had demanded they state their business, unwilling to let them in. Richard did not recognise any of them and so did not begrudge them this. They were, after all, ten armoured men. He told them his name which they sent word to Gonzalo who told them they must let him in immediately. He left Paulo and Gringo with the men-at-arms who tempted some of the guards into a game of dice. Joseph, Alexandre and Richard made their way to see the captain.

It was a moment Richard would never forget. Despite having aged considerably, the joy of being reunited brought a youthful smile to the General's face. His hair was cropped, more white then grey now, but his features were still the same albeit with a few more lines across his brow. They came together in a long embrace.

"Richard, it is so good to see you," Gonzalo whispered in his ear. "I thought you'd never come."

"Alas, I thought I never could," Richard said as they broke apart. "But sad tidings bring me here to see you, and I am afraid we cannot linger long."

After providing an introduction for his men, Richard told the General his story. He listened intently, and though it took Richard the best part of half an hour, Gonzalo never once interrupted. For a moment afterwards he sat in thought.

"My dear boy," he said at last. "I am so sorry. Louisa, Maria, they were wonderful girls."

They are wonderful girls, still. They are alive, Gonzalo, have faith.

He went on, saying, "Tell me, you say the Duke holds you responsible for what happened?"

"He does."

"Richard, do you know the Duke's wife?"

"Juana? My wife knew of her, but I've never met her myself."

"Do you know who her father is?"

"No, but she has royal connection, does she not?"

Gonzalo nodded. "Her father is Alonso of Aragón."

"The King's illegitimate son?" Richard asked, a little surprised.

"Aye, the very same," Gonzalo replied, a look of concern etched across his ageing face. "Richard, I must tell you something."

"What is it, Gonzalo? If you know anything, please tell me."

Gonzalo took a deep breath. "I served him, Richard, I served the King and I served him well, yet this is how he would repay me." He raised his hands and glared around the room. "You think I am enjoying a well-earned retirement? No, I do not belong here. There is strength still in me, Richard, I belong on the battle-field, not here."

"Then why did the King see reason to put you here?"

The captain thought about that for a moment. "I loved his wife, you know, Isabella. Not that I would have ever acted upon it for I was always loyal to the crown, to him. But I fought for her as much as I did for him. She was the one that had real faith in me, never him. Now she's dead and I never got to tell her that I loved her, my Queen."

"And the King found out about, this love?"

"King Ferdinand was always jealous of me. I was away fighting wars on foreign lands, expanding the realm. He hated it, he hated that the people loved me but most of all he hated that she loved me. Yet after she died I had no protectorate. I was no longer General Córdoba, I was just a man despised by the King."

"What does Alonso have to do with any of this?

"The King held his bastard in high esteem. All he wanted was for Isabella to treat him like a son but she never did. Alonso hated that she loved me in a way that she would never love him. He was jealous, Richard, as was his father and they conspired against me. I was recalled from Italy, Alonso replaced me as viceroy of Naples and Ferdinand brandished me with all these titles and fine words. Oh, it all looks pleasant, I'll grant you, the people fell for it but I'm nothing more than a prisoner in my own home."

"Do you think Alonso might be behind the attack?" Richard asked.

Gonzalo offered a weak smile. "That pile of shit? God no, he doesn't have the brain power to come up with such a ploy, but I have no doubt he will see the destruction of his son-in-law's castle as my doing. He is paranoid that I sit here plotting revenge against him and he will know that you once served me." His smile faltered, and caution returned to his face. "No, these assailants are someone else, someone far more dangerous I fear. You must be on your guard, Richard, you have enemies on both shoulders. Alonso won't want to get his hands dirty but he'll make sure the Duke hunts you down. He will want you to confess to acting on my behalf. I know you didn't burn the castle but that bastard will use any means possible to have me arrested and you are the key."

So that's why the Duke holds me responsible, because of a grudge his father-in-law has against my mentor. "We are hunting, yet being hunted."

"You must leave the country, Richard, they will not be able to pursue you, after all the country is still at war. Besides if these other men are English as you say then needs will have you go. I wish I could come with you. Look at me, Richard. I'm wasting away. Who will remember El Gran Capitán?"

Richard looked at Gonzalo with all the respect he could muster. "I do, Señor Córdoba, the greatest general I ever served." He bowed his head in recognition as did Joseph and Lord Jiménez.

Gonzalo waved away the gesture with his hand but he smiled nonetheless. "Aye, we had some spectacular victories did we not? But Cerignola, that was my favourite, one of the greatest victories in Spanish history!"

"The finest," Richard replied.

"But you left us and missed the battle at Garigliano, a night assault; did you hear? I was praised for my tactical genius- oh, I envy you, Richard. I have my past achievements to give me credit, that I don't deny. But to have a family of my own, to love and to share with them the tales, that's what I want. Yet I don't suppose I ever will."

"General!" Richard found the best way to communicate with the captain when in such mood was by referring to him by his title and thus affirming his superiority. "There is still time. You have a daughter, why not reconcile?"

"You do not understand, Richard. Isabella - she was the only one I ever loved and will ever love and you were the son I always hoped for. My daughter will never forgive me that sin, I fear. But still as I have none of my own, I shall help you and yours. Let them say this was our swan song."

"What about the King?"

"He can go to Hell for all I care. Do you remember our good friend Christopher Columbus?"

"The Great Explorer? How could I not."

"He kept writing to me up until the time of his death. They got him too, Richard, the bastards, the King left him with nothing and he was left to rot, poor until his death at his home in Valladolid. After all he did for the Spanish crown in the name of Ferdinand and everything the Queen promised him, the King withheld. I heard it from his son Diego's own lips that they had never expected him to return. The only possession he was left with was his flagship, the Santa Maria. He knew what the monarchy was a long time before I did and he tried to tell me. I didn't dare to believe it but I soon found out to my cost. The King confiscated all of my ships and left me with only a small garrison of men. However-" He paused, and for the first time since Richard arrived, Gonzalo laughed. "Christopher left me his ship in his last will and testament. It is harboured at Gibraltar and I issue it to you, so take twenty of my best men and do what you must."

"My lord, you offer too much."

"Richard, if I could give you more, I would, but I fear raising suspicion. The longer we keep the Duke's men at bay the better. I would like nothing more than to follow you. Oh, how I dream of meeting death with glory on the battlefield, but needs require me to stay here in Córdoba, in my seat, to wither away an old man."

"But if they should know you played a part in my escape, they will execute you."

"Then so be it, but the wrath of the small folk will be too much for the King to bear, I think. Alonso tried to have his father kill me a long time ago, but even the King would not be so ignorant as to ignore the people's love for me. He would confine me away to my bedchamber and throw away the key no doubt, but it can be no worse than what it already is. No, Richard, you have my full support, but I will keep this hidden as best as I can."

"There is one more thing I must ask of you-"

"Ask and it is yours."

"The men we track, as I have said, it is my belief they came here by ship. To your knowledge, have any foreign vessels entered Spanish waters?"

"There have been many, Richard, we are a trading nation after all, but there was one in particular that stood out. I had word from my contact in Gibraltar that the Scottish ship the Great

Michael entered the Mediterranean under a flag of truce. It was rumoured to be heading toward Valencia."

"The Great Michael?" Richard said.

."You do not know of it? One of the grandest ships in Europe, hired by the French if the rumours can be believed. Biggest bloody boat he ever saw, my man swears, should have known the Frogs would be in on it. Had I still been General I would never have allowed it to enter. Someone in Spain gives them favour."

"Aye, but that doesn't explain how it ended up in English hands. But it must be them, it must be!"

"Richard, I agree. You must hurry; they would have set sail by now. It's a five day ride to Gibraltar if you ride hard and fast. I will send word by carrier pigeon to my man down there-"

"I have heard tales of such birds," Joseph cut it with excitement, causing everyone to turn and look at him. "But I did not know they were actually in use!"

Gonzalo glanced at Richard for support, an air of amusement spread across his face. "Humour him," Richard replied.

"Well," the General said to Joseph. "It was a good friend of mine, Pedro Tafur, born in this very city in fact, although he died a few years before Richard came to me. He was a fascinating fellow, a traveller of sorts, but we've not the time to speak of his many great adventures now. When he was visiting Egypt in 1436 he saw them being used in the city of Damietta near the mouth of the River Nile. He was so impressed that he brought the idea home with him and set up a pigeon post. Columbus spoke highly of them too as they were also in use by the Republic of Genoa who equipped their watch towers with such posts. I have been using them ever since, very handy little devils."

"Interesting indeed," Lord Jiménez added with a hint of annoyance.

Richard, on the other hand, could only smile at Joseph's innocence. "You were saying about your contact?"

"Alas, forgive me, I will send word to him. He will do his best to hold them, I have no doubt, but if that ship is as big as he says it is, it will be a struggle even for them. If you-" the captain broke off, interrupted by raised voices coming from outside in the courtyard. At that moment one of the General's guards burst through the doors, the same man that had escorted them there earlier.

"Señor," he said, extremely out of breath.

"What is it, Santé?"

"Duke's men my Lord, they know Señor Ricardo is here. They say they have no quarrel with El Gran Capitán, but you must hand him over, in the name of the King."

"Oh they do, do they? And in the name of the King?" Gonzalo replied

How did they get here so quickly? "Gonzalo, my friend, I am sorry to have brought this upon you," Richard cut in.

"Richard, you have served me well. Now let me return you the courtesy. Get out of here and quickly!" The General turned to the guard. "Take twenty of our best men and go with him."

"Señor, I must protest," the man cried. "You need me here!"

"Santiago!" the General cried. "You have always been loyal, for this I raised you to captain of my guard, in return I ask only one thing of you, so do this and do it now, go!"

He nodded. "Sí Señor Córdoba."

It had been so long since Richard had seen his mentor and now his brief visit was over and all too soon. There was so much he had wanted to say to him, and so much to thank him for but there was no time. It would have to wait for another day. If there would ever be such an occasion; Richard had his doubts. He looked into the face of the man he owed so much to, and only hoped his eyes could tell him what his words could not.

"God speed, Richard, kill the bastards, and kill them all!"

They were ushered by Santé back to the courtyard where they found Paulo, Gringo and Jiménez's men horsed and ready. Santé called for his guards. It was only a small garrison the captain had at his disposal, a mere forty men but they were all armed and ready.

"Twenty of you are to follow with me, and the rest of you will stay here and defend the General. There are fifty Duke's men outside the gate demanding we open in the name of the King, but we ain't King's men, are we boys? We're men of El Gran Capitán." This brought a roar from the guards. "It won't take them long to break through, so hold them off for as long as you can. They will outnumber you two to one, but we like those odds, don't we boys!" The guards started to smash their swords and spears against their shields. "Let's go!"

Twenty of the guards filtered out to join their ranks. The rest headed towards the palace main gates chanting as they went, 'Cór-do-ba, Cór-do-ba, Cór-do-ba!' Richard wanted to stay. With the addition of his men, the two opposing forces would be evenly matched but it was too much of a risk and one the General would never forgive him for, considering the sacrifice that he was making. Richard knew in his heart that there was no choice. Santé led their sortie in the other direction out into the palace gardens towards the south. On another day Richard would have stopped to admire its beauty, flowers of all colours, beautiful smells and a fountain to match any other he had ever seen. They rode on past the fountain and headed towards the south gate but behind them they heard the unmistakable clash of sword and shield.

Chapter Five

The Great Michael
Gibraltar, Crown of Castile. July, 1513.

"In the same year the King of Scotland built another great ship called the Great Michael and he was the greatest ship and master of strength that ever sailed in England or France."
Robert Lindsay

Richard and the men of his company rode hard for four days, stopping only to relieve their bladders and when necessary to empty their bowels. They did, on Joseph's recommendation, take time out during the early hours of the third day to replenish, eating what little food they had and some of the men got some much needed sleep. They made it to Gibraltar on the morning of the fifth day in relatively good time, but they were all tired, extremely hungry and a little short tempered. The horses too were frothing at the mouth in exhaustion. But Richard supposed they could not complain, the horses were still alive and they had mainly travelled over flat country and dry farmland, making the journey for them straightforward. The downside was they roasted in the Spanish summer sun. It had made it somewhat wearisome for the men, with the heat and the lack of water, few streams on their journey and they were in short supply. They all knew it was hotter in the south but none of them had expected the furnace that they endeavoured to put themselves through.

They did get some reprieve as they neared the south coast. Here the land started to rise and they were met with the sight of mountains and with the mountains came trees which made their journey through the valleys a little cooler, adding some much needed shade. As well as the shade, the mountains forced the wind from the sea to blow up through the valleys and they were greeted with a cool breeze bringing an end to the hours of fierce blistering heat. As they passed down through the last valley towards the sea they could see the coastal town of Gibraltar. It was once part of the Moorish Kingdom of Granada but now it belonged to Castile and Spain. It was a small town on a narrow tip of land that pointed itself away from the mainland and out into the sea. To Richard, it seemed like a broken twig attached to a tree. Any slight sudden gust of wind and it looked like it may well break away.

They made their way into Gibraltar and there was no ignoring the unmistakeable sight that was the rock of Gibraltar, a mini mountain that overwhelmed most of the eastern tip. It formed a formidable backdrop to the town at its base on the western side. Complementing the rock was an awe inspiring view over the bay, where in the far distance was the town of Algeciras. The town had its own harbour, which right now harboured few ships, one or two trading galleys but mainly fishing vessels. To the left of the harbour, north of the town, was the Moorish castle, which had a high vantage point with both views over the harbour and bay, and out over the strait of Gibraltar as well, where the Atlantic Ocean met the Mediterranean Sea. On a clear day, the distant shores of Morocco were visible. The last time Richard had been here, it had been a mere grey line in the distance but today he could see green and what must be the Portuguese town of Ceuta. It once belonged to the Moroccan Kingdom of Fez after they conquered it in 1387 with the help of the Spanish Kingdom of Aragón. But in 1415 during the Battle of Ceuta it was captured by John I of Portugal and in Portuguese hands it remained still.

They made their way to the gates of the Moorish castle as they knew this would be where the town held its garrison. The castle itself was constructed three hundred years previously during the Marinid Dynasty that ruled north Morocco, therefore making it one of the most unique buildings of its type in the Iberian Peninsula. Its Kasbah was one of the largest in southern Spain.

They entered it with the guards letting them pass upon stating their business.

"I am Señor Ricardo de Guadalest and I am here to see your commander by request of General Córdoba." There was no hesitation once the Great Captain's name was mentioned. From inside the fortress the castle looked magnificent but the real focal point was its tower, the Tower of Homage. It was the tallest Richard had ever seen, making it the perfect watch tower.

They were met at the entrance of the castle by Gonzalo's sworn man. The town of Gibraltar was under Spanish sovereignty and this man was a Spanish soldier and therefore his allegiance lay with the Spanish monarchy and King Ferdinand II of Spain. However, despite retirement, General Córdoba still commanded a lot of respect. This man was one of many that were still loyal to the General. He had long served him and had fought for him at the Battle of Garigliano, Richard was pleased to hear. *It takes more than the needs and wants of a man that you've never met, that sits in a chair hundreds of miles away in a palace in Madrid, and commands you because he can because he's your lord and king, to put him before the love and respect that you have built up for a man that you've known and fought for over years of loyal service.* The man agreed with Richard's sentiments and his love for the General was great. He was a pleasant man with brown hair and a closely cropped beard. His name was Guillermo Sánchez.

At that moment there was an almighty boom and the very ground shook as a cannon was fired. Richard had only heard such a sound once in his life and that was at the Battle of Cerignola. Cannon and guns were only relatively new additions to the Spanish arsenal and were very expensive to get hold of, making them still rare in some parts of the world. They made a terrible noise, an unnatural thunderous sound that even the heavens could not contend with. Men all around covered their ears, sea gulls squawked and fluttered and Joseph even had to take a seat.

Guillermo took his hands away from his ears. "You have come in time, my friend," he said. "I received the General's message the day before yesterday. The ship Michael that you seek entered our waters a few hours ago. We have tried to slow her down but I do not think we will be able to stop her here. We have had her under constant fire from our fortress ramparts whenever she's come within range and I sent out two ships to intercept her but they are nothing in comparison to that ship. She's a monster!"

She is still here! It had taken Richard and his men fifteen days to reach Gibraltar. A nagging concern in the back of his mind had told him that she would be long gone. But he just had a feeling these men were in no hurry, they would not leave until they had made sure that Richard knew they had passed this way. "I thank you for your help, Guillermo. God knows this is not your fight. How do your ships fair?"

"If there is anything I can do to help the Great Captain and his friends then I will gladly do it. Besides, nothing much exciting happens down here other than the odd skirmish with Moroccan pirates. The men are bored and want to fight. Both ships are at present still afloat but I fear this is a fight we cannot win!"

"Is the Santa Maria ready to go?"

"She is, Señor, as the General commanded. But I must be honest with you; she won't be able to put up any sort of fight. She's half the size of my ships and even the two of them put together are no match. She only has two guns and they are nothing in comparison to the Michael's." Guillermo paused, aware he wasn't painting a good picture. "Aye, but she's a good ship and she's swift, I'll grant you that. You could chase this Michael but she will blow you out of the water if you get too close to her."

They made their way up on to the fortress ramparts and from there they gazed out over the strait of Gibraltar, watching as the fight unfolded. Even at a distance the Michael looked huge and she had a raw power that even the two Spanish ships together could not match. Richard doubted if there were any two ships in the world that could match her, apart from maybe the English flagship the Mary Rose, and her sister ship the Peter Pomegranate. Everyone knew that the English were famed for building warships and even they would be impressed by the might and power that the Michael possessed. She was built in Scotland on the order of King James IV and was so named after the archangel Michael. This ship was intended to lead a great crusade in an attempt to reclaim Palestine from the Ottoman Empire for Christendom. But it appeared that this idea had been thwarted, presumably by the French calling the Auld Alliance into effect, which was an alliance between Scotland and France.

None of the ships were looking to get too close or at least not within shooting range of each other. The Spanish simply kept firing warning shots to keep the Michael in the strait and force her into the bay within range of the fortress cannons, which so far had done little other than disturb the water. The Michael could have blown the Spanish ships out of the water had she dared to try but there would be a heavy risk of taking on possible damage and with a voyage ahead the ship refrained from doing so. It was at a stalemate.

Then it started. The two Spanish ships had drifted too far apart and the Michael wasted no time in seizing the initiative. She pounced and swiftly descended upon the nearest Spanish carrack coming up alongside her. The ship barely had time to react before the Michael fired her guns broadside and twenty four cannon ripped into the hull of the Spanish vessel tearing her apart. There was an explosion of noise as guns were fired, wood was splintered and masts cracked and crumbled. Men screamed as limbs were lost and bodies were impaled by flailing bits of wood. Those few that survived the initial onslaught tried jumping from the ship as fire spread on the deck. The hold started to flood with water and the hull dipped lower into the sea. The Michael just kept firing and pounding on the misery; it was total destruction. The other Spanish ship, despite knowing all was lost, approached the Michael on its other side in an attempt to take her unawares whilst she was busy firing on her sister ship. But she had taken the bait. The Michael had anticipated the manoeuvre and was ready to strike. She opened up her gun ports on the opposite side and the cannons erupted. The Michael fired double broadside and with all forty eight guns annihilated the Spanish ships within minutes were heading to the bottom of the ocean.

My God. Never had Richard seen anything like it, so many guns firing all at once and from a ship at sea. The sound was overpowering and the explosions erupted and the sky lit up with flame and fire and for a moment he thought he was looking into Hell itself; and then it stopped.

The Michael, job done, made her way through the strait and headed as far away from the fortress and its cannon as the wind would allow her and out towards the Atlantic Sea. The fort of Gibraltar kept firing but little or no damage was being done. Most efforts just hit the water and were lucky if they even made a splash on the side of the ship. Richard and his men, with Guillermo's assistance, made their way down to the harbour. The Santa Maria was waiting for them and they needed to get aboard her and fast before the Michael got away. She was not a ship they could hope to challenge, but they could follow her and if they kept a safe distance, they might just succeed. *But first we must catch her*, he thought. Richard's family were on that boat and he needed to find out where it was going.

The Santa Maria was not a big ship but she was big enough to house his men and there was room enough for their horses in the hold. It took them the best part of an hour to get everything on, by which time the Michael was out of view and around the coast line. But thanks to Guillermo and the help of his men, the Santa Maria was soon ready to set sail.

"I cannot thank you enough, Guillermo, you risked the lives of your men to help us!"

He took Richard by the arm. "Think nothing of it, Señor Ricardo. They wanted to do it. Just promise me you'll kill the fucking turds!"

"That, I can promise."

Guillermo removed his hand from Richard's arm. "I would come with you but needs must have me explain to the King how two of his best vessels just found their way to the bottom of the ocean floor." He smiled then faltered as he looked up to the sky. Richard had not noticed as they boarded the ship but the sky had turned grey as dark clouds passed overhead. Looking out to sea they could see it was even darker still. "Looks like a storm Ricardo, so take care and God be with you."

"Aye, and with you, brother."

The Santa Maria was an old ship but she was sturdy. Three times she had crossed the Atlantic Ocean and lived to tell the tale. If there was to be a storm Richard had no doubts that the Santa Maria could handle it. She was a medium sized carrack, nimble in the water but large enough to carry cargo on long journeys. She had a high rounded stern making her stable in heavy seas, which despite not being designed for it, had made her suitable for exploration. She had a forecastle at the front of the ship to provide living quarters for the men and a larger aftcastle at the back where Lord Jiménez, Santé, Joseph and Richard took up residence. Richard offered a place to Paulo and Gringo also but they had become quite taken with the other soldiers and chose to muck in with them. The ship had three masts; the largest was the main mast situated in the centre of the deck and the mizzenmast above the aftcastle and the foremast above the forecastle. There was also a bowsprit, a wooden pole that extended from the front of the ship, which worked as an anchor point for the forestays coming from the masts. The ship was a single decker. Her deck measured a mere sixty feet in length but the ship as a whole weighed about one hundred tons.

Most of the men, like Richard, were not sailors but soldiers born and bred. His feet were made for the battleground and they felt uncomfortable on the deck as it rolled in the sea. Fortunately some of the men had sailed before and a few of its original crew were happy to join them. "It's not about who's in command but the ship you serve, they said. We will serve you until we die or God help us she sinks," the helmsman said. There were six of them in total and Richard was glad to have them and it was good to know the ship was in safe hands. The three sails were raised and they headed out of the bay and into the strait. It was slow going, a lot slower than the Michael had been. There was a stiff wind coming from the south east that was bringing the dark clouds closer towards Gibraltar and so sailing east was proving difficult. But the sailors aboard had been through worse and by angling the ship north east were able to catch a slight wind strong enough to take them out of the strait and into the open sea. They turned north. The Michael was not in sight but they knew she had headed this way. Their best chance was to follow the coast line and hope they found her before she reached the English Channel. If the Michael got as far as that, then she could head anywhere, France, England, Scotland or anywhere else in Europe for that matter. They needed to find her before she rounded France, and follow her to her lair.

But then it started to rain.

By the afternoon they had made their way passed Cadiz and come evening they were nearing the southernmost tip of Portugal at Portimáo and all the while the rain kept falling. By now, most of the men already feeling unease at being at sea had fled into the forecastle to avoid the rain. Some, however, went into the hold to comfort the horses. Richard remained on the deck, feeling more and more uncomfortable by the minute. The rain was falling heavier now and the wind had picked up and made his wet clothes feel bitter cold against his skin. The sailors and a few of the soldiers that had braved to help out were scurrying across the deck pulling on this rope and that trying to help the ship maintain its course. It was difficult, for the deck was so wet now that the men were slipping in their worn boots. Richard looked out towards the coast of Portugal and already it was starting to fade. He was sure that they were not far from land but the rain was falling so hard now that it was difficult to see more than a few metres in front of himself.

"Señor Ricardo?" the helmsman cried from the poop deck at the stern of the ship. "Señor, I must take her farther out to sea, I fear in this weather we will not see the rocks until we are on top of them and by then it will be too late!"

He had feared that himself the moment he saw Portugal disappear into the grey. In this weather it would be too easy to run aground, and despite his reluctance to head out to sea and out of sight of the coast, putting them farther away from the Michael, he knew they had no choice. "Do what you must!"

The helmsman took them out to sea and as he did, the wind picked up and the waves rose and crashed against the hull, spraying foam across the deck. The ship began to rock ferociously and the horses began to scream. All he could see around him was a solid grey wall of cloud, rain and sea, all merged together to form one dark mass that surrounded the ship as the storm took hold. The ship swayed to and fro and up and down as the sea gripped them in its embrace, flinging them about. The sails were caught in the wind and threatened to tear, or worse; capsize them.

"Sails down, get them goddamned sails down!" the helmsman screamed.

With much difficulty in the conditions the sailors and soldiers got the sails down but not before one man was flung way over board and swept away. The sea was a monster and there was nothing that they could do to avoid it or stop it; they were in God's hands now and only He had the power to save them.

"Get inside, all of you inside," Richard called to the men.

"There is nothing more you can do!" He was clinging on to the side rail for dear life and had he not got his foot tangled in some rope may well have been lost to the sea himself. He pulled himself along the railing slipping as he went making his way to the aftcastle above which the helmsman was still trying to control the ship. "Forget it man, come down!"

"Forgive me my Lord, but we've fought through worse, I'll stay up here a while longer if it's all right with you!"

There was no use arguing. He was, after all, the expert but Richard couldn't help but think he was trying to be the hero. *God knows we need one*, he thought. At that moment there was a sudden flash of lightning which lit up the whole sky and reflected off the thousands of rain drops that were pouring from the heavens. He had to close his eyes to avoid the brightness and as he did he heard the crash of thunder that left his ears ringing.

"What the hell was that?" the helmsman called.

"What was what?" Richard responded, whilst trying to catch his bearings. He looked all around but all he could see was darkness.

"Over there," the helmsman said, pointing a little to their right. "I saw something."

Richard tried to look where he was pointing but his eyes were still recovering from the last flash of lightning and he couldn't see more than ten metres through the rain anyhow. "Are you sure you saw something?"

Then it happened again; the lightning flashed behind them and lit up the sky as it did before. This time he was expecting it and managed to keep his eyes open long enough to see what the helmsman had seen and since he had seen it last, it had moved closer. *Sweet Jesus Christ*, Richard thought. "Watch out!"

The helmsman slammed the ship's wheel down as hard as he could, steering them to the left. It didn't go far. They could try their best to manoeuvre the ship but in the end it was the sea that was in control now. They had to do what they could to avoid this new phenomenon that had presented itself but once again it had disappeared into the darkness. *We must have missed it, we must have.* Time passed and still nothing happened. Richard braced himself for impact but none came. But the lightning did and for a third time it lit up the sky and there she was, the Michael, stuck in the storm the same as they were. They passed him with no more than a few feet between them. Then she was gone, lost in the darkness.

God damn, where have they gone? "Can you see them?"

"No, nothing!" the helmsman cried.

"Shit!" But it was no use. They were both stuck in a storm being ravaged by the sea and whatever they wanted to do could not be done. All they could do was wait and hope and maybe, just maybe, they would all survive. After a while the lightning flashed again but this time the Michael was gone. They had lost her again but at least Richard knew she was still afloat and at least for the time being his family was safe and when the storm passed they would find it again. Despite near fatal death for all of them he took some encouragement from that, saying to himself, *tomorrow will be a new day.* Darkness engulfed them as the night took over from the day and still the storm raged on. He entered his cabin and locked the door and tried to find somewhere to sit, but it was impossible; everything was getting tossed about. He was cold, he was wet and above all else he was tired. He lay on the floor and tried to get some sleep but that was to be the longest night of his life.

Chapter Six

The Tournament
Bordeaux, Kingdom of France. July, 1513.

"There see men who can joust and who can ride. There shafts are shattered on thick shields. They feel the blows though the breastbone."
Geoffrey Chaucer

The voyage was long and tedious, the weather even worse. Richard had never liked travelling by sea, and the wind and rain had done nothing to ease his stomach. He had kept little down over the past four days and therefore thought it wise to decline the offer of food from his companions. His thoughts trailed the Michael and where she might have gone. They had lost her in the storm, but she surely couldn't be far. *The Santa Maria is swift, and we will catch her.*

"You will need your strength, Ricardo," Gringo said, clearly concerned at the state he had become. He did not look himself, even Richard had noticed. He seemed thinner, felt weaker and had bags below his eyes. Not only was he not eating, but he was not sleeping either.

"I will, but right now it seems my stomach does not agree with me and neither does the sea. It sets its will against us. I fear for my family, Gringo; food is the last thing on my mind right now."

Gringo left him alone and went back into the cabin to enjoy his supper with the other men, to no doubt join in with the singing and gambling. Richard praised them for finding ways to pass the time but it didn't help the constant ache that he had in his head. *They don't understand. It's just an adventure to them, a chance of glory. But this is war. They have not seen it like I have, felt it, watched the light leave a man's eye. They will all die.* A dark cloud resided over his head; he could feel it. His body was drained and he half wanted to offer his body to the sea. There was no hope for him, and he could see no light at the end of the tunnel. *When will this terror end?* He pressed his hands against the side of the ship and gripped tightly. He had received his fair share of splinters whenever he felt his stomach churn.

"Land-ho!" he heard Santé call.

Richard raised his head to glance over the water. A few miles north east he could see the coast of France. They had attempted to follow the coastline of Portugal until the storm had drawn them further out to sea, but finally they were back on course. *We've made it.* The sight was enough to make him smile for the first time in days. Even a ray of sunshine had forced its way through the clouds to shine down and glimmer off the water. It felt like a great weight had been lifted from his shoulders and for the first time since the fort he felt that God was with him.

"Stop off at the next port, and let's see if the Michael has been sighted."

It was incredible the difference that Richard felt the moment his feet touched firm ground. The instant he did so, his wits and senses returned to him.

"Gringo?" he said, turning to find his companion leading their horses from the ship. "It appears I have a sudden desire to eat something. See if you can find us a quiet inn where we might replenish ourselves and get a good's night sleep."

"Sí, Señor," Gringo replied with a smile on his face. He swiftly faded into the crowded docks. It seemed unusually busy even for a port such as this, and Richard noticed there were several groups of men all sporting banners of different colours and sizes representing knights and noblemen. There were one or two Spanish he half recognised, Don Pelayo, the Visigoth who started the Reconquista nearly eight hundred years ago and now a symbol: Gijón and the two black wolves of Bilbao. But mostly they were French. He heard the Italian tongue and could only assume they were here too. A few he knew but most he had not seen before. *What's going on?*

"Señor Jiménez, where are we?"

"Bordeaux, I believe."

That made sense. Bordeaux was famous for its jousts. *Ah, there is a tournament on, then.* It had been many years since Richard had ridden in a joust and for a few moments the thought appealed to him greatly. Memories of long forgotten victories returned to him, but no, he had more pressing matters to contend with.

"Come to compete, have you?" A greasy French voice called from behind him. Richard understood the gist of what he was trying to say, having learnt a bit of French whilst squiring for the General. Alexandre and Richard turned to spot a short balding man smartly dressed in a light yellow and jade silk, with shiny black boots. He smiled at them and he noticed a few of his front teeth were missing. *Charming.*

"To compete? No, I'm afraid I have not. I have business here to attend to," he replied in Spanish.

"A Spaniard," he said, in surprisingly good Spanish himself. "And what business might you have in France, might I wonder?"

"We come here under a flag of truce. We only seek food and shelter."

"Ah, so you are deserters, no?"

"No, we come searching for a ship that may have passed here, so named Michael. You would remember her if you'd seen her. We seek the men on board. They are Englishmen, perhaps you may have seen-"

"You will not find many Englishmen in France, Monsieur, you may remember we are at war. However there is a tournament on, and any who so wish to compete may be allowed to enter, as my lord commands," he replied. "Yet now that you mention it, a ship of such description did pass by here yesterday."

"Where was she heading? When did she go?

"The ship went north. She returns to King Louis. The English King Henry has invaded France and sacked Thérouanne, and Louis surges forth to meet him."

"King Louis? But that doesn't make any sense. Why would a ship under French rule be carrying the very men they are at war with?"

"That, my Lord, is a question that you will just have to ask them yourself."

"What?"

"I said the ship returned to the King; I did not say the men did."

What is he saying? "They are here?"

"Aye, most of them stayed, as their commander is to compete in the joust."

"Was there a woman with them, and a girl?"

"Not to my knowledge. If they carried such cargo they did not leave the ship."

Damn it, where are they; what have they done with them? If I have any chance of finding my wife and daughter I must confront these men.

"What is their commander's name?"

"He did not give a name, only that he would compete in the joust. He bore a green leaf on his banner; do you know of him?"

"Not yet, but I will."

"So shall I say that you will compete?"

"Aye, I'll compete."

"What is your name?"

Richard thought for a moment. He had so far presented himself as a Spaniard and it was not wise for an Englishman to reveal himself so deep in the south of France. But Richard didn't care anymore. He wanted answers, so his response was in English. "I am Sir Richard, Sir Richard of Guadalest and the Baron of Alcalalí."

The man smiled. Clearly, he had understood. His response too was in English, though the words were not as fluent as his

Spanish had been, and his French accent was thick. He said it slowly and Richard heard every word. "You had better get some rest then, Sir Richard, you sure as hell are going to need it."

That night spent in the inn was a quiet one. All of the men were anticipating the following day's events. Some of them had never seen a joust before and the prospect of one was quite exciting. But on the other hand they all knew it could erupt into battle and certain bloodshed at any point. A lot was at stake. Tomorrow could make or break them. For the first time since the fort they would come face to face with their foes and in a public setting. They had no idea that Richard and his men would be there of course, or did they? Maybe they had planned this all along. *How are they going to react? How many of them are there?* All Richard knew was that if needs be he would take the fight to them. It was time to make a stand.

He sat alone near the hearth deep in thought. He was prepared and he was hungry for revenge. It had been years since he had jousted but with the fire he knew he had in him, there was no way he would not prevail. *I must.* He would defeat them in the joust and confront them and demand to know what they had done with his family.

"Richard, how are you feeling?" Joseph asked as he sat down on the bench beside him, taking a long swig of his ale. "You've eaten well, I see."

"Yes, a good meal was needed, but I'm eager to see tomorrow over and done with."

"The boys are worried for you, Richard. Of course they wish nothing more than to see you uncover the truth behind these evil men that have torn your family apart. But what if you are hurt? Or worse yet, killed?"

"They shouldn't worry for me, Joseph. Did I tell you I won a joust in Toledo when I was just eighteen?"

"You did, many times," Joseph replied and then burst into laughter. Richard couldn't help but join him.

"The boys have made you something." Joseph turned to Paulo and Gringo on the far table and gave them a whistle.

As they approached the table, Richard could see they were carrying some kind of black cloth under their arms. As they got near, they unravelled it and let it drop to the floor. He had to gasp in appreciation. It was a caparison. An ornamental cloth covering that would be laid over a knight's horse featuring his heraldic signs. Sometimes these would be used in battle but these days more often than not they were used just for jousting. This particular caparison was beautiful, Richard observed. It was chequered and full of life. In several black squares trimmed with gold were emblazoned the sigil of the Guardians of Guadalest. The other squares were striped with red and gold upon which stood the Tower of Alcalalí. Just looking at the stone tower gave Richard strength.

"We made it," Paulo said, smiling. He couldn't help but appreciate his own handiwork. "I sewed the emblems on myself."

Richard was at a moment lost for words and then a smile spread across his face. "It truly is wonderful, thank you, but we've not yet been here a day, how did you-"

"Ah," Gringo cut in. "We've been working on it for a few days. We wanted to cheer you up, and the only cargo the ship carried was cloth. It would seem the General is somewhat of a tradesman these days."

"He must have known it would come in handy!" Paulo remarked.

"So all that singing was pretence?" Richard said before smiling. "Well, we still have one problem."

"What's that?" Joseph asked.

"I haven't got a lance."

That brought laughter from all the men. He was pleased to see them in healthy spirits. There were thirty one of them now. Señor Jiménez and his five companions, Santé and his twenty guards and Richard with his three new additions to the Guardians of Guadalest. Together they formed a formidable force and all of them had pledged themselves to his cause. When he stood to salute them for their courage, they began to bang their fists on the table and what a noise it made. The innkeeper, an ageing Frenchman, was so scared he put his hands over his ears and cowered behind his bar. When the noise reached fever pitch, they began to chant, 'Gua-da-lest! Gua-da-lest! Gua-da-lest!'

Richard went to bed that night jubilant but more importantly, ready.

The following morning saw Richard sat atop his destrier. Lonzo was such a powerful horse and Richard could feel the strength of him between his thighs. He was itching to get started. *What a pair we make.* Lonzo had been equipped with his own armour including a chanfron to protect his face and with the caparison he was fully barded. Richard himself felt almost kingly in his plate armour given to him by Joseph. The visor on his bacinet was raised, his gauntlets were on and his surcoat rippled in the light breeze. The symbol of the Guardians of Guadalest he wore proudly over his heart in memory of his fallen comrades. He had Simon's shield in his left hand and his right hand awaited a lance.

"Where did you get the lances from?" Richard whispered out of the corner of his mouth. "And how did you pay?"

"Why Ricardo, I sense you think I may have come by them in some un-gentlemanly like manner! I am quite offended," Gringo replied, looking affronted.

"I am sorry. I didn't mean to suggest-"

"Well, you're right, I did!" Gringo gave Richard a wink before tapping his right greave with his knuckles.

"What did you-?"

But Richard never had the chance to finish his sentence. All went quiet as the Lord of Bordeaux's herald cried out.

"My Lords and Ladies, I give to you, captain of the Guardians

of Guadalest, sworn sword to the Duke of Gandia of Spain and
Baron of Alcalalí, Monsieur Richard of Guadalest!"

Boos rang out from the crowd; they knew who he was and
they despised him. But he took no notice of them, as he hated the
damned French. The joust had been set up in the fields outside
the walls of Bordeaux, and if Richard squinted to the right he
could see the sea and the distant port where the Santa Maria
bobbed up and down on the waves. Wooden benches had been
put up to the left to sit the nobility. *Pompous arrogant bastards all
of them.* To the right stood the peasants. *We will see who's jeering
at the end.* He looked down the list and spied his opponent. A
French knight, comely, in a green surcoat displaying a yellow
sun. The knight nodded to Richard in recognition and he
returned the courtesy before slamming his visor shut.

"Lance," he called.

Gringo handed Richard a lance and he waited for the signal.
Lonzo was restless, frothing at the mouth, dragging his hooves in
the dirt. The herald stood with his arm raised, flag in hand and
after a moment's pause dropped it to the ground. In a sudden
chorus of noise Richard and the sun knight spurred their horses
on. Lonzo galloped down the list, Richard raised his lance and
braced his shield as the two of them came together. There was an
almighty crash as lance and shield met and splintered. Both of
them made direct contact and Richard felt a sudden shock wave
of pain shudder up his arm. He did not care; he brushed it aside
and within seconds it was little more than a dull ache, a distant
throb in his muscles. He was here to win, and after the first
charge, they stood a lance apiece.

"He keeps his lance low, aim higher!" Joseph called to
Richard as he came back around. Gringo handed him another
lance.

The herald dropped his flag for the second time and horse
and rider thundered down the list, black knight on one side,
green on the other. Richard could see Joseph was right, the other

knight did aim low and he was slightly off balance. Richard took full advantage and smashed his lance high into the green knight's chest, whose own lance missed Richard's midriff by inches. The green knight flew backwards in his saddle and just managed to hold on tight enough to stay seated. There was a roar from the crowd. *Funny how they like me now.* Richard was in the lead by two lances to one with a further round left to go. The two of them came around for the final stint, horses pounding, hearts hammering and the crowd's roar still ringing in their ears. Sweat ran from Richard's hair. It trickled down his face, running into his mouth and dripping from his chin. His breath too was heavy, almost stifling. He raised his visor and spat on the floor. He closed his eyes and breathed in the crisp sea air, tainted only by fresh horse dung. Richard opened his eyes and focused them on his opponent. The green knight was also enjoying a moment of reprieve, though he winced when he touched his bruised ribs. He smiled through the grimace when he realised Richard was looking. The herald raised his flag for a final time. Richard closed his visor and took his lance. The cheers of encouragement from his comrades were little more than a distant hum. He dug in his heels and Lonzo leapt forth. The green knight had learned his lesson, as he drew nearer Richard noticed his aim was higher. They clashed, both of them making contact. The green knight reeled in pain as he was struck again on the chest, Richard on the other hand grunted in discomfort. His abdomen felt as though it had been struck with a hammer. The two men licking their wounds trotted their mounts back down the lists, saluting one another as they passed.

The joust was over and victory went to Richard by three lances to two and the crowd gave both of them a generous round of applause. Richard bowed to the Lord of Bordeaux before returning to his men, all of whom were cheering.

"Well done, Richard. I see you haven't lost your touch after all," Joseph said, smiling as he approached and dismounted from his horse.

"Yes, very well done, Richard," Señor Jiménez called, "Now let's see what the enemy can do!"

So far that day they had not been visible and Richard had half thought they may have fled during the night. But he had that gut feeling they would not pass up the opportunity to mock him publicly and sure enough they had appeared at the other end of the list, taking up the place of the Green Knight and his men. Their lead man was on his horse and wore a black surcoat emblazoned with the green leaf of his house. *That's them all right, I see you, you bastards.* He wore very stylish armour inlaid with emerald green. His helmet was closed so Richard could not see his face. He had a destrier, as big a horse as Richard had ever seen, barded with their coat of arms. Richard stayed to watch the joust. He was not going to let them out of his sight. He watched as the knight knocked his opponent's helmet off in the first and unhorsed him in the second. As he came passed the second time he approached Richard and pointed his broken lance towards his face. Richard made to leap forward, but Joseph restrained him.

"No, you must wait, don't rise to their bait. Do you want to get arrested?"

"I'll kill him, Joseph, I'll kill them all!"

"You will, but now is not the time!"

Richard had to settle for taking out his aggression on all the other unfortunate knights as the day wore on. He was victorious in all of his next three matches. Beating the first by three lances to none, crushing the second having knocked the knight's helmet off before unseating him and his third and final opponent he unhorsed in the first attempt. The leaf knight as they had now taken to calling him was also winning, as they expected, and he did so with an effortless grace.

"Who does he think he is? Saint George!" Richard raged.

"Well, he hasn't met you yet."

But he was about to. The final of the joust would take place between two Englishmen, Richard of Guadalest, Baron of Alcalalí and the Black Knight as he had proclaimed himself from the House of Ashbourne.

"Ashbourne? Do you know that name?" Joseph asked Richard.

He had to think about it. "It sounds strangely familiar, but I have no recollection."

The Lord of Bordeaux's herald called them forward and they prepared to joust. Richard made sure his gauntlets were straight and his shield was in position. He slammed his visor shut and called for a lance. *Now is my time.* It was the battle of the knights in black. They eyed each other down the list, waiting. The herald signalled the advance and both of them spurred their horses on. The spectators were quiet and everyone was still, watching in anticipation. Breaths were held as the two of them sped towards each other on their great warhorses, the only sound the thundering of their hooves. As Richard approached his target, the Black Knight of House Ashbourne, let out an almighty roar, and as they came hurtling together Richard aimed high and true, putting all his weight and strength into the thrust, smashing his lance square into the man's face. The black knight's helmet was hit with such force it flew from his head and was caught by a spectator in the crowd, and as he passed him he tumbled backwards and fell from his horse. Richard continued on, Lonzo surging straight at Ashbourne's men who had to dive out of the way to avoid being trampled on by the great black beast. With a tug of the reins he turned Lonzo away and trotted back down the list. *Now let me see the face of my enemy.*

As Richard approached Ashbourne he was standing with his back to him. He had a sweaty mop of long blond hair that was strikingly familiar and almost for a second Richard thought, *no, but it couldn't be; it's impossible.* His head turned to face Richard and he gazed into those deep green eyes that he had seen so many times before. *No, no, nooooo.*

"Traitor!" Richard cried as he swung down from his horse. He flung himself at Simon and grabbed him by the throat and began to throttle him. By now, men had arrived from both sides and a mass brawl ensued. Richard heard a lot of noise and felt hands clawing at the sides of his face, but he only had eyes for one man and he was not letting go, until finally Joseph managed to pry him away.

"I'll kill you, you hear me, I'll fucking kill you!"

"You will regret that," Simon replied, rubbing his neck. "Friend," he added sarcastically.

"Where are they? What have you done with them?"

But Simon did not answer him. He just smiled at Richard as his men pulled him away.

"What is the meaning of this outrage?" the Lord's herald demanded of him, signalling to the guards. "Fighting in his Lordship's presence will not be tolerated!"

"Just a slight disagreement, I assure you," Richard answered.

"Well, you can think about your disagreement in the stocks!"

"That will not be necessary, Rémy," came the greasy voice of the balding man they had met on their arrival at the docks the previous day. He was sporting his shiny black boots again and a rather long red tunic and green hose. *Someone should really tell this guy how to dress.* "As it happens his lordship commends their spirits, but urges them to save it for tomorrow's tournament battle."

Richard looked up at the Lord of Bordeaux, a fat man with three wobbly chins who did seem to be in rather good spirits. Richard nodded to him in thanks for his compliments and he returned the courtesy. He was a man who clearly loved his food but a man that liked to watch a good scrap as well. No doubt he had never been in one and like most rich people got the joy out of watching others smack each other about instead.

Rémy looked quite affronted at being contradicted. "Be that as it may, they had best turn up for the battle tomorrow or I'll have them arrested."

"Oh they will," the greasy man replied. "Won't you, Sir Richard?"

"Aye."

"And you, Sir?" he called to Simon.

"Aye."

* * *

That night back at the inn, Richard sat at a table with Alexandre, Santé and Joseph. They were discussing the day's events and how best to proceed with tomorrow's tournament.

"I can't believe the bastard! Who the hell does he think he is?" Richard still couldn't get over seeing Simon, alive first of all but with the men who attacked their castle, who stole his wife and daughter from him and to make matters worse he looked like their leader. *How long has this been going on?* He asked himself. *Was he ever my friend?*

"You say he was your closest companion?" Alexandre asked.

"That he was."

Santé let out a low whistle. They were all as shocked as he was. None more so than Joseph, who had also been tricked into believing Simon was a friend. Two years they had known him; they used to drink with him, share secrets with him and Richard even introduced him to his family. Maybe he should have known something was wrong; Simon had never talked about his past or where he came from.

"I know something of such betrayal; I myself was betrayed by my own brother," Alexandre went on. "Such hatred can burn away a man's insides. You must push that from your mind and focus on what needs to be done. I know one day that my brother will get his just deserts but I do not spend every waking moment dwelling on it, for it will just eat away at you, Richard."

Señor Jiménez was right. The intensifying passion of hatred that he now felt for his best friend must be swept aside. His day would come but first and foremost he must find out where they were holding his family captive. "We must get him on his own tomorrow, and force him to speak."

"But how will we do that amidst a tournament battle?" Joseph asked.

"I have an idea," Santé said. "If we work as one it can be done. My boys are strong fighters, and we can keep his men at bay. If Señor Jiménez and his men can cut Simon off and surround him, it should give you enough time to extract the information you need."

"And what part do we play in all of this?" Gringo asked as he and his brother took a seat at the table.

"You," Richard said, "can hold the bastard down."

* * *

The tournament battle was to be fought on the same ground where the joust took place on the previous day. The wooden benches had been taken away and instead a mock castle had been put up in their place. It was a fifth the size of any normal castle and made entirely of wood. It had a fake drawbridge with red flags running along the top of its walls. The battle was to be fought between two teams, a red team and a blue team. All the different knights and lords who wished to compete with their retinue of men were designated a team colour and they all wore ribbons on their arms depicting that colour. Richard's band of men were drawn on the red team who would be defending the castle and Simon's men were on the blue team who would be attacking it. They had all been relieved of their weapons and no horses were to be used but they were allowed to keep their shields and wear armour. In place of their weapons they were all given wooden swords. They were not to kill a man but they could still hurt one.

As this was a battle the whole area had been cordoned off and spectators had to watch from behind a rope at a safe distance. Today it felt like there were thousands watching and there were hundreds of men who would be taking part. They were all huddled inside the pretend castle and on the hill opposite they could see the other team bracing for the assault. Amongst them they could see the black and green of Simon's house. These mock battles were brutal and it would be tough to get to him but if they stuck together, hopefully they could carve a way through. Santé's plan would work.

Rémy, the Lord of Bordeaux's herald, entered the space between the two armies on horseback with flag raised aloft. "There will be a prize awarded to the house with the most men remaining," he shouted out, bringing a loud cheer from the men taking part. *My prize has long blonde hair and a pretty face,* Richard thought. He was over there somewhere and Richard would find him.

"Let the battle begin." Rémy dropped the flag to the ground and fled the field in a hurry.

Richard never took his eye off the banner with the green leaf. He could see men and different banners charging towards him in the corner of his eyes but still he focused on that banner; yet still that banner didn't move. *What's he doing?* As the blue team charged down the hill to attack the castle, the men in black stood their ground. Then without a second thought they turned and left the field. *No! The Lord of Bordeaux will not stand for this! He wanted to see us fight.* But then it hit Richard. All of the Lord's men were competing in the battle. There was no one to stop them from leaving. *How could I be so stupid?*

"Men to me," he cried, surging forth to the miniature drawbridge. "Push it down."

They sprang from the castle entrance in what the other men on their team could only presume was a daring counter attack and so some of them followed. They needed to get to the top of that hill but with an army of men bearing down on them it would not be easy. They met the opposing sides centre head on in a splintering clash of wood. Men were knocked from their feet, others were bundled over with big shields and some were already sporting bloody noses where they had been clubbed in the face. Richard barrelled his way past men as they poured on down to the castle, forcing people back with his shield and sweeping legs with his sword. He had to slow down to a walk as more and more men piled in and were forced together. Richard tried to push his way through but it was impossible.

He looked up at the hill and could no longer see Simon or his men. They had fled and Richard's men were unable to pursue them. "Push men!" he cried. "Push!" But it was no use, he had been cut off from the others, and there was no way out. Richard had decided not to wear his helmet as it narrowed his vision but it was a mistake, as he now felt vulnerable. Richard sensed the blow before it came, hard and fast. A wooden blade struck him hard on the back of his head, he felt the blood trickle through his hair and he saw Simon's face glaring at him. Then he watched as the face laughed and laughed until darkness surrounded him.

Chapter Seven

French Encampment
Tournai, County of Flanders. July, 1513.

"One weeps not save when one is afraid, and that is why kings are tyrants."
Marquis de Sade

King Louis XII of France had been sent word from his spies in Calais that Henry of England had invaded, but sources' information about his army's size and strength varied. All that was definitely known was that from Calais, Henry was proceeding south to the town of Thérouanne and would put the place under siege. Louis, in a bid to stop the English, requested the Duc de Longueville to raise an army to march to the town's relief and to quell any further advancement into French territory. The Duc relished the opportunity to show his worth to both king and country. Outside the walls of Tournai, the French force gathered and within the week had over seven thousand troops. The King himself had said he would travel forth from Blois to inspect his army and to see them to the battlefield, hopefully raising the men's morale in the process. Although the Duc had his suspicions that there was another reason entirely as to why the King had wanted to be there.

He was right, of course. The King had sent a band of men on a secret mission to Spain and he was eager to hear any news of their success. Their leader, a man named Grenwick, had not himself travelled but was at present camped outside Tournai, readying the rest of his men for the imminent battle. The King had other plans for Grenwick and his men. As soon as the Michael returned, Louis would send her back to King James IV of Scotland and the Ashbournes would see it done.

"He followed you?" Grenwick smiled, his crooked yellow teeth glinting in the evening fire light.

"Of course, father, he has made his way to Thérouanne to the English camp."

"You are sure?"

"Yes, father. Some French bandits followed them there. They hoped by delivering this news the King might reward them with armour and some coin."

"And did he?"

"No, he had their hands and feet cut off. He hates bandits, a plague he called them."

"I shouldn't think that went down too well?"

"No, their leader said we would burn in the deepest pits of Hell when El Cazador and his demon huntsmen come for us."

"Who the hell is El Cazador?"

"He described them to me. I have no doubts that it is Richard and his merry band of men."

"Good, then the French will capture him and our hands will stay clean."

"Do you not intend for us to fight in the battle?"

"No, the King has better need of us. He is sending five thousand men to aid the Scots in their invasion of England. He has granted me the special honour of leading them. Finally, we get the chance to take back what is ours and it's no thanks to the damned French!"

"When do we leave?"

"In the morning, but not you; I have another task for you."

Grenwick and his score of men were welcome with the French and had been since they fled across the channel following the aftermath of the Wars of the Roses. Over a period of time, having successfully shown their loyalty to King Louis, they had been awarded special recognition and were now a branch affiliated to the French army. Their main purpose was simple; they were spies, but they were equally adept assassins. They could even be relied upon in battle. Although only a small retinue, they were experienced warriors and their services could always be relied upon, often to devastating effect. Grenwick was proud to say that he had provided the King with some of the best spies in all of France. In return for their service the King had promised him land and plunder, but more importantly the return of his English estates.

"I will not rest till he is dead," Grenwick had said through gritted teeth the night they met in the Château de Blois. The King seemed startled and Grenwick followed the King's gaze to where his fist was balled into white rage on the table. He tried to relax, to keep his fury to himself, but it was no use. His anger ran too deep. "Help me find him, your Highness, and my men are at your command."

"What was his name?" the King whispered, instinctively glaring around the private chamber.

Grenwick did not blame him. He knew from experience that palace walls had ears, as did the two guards that stood watch either side of the room's door. He leaned in closer. "His name, I believe, is Richard Longsword though he might not go by it. My sources tell me he is in Spain but that is all I know."

The King appeared deep in thought, muttering to himself. Grenwick caught the words 'Ricardo de Guadalest.' "I'm sorry, your Grace?"

"It has come to my attention before that there may be an Englishman in Spain that goes by the name of Ricardo de Guadalest. Could this Richard that you seek be, in fact, this Ricardo de Guadalest?"

"You know of him, my Lord?"

"He was the hero of the Battle of Cerignola. Have you heard the story?"

"I have not."

"Then I shall educate you. Ten years ago nearly ten thousand French troops stormed against the fort at Cerignola. The Spanish, led by Gonzalo Córdoba, with a mere six thousand men and out gunned, destroyed the French army and killed the Duke of Nemours in the process. It was Ricardo of Guadalest that led the Spanish counter after two of our charges failed. Thanks to their use of arquebuses they killed four thousand of our men that day. The first ever battle decided by the use of gunpowder. We will be remembered in history as the losing side!"

"So he is a captain in the Spanish army, my Lord?"

"He was once the General's squire and later second in command until he was knighted. He's now a mercenary, and one of the best too, so I hear. He was hired by Juan Borgia, the Duke of Gandia." The King paused for a moment, sitting back in the ornate chair. "That battle was a stain on the history of this great and proud nation. I will always remember that name, Ricardo de Guadalest, the Englishman who led the Spanish to victory against France."

"Then surely, my Liege, you will want to help my cause?"

"Help? I'd do it myself if I had the chance." The King grinned. "A welcome opportunity has presented itself. I would be remembered for this great deed, the king who avenged the Battle of Cerignola and returned honour to France. It seems we share a common enemy, Grenwick. It may take some time, but I will find him, and you will dispose of him."

Grenwick was deep in thought. He rubbed his chin as his mind wandered and he felt the bristle that concealed his chin rough under his fingertips. *I must remember to shave.* As his fingers moved he felt the lines that were etching into his cheeks. *I am getting old.* He took in a deep breath, then suddenly he was roused from his thoughts by his son's voice.

"Father? Father?"

"Yes, what is it?" Grenwick heaved a deep sigh. Glancing up from the table he noticed a new face had joined them in his tent.

"The King's steward is here," Simon replied.

"The King is asking for you, my Lord," the steward said.

"Thank you, François, I shall be with him presently." But first Grenwick needed to speak to his son. When François left he spoke. "Did you have any trouble on the road?"

"Piece of piss! They were too few to put up a decent fight and Richard suspected nothing; he didn't even know we existed."

"Did he say anything of the gold?"

"No, he denies any knowledge."

"Does he speak the truth?"

"It's hard to tell, but I say he's lying!"

"Well, we have his daughter now, so one way or another we will find out." Grenwick thought on that for a moment. Perhaps he could try extracting information from her. She would squeal at the thought of torture and would reveal all. But what if Richard had never told her? Grenwick was an animal and he never cared to hide it, but one thing he had never done was harm a woman. No matter, Richard had come for her and it was only a matter of time before he was caught. *King Louis would see to that. We will find what we seek soon enough.* Grenwick glared at his son. Despite his thoughts he had not failed to notice Simon shift uncomfortably when he had mentioned Richard's daughter.

"What is it?" Grenwick demanded. "Am I about to find out why you have come back with less than half the men I sent you with?"

"They are my men," Simon blurted in defence. "They are mine to do with as I will."

"Who is your commander?" Grenwick roared.

"You are," Simon replied, defeated.

"Goddammit Simon, they are my men and if you wish to keep your command you will take better care of them!" He lowered his tone. "Now, what is it that you are afraid to tell me?"

"We have his wife too."

"That was not the arrangement! After her capture you were to escort her to the Duke of Gandia. That was the deal. Did I not make that plain? Were your orders not clear? We have enough enemies as it is without another. You fool!"

"But we were attacked!" Simon protested.

"By who exactly?" Grenwick growled.

"The Duke's soldiers. We returned to Guadalest as planned with the Duke. Though I can't fathom why, as Gandia was on our way back to Valencia. I was personally escorting the woman to the castle where he wanted her taken, when my men found me. They were attacked in the forest by the Duke's soldiers."

"He betrayed us?"

"Naturally I assumed so and therefore kept her as a hostage."

"Then you did right for once. I have no idea what Juan Borgia thinks he's up to but we will deal with him later. As it stands we have what we wanted from the bargain, and he does not."

Simon smiled, looking pleased to have made the right decision but he was not out of the water yet.

"Anything else you care to share with me?" Grenwick asked, spying him suspiciously.

"No, but I'm glad to be back. Two years I spent in that shit hole-"

Grenwick cut across him. "Only I heard word that you ran into some trouble in Bordeaux."

"No, we-"

"You damned fool, Simon! I told you not to compete in that bloody tournament. You risked everything!"

"I brought him here, didn't I?"

"He could have killed you and you risked the lives of my men all for the sake of your pride!"

"You have little faith in me, father. I would have killed him!"

"Would you? I heard that you and he had formed quite a friendship."

"I only ever acted upon your orders. He means nothing to me, and I will prove it to you; I will kill him."

"You will kill him only when I say you will kill him. First we need to find the location of the gold, understand?"

Simon nodded. "Does the King suspect anything?"

"He has no idea. He believes it's only revenge I seek. If he were to learn of the gold he would only claim it for himself." Grenwick spat on the floor in disgust. "No, after we have retrieved it we will leave this godforsaken country and claim back what is ours. But for now the King awaits and needs must have me go kiss his arse."

* * *

It was cold, damp and dark on what was proving to be a wet summer in northern France. Louisa and Maria sat shivering, hands bound, inside a wooden cage that had been crudely erected in view of the guards, who were seated around a warm fire and tearing chunks of meat off the bone with their teeth. The two women were made to watch on in hunger, their stomachs rumbling. They had not been fed or watered all day, and they were forced to relieve themselves where they sat. It was a horrible and uncomfortable situation they found themselves in, and one they didn't understand.

They had come in the night and dragged them from their beds and set their home on fire, men in masks wearing black cloaks. They had said nothing and ignored their pleas. "What have you done with my husband, where is Richard?" Louisa had screamed but to no avail. She wasn't even sure they had Richard. She had no idea whether he was safe behind the walls at the castle or if he was dead, but she daren't not think of the latter. These men, God damn them, were after something, but whatever it was they were not letting on. Richard, if he was alive and she knew it must be true for she felt it in her heart, would come for them. *Then these bastards would pay, by God they would pay.*

For nearly two weeks they had been dragged to and fro until they had made it to this French town. They had spent days at sea locked in a cabin and many hours sitting on a horse, with nothing other than the inside of a sack to look at. The time spent riding on horseback had left them aching and pained with saddle sores. They had tried screaming out, protesting and even fighting their captors but they always came out second best. Their throats were left raw and parched to add to all their other miseries and now they were stuck here. Bloody, cold, hungry, no idea where they were or what they were doing there and still not a single soul had uttered a word to them.

"What do they want from us, mother?" Maria asked her for the hundredth time.

"I don't know."

"I want father. Why hasn't he come? Will he ever come for us?"

"He will, darling, he will." But Louisa wasn't so sure, she wasn't sure of anything anymore. Her defiance was slowly drifting away like a dandelion seed on a summer's breeze, only for dread to seep forth in its place. "We must be brave, Maria, your father will come, so have courage."

"What will they do to us?"

Louisa was spared the torture of trying to answer her daughter's question as they were interrupted by a man wearing blue robes emblazoned with the emblem of the French king, three gold fleurs-de-lis. He was well groomed and had dirty blonde hair and spoke in rather fluent English.

"My name is François, and I am servant to his Royal Highness King Louis XII of France. You must be Louisa Longsword?" he asked, looking at the older of the two women.

"Longsword?" Louisa replied, having learnt English from her husband. "I do not know this name you speak. I am Louisa Rois of Llaurí and the wife of Sir Richard of Guadalest. He has no family name, having never known them."

"I see," François said, thinking for a moment. "But he is the same Señor Ricardo who fought so valiantly against France in the Italian wars, no?"

"Once maybe, but he retired. He fights no more, we have no enemies, please."

"Ah, it is not so simple, one cannot just walk away from a life of treachery against the crown of France."

"But-"

"I am afraid, my dear, that your husband's life is not in my hands, but in the King's, as is yours. You will come with me now. You can save your pleas for him."

* * *

The King sat in his velvet cushioned chair which he'd had brought all the way from his palace in Blois, deep in the shadowed confines of his luxurious tent. It was a cold evening so a fire had been lit. *Damn this miserable summer,* he thought, *the English come and they bring their shit weather with them.* He wore thick fur on his robes and sat snuggly in his chair. He wondered if Grenwick had been successful in his quest; in fact he had thought of little else. He was glad of Grenwick's return. He needed his men with the battle fast approaching. *Not only must I defeat the English here but I must help the Scottish attack their rear. If all goes to plan they will retreat back to England leaving me to stake my claim in Italy.*

"Your Grace, Monsieur Grenwick to see you."

"Send him in, François," he replied. "That will be all."

The King watched as Grenwick entered the tent. He looked tired. His years were finally starting to appear on his face. Despite this, he had an aura of good news about him and he smiled as he bowed.

"You wished to see me, sire?"

"I trust all went according to plan?"

"To a degree, your Grace. Richard Longsword is at present in the English camp. My son has taken his wife and daughter captive."

The King rose from his chair, thoughts starting to race through his mind and his heart beat a little faster. A bead of sweat trickled from his temple and suddenly it felt hot in the tent. *I have Ricardo de Guadalest's own family within my grasp, to do with as I will.* A few years ago, the King had heard of Richard's wife and her beauty, no less from the Pope himself. She was once his maid, what was her name? *Lisa, Louise. No matter, I will find out soon enough.* He had no doubt her daughter would grow to be the same. He felt a sudden stirring in his loins. *They will be mine. They are mine.*

"Your Grace?"

The King realised that he had risen from his chair. His peculiar behaviour had not gone unnoticed. Grenwick seemed somewhat taken aback and could not fail to hide the bemused expression on his face. Slightly flushed, the King sat back down.

"His wife and daughter, you say." The King tried to sound casual.

"Yes, we thought Richard would follow-"

"Well, it appears you thought right. We will destroy the English in due course. Richard Longsword is a dead man. You have my word."

"Thank you, your Grace." Grenwick sighed.

The King noticed Grenwick shift uncomfortably. "You have served me well, Grenwick, no one can deny it. Now let us share in the spoils."

Grenwick's face creased into a horrified expression, causing the King's lips to curl into a smile.

"Your Grace?"

* * *

Louisa entered the King's tent. Her face was pale, her lips were almost blue and her hands were shaking. She was cold to the bone from being left outside, caged up like some sort of animal.

Her clothes were soiled and torn, and her wrists and ankles were red where the rope had broken the skin. The warmth in the tent stabbed at her skin like small needles, the stinging making her eyes water. The King really had himself well looked after, she observed, there were velvet and silk cushions and furniture made from expensive wood, and his bed wasn't far off from what you would expect to find in a castle let alone a tent. There was another man there, whose face was oddly familiar. *I know those eyes, he has very similar eyes to someone I know.* She knew they wanted Richard. It all made sense now and taking her was the only way they knew he would follow. She hoped Richard wouldn't, they would only set a trap and he would surely be tortured or worse, killed.

Richard stay away, please don't come. If Louisa had learnt one thing about herself it was that she was a strong willed woman, stubborn and defiant. Richard had found that out the hard way. *Oh, I must not think of Richard.* It hurt every time she did. All the fight that had left her over the last few days seemed to come flooding back to her. *I can look after myself. I must be strong for me and Maria.* Being held captive was not the worst situation in the world to be in, she decided. *Surely it would not be too long,* she thought. *I will find a way to escape, for men are vulnerable and I am beautiful, so maybe I can use that to my advantage, lure the guards perhaps.*

"Louisa, is it?" the King spoke in surprisingly good English, rousing Louisa from thought.

"Yes," Louisa replied, trying to sound as defiant as she felt.

"You are in the presence of a King!" the King shouted. He rose from his chair swiftly and approached Louisa, his cloak brushing the floor. She edged back but not quickly enough. The King raised his hand, where he wore his sovereign ring. He swung with incredible force and slapped Louisa across the face. The ring split her lip and blood leaked down her chin, the blow making her dizzy and lose focus. She swayed and nearly lost her balance, but she regained her footing and stood tall.

"You will therefore address me as one." The King held out his hand with the bloody ring. Louisa stood unmoved. The King nodded at Grenwick. Louisa had almost forgotten his presence, her loathing completely focused on the King. Grenwick grabbed a chunk of her hair and pushed forward, forcing her down into a bow. The King's hand was inches from her face, and he waited.

She realised she was in a position she couldn't win, so she pursed her lips, closed her eyes, and longed for her husband. Leaning forward, she kissed the King's ring. Grenwick let go of Louisa's hair. She slowly raised herself into a standing position. She looked down at the floor, feeling ashamed, unable to look the King in the eye. She knew full well she was a captive but thought she would be shown some sign of chivalry as a woman at least, particularly from the King.

"You are a goddamned whore, Madame Longsword, the spouse of an enemy of France. You have acknowledged me as your King, but still you are a whore and therefore shall be treated as such."

Louisa raised her head to look at the King. He had a terrible smile and his eyes looked at her in hunger. *Oh God no, please.* The King descended on her, and though she tried to back away, it was no use. He pushed her to the floor with brutal strength. Louisa tried to crawl away but he just grabbed her by the feet and pulled her back. With one hand he held her throat, choking her, and with the other he savagely ripped at her soiled clothes. She stank of her own piss but the King didn't even care, even in her disgusting state. His lust for her was incredible, Louisa could feel it emitting from his skin like an invisible force. He groped at her in desperation, and the fact that she was Richard's only drove him further into a frenzy, she knew. He wanted to punish him through her. He hated the fact that she wasn't his and it only made him want her all the more, to attack her, to punish her. He clambered on top of her, and she couldn't breathe. The King held her neck with such force her face started to burn, her cheeks itched and her eyes watered. She wanted to scream but she couldn't get any words out and when she thought it couldn't get any worse, the real pain started.

After he was finished, the King stood and pulled up his hose, panting somewhat but looking overwhelmingly satisfied. Looking down, he smirked at the pitiful sight. Louisa sobbed with her head buried in a pillow. Her clothes were torn and hanging from her body, her neck was sore where the King had groped at it and her throat was left feeling raw. She wanted to move, to get up and to run away but she couldn't. She was frozen to the floor in shame. All she could feel was the King's seed as it trickled down the inside of her leg. Sickened, she just laid there and began to cry.

"Hush now, you enjoyed it, I have no doubt. After all, you are a whore." The King spat on her. He put his hand into his pocket and pulled out a coin. "Never say the King does not pay his way," he said as he dropped it on the floor. "Grenwick!" he said, as he turned.

* * *

"Your Grace?" Grenwick moved forward, having watched on from the shadows of the tent in stunned, horrified disbelief as the King ravaged her again and again. He hated the Longswords more than anyone. Still this didn't feel right. *Does she deserve this? What truly has she ever done to me? Or him?* But yet he kept his calm and his silence; it was not his place to question the King.

"Delightfully tight. It is my wish that you try for yourself Grenwick."

"I'm afraid — I — should not sire, I must prepare my men."

"This is the wife of your enemy, the same enemy that took everything from you and left you with nothing, nothing! She is a whore, Grenwick, and she deserves worse! This is the reward I give you, feel her wetness on your cock, take her now, I command you!"

"Yes, if it pleases your Grace..."

"It does."

Grenwick stared down at Louisa. She looked a savage mess. She was red and bruised, her face tearful and swollen. Her breasts were bare and her pink nipples were hard from the cold and Grenwick could see the teeth marks from where Louis had bit at them. Her legs were spread, making it appear she did not care. All dignity had left her and so Grenwick stared at her cunt. He had felt sorry for her, felt her pain. He had wanted to leave, to have not seen what he did. But now, like the weakness of all men, he was taken over by the sudden impulse to fuck her. She was so vulnerable, so innocent and ready to be taken. He could smell it, the sweet smell that could only come from between a woman's thighs and as the King's had done, his own eyes filled with hunger. He watched as she gasped the moment she noticed the sudden change in his eyes that for one moment had seemed to gaze upon her in pity but now fiercely in lust. Now she knew what was about to come and that only made it more satisfying. He lay down on top of her, their face inches apart. She recoiled at his breath.

"Richard, oh god Richard, forgive me," she whimpered. "Please no."

But Grenwick just smiled at her, showing off his crooked yellow teeth. He felt her shiver in disgust and heard her retch. He did not care, and before she could say or do anything else, he forced himself inside of her and this time she did scream.

Chapter Eight

The English Camp
Thérouanne, Habsburg Netherlands.
July, 1513.

"My Lord, if it were not to satisfy the world, and my realm, I would not do that I must do this day for none earthly thing."
Henry VIII

I could see Louisa. She was beautiful, so young, so pure. Her sleek black hair that travelled down her back, her blue eyes that delved deeper than even the largest of oceans. Her small pink lips, ever so sweet. I kissed them and I held her in my arms.

We stood in a field beneath an olive tree and we gazed out as the sun set in the distance and it was mesmerising. I had all I ever wanted, a woman that I loved, a daughter to care for and a home of my own. I ran my fingers through Louisa's hair.

"What do you think of her?" she asked me.

I smiled and gazed upon Maria's face, as she lay asleep on the grass. "She is beautiful like her mother."

"She has her father's eyes," she replied. "I am sorry to have sprung this on you. Every day I wanted to tell you but I thought you'd never come back."

"Think nothing of it, Louisa, I loved her the moment I saw her just as I fell in love with her mother the first time I laid eyes upon her."
Louisa looked at me with a tear in her eye. "Mind you, I would have liked a son," I added.

"Richard!" she said and hit me on my arm. "You shall have to wait!"
That did make me laugh. "I am glad that we are here, together."

"I thank God every day for bringing you back to us," Louisa said. "For two years I cried myself to sleep every night." She clenched my hand in her own. "I love you, Richard."

"And I you, Louisa."

We had just moved into the small palace in Alcalalí set in the heart of the Xaló Valley. Louisa had fallen in love with it the moment she laid eyes on it. I, too, could not have wished for a better home to raise my daughter. The village that surrounded it was small but the people were welcoming. I had great hopes for the place. I wanted it to become a trading town so that my people might prosper and I had an ingenious plan as to how I could make that happen; I wanted to grow oranges. I genuinely looked forward to a life of honesty and hard work. But before that could all take shape there was one thing I felt I needed to do, and that was make the short trip to the neighbouring Valley of Guadalest to visit the home of the elderly couple who raised me. We made the journey on horse and cart, passing through the mountains. We stopped first at Castell de Castells to introduce myself to the Calatrava Knights who had long kept watch over our valley. Then finally after half a day's ride and crossing through the forest of Els Arks, on the road outside my old home.

It was a small house, a farm of sorts and one of many that spread across the hillside surrounding the village of Guadalest. I had told Louisa of my upbringing and she was eager to see the house that I had grown up in as a boy. She too was looking forward to returning to Llaurí to see her father. At least she had a father. I still had mixed feelings about this place. It was a lonely time in my life, a time when a boy needed a father and a mother to teach him and to tell him everything was going to be all right. But I had neither and no answers as to why that was. All I had was an elderly couple who seemed more interested in their animals than they did me. I was just a burden to them and I never felt loved. Yet all the same this had been my home and whether they had loved me or not they showed me kindness by taking me in, a helpless boy with nobody left in the world. They had fed me, clothed me and provided me with shelter and for that at least I was grateful.

I don't know why but on my return to Spain it was on my mind to visit this place. I was drawn to its memories. The fact that we now lived so close meant I had no excuse but to do so. I had hoped that perhaps

Señor Mario and his wife Señora Sofia still lived and that I could speak to them and tell them of the man I had become and try to repay them in some way. I felt I owed them that much at least. I don't know what I expected to find when I got there but they were gone. I presumed they were dead; perhaps they had been for many years.

The house was abandoned and I spoke to a man in the village who said that Sofia had died years ago and Mario soon after went mad and disappeared. So the house had been left untouched as the folk in these parts were superstitious and therefore didn't want to go anywhere near it. "A bad omen if you ask me," the man had said. "Stay away from that place if I were you."

I did not tell this to Louisa but instead paid a visit to the Castellan at the castle who was governor of Guadalest. He was an old man but polite, and he said the house was up for auction but nobody wanted it and that he would let me buy it there and then for a reasonable price. So I did. I have no idea why I did this. I have not even mentioned to Louisa that I did, but it just felt like the right thing to do.

"Good man, good man," he said. "So you're a soldier, are you?"

"Was," I said.

"Well, we're always in need of good men around here and I'll soon need replacing. I'm not what I once was and the men here are useless. All they do is sit on their arses. We could use a man like you."

"I am afraid my fighting days are over."

"Fighting? No fighting around here. All we do is guard the castle and get drunk!"

"Who is your liege lord?"

"The Duke of Gandia, Juan Borgia, snot nosed grandson of the Pope. Mind you, he's never been here and his father before him only visited once or twice."

I couldn't help but smile. I remembered the little boy who tried to stop me taking Louisa.

"What's so funny?" the Castellan asked.

"I met him in Rome."

"Who, the Duke? You've been to Rome?"

"Aye, I fought in the battle at Cerignola and was lucky enough to have an audience with the Pope."

"Sweet Christ, you're Señor Ricardo de Guadalest aren't you?" the Castellan said, sounding surprised though his eyes portrayed a different picture. They looked as though they were staring at a man they long knew. A man that had gone on a faraway journey but had finally returned home, safe and sound. His eyes showed no surprise to see me before him but they did look at me fondly and with a sincere sense of joy. "Never dreamed you'd come back to this place."

I thought it odd, though the man was strangely pleasant. I felt like I knew him somehow but I could not place his face. "The very same, but I'd appreciate it if you didn't tell anyone. I seek a quiet life these days."

"Señor, it's an honour," he said as he lowered his head.

"Please, you are Lord here."

"Ricardo, then, join us. The Duke will be proud to have you, and I will recommend you as my successor personally. The Guardians need a man like you!"

"I am not sure he will want me after our last encounter. However, I will think on it, but first I must speak to my wife. It is she that needs persuading."

Louisa was thrilled that we had made this journey together. She told me that she hadn't felt so free in a very long time, not since she used to visit Guadalest with her father all those years ago. When I returned from the castle I found her under the olive tree under the watchful glare of my old home, singing softly to Maria. I did not mention what had happened to the previous owners nor did I inform her that it was in fact the boy whom she'd spent the last few years of her life caring for that was lord of these lands. She was far away from that life now and what we wanted was a fresh start and to be happy.

And so far we were. But it was strange, being here in the place of my childhood and memories. Strange memories, that I didn't even know I had, came back to me. The most vivid of which was following Mario into the trees when I could have been no more than five years old. He had turned and found me and he had been furious. He shouted at me

and said, "You must never come here, ever, do you hear me boy, never
follow me to this place again. Ever!" I had run from him and I never
once went back. I had been scared, so scared.

I looked over Louisa's shoulders to the trees and watched as the small
boy followed the old man.

"Richard," Louisa spoke softly. "Richard..."

* * *

"Richard, Richard. Goddamn it man, wake up!"

He stirred. Everything was blurry and his head pounded. He
heard a voice and he recognised it. He tried to raise his head but
it was no use, it hurt too much. He lay back down, feeling dizzy
and he felt sick. "Joseph?"

"I am here, Richard. How do you feel?"

"I've felt better. That's the second time in as many weeks I've
taken a blow to the head."

Joseph chuckled. "You're getting old, but we all are. How old
are you now?"

"I am thirty seven," Richard replied.

"It could be worse I suppose, well it's good to see you alive
anyway." Joseph smiled.

Richard could see as the blurriness started to fade away and
he made out Joseph's face although the light was sore on his eyes.
He could see a green blur that must be grass. *Thank God, we're not
at sea.* He heard wheels grinding their way over the road and hoof
beats, and knew he must be in the back of a wagon. "How long
have I been gone for?"

"A few days. That must have been some blow. We feared we'd
lost you. But I told the men you'd be back. You've got unfinished
business to attend to."

"Where are we? Where is Simon?"

"We are in Normandy, a few miles inland from Le Havre. As
to where Simon is, I cannot say, but we do know that he went

north. While we were stuck in the tournament battle he made good his escape, and by the time we were ready to pursue he was long gone. It seemed unwise to make a fruitless attempt of tracking him, so we took to the sea. We knew the Michael sailed north to King Louis and if the rumours can be believed he is in Flanders with his army at Tournai. It seemed likely that Simon would go there. Our intention was to sail the Santa Maria to Picardy and try and head him off before he could reach Flanders. However, we sighted the Michael at Honfleur and so we boarded her."

"You did what?"

Joseph smiled. "Well, the ship was there, so why not? We needed answers, Richard. We anchored the Santa Maria at Le Havre and when night fell, we took three rowing boats across the Seine and into the harbour at Honfleur. Unfortunately, none of the men we seek were on board but there were two French soldiers. We questioned them and they told us that the French King had hired the Michael from King James of Scotland and that it was too big to be kept at the port at Dieppe and so it was brought to Honfleur. They confirmed our suspicion that Simon has gone to join the French King and his army at Tournai. Your wife and daughter are there also."

Richard let out a sigh of relief. "Then we must go to Tournai. But what do you suggest we do? Go there with thirty men? We cannot take on the whole French army, Joseph."

"My thoughts exactly. And that is why we are not going to Tournai."

"Where are we going?"

"To Thérouanne, to see the King of England."

* * *

King Henry VIII of England had landed in the city of Calais during the month of July. The city had long been in the hands of the English monarchy since its capture nearly two hundred years previously by Edward III in 1347. After his success at the famed Battle of Crécy, Edward marched his army back north where he laid siege to the town and after eleven months the city was captured. Since then it had been a valuable trading port particularly for materials such as tin, lead and wool. For this reason, Calais was often referred to as the brightest jewel in the English crown. Recently, however, it had been the perfect place for Henry to raise his army and invade France. He issued Thomas Wolsey his almoner with orders to muster together an army of near thirty thousand men and keep them supplied and equipped during the war. Henry was in an alliance with Spain, the Holy Roman Empire, Switzerland and the Papal States as part of a Holy League and as such was joined by the Holy Roman Emperor Maximillian, who brought with him his own army. But rather than fight as an ally he told Wolsey he would be a general under Henry's command, thus making him a mercenary, and King Henry would have to pay him.

They marched south through the County of Artois, the south eastern most part of Flanders, which despite the French laying claim to it was actually part of the Habsburg Netherlands. The Habsburg Netherlands formed part of the Burgundian Circle which was ruled by the Duke of Burgundy, Charles V of the House of Habsburg. This circle was one of many that constituted the Holy Roman Empire of which Charles' grandfather Maximilian was emperor. Despite relinquishing these lands to the Empire under the terms of the Treaty of Senlis, France still occupied several of its strongholds. Any lands, farms or villages in French hands were pillaged and destroyed. After a few days' march they arrived at the town of Thérouanne and in the month of August besieged it. It wasn't long before the French Army, under the Duc de Longueville, arrived from Tournai to aid it but the English had a far superior force and Henry knew it. Defeat them here and there would be no one to stop him marching all the way to Tournai, which the Duc had left lightly garrisoned. It would soon fall into English hands.

The French kept a safe distance, choosing to occupy the town of Guinegate and the English knew that they would not be stupid enough to meet them in open battle so the French had taken to harassing the English siege lines using their experienced horsemen. There were a few skirmishes over the next few days, but nothing major. There was a victorious moment when the French heavy horse attempted to resupply the town and feed its hungry garrison by throwing sides of bacon over its walls. The English, led by Henry Percy the Earl of Northumberland, in a spontaneous pursuit took his men and surprised the French horse by attacking them from the rear. Huge cheers went up from around the town of Thérouanne as the French horsemen fled.

After that, the days passed quietly and the French did not risk another assault, instead waiting for the English to come to them but the English would not be so accommodating and therefore were happy to let the French wait harmlessly at the other side of the field. Days passed and nothing happened.

"Gentlemen, what do you suggest we do?" the King asked his barons. He had summoned his war council in his great pavilion and he was eager to discuss the next move. Henry was far from foolish, and he was strong, both physically and mentally but he was impatient and he wanted this situation dealt with sooner rather than later.

The Earl was the first to speak. "Your Grace, take the fight to them. We showed you how weak they are when we chased them from the field. Send out your full force and annihilate them."

"I have to disagree with Sir Percy, your Grace. The French want you to attack, they may be small in numbers but we will lose many men if we try to assault Guinegate. They have put a stout defence in place. We should be content to carry on the siege; we risk jeopardising that if we were to meet the French army head on," the emperor Maximilian added.

The King took off his silk hat which was decorated with bilaments and scratched his head. "You are right, of course, but while they are there they will be a thorn in our side. We must dispose of them and quickly if we are to make progress before autumn. But I will not risk men needlessly."

"But your Grace, if we-" the Earl tried to chime in.

"No, Sir Percy, we must take caution. But by all means have your men ready. If the French attack I want us ready to counter them at a second's notice." The King turned to the emperor. "Maximilian, have your artillery turn from Thérouanne and point them towards Guinegate. We will strike when the time is right and we will strike them hard. But for now we must wait and hope an opportunity presents itself."

"Yes, your Grace," Sir Percy replied. He sounded disappointed but he knew his King spoke the truth. He bowed and left the tent.

"He wants to prove himself worthy of your loyalty, sire," Maximilian said.

"Aye, he's a good man; just hungry for battle, as are we all. His time will come and so will yours, my Lord. So have your men readied, because soon I feel the battle will begin."

* * *

By now Richard was feeling fit enough to ride on his horse. Lonzo seemed in good spirits, obviously pleased to have him back. It took them a little over seven days to reach Thérouanne. They made their way east across Normandy, and from Le Havre they followed the coast line as far as Dieppe. They wanted to avoid the big towns as much as possible so from there they went inland and stuck to the country as best as they could, using woodland wherever possible. They met little resistance as most of the knights and soldiers of the land were either mustering at

Tournai or in Italy fighting in the latest Italian War, the War of the League of Cambrai, so there was no one to intercept them. They met a few sell-swords on their journey and were shadowed by bandits here and there but they were too big in number to be challenged. Most people chose to avoid them and they did their best to avoid them in return. One large group of bandits did dare to test their resolve however, just outside the forest of Crécy. After reaching Picardy, they crossed the River Somme just south of the town of Rue and as they neared the forest where the bandits were hidden, they tried to ambush them. But before a skirmish could even break out, Richard and his men chased the bandits back off into the trees. No doubt their armour and horses would have fetched the bandits a nice price but none of that was good to them if they were dead. Richard's men were in no mood to be trifled with.

"Qui êtes-vous?" came a Frenchman's voice from behind the tree line. It stunned Richard for a moment.

"What did the damn bastard say?" Gringo asked Richard.

"Who are you," he revealed.

"El Cazador!" Gringo cried in the direction of the trees.

Richard looked at Gringo with an air of amusement. "The Hunter? Is that the best you could come up with?"

Gringo shrugged. "It was the best I could do in such short notice."

Richard shook his head but spurred his horse on in front of his men and held his sword aloft. "Je suis Le Chasseur et l'enfer viendra à ceux qui se dressent sur ma route!" he cried to the man in response. *I am The Hunter and Hell will befall those who stand in my way!* If Richard wanted his enemy to fear him, then he would have himself a name worth fearing. So on that day, in front of the frightened French bandits who cowered in the trees, he became El Cazador and his men his Cazadores, and they roared his name.

"Caz-a-dor! Caz-a-dor! Caz-a-dor!"

They still had the majority of their strength. One of Santé's men had fallen ill just south of Dieppe and was in no fit state to continue the journey. They had no choice but to leave him behind. They found a Cistercian convent in the small village of Saint Saéns, south of the Forest Eawy. It had been founded by nuns from Bival Abbey, just a morning's walk away, under the Patronage of Empress Matilda in 1167 and it was dedicated to Mary Magdalene. After speaking to Paulo and Gringo, former monks of the same order, the nuns were more than happy to see to his care. It was that, or risk the rest of the men catching whatever he had. At least at the convent the poor man could die in some peace and comfort, unless of course he made a full recovery, in which case Richard left him orders to follow them to Thérouanne. Another of Santé's men offered to stay with him in case he did, but Richard was not sure that had so much to do with his friend as it did the pretty girls they had passed in the village. The sailors that had accompanied them to La Havre were given the orders to sail the Santa Maria back to Gibraltar, to the General's keeping. They had little need of her now. Their plan was to head cross country and join with King Henry and his army. There was a battle approaching and Richard intended to be in the thick of it.

He had made sure to eat well during the journey. It took his body a few hours to adjust on the day he had woken up with a tremendous lump on the back of his head. It wasn't long before his body had realised how hungry he actually was, having not eaten for a few days, but he had made up for it. They were still reasonably well provisioned and the woodlands provided plenty of nourishment including wild deer and one night a boar. Having crossed the River Somme on their journey, it provided them with an opportunity to refill their flasks. It was a pleasant journey all in all. The men were motivated and driven by the desire to confront their foe. One thing that had pleased them was that it was nowhere near as hot as when they had travelled to Gibraltar, but after Rue when they had turned north and approached the County of Artois it got wet, and the wetter it got the colder it got.

They made their way through Flanders until they stopped at a small village called Bomy. It was situated to the east of a small woodland that perched atop a cliff. There was a little stream where they washed and took a moment's rest while their horses had a drink. *What a beautiful place, Louisa would love it here,* Richard thought. He could just picture his wife sitting by the stream. From the trees they could see across the fields of Guinegate and the village was clearly visible, made much bigger by the camp that surrounded it. The French had occupied the village but it wasn't large enough to house all of them. The French royal standard flew from its centre and around it were the banners of dozens of French knights and noble houses. Their number, Richard guessed, was about ten thousand strong but compared to the English camp surrounding Thérouanne in the far distance it looked relatively small. That was a pleasing sight. The English outnumbered the French considerably and it seemed the French were in no mood to attack to save their besieged town. More likely they would wait for the English to come to them and if they didn't, they were perfectly placed to make an organised retreat.

Amongst the French banners Richard could see the blue and yellow of Pierre Terrail, the Chevalier de Bayard. Richard had never met him in battle personally but he had proved to be a worthy adversary to his mentor the General Córdoba, particularly at the Battle of Garigliano. The man's bravery had preceded him and even in Spain he was well known as a soldier who fought with no fear. As Richard watched his banner float in the breeze, a small patrol broke from the French camp and made its way across the fields. They were warming up the horses and preparing them for a possible charge. There could have been no more than ten of them and they wore red and white striped jupons representing the men of another man Richard knew,

Jacques de la Palice. He would recognise his men anywhere, having fought against them before. Richard, along with the General, had taken Jacques prisoner at the Battle of Ruvo ten years ago. They destroyed his force, killing or capturing all of his men along with all his horses. Another of Richard's great achievements. Jacques was always too eager to enter the fray with no thought for caution. Richard knew if he was to meet either of these two men on the field of battle which one he would rather face.

"Santé," Richard called.

"Ricardo?" he replied, coming up to stand beside him.

"You see those men down there?"

"I do."

"They are sworn enemies of the General Córdoba, your Lord and Commander."

"Oh, are they now, are they indeed?"

"What do you say we pay them a visit and say hello on the General's behalf?"

Santé smiled. He had come all this way to help Richard at the General's request and he had never once complained, despite his hesitance to leave his commander's side. If there was one thing that would make him happy, it would be to kill men who had previously fought against the General. "I would love to."

"Cazadores," Richard called. "Charge!"

They swarmed down on the French horsemen from the trees. It was the Frenchmen's horses that picked up their arrival first. Their ears lifted at the sound of hoofs rumbling the earth. They began to whinny and drag their feet uncomfortably, much to the displeasure of their riders. Then quite suddenly the Cazadores had them surrounded. The French horses tried to bolt and many of the riders were lost and crushed beneath the stampeding hoofs. Those that remained seated had little choice but to put up a fight. One or two tried to surrender but the Cazadores had swooped in for the kill and only blood would quench their thirst.

Richard knew they had to move quickly because the French would not sit idle while they slaughtered some of their men. He was not wrong. Jacques de la Palice was outraged by the sudden assault on his small party and within minutes the French heavy horse under his command came surging forth from the camp. There were hundreds of them and they would show no mercy.

"To Thérouanne," Richard cried.

They raced across the fields to the east of Guinegate. Their target was the town of Thérouanne which lay on the northern side. As they got closer, the English camp seemed to grow in size; there were thousands of them. By now, most had noticed what was going on. The cheers that erupted spurred them on just as the jeers from the French camp had. The horses' hoofs thundered across the dirt and the men in pursuit screamed their French war cries and they were gaining on them. But one thing they had forgotten about in their moment of anger and blood lust was the English longbows, which when the French came within range let loose. Soon, cannon fire was added to the assault and several Frenchmen were killed before they could organise a retreat. The English horse came forth to meet Richard's party and whatever spirit burnt within the French was swiftly snuffed out.

A man came forward on his courser, removing his helmet to show his thin face. He had a closely cropped brown beard and could have been no older than Richard. He sat atop his horse with an air of authority and was clearly a captain in the King's army who led a large retinue of men. His standard bearer followed him and his coat of arms showed a blue lion on a sea of yellow.

"I am Sir Henry Percy, fifth Earl of Northumberland and Lord to his Majesty the King. I see you carry the royal standard of Castile and-" he said, pointing to a claret banner that Santé carried, "the colours of General Córdoba. So tell me, has the Great Captain come to aid us, and where is his army?"

"No, my Lord, he has not. There is no army but us. We have

come to join you nonetheless, if you would have us?" Richard replied.

"You are English? Who are you, Sir? I do not recognise your banners," he said, looking up at the two banners held by Paulo and Gringo that were flapping in the breeze. One was made of black cloth and bore the sigil of the Guardians and the other was of red and gold and bore the Tower of Alcalalí.

"My men call me El Cazador but if you would have my name, it is Sir Richard of Guadalest, formerly General Córdoba's second in command and at present Baron of Alcalí and captain of the Guardians of Guadalest, warrior knights who serve the Duke of Gandia," Richard said, pointing to his few men, all three of whom looked amused by being described as warrior knights. "Beside me is Santiago, captain of General Córdoba's personal guard and to his left-" indicating Alexandre, "is Señor Jiménez of Albacete. Together we are the Cazadores, the huntsmen, and we come to aid you in this fight."

"God almighty, Richard of Guadalest. I've heard of you, Sir. What a privilege. It would be an honour to have you on our side, after all, you are an Englishman, and this is where you belong. But pray tell me, why have you come to us now?"

"My Lord," Richard replied. "Where else would I get to kill Frenchmen?"

The Earl burst into laughter and was joined by some of his men. Soon Richard was laughing too and so were his men. It was a strange moment that they found themselves in but the relief amongst the men having made it this far, to have their foes so close and to be on the verge of battle, which is what they were born and bred to do, was evident. The men were ready and for the first time in days were in high spirits.

"Well, Sir Richard, you've come to the right place. The King will be honoured to have you."

Richard approached the King's tent and above it flew the royal standard of the Kingdom of England. A flag split into four quadrants; in opposite corners were three golden lions on red representing England and in the two other opposite corners were three golden lilies on blue representing England's claim over France. Two men guarded the entrance to the tent and on their surcoats were emblazoned the red and white rose of the Tudor House to whom King Henry belonged.

The King himself Richard found pacing up and down inside his tent. Perhaps, thought Richard, the King was keen to meet him. He was a large man, with a round stomach and chubby cheeks, that weren't too dissimilar from those of King Ferdinand. *Is this the effect war has on a king, impatience and saggy cheeks?* Despite his appearance he was built strong, with wide shoulders and thick arms. Over his mail he wore a red jupon emblazoned with the three lions of England. He smiled when he saw Richard.

"Richard!" he cried, grasping his hand and shaking it fiercely, addressing him like he had known him for years. "You are well, I take it?"

"I am, your Grace, as I hope are you?"

"Ah, nothing a good French defeat wouldn't cure." He laughed to himself. "I have heard of your own exploits against the French," he carried on. "Why the bloody hell didn't you fight for us, you sly dog, ey?" He laughed again. "But no matter. You are here now. So my father in law finally decided to get Spain involved in the war, did he? How many of you did he send?"

"King Ferdinand did not send me, your Grace, I came of my own free will. I have twenty eight men at my command. I apologise that it is not a great number but they are all stout fighters."

"He didn't send you? Then why the bloody hell are you here? Sir Percy tells me you carry the colours of General Córdoba, so did he send you, then?"

"In a manner, your Grace. I am here on a secret mission but I have the General's full support. I was hoping you may be able to help me, your Grace, and in return I will fight for you in the upcoming battle."

"Ah, so you haven't come back to us, then? You bloody want something. Damned Spanish, I knew it was too good to be true. Well, out with it then, what do you want from me?"

"Have you ever heard of the House of Ashbourne, your Grace?"

"Ashbourne," he shouted. "Of course I know of House Ashbourne. Those bloody bastards fought against my father, didn't they, in the civil war, turned traitor when he secured the throne and fled to France. Those turd face cocks are probably over at Guinegate right now for all I know!"

"As it happens, your Grace, they are."

"What! I'll rip their fucking hearts out!" he shouted, slamming his hand on the table. "Anyway, what have they got to do with you?" he asked suspiciously.

"They kidnapped my wife and daughter, your Grace."

"They did what? Those fucking bastards! Why did they do that?"

"I do not know. All I know is that they are Englishmen and they represent the House of Ashbourne. I was hoping, as the King of England, you might know who they are and what they want with my family."

The King, his rage easing, sighed and spoke to Richard softly. "That is grave news, Richard, very grave indeed. I can't imagine what you're going through. Yes, I know of them, by God I do, but I have no idea what it is they're planning or why they took your wife and daughter. But I can tell you this for nothing; whatever it is, it won't be good."

Chapter Nine

Louisa Rois of Llaurí
Bomy, Kingdom of France. August, 1513.

"There is no greater pain than to remember a happy time when one is in misery."
Dante Alighieri

Louisa sat close to the stream edge, alone. Most of her days were spent alone. It seemed the King didn't even care whether she came or went anymore, now that he had reduced her to nothing. But where could she possibly go, even if she wanted to leave? She had no intention of leaving without her daughter but where she had been taken was a complete mystery. Since the night she was taken from the cage to see the King, she had not seen her daughter. Many days had been spent searching the town of Tournai and the surrounding camp looking for her, but never once did she see her. After several weeks searching she had almost given up hope of finding her and that's when the army struck its banners and marched out to war. Louisa had no choice but to follow and it was on that journey that the morning sickness started.

Louisa watched the slow trickle of the stream as it rippled on by, her mind drifting a million miles away. She took mild interest in the hoof prints that were visible on the bank. A band of men had been there before, and recently. She wondered who it had been and only wished in her aching heart that it had been her Richard. Feeling a sense of dizziness she closed her eyes, wincing she held her breath and hoped it would pass. But suddenly she had the urge to be sick, and leaned over to vomit on the grass. She clambered forward on all fours, crawling her way through the grass towards the water's edge. She took in the soft touch the green blades made upon her finger tips, trying to will her mind away from how she felt. She put her hands in the cool water and took pleasure in the icy biting on her skin. She splashed water on to her face and washed it clean, rinsing her mouth out as well.

She felt slightly refreshed but it was nothing, nothing could hide the sorrow she felt. No matter where she went, no matter what she did, it would attack her insides like a disease. *There is no escape.* With that in mind she began to sob. She had only felt like this once before in her life and she knew what was wrong. That day had been the happiest in her life; this was definitely the worst. She felt grief, she felt ashamed and for the first time in her life she only wanted one thing, to die...

Rome, Papal States. May 1503.
It was a lovely mid-May morning when Louisa awoke in her room at the Castel Sant'Angelo in Rome. She heard the chirping of the birds outside and there was a ray of sunshine gleaming through her small window, lighting up the room. She rose from her bed and proceeded to her water basin to wash. She looked into the small mirror on her table and admired her beauty. She, along with the other servants of the Pope, had been ordered to look their best today. It was a special day, he had said, for the Spanish had been victorious at the Battle of Cerignola in their bid to seize full control of the Kingdom of Naples from the French. He had therefore invited the Spanish General along with his battle commanders and war heroes to visit the castle in Rome.

Pope Alexander VI, who had taken to confining himself within the walls of the Castle of the Holy Angel ever since the death of his son Giovanni Borgia, second Duke of Gandia, was quite looking forward to the arrival of the Spanish consort. After all, he was once the Archbishop of Valencia and a Spaniard himself. But it was widely known that he was waiting to see how the war turned out before he offered his allegiance to either side. It was rumoured he might have offered France his backing in return for Sicily before offering Spain help in exchange for Siena, Pisa and Bologna.

However, it was King Ferdinand II of Spain who had the initiative in the second Italian War and it was his army, led by General Gonzalo Fernandéz de Córdoba, who was successful at the recent battle in Cerignola and it was Gonzalo and his men that would be visiting this day. Rumour also had it that the General's second in command, Ricardo de Guadalest a young Englishman who led the charge, was the real hero of the battle. Tales had reached Louisa's ears of his valour and it was often whispered amongst the servants how handsome he was. She could not deny it, for she had met him before.

She had never mentioned her last encounter with the English knight and it hurt her every time he was mentioned in idle gossip. The truth was she loved him but that truth had no foundation; the only truth she had come to know was that of death and despair. That was something that was real, something that happened everyday all around the world. Louisa hated it; she didn't see why everybody needed to fight each other, to kill. Can there not be peace in the world? Did God really put us on this earth to resort to such extremity? Her father, a lowly Lord from the Kingdom of Valencia, had already lost a son and feared to see his daughter caught up in such grief that surrounded the wars. He wanted a better life for her and offered his eighteen year old daughter to be of service to the Archbishop of Valencia. Taken by her young beauty, the Archbishop agreed and she became one of his servants. Six years later, the Archbishop was Pope of Rome and she was twenty four years of age. She had changed; the world, she felt, had not.

There was a knock on her door.

"Come in," she said.

Juan Borgia entered. He was the son of the deceased Giovanni Borgia, grandson to his Holiness and third Duke of Gandia. He was just a boy, sixteen years Louisa's junior. He was a skinny thing but tall for a boy only eight years of age. He had the same longish brown hair his father had, a small thin nose and a similarly small mouth. The Pope, having lost his son, had demanded his grandson be kept close. Juan, however, seemed completely disinterested in the death of his father. Despite his young years, he was both intelligent and sly and like most highborn males he would know that upon death all his father's lands and titles would pass to him. This evidently pleased him and it was news he was eager to share with Louisa.

"I will be a great lord one day," he told her. "I will lead men in battle just as my father did before me."

Louisa did not doubt he would. He was too clever not to, but she knew where this was heading.

"One day I will marry a beautiful woman."

This was not the first time that he had hinted at such. She knew the boy was taken with her and had been ever since the tender age of two when the Pope had asked her to care for him. She had seen to his every need, bathed him, clothed him and fed him. She had gradually become fond of the boy in a strange sort of way, but there was something about him, something menacing that she did not like.

"You will be my wife one day, Louisa," he went on.

"You flatter me, my Lord," she replied, giving a little curtsy. "But wouldn't you prefer a girl your own age and one without a daughter?"

Juan looked at her for a moment. She could sense what he was thinking behind those eyes. He loved her, she knew, but the fact she had a daughter by another man that she refused to speak of irritated him beyond belief. He was jealous of the infant girl. So much so that when the babe was first born and Juan had found it suckling at her mother's bosom, he had demanded the same treatment. Louisa was horrified by the thought but she had little choice if she wanted to placate him. Disturbing though it was, she became the six year old boy's wet nurse. Even now, he tried to persuade her but she resisted the temptation to give in to his sickening desire. She had to be firm.

"It's you I want!" he blurted out, suddenly. Louisa could sense one of his tantrums coming on.

"My Lord, nothing would please me more than to one day be your wife. But I am the Pope's servant and he would never allow it. Besides, you are betrothed, as you very well know. The Pope has made plans for you to marry Juana, daughter of Alonso the Archbishop of Zaragoza who is in turn son of King Ferdinand II of Spain. This is a great honour."

"I won't marry her, I don't want to. I am a Duke and I will do as I please."

"You are a Duke," she said. "And you will be a great Duke, but even a Duke must do what is expected of him and you are expected to marry Juana of Aragón. I am told that she possesses such beauty that not even I could hope to match it."

"Really?" he replied, his tone quickly changed. "More beautiful than you?"

"She is, my Lord."

"Then I will take this girl to be my wife." He spoke more to himself than to Louisa, seeming satisfied. Then his face dropped. "But, I will get to keep you, won't I? You will still look after me?"

"I will serve you, my Lord, as long as you require me."

He smiled. "Good, then I will have the two most beautiful women in the world."

Louisa sighed. "Come my Lord, his Holiness will be displeased if we are late for our guests."

Outside the Castel Sant'Angelo Louisa and the other servants, the Pope's personal guard and his family formed a welcoming party for the arrival of the General and his entourage. She could see Juan standing with his cousins. Cesare Borgia, the Duke of Valentinois, was there standing next to his holy father. He reminded Louisa of an older Juan, not just in looks but they shared the same cunning. It was also whispered amongst the servants that he may have played a part in his brother's death. That was why the Pope's avid search for his son's killer had suddenly stopped. With him was his military engineer, Leonardo da Vinci, a man of many talents, a genius of sorts but it was his paintings that Louisa was fond of. Next to them was Cesare's sister, Lucrezia. Louisa had never really liked Lucrezia but there was no denying how pretty she was. She was slim, with golden hair like the sun and blue dazzling eyes that kept darting to her brother who she smiled at admiringly.

Drums sounded to signal that the Spanish had arrived. Louisa *watched as they approached crossing the Ponte Sant'Angelo, the bridge that ran over the Tiber River leading to the castle's front. There were three men on horses at the procession's head followed by one hundred foot soldiers. In the middle was a slightly older man on a grey stallion that Louisa assumed must be the Great Captain Córdoba. To his left was a middle aged man on a brown courser that must be Prospero Colonna, the commander of the Spanish horse. But to his right was a young man with jet black hair, not too dissimilar to Louisa's own. He had piercing brown eyes and a long nose, but he was incredibly handsome. There he is, she thought, the father of my child. It had been two years since they had last seen one another. She watched in awe as he approached on his black destrier before coming to a halt.*

"Welcome, my friends," the Pope called out, his hands raised. "To the Castel Sant'Angelo."

"We thank you, your Holiness," the General replied in turn. "It is an honour to be here."

Louisa ignored the pleasantries. She only had eyes for the Englishman, except he didn't really look English, not like most she'd seen. He had golden brown skin that almost shone in the sunlight. He wasn't battle scarred like most men either; he looked fresh, almost untouched. It wasn't long before she caught his eye. He looked at her for a while, his searching brown eyes staring into her blue ones. She felt so vulnerable under his gaze. He smiled at her and she shivered, except she wasn't cold, she was hot, extremely hot and she started to sweat. What's happening? She thought. Only once in her life had she felt the way she did now and just like then Richard caused her heart to flutter and he did so without so much as uttering a word. Her breath was heavy and her heart started to beat faster. Then he looked away. She took a deep breath and composed herself. She needed to realise her place; she was a servant girl and nothing more. Louisa followed the other servants back into the castle. There was a feast to be prepared and she needed to clear her mind from such childhood fantasy.

Later that evening, Louisa sat alone in the castle gardens. She had been dismissed from her duties and followed most of the guests who were now enjoying a stroll around the grounds, making the most of a warm night and a star filled sky. She secluded herself in her favourite spot in one of the garden's more intimate corners, surrounded by trees in blossom.

She thought of her daughter, who she missed dearly. She remembered back to when she first realised she was with child and how it had filled her with fear. But the moment Maria was born she knew it had been a blessing. Maria was an angel, a gift from God. Louisa was happy, but she knew the Pope would be furious. It was a sin to have sexual relations with a man outside of wedlock and who would uphold God's will if not the head of the Christian church, Christ's vicar on earth? But to her surprise the Pope had been lenient. He did have his very own mistress after all and he understood all too well the lesser sins and temptations of everyday folk. Even so, it was not acceptable to have the child seen in his household. He therefore sent Maria to the convent of Santa Brigida in Rome to be cared for by the Bridgettine Sisters. It was only a short walk, when Louisa was permitted, just the other side of the river. But it had been many weeks since she had seen her last.

Silent tears flowed down her cheeks as all her emotions came seeping out of her. Would she spend the rest of her life here? Would she ever know what it felt to be loved? One thing she knew for certain was that for a brief moment she was in love with the young man from Guadalest all over again. It had lasted mere seconds but it was there nonetheless. She had kept glancing over at him during the feast as well whilst she walked around filling up cups with wine. He was sitting on the high table in between Cesare and Lucrezia. Louisa hoped that he would see her and smile that beautiful smile once again, but he never did. He only had eyes for Lucrezia who was keeping him more than occupied.

There was a sudden rustling in the bushes behind her. "Who's there?" she asked, quickly wiping her wet cheeks on her sleeve before looking around to find the source of the noise. But when she got a response it came from in front of her.

"I am sorry to have disturbed you, my lady," a soft voice said. Louisa turned to see the face that had been on her mind all day. "I will

leave you to your thoughts."

"Sir - Richard-" she stammered. "I - no - stay."

He smiled that wonderful smile and Louisa felt a tingle go up her spine.

"Please, just call me Richard," he said. "I am no Lord."

"But you are a knight, Sir."

"I am a knight, yes, I was knighted after the battle but I am no great lord. I hold no lands, so I am just a commoner really, not like you," he said and smiled. "Do you not remember?"

"Yes, I remember. I remember a farmer's boy that came to the aid of a lord's daughter. But that was a long time ago, and much has changed. I am a mere servant and you, Sir, are no commoner."

"You are too kind, but I beg to differ," he replied, pointing to a seat beside her. "May I?"

Louisa nodded, unable to find the words to answer him. He was so close to her now she could feel his warmth, and her hands started to shake.

"Can I ask you a question?"

"Anything," she said, trying not to look in his eyes.

"Why have you been staring at me all day?"

So he had noticed her during the feast. He was obviously better at concealing it than she was. "You are a knight. We do not often see men of your stature here."

"Is that all?" he said, sounding somewhat disappointed. "And there was me wondering why the most beautiful woman in Rome had eyes only for me."

"I-" was all that she could utter. She thought of her daughter and the tears started to trickle down her face once again.

He gently wiped away the tears from her face. "Do not fret, Louisa," he said and kissed her.

For a moment Louisa was in heaven, all else in the world had left her and did not matter. Then she heard another rustling in the bushes, only this time it was followed by running footsteps.

The two of them were summoned along with the General to the

Pope's quarters to explain their unruly behaviour. Juan watched from behind his grandfather's chair with a happy expression on his face. Louisa knew the second she laid eyes on him that he was the reason for their being there and she suddenly felt ashamed of the boy that she had taken care of for so long. Am I not allowed to experience my own happiness? Louisa was saddened and stared down at the floor, unable to face the Pope's accusation. But what the Pope said was nothing along the lines of what any of them expected him to say.

"So, you two have taken a liking for one another have you?" They both nodded. "Well, as it happens, the Pope is not a monster, though some may be of that opinion. But I reward good men. Señor Ricardo, you have fought valiantly in the war against the French. Louisa is your prize, should you wish it?"

"What!" Juan cried out.

"You will hold your tongue, boy!" the Pope told his grandson. "You are in enough trouble as it is."

"Your Holiness?" Louisa asked, shocked by the Pope's words.

"For heaven's sake, girl, is this what you want or not? You have served me well, but I can't keep you here forever. This man can offer you and your daughter a good life, so would you take it?"

"I would, your grace, I will, your grace, but-"

"What is it, child?"

"I have already lost a brother to the war, your grace, my only request is that if I am to go with this man, that he choose a life away from war. I could not suffer to lose him as well."

"That is something that you had best ask him."

Louisa looked at Richard and those piercing eyes of his looked at her and they knew in that moment that they were in love. There was nothing else that mattered in the world other than that they should be together. Richard turned his gaze to the General, who had been anticipating this day for a long time. He knew the moment he knighted Richard that he would be free to follow his own path and if this was the life that he desired then the General was not going to get in his way. He smiled and clapped Richard on the shoulder with a big hand.

Richard turned to Louisa. "I am your man," he said. "There shall be no more war."

"Then in the eyes of God, I marry you," the Pope beamed. "Señor Ricardo de Guadalest and Louisa Rois of Llaurí. Do you have a family name, Señor Ricardo?"

"I do not, your Eminence."

"I see," he replied. "Well, that won't do, you must have a name. Will you accept your wife's? It is not uncommon for a man to add his wife's name to his title."

Richard smiled at Louisa. "I would be honoured," he replied, then his smile faded. "Though where we will live, I do not know."

"Where will you go?" asked the General.

"We will return to Spain of course, perhaps to Guadalest." It was after all where they had met.

The Pope watched the conversation with interest, and then seemed to be struck with a sudden thought. "It seems a waste for such a talented young man to be lost but perhaps my family can make use of you, Sir Richard. Hmm. I may be able to help you." They faced him. "The Kingdom of Valencia is owned by the Crown of Aragón but it is ruled in most parts by my family, including I might add, Guadalest. Tell me, Señor Ricardo, what do you know of the Xaló Valley?"

"It is the valley on the far side of the Morro Blau Mountain. I have been there once but only as far as Castell de Castells," he replied.

Juan Borgia, whose plan had failed miserably stood almost forgotten behind his grandfather's chair, listening eagerly to what was being said. Louisa saw him grin sheepishly. By family, the Pope meant him of course, and he knew where the conversation was headed. The Duke of Gandia owned those lands and when Juan was of an age to claim them, they would owe fealty to him.

"Well," the Pope continued. "If you follow the Xaló River from its source at Castell de Castells it will take you through the valley around the Mountain of Cocoll into a beautiful expanse of land where there are several villages. One of which is called Alcalalí. There is a great tower there built by Don Pedro de Castellví over a hundred years ago who sold

the land to Jaime Verdaguer. Alcalalí stayed in Verdaguer's family's procession for several generations, and they even built a palace." He smiled. *"The land, of course, is now in our possession and it is my wish that it be elevated to a barony, with the King's authority of course. But he won't say no if I threaten him with excommunication, will he? How would you, Señor Ricardo, like to become the Baron of Alcalalí?"*

Richard's jaw dropped but he found himself on one knee. *"Your Eminence, you honour me."*

"Then rise Señor Ricardo de Guadalest i Rois de Llaurí, Baron of Alcalalí."

* * *

Louisa meandered her way through the trees, each one staring at her eerily as she passed, taunting her. She could feel the moist dirt between her toes and hear the crunching sound the leaves made as the soles of her feet gently pressed against them. There was a cold breeze lapping against her face leaving her cheeks and lips feeling numb. It seemed strange that she could feel the wind in her hair and the earth at her feet, yet inside she felt nothing, she was hollow. Over a month had passed since she was taken captive along with her daughter and during that time her will to live had slowly seeped away from her as easily as blood seeps from a wound. Her soul, if she even had a soul anymore, was no doubt as dry and shrivelled as the leaves that scattered the floor around her.

As she walked her night dress billowed in the breeze behind her. It was a dark day, even more so beneath the foreboding canopy above. Even the trees seemed to share her emotion. The wood almost seemed alive to her, calling to her, drawing her in to the darkness. The only strength left to summon was her will to keep moving on and to do what she knew must be done. As she walked her footsteps quickened. Until suddenly, searing pain engulfed her. There was a terrible agony stabbing at her shoulder. A wild branch had ripped into her dress and torn into the skin. She fell to the ground. Her knees pressed into the cold damp earth. She screamed. Then she remembered.

She remembered the moment that haunted her dreams, the moment that flooded her with anguish and fear. *His breath on my neck, the strength in his arms as he holds me down. The ease with which he tears away my clothes whilst holding my throat, choking me, killing me.* She raised herself, her shoulder throbbed and blood dripped down her arm. There was pain there, she knew, but she had no time for pain. She wiped away tears from her eyes with the back of her hand and stumbled on. Each step was taken with a heavy heart and her legs felt like stone.

Richard cried out, startling himself from sleep. He was sitting bolt upright in his bed again. He lay back and rested his head upon the pillow once more. The air felt awfully cold against his skin, yet he felt unusually warm. Cold sweat sprinkled his brow and his breath was heavy. Closing his eyes, he tried to think back to his wife, but she was just a blurry figure fading into blackness. Richard opened his eyes. Louisa again had plagued his dreams. He was sure she was trying to tell him something, but what?

Stretching the weariness from his legs Richard got out of bed and made his way to the water basin. Looking in, he could see his own haggard reflection. His black hair stuck to the side of his face. His appearance was more gaunt these days. He had lost weight since the kidnapping. But he still had that fire burning deep in his dark brown eyes. Putting his hands into the basin he felt the cool sensation as they submerged into the water. He splashed water on to his face and rubbed off the sweat. His reflection rippled in the bowl. Something was horribly wrong. He knew it. He could sense it. He had that clenched feeling in his gut every time he thought of his wife and it was only getting worse. He stood for a moment, water trickling down his chin. "I must find her, I must!"

"Richard!"

Richard turned to see Joseph's head poking just inside the tent.

"What is it?"

"The men are rousing. There is a commotion over in the French encampment that has them all intrigued. Something is surely going on. You don't think they are preparing to attack, do you?"

"No, they will wait. I fear they underestimated the size of our force. Henry now has fifty thousand men at his command, thanks to the arrival of Maximilian, and the French will not meet us in open battle."

"Is it true Henry is paying him a hundred ducats a day for his service?"

"It most certainly is. Let's see what all this commotion is about."

With Joseph's help Richard put on his armour and exited the tent. It was a beautiful sunlit morning and the rays glistened off the dewy grass. Even so, there was still a stiff breeze with an icy chill to it. Richard took in a deep breath. *The smell of battle*, he thought. Dirty soiled men, horse shit and burnt sausages coming from a nearby fire.

"Richard, a sausage?" Gringo called.

"I'm afraid not, my stomach does not agree with me this morning."

"Ah, all the more for me then." Gringo winked at Richard and carried on burning his breakfast.

Richard surveyed the scene. Who would have thought it a few months ago that he would be sitting here on the verge of battle with his friends and men at his command? Despite himself he couldn't help but suppress a smile. This is where he belonged; this was what he was.

Richard gazed across the plain to the French camp. Since he had arrived he had done little else. The town of Guinegate looked like a buzzing hornet's nest full of activity. The French were up to something. He hated the tension that came with waiting. Like Earl Percy, he wanted nothing more than to attack. The French did not have the numbers or the defences to hold off a full English assault but as the King had pointed out they would probably run, and when he marched on Tournai they would return and harass them on their journey, using guerrilla tactics. Richard had to agree that until they had captured Thérouanne there wasn't much they could do, unless an opportunity presented itself. The King had his men to think about, after all, but all Richard could think about was Louisa. She was over there, he knew it, he could feel it.

"Can you see what is happening?" Joseph asked Richard.

He had to squint but below the wooded cliff to the west of Guinegate, beyond which Richard knew laid the village of Bomy, the French horse were circling. *What are they up too?* He tried to focus his gaze on the horsemen. Many of them were jeering and laughing. Then he spotted King Louis standing amidst his men. He was looking up, arms raised, and he was shouting. Men around him were also pointing up. Richard raised his gaze, wondering what on earth they were looking at. Then suddenly, he saw her. There she was, all alone in her night dress, his Louisa, standing on the cliff edge.

She's alive, he thought, a weight lifting from his heart. But then, what he saw next, made his stomach turn.

* * *

Louisa looked down and across the field of battle. It was beautiful. The way the sun shone and glimmered across the green grass. She could see men, thousands of them, so many banners, so many colours, but they were ants to her, and nothing could touch her here. For a moment she was at peace. She thought of her beautiful daughter, so innocent and pure. She thought of her wonderful husband, so strong and handsome. Then she closed her eyes, clasped her hands and prayed.

"God protect them. Please watch over them, for I cannot-"

"Whore! What are you doing, whore?"

"Forgive me my sins, please, forgive what I have done-"

"Whore!"

"I am defiled. This thing that grows inside me ... forgive what I must do-"

Louisa opened her eyes when she heard that voice which she had hoped she would never have to hear again.

"What's the matter, whore, was I not to your taste?"

Louisa looked down to lay eyes upon the King of France one last time. Such a vile creature, he would meet his end soon, she knew. His men jeered at her, their voices ringing in her ears. But she took confidence from it. They could no longer touch her; this day belonged to her.

"Come down, we shall have to go another round!" Louis called as he lowered his hose to reveal his turgid manhood.

"You will never lay your hands upon this body ever again!" Louisa cried out. "No one will," she said softly to herself.

She felt the squirm in her stomach that had plagued her of late. Doubling over, she fell to hands and knees and retched. The men below laughed and she could hear the King laughing loudest of all. Her thoughts turned to her husband. *He will come for you, for all of you!* Mustering all the strength and courage she could, she got to her feet again, standing tall with her face held high.

"I love you, Richard," she whispered.

And fell.

* * *

Joseph watched as her body tumbled. He felt the sickening crunch as her body impaled on the rocks below. He heard as

Richard let out a terrible scream. He turned to look at him. All the men who had watched on in horror had turned to face him. There was nothing more bone chilling then the scream of a man who had lost everything. As Richard howled in despair Joseph watched as it took the combined strength of both Gringo and Paulo to hold him back.

"Let him go," Joseph called.

"But, but Joseph," Gringo stammered.

"I said, let him go."

They let go of Richard's arms and with an ear splitting roar he charged the field, alone and seemingly unafraid.

"Louisaaa!" he screamed as he ran.

"There would have been no stopping him," Joseph explained as he drew his sword.

"We all have to die sometime right?" Paulo replied, as he and Gringo both unsheathed their own swords.

Joseph looked around at the small retinue of men that Richard had at his command. They were all tired and they were all hungry, but yet they were all standing and they all had the look of hatred burning bright in their eyes. He couldn't help but smile. *God bless them*, he thought.

"Cazadores charge!" he cried, and so they did. Twenty nine men stormed the battlefield surging towards the French army. Except they were not alone; all over, men from other retinues followed suit and screamed as they ran.

"El Cazador! El Cazador! El Cazador!"

"Sire?" The Earl of Northumberland turned to the King. "The men are charging. What should we do?"

"What do the men chant?" Henry replied.

"Your Grace?"

"El Cazador, what does it mean?"

"It is Spanish for The Hunter, your Grace."

"Ah, that's right and whom do they speak of?"

"They speak of Sir Richard of Guadalest, your Grace. That was his wife that fell from the cliff, he led the charge-"

"I saw with my own eyes, damn that man, but by God do the men love him and so must I!" He tilted his head back and roared with laughter. "God have mercy on those he hunts, because he bloody won't!"

"Sire? What do we do?"

"Milord, take your middle down the centre." He turned to his ally Maximilian. "You must concentrate on the flanks, Sir. Take a detachment of archers and a battery of light artillery."

Maximilian nodded. Henry turned back to the Earl. "It ends today, milord, by God it will. The men are ready, just look at them!" He slammed his visor shut and drew his sword.

"Guards!" Henry's personal guard, all horse, mustered around him.

"For Richard, for England and for St George, charge!"

The English army flooded the battlefield with Richard still at its head. They took the French horse completely by surprise. The French King watched on in horror as the horde of English soldiers rained down upon him. It was too late to sound the retreat. He was gripped by sudden panic and fear. He knew then that all was lost before it had even begun.

He knew then, that *she* had won.

Chapter Ten

Battle of Guinegate
Guinegate, Kingdom of France.
August, 1513.

"A hundred men of arms were left upon the field, and more than a hundred taken prisoner, of the best men in France."
Baptiste de Tassis

In the midst of battle, Richard could see Louis fleeing the field on his destrier. The Duc de Longueville was trying to organise the French horse to counter the English advance and make a stand. Richard rolled out of the way of an oncoming horse and managed to pull the rider from his saddle with his free hand. Before the knight even had time to hit the floor, Richard plunged his sword deep in the man's chest with a sickening crunch. Another knight, this one unhorsed, surged at him from the side, his sword raised and screaming. Before the knight could attempt a cut at Richard, he turned and sliced his sword straight across the man's stomach. Richard watched as the man's guts sprawled on the floor and the knight fell to his knees and crumpled face first into the muddy ground. There was a fire burning inside Richard that he had not felt for a long time. He moved with incredible ease and an effortless grace. As the enemy around him tired, he grew stronger and slew down knights and men-at-arms alike as if they were merely peasants, stable boys unfit to stand against his mighty sword.

A sudden booming sound ringing in his ears alerted Richard to the presence of the artillery fire. Looking up to the sky he saw hundreds of arrows as they flew from the English longbows and came crashing down into the enemy flanks. French knights and horses alike fell under the sudden barrage sent forth from the

English archers and the Emperor's artillery. The French heavy horse were being forced into a bottle neck, their vulnerability making them easy targets. Now was the time to press the attack. Richard pushed on. As he approached the nearest horse it reared on to its hind legs, and with a roar Richard slammed his blade into the beast's underbelly. Tipping backward it crashed to the floor trapping its rider beneath. As the man screamed, Richard pounced and drove his sword into the man's throat to ease his passing. Seeing his advance, the Duc de Longueville spurred his horse towards Richard. As the Duc approached at galloping speed to run him down, Richard had just enough time to hurl himself out of the way. The Duc turned his horse and reined in for another attack. Lying next to Richard was the lance of the man he had just killed. Without thinking he rolled over and dug the hilt of the lance into the soft earth. The horse's scream was loud and short as its chest impaled on the lance, killing it almost instantly. The Duc was catapulted through the air and landed with a dull thud as he hit the ground. Acting instantly Richard was upon him before he could even unsheathe his sword.

"My Lord, do you yield?" Richard held his sword to the man's throat.

The Duc looked across the field of battle. It was at this moment that Henry and his personal guard smashed into the remnants of the French horsemen. Those that could turned and fled the field as fast as they could spur their horses on. With a sigh the Duc looked Richard in the eye.

"Oui," was all he said and offered Richard up his sword.

"Paulo! Gringo!" The two men came to Richard in a hurry. Neither showed any sign of injury but both had swords dripping red with the blood of Frenchmen. "The Duc is my captive. Escort him back to camp if you would and bring me my horse."

* * *

King Louis stood on the bridge that crossed the river between Guinegate and Bomy, watching as his army was routed in disarray. His men tried to flee the field by any means possible but wherever he looked they were being chased down and hacked to death by the hungry English horde.

"Your Majesty!" the Chevalier de Bayard called. "You must go! I can hold them to give you time but you must go!"

"Yes, Pierre, hold them." Louis turned and fled. A loud cheer went up amongst the English ranks as they watched the French horse flee the field.

"Men to me!" the Chevalier cried. "To me!"

Those that were within earshot and not too scared to fight and to die if needs be, ran to his side. Despite defeat there was glory to be had and French knights and men-at-arms flocked to his side. They were only about forty in total, but on foot, shield in hand they were a formidable force crammed into the entrance of the small narrow bridge. Behind them, those that remained of the French army retreated to safety.

The English heavy horse tried to run them down but it was to no avail; the French held strong. English knights had to drop their lances and resort to attacking the small force with swords, on foot. They were joined by men-at-arms from the Earl of Northumberland's division and the two companies came together, shields locking and swords stabbing. Men died, holding their wounds, entrails spilling out and afterwards their bodies were trampled on as blood ran from the bridge and into the river below.

* * *

Yet still the French held strong. Richard had joined the melee with his men and together with the other knights and men-at-arms they pushed with all their strength. The French, their numbers slowly dwindling, were starting to stutter, their foothold weakening. Swords were still jabbing through shields and the French were holding on for dear life, then suddenly their strength gave way. The English broke through their line and a bloody massacre ensued. Richard forced his way through and stabbed the first Frenchman he passed in the side of the body, blood spurting from the wound as he removed his sword. Another Frenchman unwilling to give up the fight screamed his war cry as he came running towards Richard. They met swords raised and exchanged blows. As the Frenchman lunged and missed, Richard kicked out and swept the man's legs from under him and he crashed to the floor. Richard raised his sword for the killer blow but then he felt cold steel at his neck.

The English, who had now subdued the last of the French resistance began to cheer, but it soon went quiet. Word spread and all the men turned to see what had drawn everyone's attention. Richard the fearless hunter who had led the charge was now at the mercy of the Chevalier de Bayard who had his sword pressed against Richard's throat.

"What is your name, Monsieur?" Pierre asked.

"Sir Richard of Guadalest," Richard replied with dignity. "And you are, Sir?"

"Ah, the famous knight. It is an honour to meet you, Sir Richard. My name is Pierre Terrail, the Chevalier de Bayard. Do you yield?"

"My lord, the battle has been won. You are surrounded."

"I said, do you yield?"

"Aye, I yield," Richard responded as he offered his sword to the chevalier who had put up such a brave and valiant fight.

"Good, then I can surrender with my honour still intact. I am your prisoner, Sir Richard." The chevalier offered Richard back his sword and gave him his own. "I compliment you on your victory."

Henry VIII rode in amongst his men and they all praised him as he passed. "Long live the King, long live the King," they cried.

Henry was jubilant with this resounding victory. Richard watched as the King approached, sensing his mood change as he neared.

"Richard, you bloody bastard! You attacked without my authority!"

"I did, Sire. Please forgive me, Sire."

"You may come to rue the day you undermined my command! But for now, I think a promotion is in order."

"Your Grace?" Richard asked in bewilderment.

"How would you like to become one of my barons, Sir?"

"But I already hold a barony in Spain, your Grace."

"What are we if not allies, ey? You can keep your damned Spanish land for all I care. It's you I want!"

"I-I-" Richard stammered.

"No need to thank me, just serve me well. Ah ha, now I know this chap!" The King turned his gaze to the chevalier. "Right pain in the arse, you, Sir."

"Merci, your Majesty," Pierre replied with a bow.

"You've got balls, Pierre, I'll give you that, bloody big balls. Not a braver man I'll warrant, not even in my lot. You put up a good showing today, Sir. I do admire courage in a man and you had my new baron here surrender to you, is that right?" he said pointing to Richard and shaking his head.

"Oui, your Majesty."

"Ha-ha, and Sir Richard, what do you intend to do with your prisoner?" the King asked Richard.

"Let him go," Richard replied, leaving the chevalier looking a little surprised.

"Good lad, good lad. Shame though we'd have got a bloody good ransom for this one ey?" the King laughed. "But I know a bloody good show when I see one. You hear that Pierre? You're a free man! Go and be a nuisance to me on another day!"

"Merci, your Majesty," Pierre replied before nodding his appreciation to Richard. "Until we meet again, Sir Richard." The

English men-at-arms made way for the chevalier who walked from the battlefield of defeat not in disgrace but with his head held high.

Richard turned to the King. "My Lord, I regret, but I cannot accept your generous offer."

"You can, Sir Richard, and you will, but first let's see if we can get your daughter back." He smiled. "As it happens the Scots are invading England and I want you to be there to meet them and I think in England you may find the answers that you seek."

"I understand, your Grace."

"Help me, Sir Richard, and I will help you. I will have the Mary Rose made ready, and I will leave her under your command. Sail her home, Richard, and see to the bloody Scots for me!"

By now the Earl of Northumberland had come to the King's side. "My lord? But the Mary Rose, she is your flagship, Sire, one of the greatest warships in Europe. You must not let her go…"

"Ah, one of the greatest. You said it yourself, Percy. You know me, Sir, I will not be outdone by the bloody Scots and this Michael of theirs. I had a ship ordered in secret, the Henry Grace à Dieu. She's a double decker and weighs one thousand five hundred tons and has over a hundred and fifty guns. Bet you didn't know that! Ah huh, now she is the greatest ship in the world, you'll see!" Henry gave Richard a wink. "So you see, Percy, I have a new flagship and the Rose will escort my new baron here home."

"I thank you, your Grace." Richard bowed to the King.

"God speed, Richard, and good luck," the King said. "But before you go, one more thing." He turned to his guards. "Bring the prisoner!" They brought forward a young man with dirty blond hair. He looked well-kept and dressed well for a man his age. His tunic displayed the blue of France and the golden fleurs-de-lis. "This is François. He is the steward of King Louis XII of France, and he says he has information concerning your daughter. I thought you might like to see what you can get out of the bastard yourself." The King nodded to his guards and they threw the young man to the floor.

Richard smiled and called to his men. "Take this stinking cockroach to my tent."

It had been a very long time since Richard had interrogated anyone and it wasn't something that he particularly enjoyed doing either. However, Señor Alexandre Jiménez had lost one of his men in the battle and was therefore more than willing to offer his services forward for the task. To him this was just another stinking Frenchman, someone whom he could take at least a little bit of anger out on and serve some justice for the man that had followed him for the last ten years.

The young man, despite his youth, was brave and put up a strong resistance for a time. At first he refused to speak at all and then it turned into curses. "Fuck you, you bastard English dogs!" Then he started to spit at whoever went near him. But after Jiménez had smacked him across the face a few times he soon stopped doing that. François was his name and he was steward to the King of France. He clearly knew he would be ransomed and he knew the English would not torture him because of who he was.

Except he was wrong. These were not Englishmen, they were a band of Spaniards and not only would they torture him, they did torture him. Things got a lot worse for François after that. They had his head plunged into water and held until he could almost breathe no more and when they finally pulled his head up for breath, when his head started to daze and things started to go dark, they did it again. Again and again and again they did it and at this point François almost welcomed death. So far he had revealed nothing and he didn't intend to. He would rather have died than betray his King. "This didn't hurt so bad, you will kill me and I will tell you nothing, nothing!" he whispered.

Then came the red hot pokers and not only did these cause the most excruciating pain that François had ever felt, but they woke him from the unconsciousness that had been taking hold of him during the drowning. He was now wide awake and experiencing the worst moment of his life. There were three of them and they had been heated in the fire outside Richard's tent, where his men sat waiting, listening. After they had been heated until they glowed orange, they had one at a time been pressed against his body. Refusals to speak turned into screams of pain and anguish and the more he screamed the more they tortured him. Running the tips of the pokers down his chest and along the insides of his thighs until François, writhing in agony, could take it no more. "Yes. I will talk, please, just no more, no more."

He could have talked from the beginning and I would not have hurt him. He brought this upon himself. I had no desire to do it but I had to, I had no other choice. Richard tried to justify what had just happened but whatever way he looked at it, he just felt guilt. *Oh God forgive me!* "You have seen my daughter, Steward?"

"I- I-have," he replied, somewhat hesitantly. "She was brought to my camp along with your wife." The words started to flow from his lips more fluently, and the more François spoke the better he felt.

Richard felt a pang of heartache at the mention of his wife, but he didn't dare dwell on the thought of his lover, not when his daughter had need of him. *I must not look weak in front of the men.* "They were taken by Englishmen. Who are they and what do they have to do with you?"

"They were once soldiers of England but now they serve my noble King Louis. Their leader is a man named Grenwick from the House of Ashbourne. He was a lord under the banner of Richard III when he held the English throne. After his downfall at the Battle of Bosworth Field they came to us."

"What do they want?"

At this François laughed. "What they want, Sir Richard, is your death!"

"Why? What have I done to them?"

"To them? I have no idea. That you will have to ask them yourself. But to France, you humiliated us at Cerignola and for that the King wanted your head."

"Then why not just take it? Why take my wife and daughter?"

"Why else? For love. They knew you would ride to the ends of the earth to save them."

"Do you know about the gold?" Richard asked.

"What gold? What are you talking about?" François said, somewhat confused.

"When they came after me in Guadalest, they asked me where the gold was. They think I know something that I do not. What do you know of it?"

François shook his head. "I knew they were after something else, something more, and I knew they could not be trusted. My King will not be pleased. They have never once mentioned anything of gold to him. They only requested that my King find you and let them kill you."

"Where is my daughter now?"

"They have her," he replied. It was easy for him to give up the traitor Grenwick. "They took her with them to Scotland."

"To Scotland?"

"Aye, on my King's orders, they are to invade England with the Scots."

So Henry was right. If I go to England and help in the war against Scotland I may just find my daughter and the truth behind all of this. It was a lot to take in. He had travelled so far in such a short space of time and he had even further to go. He had watched his wife die in front of his very own eyes and he had become a baron to the King of England and now had command of the famous Mary Rose. *So to England we will go and again to war must we ride.* "Señor Jiménez, ready the men, for tonight we set sail for England."

Before Richard could do anything else, François burst into laughter.

"What is so funny?" Richard asked.

"You'll never get her back," he said. "At least not whole anyway."

"What do you mean?"

"Oh, they'll do to her what they did to your pretty little wife."

"I'd choose your next words carefully, Steward!" Richard warned.

"I listened outside, oh yes I did, as they fucked her over and over again, while she just moaned like a whore. Oh, she was taken well care of, you can be assured of that and now it will be your daughter's turn. They'll rip her tight little cunt apart!" Then he laughed again, a cold high pitched laugh and he didn't stop until Richard picked up one of the pokers and thrust it straight into his right eye.

He deserved to be tortured and in the end he deserved to die. Richard felt no remorse for the man, only hatred for those still yet to face his wrath, but their time would come. Richard took one last look at the dead man in front of him and smiled. *To war,* he thought, and made his way from the tent.

It took them less than a day to ride to Calais from Thérouanne and for the first time in days the summer sun came out to greet them. They took their time and Richard's men, battle weary, just sat in their saddles and enjoyed the journey. The Michael, once hired to bring assassins to Richard, was now transporting them to Scotland to help King James IV and his invasion of England. By now Grenwick and his men might even be there and it would be pointless for Richard to pursue them, not to mention reckless. They would meet them soon enough. But in the meantime Richard had other plans. He had every intention of going to London, and maybe there he would find some answers to this riddle.

François had said that Grenwick and his men had served Richard III when he was King of England. Richard III from the house of York fought Henry VII from the House of Lancaster during the War of the Roses. If Richard's father was Grenwick's enemy then it would only make sense that he fought for Henry VII who was the father of the present King of England, Henry VIII, who just recently raised Richard as one of his barons. *So my father served the father and now I serve the son.* He just had a gut feeling that if he went to the city where all this had taken place then there had to be something, just something, that would point him in the direction of his ancestral family.

It was night when they reached Calais and the men were tired. They would need all their strength for their journey across the sea so Richard forbade them to explore the town or visit its taverns. Calais may be in English hands but it was still a dangerous place and he needed all his men alive and in good fighting condition. They headed straight for port and to the Mary Rose. She was an incredible warship unrivalled by none. Even the Michael, although much bigger, did not have her grace, elegance or beauty. But it was hard to assess her in the dark. Richard could just make out her masts in the moonlight.

"We will board her tonight but set sail in the morning, to let the men get a good rest. There will be ale on board so let them have a drink, but warn them we sail at first light," he said to Joseph.

"Aye, aye, Captain." He gave a smirk.

Joseph had really come along since the day Richard stumbled into his shop looking for armour. It had only been a matter of weeks but he had turned into a man. He was fitter, looked stronger, and he had been fighting regularly with Paulo and Gringo. The clumsy Joseph that Richard remembered had been replaced by a man that had experienced battle. *Battle changed a man; you had to embrace it, learn from it and deal with it or the truth was you ended up dead.* Richard had feared for Joseph at the start of this journey but ever since he killed that man in the forest he had changed, and now Richard was proud to have Joseph alongside him. Although Joseph had no official position, Richard considered him his second in command, something which didn't seem to bother Santé or Lord Jiménez. On the contrary, they seemed impressed by his leadership in the recent battle at Guinegate. The three of them together formed a formidable trio of officers that any commander would be grateful to have. Richard could count on their advice and counsel and he hoped that maybe after this was done, they would stick with him.

That night on the ship was an unpleasant one. Richard was never too good at sea as his experience on the Santa Maria had proved and it did nothing to aid his already troubled thoughts. He had for a few nights now been having some very vivid dreams. But he wasn't sure if they were dreams or perhaps they were memories. In all of them he could see his father and he was taking him somewhere, leading him, but he could never see his face; he always had his back to him. Somehow Richard felt like he remembered him, like he knew him. His mind was bringing back experiences from when he was a child that he never knew even existed. He held his father's hand as they walked through the countryside with his mother. He heard his voice as he sang him to sleep. He watched as he went away on his horse never to return again. Then Richard saw his face, clear as day; he was here, there right in front of him. "Father, Father!"

Richard woke, but he was alone.

Chapter Eleven

Alexandre Jiménez
Mary Rose, English Channel. August, 1513.

*"You shall find out how salt is the taste of another man's bread, and
how hard is the way up and down another man's stairs."*
Dante Alighieri

The Mary Rose was a grand war ship, built on Henry VIII's orders
in 1511 along with her sister ship, the Peter Pomegranate. She was
so named after Henry's sister Mary and the Tudor Rose. She was
to become the flagship of England and was present in several
wars against Scotland, France and Brittany. The ship, like most of
her time, was built in the style of a carrack with high castles at
both the bow of the ship and at the stern, between which was a
low deck. The ship carried a staggering ninety-one guns, causing
the hull to be designed in such a way that it narrowed to
compensate for the weight of the guns. There were four levels to
the ship which included three decks; the lower deck, the main
deck and the upper deck. At the farthermost was the hold where
the kitchen and the provisions were kept and above that but still
below the water line was the lower deck, known as the orlop,
where the spare sails were stowed. The main deck housed the
biggest guns and had seven gun ports on each side. The upper
deck was mainly dedicated to fighting and had a mix of heavy
and light guns. It was one hundred and five feet long and
weighed nearly five hundred tons.

The impressiveness of the ship was lost on Richard as he
glumly faced another miserable sea voyage. He was a fighter; he
always had been and he always would be, his feet designed for
the battlefield. Yet if this ship was what he needed to take him
there then so be it. Richard often thought God worked in myste-

rious ways and he couldn't help but think God was on his side, guiding him to his goal, and for that at least he was grateful.

The ship, like the Santa Maria, had her own crew so fortunately the running of the ship was none of his concern. The crew had sailed the channel and back hundreds of times and for them this was just a straightforward stroll in the back garden. The ship was large enough to house four hundred men. The crew were two hundred on their own plus thirty gunners whose sole purpose was to man the guns. On the previous journey she had housed near two hundred of the King's soldiers, now replaced by Richard and his Cazadores. They, of course, were not even a sixth of that number but at least there was plenty of room for everyone. Richard had taken up quarters in the aftcastle in the King's old cabin and had so far not left the confines of its sheltered walls. The journey took the best part of a day so he didn't have to stay cooped up for long, but he was lucky in that Señor Jiménez, like himself, was not overly keen on the open seas. Richard shared several hours of company and conversation with him.

"Never liked the sea myself," Alexandre said. "I was raised in the country, never even saw the sea until I was near twenty. No, if God had wanted me to explore the sea he'd have made me a mermaid!" He roared with laughter.

Even in his queasy state Richard had to chuckle. "Merman, you mean?"

"Ah, I stand corrected. You could just picture me now, couldn't you, with a green beard and a trident!" he replied. "Mind you, this wouldn't do," he said, gesturing to his stomach and giving it a wobble with two hands. "That would put the mer-ladies off!"

Richard's time spent in Alexandre's company was enjoyable and the more he spoke to him, the more his fears and worries of the sea left him. Richard felt comfortable in his presence as he was sure Alexandre did in his. They shared an experience and in

Richard's mind it was that which spurred their friendship on. They were once men of stature; Alexandre was Lord of Albacete and Richard was second in command of the Spanish army. Where Alexandre had once owned land it was taken from him as was Richard's back in Alcalalí, where it had been put to the torch by Simon. Alexandre had lost his family as had Richard, but most importantly what they had both faced was betrayal by ones they thought close to their hearts. *Now that really changes a man's perspective on life. It's a hard lesson to learn, but you really can trust no one.*

Richard had spent too many days brooding over his misfortune whereas Señor Jiménez was a man that seemed to hide his pretty well. Richard was under the impression that despite his warm and honest smile, beneath it was tearing away at his insides desperately trying to find an escape. Richard was eager to hear this man's story and he was surprised at how willing he was to tell it.

"You only needed to ask," Alexandre said...

Albacete, Crown of Aragón. October, 1507.

My home town of Albacete is a beautiful place, Ricardo. It is where I was born, on the fifth day of April in the year of our Lord 1470 and it is there that I was raised. Many years before my birth, however, this glorious town was nothing more than a small Moorish village and for a long time had been dependent on the neighbouring town of Chinchilla. Back then, Albacete was considered part of the Kingdom of Murcia. It was not until the famous writer Don Juan Manuel, the Prince of Villena, became Governor of Murcia and Lord of our lands that our small town started to flourish. Gradually, over a period of time, our town began to thrive and our population increase. We are famed for making daggers, something we have perfected over many years. See, here is one that was given to me by my father. It is unequalled in splendour; those are sapphires. Take it; no, keep it.

Now in 1296, Murcia and its surrounding region were swallowed up by the expanding Kingdom of Aragón. However, in 1304, it was incorporated into the powerhouse of the Iberian Peninsula, the Crown of Castile, thanks to the Treaty of Torrellas. From that day on we were governed to appoint our own lord and as such have been a town under our own rule ever since, answerable only to the King of Castile. For two hundred years Albacete has been ruled by a member of my family, an honour that only a Jiménez could fully understand. For our long serving and unquestionable loyalty the crown granted us a license to host a market once a week, where we would trade in many goods, especially our daggers. It brought prosperity to our town.

My father, the rightful Lord of Albacete, was the most beloved and respected of all the lords who had ever held the titled. I envied him in many ways but I always looked up to him. Every good virtue that I possess I gained from my father. Despite this, I never wanted, sought nor aspired to the position that he held, yet I was honoured the day he saw fit to pass it on to me. As you can imagine my brother, however, was not. He is, after all, as the elder by right the lawful heir to the town but he lost my father's love several years previously and my father had a right also to deny him this if he felt it was not in the best interest of the town. My father had never wanted my brother to succeed him and he told the captain of his garrison as much, who had it put down in writing.

My brother, though it kills me to say it, Ricardo, is not a nice man. When we were boys he was my closest friend and companion. I would follow him everywhere and do all the things he did because back then he was pure of heart, but as we grew older we grew apart, and he changed. It started when he would beat and bully my sister, and it escalated when he raped several women. Only few are known but I am sure there were more and to make matters worse, he and his friends would kill men for sport. God only knows all the things that he got up to and though my father tried to discipline him and keep his acts of evil quiet, it all spiralled out of control the day he hit my mother and for that my father banished him.

To this day I have no doubts that my brother was responsible for my *father's death. I think it no mere coincidence that he was present during the Granada War and after the great Spanish victory at the Battle of Illora in 1492 led by the famed General Córdoba and his squire Señor Ricardo de Guadalest, that both my father and his horse should unceremoniously find themselves at the bottom of the El Chorro gorge. My brother had hoped, I am sure, that if my father was out of the way then on our return home he would be made Lord of Albacete. However, he had no idea that my father had already put his wishes that I succeed him into his will. When we returned, I was made Lord of the town and my brother would stay banished. He has hated me ever since but for fifteen years peace ensued and I am proud to say the town lived in harmony.*

In 1507 my brother went to see Pedro Fajardo, first Marquis of Los Veléz, a greedy but ambitious man who is Governor of Murcia. As my brother had hoped, Pedro was a man of like mind, keen to expand his territory and the thought of regaining Albacete and its surrounding lands back under Murcia's domain like it had been several hundred years previous appealed to him greatly. My brother, who it has to be said was always very convincing, no doubt persuaded the Marquis into believing that Albacete was rightfully his. So, they struck a deal. My brother would lead a party of the Marquis's men who would capture the town replacing its garrison and he would become the Lord of Albacete. Albacete, however, would be reinstated under the rule of Murcia and the Marquis to whom my brother would make annual payments. It was a deal that worked for them both and in the autumn of that year they came, and in the night the massacre began.

I remember the events like they took place yesterday, I was praying by the altar in the cathedral, one of the most wondrous buildings in all of Albacete and always a tranquil place to visit, but it was not so peaceful on this night. We rarely had trouble in Albacete so the town entrances were only manned by a few men, travellers were welcome and we always made an effort to accommodate them. They were free to explore at their leisure. Perhaps this was naïve on my part; I knew my brother, I knew what he was like and I knew what he was capable of. I could feel it in my heart and the uncomfortable squirm deep in the pit of my stomach that he was out there plotting and scheming, just biding his time, waiting for the opportunity to exact his revenge but I had never expected this. I should have been more vigilant, I should have fortified the town.

I heard the hoof beats first as they thundered down the streets. The guards manning the perimeter did not stand a chance and were cut down before they could even raise the alarm. Then came the screams, oh God the screams. Men were butchered, hacked apart as though set upon by savage beasts, children were shown no mercy and slain in the hundreds and woman were dragged from their beds and forced to do unspeakable things. I will never forget the images of that night, they hound me like a poisonous nightmare but one that I never wake from. Yet it is not what I saw that night but what I heard that truly haunts me and plagues my mind. That is what keeps me awake at night. Any man can cover his eyes and refrain from seeing what he does not want to see but no matter how hard he presses his palms against his ears, he cannot stop from hearing what he does not choose to hear. I knelt at the altar and I just listened to the onslaught until I was roused by the captain of my garrison.

"My Lord, we are under attack from your brother!"

"Aye, muster what remains of the men. We must save as many as we can."

We had no choice but to make a stand and outside God's holy temple, forty men stood against two hundred. We were severely outnumbered and could not possibly hope to overcome them but what we could do was hold them, at least for a while, giving the townsfolk a chance to escape the town and find refuge in the surrounding forest where they might stand a slim chance of evading my brother's tyranny. We fought, and we fought bravely and we fought valiantly but it was not enough. I watched as my men were slaughtered around me, hacked down in brutal fashion and their bodies were trampled on as their blood ran and soaked into the soft earth.

"I want my brother alive!" I heard my brother call.

It was all over in less than an hour. Over thirty of my men lay dead and the few that remained had been taken prisoner. I was forced to watch at sword point as my brother brutally tortured and killed the last of my garrison, my friends. It appeared he had a grotesque fascination with the removal of flesh. I watched as they were gelded and their very skin peeled from their fingers and toes and only when they could scream no more did he end their suffering. It was too much for any man to bear and despite my desire to stay strong I wept like a child that had lost his first toy and when I thought things could not get any worse, they did.

I had hoped that my wife and daughter had escaped the town as my father had once put an escape route in place from our home for any such time, but I should have known that my brother had known about it and he had cut them off before they could flee. I was forced to watch as the two people I held dearest to my heart were beaten to within an inch of their lives and all before the very clothes they wore were ripped from their bodies and the men, near all two hundred of them, defiled my wife and daughter on the front steps of the cathedral. No one should ever have to bear witness to what I saw that day, and when I thought it was all but over my brother took his blade and he slit their throats.

"Kill me! Kill me too, you gutless bastard!" I cried. I wanted to die, I had nothing left. But my brother just laughed at me. He would never give me the easy way out. No, he wanted me to suffer and suffer I did. They stripped me naked and as I stood shivering in the cold they burnt me.

"Something to remember me by, brother," he said as he took a torch and thrust it at my chest and back while I screamed and only when I was left red, raw and blistered did they leave me to walk from the town alone, as naked as the day I was born, with nothing but scars and a broken heart.

It is unexplainable the feelings and emotions you go through when our loved ones are taken from us and it is even harder to expect our friends to understand them. But you see, Ricardo, when I say I know how you feel I mean it and I have the scars to prove it. You asked me once why I wanted to come with you even though you did not have the money to pay me. Well, this is your answer, I was not able to save my *wife and daughter, Ricardo, not like a father and husband should have and I will bear that shame until the day I die. But I will never, never live to see another man suffer such fate and that is why you have my sword, brother.*

* * *

What can you possibly say to a man that has gone through all of that? Nothing, thought Richard. *No words of comfort, no light at the end of the tunnel, only darkness and haunting memories that plague your brain like a disease.* They both felt each other's pain and that for now was enough, that at least brought them some piece of comfort and so they sat in silence.

Since the day his family were taken Richard had thought of little else until now. It was impossible for him not to think about what Alexandre had just said and to think about his wife and daughter and the horrendous acts of violence they were forced to endure. Richard thought that his world was coming to an end until he heard this story. He thought he had had it bad, but Alexandre had had it much, much worse. Yet he had lived through it, he had survived and he had done something Richard thought unimaginable; he had come out the other side stronger.

"My Lord," Richard said, breaking the silence. "You say this happened in the autumn of 1507?"

"Aye, it did."

"Six years, that is an awfully long time, my friend. I could not imagine my life in six years' time without Louisa and Maria at my side. Pray tell me, how have you passed the days?"

Alexandre had appeared distracted with memories but he raised his head to meet Richard's gaze. "It has not been easy, Richard, but I know they are with me, here-" he pointed to his head and then to his chest "-and in here. That can never be taken from me and I know that they are waiting for me and I will be reunited with them in the afterlife."

Despite an obvious willingness to die, to be reunited with his family, Alexandre had a burning desire for revenge, that much was certain. His inner thoughts were hell bent on one thing, on someone, his brother. He alone wrought this devastation and destruction to Alexandre's life and he alone could pay for it. Richard could see it on his face.

"Your brother, is he still in Albacete?"

"He is no brother of mine, but in answer to your question, no, he is not. His men still occupy it of course, but after he ravaged my town he sacked Chinchilla as well. He has fortified the town and has over five hundred men at his command. I have but four now, so what can I do?"

"Can you not appeal to the King?"

"I already have. But he is no longer the King of Castile, only of Aragón. He lost that right with the death of his wife. He is regent aye, for now. But he has more pressing concerns on his mind, such as wrestling the kingdom from his daughter. If only Joanna's husband Philip hadn't died, we would have a new King in Castile. As it is they say Joanna's lost her sanity, Philip's sudden death has wounded her deeply I fear. She is a lot like her mother Isabella, she would have been a good queen, and she would have listened."

"King Ferdinand always was a two faced bastard. He'll get from you what he wants but he will never help you in return. He failed the General Córdoba and he has failed you too. What King treats his loyal subjects so? No, I should have known better, I was stupid to suggest it."

"And we fools fought for him?"

"Aye, during the Conquest." Richard frowned. "I had no idea you were present in Illora. Why did you not tell me? You smiled when I told you who I was. You didn't believe me!"

"I smiled because I knew you, because I had been there and I had seen what you had done. You were a hero, Ricardo, a hero to us all and even though you were my junior, I looked up to you as did all the men. I dreamed one day I'd serve a man like you, and twenty one years later here we are. When you walked into that little inn in the middle of nowhere, you can see the funny side! No?" He laughed.

The rest of the journey went smoothly as they passed the time talking of their exploits in Granada. It was fascinating hearing the events of battles that Richard was not involved in and just as exciting reliving the details of the ones he was. That was his first war and it moulded him into the man he was today. Yet somehow he had inspired the likes of Señor Jiménez, as great a man as he had ever known. All Richard had ever tried to do was be the best that he could be and to live up to the expectations of the General, serving him proudly and loyally as any knight should.

There was a knock at the cabin door. It was Joseph. "Richard, sorry to disturb you but we are nearing Portsmouth."

"Very well, thank you, Joseph. I will be with you shortly."

Joseph smiled and went back on deck. Richard turned to Alexandre. "My Lord, it has been a pleasure. I honestly cannot thank you enough for risking your life in coming with me. You have my word as a knight, that when this is all over, whatever forces I have, we will march to Chinchilla and there wreak havoc on those who dared to challenge your authority."

"Ricardo, I cannot possibly accept-"

"You are one of us now. You are one of the Cazadores and your vendetta is our vendetta; together we will see it through to whatever end."

Alexandre nodded and held out his arm, Richard clasped it. "Together," he said.

They sailed around the eastern side of the Isle of Wight and entered the Solent. Standing on the deck of the Mary Rose, Richard watched as they approached Portsmouth harbour. The city itself was situated on Portsea Island, the third largest island in Britain. The city had belonged to John de Bruges, Earl of

Winchester, until he renounced his peerage in 1500.

The harbour was, along with Southampton's, one of the biggest in the country and was chosen as the base for England's navy. It was perfectly situated for both assaults across the channel and to defend the country should it come under attack at sea. It was well protected having a natural defence from the Isle of Wight screening it from the open sea and with a narrow entrance and strong fortifications it was almost impregnable. As they entered the harbour, Richard looked up to see the Round Tower, one of the oldest fortifications in Portsmouth, built nearly a hundred years previously in 1418 to defend the harbour. It was constructed by Henry V and made of wood but was rebuilt some years later by Henry VII with stone, who also added to the harbour the first dry dock.

Their port of call, selected by King Henry, was to be Portchester Castle which was situated at the north end and was the first fortress to have ever been built in protection of the harbour. It was a castle built within a former Roman fort and as a royal fortress had been visited by several monarchs over the years. Its last visit, however, had come from Margaret of Anjou, wife of Henry VI in 1441, and since then it had been left to languish. The fort was square in shape with stone walls running along each side and the castle situated in its northernmost corner. The focal point was the castle's keep which loomed over every-thing, a tower of large proportion from the top of which was a beautiful view over the harbour and of the church in the forts southern corner. Some of the men were quite keen to visit the church named after the Holy Saint Mary upon arrival, where they could account for their sins and thank God for surviving the last battle. For others, it was a question of surviving the next. Richard, too, prayed but only after he buried his wife, whose body he had brought with him from France. It was an emotional affair and all the men paid their respects. *The sword outwears its sheath, and the soul wears out the breast. And the heart must pause to breathe, and love itself, have rest.* He sat at her grave for hours and that's when he prayed that they would be victorious and asked God to deliver him his enemies on the battlefield, whereupon he could deliver God's justice and send the bastards straight to Hell.

They stayed for three days but Richard did not dare to stay there any longer. War was coming and they needed to head north. But if Portchester was to be his seat in England then the place needed to be liveable. The castle's buildings were in desperate need of repair and with the help of some of the local men from the town of Portchester they were able to get the work underway. The fort was also poorly garrisoned so they recruited some of the locals' sons to be trained as soldiers by a handful of Santé's men who they were to leave behind to strengthen the fort's defences. But most importantly a blacksmith was needed, for if they were to strengthen the garrison they would need armour and the horses in the stables were in short supply of shoes.

"Do you really wish for me to stay behind, Richard?" Joseph asked. "I can be of use to you. My skills with a blade have improved."

"My friend, I know they have and there is no one else I would rather have by my side. But I would have you safe. Besides, I need you here. I need someone I can trust. I appoint you Castellan of Portchester and I leave the castle's repair in your capable hands." Richard smiled but Joseph did not return it.

"Can your promise you will be back to see it?"

"No, but I have every intention to be. Maria would love it here, so close to the sea, we could start a new life."

"That you could." Joseph sighed.

"Come now, Joseph, why so glum? This is a good opportunity for you and do not think I have not noticed how taken you have become with the maid!"

This time Joseph did return the smile. "I had not thought any one had known."

"Joseph, everybody knows," Richard cried out with laughter. "Anyway, you are welcome to see us to London. You can even bring the wench!"

Joseph ignored the latter part. "You are going to London?"

"Aye, and maybe there I will find some answers about my father."

Chapter Twelve

The Priory Inn
London, Kingdom of England.
August, 1513.

"Truth, like a torch, the more it's shook it shines."
Sir William Hamilton

The weather the next day was extremely pleasant, even for an English summer. Richard had awoken early that morning and was greeted by blissful rays of sunshine that sparkled from the water in the harbour. He broke his fast on bacon and bread and washed it down with some honeyed milk, and then with the rest of the men he prepared to depart. Lonzo and all the other horses were saddled and ready and all that was left to do was to say goodbye. He watched as Santé embraced his two companions that he had chosen to stay behind and they wished him well. Richard, too, went over to shake their hands and thank them for their loyalty. The worst was still to come. He was approached by Joseph who as he expected was on the verge of tears as he gripped him in a bone crushing hug.

"Promise me, Richard, that you will return," he whimpered into Richard's shoulder. "Promise me."

"Have no fear, Joseph, we will return and this place better be up to scratch when we do, or you'll have me to answer to."

Joseph released his grip and he smiled. "You can count on me for that at least," he replied.

"Anyhow, are you not coming with us to London?"

"Well..." he said, turning round and taking a look at the maid he had become quite fond of.

"Say no more," Richard replied, laughing. "You enjoy yourself." He patted Joseph on the shoulder before heaving himself up on to Lonzo's back. "Take care, Joseph."

"Aye and you, God speed, Richard."

"Cazadores, move out!" he called to the twenty five men that were packed and saddled, ready to depart, and they made their way up the church road and out of the fort at Portchester, heading north.

It took them three days to reach London. It was a city like no other in Europe. For over a thousand years it had been a fortress built by the Romans in the third century when it was known as Londinium. Its wall still stood till this day although its defences had been updated and now included the Tower of London in its south east corner and Bayard's castle in its south west. The city, however, had outgrown its walls and its population increased and spilled out of the gates and had expanded further along the Thames River. They made their way along Fleet Street and Richard felt a strange sensation, almost a tingle of anticipation, mixed with a bit of dread. He had never been to London before yet for all he knew this could have been the town he had been born in, and oddly he felt at home immediately. It was as if it was meant to be, like there was some purpose to him being here. All roads led somewhere and maybe this is where his was taking him to, to his home, to his father.

For several years, Richard had become accustomed to village life but here everything was so busy, even more so than Córdoba had been; so loud, so much more than he was used to. He could hear the sound of the market voices calling, the fishmongers, the butchers and he could smell the reek of gutted fish, the stink coming from the river, the smell of shit and human waste and the waft of horse dung casually left to bake in the afternoon sun along the crowded streets. He could smell food from the taverns and ale from the barrels. It was foul and overpowering yet somehow comforting; he was home.

"So, now that we have reached this wretched place, what do you intend to do?" Señor Jiménez asked, trotting up beside him.

"I don't know," Richard replied honestly. "I'm not sure what I was hoping to find here. But if my father was a knight then there must be records of his existence; there must be someone in the capital who can help."

"Maybe, but where to begin, Richard, we have little time as it is. Scotland is invading and we must be there to meet them when they do."

"I know, I know. Perhaps this was foolish after all. Let the men rest a while. I won't be long, then we will continue our journey."

"What will you do?"

"I did not come all this way for nothing, my friend. I will take a ride to the tower and see if therein lie any answers to this riddle."

"Do you want me to come with you?"

"No. I feel this is something I need to do alone. Enjoy your evening, Alexandre, but have the men readied by first light. In the morning we ride for Scotland."

Richard spurred Lonzo on and went through the Lud Gate, one of seven entrances through the wall and into the heart of London. He went under the portcullis and was immediately drawn to the attention of one of the most beautiful buildings he had ever seen. He had been lucky in his life to see such places as the Castel Sant'Angelo and the Alcazar de Córdoba but Saint Paul's Cathedral was breath-taking. It had sat proudly atop of Ludgate Hill since its conception under William the Conqueror in 1087. It took nearly two hundred years until it reached its entirety and was consecrated in 1240. It was designed in the shape of a cross with a tower in the centre atop of which was one of the tallest church spires in the whole of Europe.

He made his way around it yet he could not avert his gaze from it. It was far larger than any other building in London and even as he got further away and headed down Watling Street if he turned in his saddle he could still see it clear as day piercing high into the sky. Richard made his way to the river until he reached a church to the north side of London Bridge. It was named after Saint Magnus the Martyr. He wondered as he gazed upon it if his father had ever been here or if he had ever crossed the bridge. The bridge itself was fascinating; it was the only bridge in London that crossed the Thames and it had buildings running all the way along it which included over a hundred shops and a chapel, all of which looked like they would topple off at any minute but impressive all the same. From there he followed the river east to the Tower.

The Tower of London was a fortress, whose name came from its most prominent feature, the White Tower. The White Tower, a keep which provided great strength and defence for its lord, was also considered a palace that had accommodation fit for a king. The tower was built on the north bank of the Thames, a looming landmark visible to all persons approaching London on the River Thames, by William the Conqueror in 1078. Since then it underwent two serious developments by Richard the Lionheart who built an inner ward enclosing the White Tower in the late twelfth century and an outer ward built by Edward I that encompassed the whole castle in the late thirteenth century. Yet more striking was the moat that surrounded it all. Just like the Cathedral, it was a structure of no comparison, it was difficult for Richard to comprehend how men could build such things of wonder. The tower had an illustrious history that went back nearly five hundred years. This was supposedly the site where King Richard III, son of the Duke of York had his nephews, the Princes in the Tower, murdered. *Grenwick was Richard's sworn man. For all I know he killed them; maybe my father knew of it and that's why he's dead.*

Richard dwelled on that thought a moment. He knew little of Grenwick but he knew enough to suppose that he was a man willing to do whatever it took to get what he wanted, and a man like that was capable of all sorts of unimaginable things. *I wonder...*

Richard circled the tower many times and spent the most part of the afternoon basking in its magnificent aura. It was unoccupied at present for absent above the tower was the royal banner of arms and instead fluttering in its place was the flag of Saint George. It was to be expected, as the King was in France and the Queen was in the north mustering her husband's northern army. The tower had not been in use by a royal monarch since the death of the princes anyhow. Folk were super-stitious and it would not do to live in a castle where the ghosts of dead children walked the corridors at night. The Tudor kings had therefore sought alternative accommodation. Henry's father had long admired Richmond Palace but Henry personally preferred the comfort and safety of Windsor Castle.

The tower, despite seeing its last days as a royal residency, still had its uses. It had long been tradition since the early fourteenth century for the royal monarchs to lead a procession form the tower to Westminster Abbey for their coronation. Henry and Catherine had done just that before being crowned as King and Queen of England. More significantly, however, the tower itself saw use as an armoury but more infamously as a prison and place of torture. Only those that had committed high treason warranted a place in the tower.

The thought made Richard's stomach churn. Suddenly he saw the tower in a dark light. Moments ago he had stood in awe of it, then out of nowhere it was as if it had been cast under a dark shadow and he instantly felt in fear of it. He decided he had to get away.

Richard pulled on Lonzo's reins, and he obliged without hesitation. The horse too felt eager to be away from this place. They turned from it and headed across the crowded street, where the citizens of London were eagerly running about their business. There were many a horse and cart they had to navigate between but once out of the tower's watchful glare it felt as though a weight had lifted from Richard's shoulders and his spirits rose again dramatically. It was only then that he realised how hungry he was.

They trudged on for a little way. Richard had no idea where they were going but Lonzo seemed happy to keep on walking. Eventually they headed down a side street and after going down it some way the horse stopped suddenly. Richard, whose mind had been trailing along thoughts of his father, was jerked from his daze. He glanced up and noticed they had stopped outside an inn. The inn was barely recognisable and Richard was adamant that had they not stopped in precisely that spot he would not have noticed it was there at all.

There was a small weather-battered wooden sign that creaked as it swung gently in the slight breeze. Upon it, though somewhat faded, was a picture of a building that looked a lot like the Benedictines' home of St Bartholomew's that was situated just outside of town. Richard's thought was confirmed as he ran his gaze over the inn's name; 'The Priory.'

"Are you sure?" Richard asked his horse, patting Lonzo on the back of the head. "I think even we can afford a little better," he said in a whisper.

At that moment the big oak door of the inn was forced open. An old man, who must have been at the very least mid-seventy, appeared with a broom as he brushed the dust from his premises. He had not noticed Richard was there until Lonzo gave a soft whinny and he looked up from what he was doing. "Can I help you...Sir?" he added after taking in Richard's appearance.

"Are you open for business?" Richard asked.

"Rarely," the man replied gloomily.

"Today is a good day for business. You should be open."

He glared at Richard. "Who are you?" he asked.

"My name is Sir Richard. I am the new Baron of Portchester. And you are?"

"My name is James Clifford. I own this establishment," he retorted with a bow. "What brings you from Portchester?"

He could not say why, but despite his rudeness Richard liked the man. In his defence he had probably run the establishment for many years and with little custom, and it was no wonder the man was so miserable. Richard even admired his dry sense of humour. It took both courage and experience to know when to speak to a man of rank with such a tone.

"I am heading north for the war against Scotland. My men and I have stopped off in London for supplies. Can I offer you custom?"

"Aye, you can, follow me."

Richard got down from his horse and tied Lonzo to a wooden post. The stocky man beckoned him inside, holding the door open in grudging deference to Richard's rank. Richard scanned the small, boxy room. It was crammed with tables and chairs and had a small bar to the right. *I wonder if my father ever sat in here and had his supper,* he thought wearily.

"What can I get you?" James asked from behind the bar. It was only now that he found himself close up that he realised amongst the wrinkles of his face the innkeep had a rather savage scar on his left cheek.

"I'll start with ale if you would be so kind."

The innkeep nodded. "It gets quite dark in here. I will light a fire. Please, take a seat."

"Thank you," Richard replied.

"Are you hungry?" James called.

"Yes, I could certainly eat something."

James nodded again. He lit a fire in the hearth and the room brightened and warmed considerably, letting Richard relax a little. James then brought over some ale, a loaf of bread, some cheese and a few apples. "It is not much, I am afraid, but it is all I have." As he laid the food on the table James glanced at Richard curiously. He seemed to recognise something in his eyes and Richard could not fail to notice his stare. It was as if the man was seeing him again for the first time except in a different light.

"Have we met before?"

"No, I would have remembered," Richard replied, quite adamant that they had never met. Though as the words fell from his lips he was not entirely sure. A vision of his youth appeared in his mind. He remembered a priest... Father Jacob? "Perhaps you knew my father?"

"What was his name?"

"I do not know," Richard confessed. "I had hoped you could help me."

"Alas, without a name there is little I can do." He sighed, grabbing the loaf of bread and tearing it in two. "Maybe you remember something, anything?"

Momentarily Richard had been filled with hope but it swiftly drained away like dew of a late spring morning. He knew very little about his father. "I think he was a knight. He went to Spain, which is where he met my mother. That is all I know."

James was just about to take a bite from the bread when he took notice of what Richard had just said, and paused.

"Longsword!" Richard blurted out. "That's it, I remember! That's what the men called me, Longsword!"

The innkeep jumped. He was so shocked by the word he had just heard he knocked the jug of ale to the floor. He glared at Richard with his mouth open. "Richard, my dear boy! Good God, is that really you?" He clasped Richard's hand, taking no notice of the broken jug as tears welled up in his eyes. He looked at Richard and Richard looked back at him. James had a warm smile on his face. His earlier hostility was long forgotten.

"You know me, old man?"

"It is you, I knew I recognised you. Forgive my ageing eyes, Richard, but I see it now, you look just like your father. I had wondered if I would ever see you again!"

This seemed almost too good to be true. The first day he arrived in London and by chance he stumbled on the Priory Inn, owned by a man who recognised him as his father's son. *Who is this man?*

"I still write to your grandfather from time to time," he carried on, in jubilation. "He wrote to me and told me you might come to England one day, to search for your roots, and here you are." He beamed. "I never would have believed it."

Richard's heart sank. "I think you may have me mistaken, James, I never knew my grandparents."

But the man kept smiling. "He never told you, did he?"

"Who are you talking about?"

"Your grandfather lives, Richard, the father of your Spanish mother, except you do not know him as such. You know him as the old man who raised you as a boy."

What is he saying? No, this cannot be true. "No, that is not possible. That man never loved me. If you say he is my grand-father, then I say it is not true."

"It is true, Richard, that I can promise you. Believe me, there are reasons behind the methods we chose to protect you and your family."

He knows something. "Who are you?" Richard asked.

"You already know my name. I was a friend of your father's."

"You knew him well?"

"Aye, I did. I suppose under the circumstances at the time you could say he was my closest companion. It was during the Wars of the Roses. I had previously fought for him in the early stages but after the defeat at St Albans and the death of his liege lord the Duke of Somerset, we fled into hiding. That's how I came across this place. At the time, like now, I had little custom, but your father towards the end of the war came back and he liked to stay here regularly. He was an informant for Henry VII. The Priory, as you can see, is well located to the Tower of London where Henry's rival at the time, Richard III, took up residence. Also being just off the beaten track and dare I say it not the most lucrative of inns, it was never frequented by Richard's soldiers. Your father was safe here and I suppose over a period of time we became close. I liked him, Richard, he was as good a man as any I have ever met."

"Please, James, I know so little of my father. Tell me more about him; what was his name?"

"You really know nothing, do you? Well, your father was christened Robert Longsword; that is the name of your house. He was an only son born into a modest family that has served and fought for the Kingdom of England for near four hundred years. Your father was a knight and fought for King and country, although he fought for the rebels against Richard, but he was no true king. He was also present at the Battle of Castillon, the defeat that ended the Hundred Years' War with France. It was there that he met your grandfather, a Spanish mercenary. Robert was also present at the first battle of St Albans as I have mentioned. That defeat was difficult for your father to bear; the death of the Duke played heavily on his mind so not long after that he left for Spain, where he married your mother."

"You knew my mother?"

"Unfortunately, I did not. She died when you were only a babe, several years before your father returned to England. But if what your father said of her was true, then your mother was beautiful and had a heart of gold. Yet as strong willed as your father claimed her to be she was not strong enough to fight off the fever that finally took her life."

"What did my father do?"

"He did what he thought best. If I could tell you one thing about your father it is that he loved you above all else."

Richard had to suppress a laugh. "If he loved me, why did he leave? Why did he leave me alone in a foreign country with no family or at least any knowledge of them?"

"That is not true. He only came to England to make enough money to take care of you, to provide you with a decent life and he had always intended to return. He left you in the capable care of your deceased mother's parents, your grandparents. They only withheld their true identity to keep you safe."

"Keep me safe from who?"

"The men who killed your father."

"The Ashbournes?"

"Aye, the Ashbournes."

"What do you know of them?"

"Well, they are a family not unlike your own, they were powerful and respected. But they shared a feud with yours that goes back hundreds of years. The leader of their company is a man named Grenwick, a ruthless man who served Richard III. I met him once, in this very room the night he found your father."

"And he killed him?"

"No, your father had valuable information regarding Richard III. Have you heard the story of the Two Princes?"

"Only rumours."

"After the death of Edward IV, his twelve year old son Edward was brought to London and crowned King Edward V of England. He was accommodated at the Tower of London and his Uncle Richard, Duke of Gloucester was chosen as his guardian and declared Lord Protector until the boy came of an age to rule. Not long after this Edward's ten year old brother, Richard of Shrewsbury, was brought to join them. After only two months as King both Edward and his brother were declared illegitimate by an act of parliament known as Titulus Regius-"

"Why were they illegitimate?"

"They declared that their father's marriage to Elizabeth Woodville was invalid, therefore making all their children illegitimate as heirs to the throne. We have our doubts as to whether this is true or not but we believe that the boys' uncle was behind it for he was not long after crowned King Richard III and declared rightful King of England."

"Then he killed them?"

"He did. Your father broke into the tower to see what had become of them. He found them playing in the tower grounds and thought all was well, but that night he witnessed their murder. Richard lured them to a room where a knight named James Tyrell, a staunch supporter of the House of York, was waiting for them. Your father said he never saw the instruments that killed them but he did hear their high pitched screams and it was something that would haunt him until the day he died."

"What became of them? Surely they didn't go unnoticed?"

"Your father said he saw Tyrell and Grenwick carry their little bodies from that room and had them buried under the stairs leading to the castle's chapel. Of course, people had their suspicions but Richard was king so who would question him? Besides it was only Richard, Tyrell and Grenwick who knew what became of them and they were never going to reveal what they had done."

"Except my father knew."

"Precisely, and your father put it in writing and he made sure the last thing he did with his life was put it in the right hands."

"Whose?"

"Mine."

"Yours?"

"Aye, you sound surprised, Richard? After all, why would your father pass on that delicate information to a little old innkeeper like me?"

"I didn't mean to cause offence James, it just seemed—"

"—a bit odd? None taken, Richard. But your father was seen trying to escape the tower so the King sent Grenwick to flush him out. Robert knew it was only a matter of time before they got hold of him so the night Grenwick turned up here, your father gave me the letter that he had written to Henry Tudor claiming what he had seen. He trusted me, Richard, and I am honoured that he did and I believe that I may have been the last person to see him alive. In the early hours of the next morning your father rode for the tower to keep them at bay while I delivered his letter to Henry."

"And you succeeded?"

"I did. Henry used the information to rally the people to his cause and at the Battle of Bosworth field the Lancaster army overcame the York army and Richard III was killed. Soon afterwards, Henry was crowned the King of England, the seventh of his name."

Richard inhaled a deep breath, before releasing. "At least my father did not die in vain." He sat in silence for a moment. *So this is who my father was. He was a knight and died for a worthy cause. He never abandoned me but left to give me a better life, he loved me.* "Did you hear of what happened in Guadalest?"

"Yes, your grandfather mentioned in his last letter that your wife and daughter had been taken captive. I am so sorry, Richard, your father never meant for you to get caught up in all of this."

"How does my grandfather know of what happened? In Spain they think I killed my brothers and that I burned down the castle."

"Your grandfather always kept a watchful eye over you." He paused. "Let me put it this way, did you ever think it a little bit suspicious or at the very least a little odd that when you woke after your fall that night that your horse just happened to be waiting for you?" he asked, nodding encouragement at the bemused expression on Richard's face.

"He...he put Lonzo there?"

James smiled. "Of course he did. How else do you think the beast got there? He even pulled you from the water, albeit with some difficulty I might add, he's a very old man your grandfather.

"I-I-"

"Am speechless? He had to bribe some local farm boys to help him. He had them follow you to Alcalalí. They saw enough devastation in that little village of yours for your grandfather to understand the truth of what had happened. He knows you did not do it and so do I. There is only one man responsible for what has happened and that man is-"

"Grenwick!"

"Aye, Grenwick."

"When the men came they were adamant that I had been left gold by my father. Have you any idea what they were speaking of?"

"King Henry was a generous man, he paid your father well, but the information your father had for him was priceless. Your father made me promise that whatever Henry gave me in return for that letter, that I would get it to you. Henry gave me a wagon full of gold, gold that he had confiscated from Richard's vassals, Grenwick chiefly among them. It was difficult and it took some time but I got it to your grandfather in Spain."

"Where is it now?"

"That is a question you will have to ask your grandfather when you return home. There are too many ears around here, but we both agreed that it should be hidden until such a time that it would be safe to reveal."

"Why?"

"After Richard's downfall, all of his men that did not swear allegiance to Henry lost everything. Grenwick was a proud man and he could not bear to switch his allegiance. Not to mention he knew of what happened in the tower and Henry had ordered that anyone in connection to be executed. Grenwick could not take that risk so he fled, to where I do not know. But know this; he found out about the gold and he has been searching for it ever since. He sees Robert as the sole reason for his downfall and he will not rest until you are dead and the gold is his."

"And all this time my grandparents knew and told me nothing?"

"Richard, your grandparents loved you as did your father. Your grandfather loves you still. All that they have done has been to protect you. It is why they never revealed themselves to you, why they never showed you the love and kindness they should have, to keep your identity safe. It killed them to treat you so, your grandmother wept the day you left with the General Córdoba in fear that she may never see you again, but your grandfather knew it was for the best. At least in the General's care you would be surrounded by soldiers who would keep you safe from harm and you would learn the necessary skills to defend yourself and then maybe one day you would return."

"But I never knew they existed. Why would they think that I would ever return?"

"The General knew."

"What?"

"The day you left, your grandfather told him everything. Not about the gold, but that you were being hunted and you needed protection. The arrangement was that one day when you were of an age the General would reveal this information and you could finish this feud, and go home and claim what is rightfully yours."

Richard shook his head. He couldn't believe what he was hearing. "You mean to tell me that all this time the General has known about this and he's never said a word? My life, my family's lives were at risk, my wife and daughter were taken from me, my wife now lies dead and I knew nothing! Why would he keep this from me?"

"Tell me, Richard, what is your relationship with the General like?"

"He is like a father to me. He has always treated me like a son."

"Then I think therein lies your answer. The General loves you, and he has dedicated a large portion of his life to protecting you and raising you into the man you are today. He feared for your life more so than he did his own and he could not bear to lose you. He knew that one day you would be knighted and when that day came you would be free to choose your own path, and he could not bear to tell you what he promised your grandfather he would."

"Why?"

"Because he knew you would go after these men, he knew you would want to track them down and kill them, and he did not want to see you die. Can you blame him?"

"I suppose I cannot." Richard sighed. "If everyone was so eager to keep this from me, why are you telling me now?"

James smiled. "Times change, Richard. After years in hiding the enemy has finally resurfaced, your wife is dead, your daughter captive, what have you got left to lose? If your victory at Guinegate showed your enemies anything, it is that you are strong and that you are coming. You have them on the run, dear boy."

"What should I do?"

"You go after them, you track them down and you kill them!" he said with deadly conviction before standing up and heading from the room. He returned moments later struggling with the effort of lifting a heavy trunk. Richard watched him curiously.

"What is that?" he asked.

James slammed the trunk on the table and opened the lid, smiling at Richard as he did so. "This," he replied, "Was your father's. I believe it is time that it was passed on to you."

Richard had to stand to see what was in the trunk and he was pleasantly surprised by what he saw. First and foremost was the large unmistakeable shield, painted black and decorated pristinely with a single red rose. Then there was a surcoat dyed black that too was emblazoned with the same sigil, but the item that caught Richard's attention the most was the great long sword that shone in the firelight. The very steel appeared like silver, despite the obvious signs of battle use, and the hilt was as if made of gold. In the sword's pommel carved pristinely from a ruby was a rose, and the craftsmanship was impeccable. Richard held it aloft and admired its beauty.

"There is a note inside," James said.

Richard lifted the shield and saw Joseph spoke the truth. In the bottom of the trunk was an old, tattered, folded bit of parchment. He pulled it out, opened it and read the words that were hastily scribbled by his father thirty years before.

My son,
I give to you my sword as my father once passed on to me.

Long has our house stood and fought for a worthy cause. You as the sole surviving Longsword, the last of our line, I task with carrying on that tradition.

Wear the sigil of our house with honour, be proud of who you are and always remember where you came from.

Your loving father,
Robert.

Chapter Thirteen

King James IV
Burgh Muir, Kingdom of Scotland.
September, 1513.

"He said to me that his subjects serve him with their persons and goods, in just and unjust quarrels, exactly as he likes, and that therefore he does not think it right to begin any warlike undertaking without being himself the first in danger. His deeds are as good as his words."
Pedro de Ayala

A few months earlier at Stirling Castle.

Pedro Ayala, Spanish diplomat for King Ferdinand II and the late Queen Isabella I of Spain, had been their resident ambassador in Scotland for nearly twenty years. So impressed was King James with Pedro's wisdom that after a few brief visits the King wished to entertain him at court as his guest, offering to pay for his accommodation and even reserving a house and paying a year's rent towards a possible permanent Spanish Embassy in Edinburgh. Pedro was proud of what he had achieved in Scotland over the years. He had, during all that time, dissuaded James from warring with England; had visited the English court; had kept his monarchs in Spain well informed; and his friendship with the King of Scots had blossomed. Despite this, he was ageing, his health waning, and he wanted nothing more than to go home and live out his remaining days in some peace and comfort.

Standing at the foot of the King's throne in the Great Hall of Stirling Castle, Pedro gazed into the thoughtful face of the forty year old James and wondered what it was that played on his mind. He was a handsome man with long hair that he never cut and a long beard that he never trimmed and it suited him. Pedro was very taken with the King and had been astonished at how sophisticated he was when they first met fifteen years ago. Pedro had believed the Scots to be a barbaric race and although he had learnt that some in the north still were, unlike them James could not only speak their Gaelic language but could speak English which was the common tongue for most Scots as well as German, French, Italian and Flemish, not to mention Spanish which he spoke terrifically well. This allowed for the two men to speak often in private. He was a true renaissance prince and held an avid interest in scientific matters. He kept a full renaissance court which included alchemists and maintained an alchemical workshop. He allowed the college of surgeons to have a royal charter, backed the establishment of Scotland's first printing press and he had several royal palaces. He undertook building works including Falkland, Linlithgow and Edinburgh where he turned the castle into Scotland's foremost gun foundry. But he saved his grandest work for Stirling Castle, restructuring the fore work, renovating the royal chapel, establishing a college of priests and completing the Great Hall, where they now stood. James had furnished all of his castles with tapestries and was a sincere patron of the arts, which included several notable figures who were present at his court.

"I commend you, Pedro," the King said, smiling down at him. "For suggesting the development of this castle and the improvement of my court, Stirling is now a palace of European standing that any king would be proud of. It is no wonder the English want to take my country, no?" James laughed but Pedro shifted uncomfortably. It was not the first time of late that the King had mentioned England and he couldn't help but think that after he left for Spain, James may have more than just words to share with the English King. "It pains me, though, that after all this time you will be leaving us. Are you sure you will not stay, Pedro? You have a home here. You will always be welcome in Scotland."

Before Pedro could reply he coughed quite violently. He quickly raised a handkerchief to his lips, while the King watched him sceptically. As Pedro withdrew the piece of cloth from his mouth he saw a trace of blood, and he swiftly tucked the handkerchief up his sleeve before the King could notice. "I have enjoyed every moment spent at this court, your Grace. However I am unsure as to how many years on this earth God has planned for me and I wish to see my homeland once again."

"I have no right to stop you, of course, but are you fit to travel?" the King asked, somewhat unconvinced.

Pedro was adamant the King would not stop him from leaving. "I...I am, your Grace."

"Then so be it. Where will you go?"

"Hopefully Toledo, the city of my birth."

"I know not of that place. Tell me of Toledo."

"To some men it is just a town of no significant importance, but to me it is home, and that is all that matters in the world. There is no place like home."

"Aye, I can agree with you on that account."

"But it is a place proud of its heritage with a vast culture. We have a reputation for making and selling the finest blades and we also have several architectural wonders. A particular favourite of mine is the Monastery of Saint John of the Kings built by my King and Queen to commemorate the birth of their son John and their victory over King Afonso V of Portugal at the Battle of Toro."

"Fascinating. Will you visit anywhere else on your travels home?"

Pedro suppressed a cough. "I have been ordered by the King to visit the English ambassador, John Stile, in Valladolid on my way back." As soon as the words passed his lips he wished he'd never spoken them.

"The English ambassador in Spain?" The King looked taken aback.

"You seem surprised? I have visited England as well on several occasions since I have been here, your Grace. After all, Spain has an allegiance with England. King Henry married King Ferdinand's daughter, Catherine of Aragón."

"The same Catherine of Aragón that you led me to believe would be wedded to me."

"I have apologised for that, your Grace, I cannot determine what the Spanish crown will do, only advise, inform and pass on the knowledge

that I have available to me."

"I know, Pedro. I do not hold it against you. I just think Spain can prosper from an alliance with Scotland."

"As do I, but Spain has greater need of England at this current stage. Spain is at war with France over land in Italy, and England is far better located to launch an assault on France. Henry already has plans to invade France to keep them occupied while his father in law stakes his claim in Italy."

This news did not come as a shock to James. "I know of this. I have received a letter from King Louis asking me to honour the Auld Alliance."

"And you will run to his aid? Need I remind you it is not only France that you have allied yourself with? You yourself married King Henry's sister Margaret and that makes you allies with England too. Your Grace, I implore you, do not go to war with England."

The King sighed and scratched his beard. "My marriage to Margaret only makes her my wife. Yes, it brought about a temporary treaty and an era of peace but how long do you think that will last? Henry only wishes to keep me at bay while he wars elsewhere. No, Pedro, I have no alliance with England but I am honour bound to help the French. You are a wise man and an even better friend, Pedro. I accept what you say and I see the truth in it but you must know me by now, and what I am is a man of honour and that leaves me with no choice. If Henry invades France, then I will invade England."

* * *

South of Edinburgh, in the heart of Drumselch Forest at Burgh Muir, King James watched from the clearing as the very trees around him seemed to come alive. Under the shadowed canopy of the ageing oaks, the trunks began to sway and stagger in the dark. Men stirred and went to relieve their bladders and to jostle their friends from sleep. There were hundreds of them, thousands, and they swarmed through the forest like bees. There were among them lords and barons, burgesses and earls and all manner of men aged between sixteen and sixty and their number was nearing sixty thousand strong, the most formidable force ever assembled in Scottish history. As the King's horn blew it had the same effect as if a man's foot had trampled an ant hill, and like thousands of ants King James of Scotland's army poured forth from the trees and filled the clearing.

In the midst of them all, atop a small knoll, stood James. It was a mound erected for such occasions, built in part with freestone and known by all as the King's Knowe. To the side of the knoll was the Bore-Stane, a solid standing block of stone in which was planted the King's royal standard, a yellow flag upon which the red Lion Rampant of Scotland was proudly etched, embellished by a double red border set with red lilies. James let his gaze move to it and felt pride as he watched it billow in the early morning breeze. He would do as great men had done before him; he would achieve what William Wallace had done at Stirling, he would succeed as Robert the Bruce had done at Bannockburn, and he would defeat the English.

"Good morning, your Grace," a voice called from below him. He recognised the voice, it was unique and one of only a few that was English accented. He looked down to see Grenwick, the man sent by King Louis of France to command the small French contingent of his army.

"Ah Sir Ashbourne, the Englishman who leads French troops for the Scots against England. You are an odd fellow, Grenwick, your situation is rare. Tell me, are you ready to kill your countrymen?"

"I have been waiting a long time for that chance, your Grace."

"Then your time is nearly at hand. I only hope your men will not let me down."

"They will not, your Grace, they are all hardened veterans tainted by previous battles against the English. They know how they fight, they know how to face them and they know how to kill them."

"King Louis speaks highly of you and I trust your judgment. Tell me, how would you approach this campaign?"

"May I speak freely, your Grace?"

"You may."

"I would not have written to England to inform them of your intentions. If you want to hit them with their sails down, whilst their King is abroad, then it would have been wise to be cautious. Using the element of surprise you could have swept through the country unchallenged and made it to London before Henry even had the chance to react."

The King smiled and shook his head. "Many of my earls would agree with you, but unfortunately I am not so cunning and sly. No, I am a man of honour and I am chivalrous. I told my enemies that I am coming and have given them the chance to meet us in open battle. Let the men of the world know my virtues and let them know that I am not afraid, that we are not afraid. Defeat whatever they send against us, Grenwick, and then, maybe then, we can march upon London." Grenwick nodded to show that he understood. "Besides, Henry's army is in France. How many men do you think his Queen Regent can muster? We will destroy them, Grenwick, have no fear."

"You fill me with confidence, your Grace. We cannot fail."

There was a brief pause in their conversation as the King looked away to see the rest of his men spill into the clearing. "Tell me," he said, still speaking to Grenwick. "How fares my ship? You sailed her, did you not?"

"We did. The Michael is a grand ship, the grandest I ever did see. King Louis is quite taken with her and was saddened by her return."

"Well, if I die in the coming battle he can have her, but for a price of course." He laughed. "I hope you made good use of her?"

"We did, your Grace, we put her to very good use and we

took extremely good care of her."

The King brought his gaze back to Grenwick. "As you take such care of that girl you brought with you?"

"The girl?"

"Aye, the girl, who is she?"

"She is my daughter," Grenwick said, his eyes flickering to his feet unable to meet the King's.

"A daughter you keep guarded night and day? You treat her like a prisoner."

"You can never be too careful, your Grace, these are times of war."

"We are allies, are we not? Do you not trust her safety among my men?"

"Of course, your Grace, it is merely a precaution."

"Good, because you will not be amongst a better company of men anywhere in the world." The King put aside Grenwick's suspicious behaviour; perhaps he lied, but it was of no account for the moment. The King turned to face his men and raised his arms aloft.

"Men!" he cried. "Men of Scotland, my brothers, I see you all today as men unified under a single cause. Together we are strong, together we shall make the world tremble when we march south and invade England!" Cheers went up amongst the men. "King Henry of England, like so many before him, has laid claim as overlord of Scotland." The cheers turned to jeers. "Does he think that with a few choice words he can raise himself to supreme ruler of our realm? No, if he wants Scotland for himself then he will have to come and get it." The cheers returned. "But I remember that for hundreds of years English kings have sought to rule us and I remember that after hundreds of years of war and rape and murder, we are still here!" The men began to bang spears on shields. "The Pope, his great Holiness Leo X, has threatened me, telling me not to invade England and that to do so would cut us off from God's grace, and Christopher Bainbridge

the Archbishop of York has threatened me with excommunication, but of course he would - he's a damned Englishman!" The
men in the clearing erupted with laughter. "I say damn them,
damn them both. We are free men and if we are not allowed to
defend our freedom, our liberty, our families and our country,
then there is no God!"

The raucous atmosphere caused by the men hit fever pitch,
the spears and shields continued to clash and they began to
chant: 'Ste-wart! Ste-wart! Ste-wart!' They cried out the name of
the King's house, the name he shared with his predecessors, his
ancestors and it spurred him on.

"We will defend our freedom, we will defeat the English and
I tell you now, no I promise you that God, God is on our side!
Brothers we are Scotsmen, we will fight as Scotsmen, we will die
as Scotsmen and God willing we will live as Scotsmen!"

The chanting changed as the men that surrounded the King's
Knowe cried out with passion the name of their country. 'Scotland, Scot-land, Scot-land.' The King walked down from the
knoll and into the crowed and mingled with his men, each
patting him on the shoulders and back as he went.

* * *

Grenwick watched as the men of Scotland riled themselves into
a frenzy. They cheered and they chanted, weapons were raised
aloft or clattered on shields, some clapped until their hands were
raw, others shouted until their voices were hoarse. The men
hustled and jostled, patted each other, hugged each other but
most importantly, they were ready to die for one another. They
crowded around their King and still crying his name they
followed him from the clearing. Grenwick watched them go and
he smiled. He knew it in his heart that they would be victorious.
He knew the Scots were ready and he would be among them
when they took England by storm. He hoped that wherever

Richard Longsword was right now he could feel their wrath. "You hear that, Richard? We're coming for you and Hell is coming with us."

Later that morning Grenwick was called to a small council by the King and in the woods at Burgh Muir they set about discussing the plans for their invasion. Present at the meeting were four earls; William Graham, Earl of Montrose, Adam Hepburn, Earl of Bothwell, Matthew Stewart, Earl of Lennox, Archibald Campbell, Earl of Argyll and lastly the King himself.

"My Lords." The King spoke gravely. "It is high time we were on our way. We have an unbeatable force and the men are eager. Let us make haste for England."

"I agree, your Grace." The Earl of Bothwell was first to reply. "However it cannot hurt to bolster our forces. We are still awaiting Lord Home and the Earl of Angus, so I suggest we start the march but head for Ellemford and await them there. It would be wise to cross the Tweed in full force."

"Very well, Adam, send word to Home and Angus, and let them know of our intentions."

"Your Grace." The Earl of Montrose spoke next. "From Ellemford we would be perfectly situated to cross the River Tweed at Coldstream."

"Or we could cross at Norham and take the castle there?" the Earl of Lennox suggested.

"Yes, but if we cross at Coldstream, Etal and Ford will be open to us. Why take one castle when we can take two?" retorted Montrose.

Before Lennox could respond, the Earl of Argyll interrupted. "We should head to Berwick and recapture the town. It has been in English hands for over twenty years, so let us reclaim it, to raise the morale of the people of Scotland."

"Berwick is out of the way," Montrose demanded.

"Your Grace?" Grenwick cut in. "Have you considered the cause for your invasion?"

The King looked somewhat angered. "I am doing this for you and your King, am I not? I am helping France! Is that not enough?"

"It is most welcome, your Grace, but may I say you are not France, you are Scotland, a people of your own. As you know, France at this time is in short supply of allies and you yourself have been threatened with excommunication. Let the world know who England really is, find a cause. A cause close to Scottish hearts that will inspire the men to greatness. You are aiding France and it is commendable, but why are you invading; what is your cause?"

The King looked thoughtful for a moment as he fingered his beard. The earls looked at one another and then back and forth between Grenwick and the King. All were silent. "The Bastard," he whispered.

"Who, your Grace?" Adam asked.

"The Bastard!" he said, this time louder and more convincingly.

"John Heron?" asked Montrose.

"Yes, of course!" cried Lennox.

"And who might John Heron be?" Grenwick asked.

"John Heron," the King replied. "He was the brother of Sir William Heron, Lord of Ford Castle. There has always been feuding across the border but on a day of truce held by the Wardens of the Marches, John Heron and two accomplices murdered Sir Robert Kerr, the Warden of the Scottish East March. It caused much controversy amongst my people and they have been baying for justice ever since. I still hold Sir William prisoner but that is not enough to quench their thirst."

"Then I believe you have found your cause."

"Let it be known that we invade England to avenge the death of Sir Robert Kerr! We march for Ford Castle."

"What of Norham?" Lennox asked.

James smiled. "We will take Norham too. With Henry abroad

I expect to go relatively unchallenged, so let us take what we can when we can. Matthew, from Ellemford take your men and lay siege to Norham. We will cross at Coldstream and take Etal and Ford; when the castle has fallen put a garrison in place and meet us at Ford."

"Yes, your Grace."

The King looked over to the Earl of Argyll. "Berwick can wait, but I promise you my Lord, that when this is done, we will march on Berwick and reclaim it for Scotland." He nodded in response. "My Lords, you have your orders. Ready your men; we make for Ellemford."

Grenwick made his way back to his tent amongst the trees. Two of his men stood guard outside, clad in black with the green leaf of his house sewn on their chests. Those leaves were faded, as was the memory of his past life; so many years had he spent in exile that he wasn't sure who he was any more. *It will all come back to me soon, of that I am certain.* As he approached his guards they looked at one another nervously.

"What is it?" he asked, looking from one to the other. "Has she told you the location of the gold? Does she know anything?"

"No, my Lord," one of them replied. "I think she does not. Perhaps if we used more force we could make her talk?"

Anger flashed across Grenwick's face. "No! I told you to rough her up a little but that is all. She is not to be seriously harmed. She is a girl of twelve, for Christ sakes! She's scared for her life and if she knew anything she would have told us already."

"Then why not kill her, my Lord, and be done with it," the other man suggested.

"It seems the only one that knows the location of the gold is Richard. He will come for his daughter and when he does we must be ready. Until such time, she stays whole. If Richard was to find out she has been harmed, it will seriously affect how he approaches us. If she is alive and well he will be cautious. He will not want to risk her being harmed, and he may even trade his life for hers. But if we kill her, he will be wroth and his retribution terrible, and he will not rest until we are all dead."

"Then let him come. We will take him and when we have what we want, we will kill him."

"Easier said than done," replied Grenwick. "Only a fool doesn't fear his enemy, remember that."

"Sir?" the first man asked. "Is it possible that Richard does not know where the gold is?"

"Of course he does, you damned fool! Never trust a Longsword!"

"She's a Longsword," the second man said.

Grenwick smiled. "Only half," he said as he pushed passed them and into the tent, ignoring their protests as he went. He was greeted by an unpleasant scene. "What in God's name is going on here?"

Maria was on all fours, her wrists bound and tied to a post. Her skirts had been raised and one of the men supposed to be keeping watch over her was knelt behind her, trying to lower his hose, while another stood watching and laughing. She looked up at Grenwick when she heard his voice. Her face was bruised and there was blood coming from her nose and lip. "Please," she whimpered.

"My Lord," the man on his knees replied aghast. "We had not expected you back so soon."

Grenwick was outraged. "Get up! Get up, God damn you!"

The man stood up, struggling to steady himself as he attempted to pull up his hose but before he could do so Grenwick's sword was already free from its scabbard and hurtling towards the man's stomach. There was an almighty squelch and the man's eyes rolled back into his head, before he collapsed into a heap on the floor. Grenwick raised his sword to the other man's throat.

"Get out," he said. "Get out!"

The guard couldn't flee the tent quickly enough. Grenwick

lowered himself to where Maria was crouched and he cut her free from her bonds. "Go and clean up," he said.

Maria went to the water basin and took a cloth and dabbed at her bloody face. Even at such a young age and in the sorry state she was in, she was still beautiful like her mother. "I had the good fortune to know your mother," Grenwick said.

"You did, my Lord?"

"Aye, you could say we got very close, once." Grenwick smiled that awful smile. He walked up behind Maria and took a handful of her hair and raised it to his nostrils, sniffing. "You remind me of her," he said. "I hope to know you in the same way, one day."

"My father will come for me," she replied defiantly.

"I have no doubts he will, but when he does I will take from him what I want and then I will kill him." He tugged on her hair and then whispered in her ear. "I made a promise that I would not stop until all the remaining Longswords are dead."

"So you will kill me, too?"

"You are very fortunate, Maria, that you were not born a boy. The Longsword family name will die along with your father. No, I have a better use for you, my dear. We will breed you out and you will provide this world with sons and prolong the Ashbourne name. After I have had my way with you, you will marry my son."

"Who is your son, my Lord?" she asked sarcastically. "Have I had the honour of meeting my betrothed?"

"You have." He laughed. "He has blond hair and blue eyes. His name is Simon."

The look on Maria's face said it all.

Chapter Fourteen

Catherine of Aragón
Wooler, Kingdom of England.
September, 1513.

"Nature wronged her in not making her a man. But for her sex, she would have surpassed all the heroes of history."
Thomas Cromwell

The Queen was offered help up on to her horse but she refused it. She hated that. She gracefully pulled herself up and swung a leg over her mare and seated herself in the saddle before trotting off towards her army, closely followed by the men of rank. She could see a sea of men encamped outside the town of Wooler, thousands of them all preparing and arming themselves for battle. There were hundreds of different banners but proudest of them all was the banner of Saint Cuthbert that she had retrieved from the Cathedral of Durham, a symbolic icon that the men could rally around, as it had been present at victories against the Scots in 1138 and 1346. Hopefully it would bring her victory too.

"It is an army to be proud of, is it not, your Majesty?" a voice called from just behind her.

She turned. "It is. You have done well, Sir Thomas, and you have my compliments."

"Your Majesty, Sir Richard Longsword, the new Baron of Portchester to see you," another voice called, coming over to join them.

"Who?"

"I think you will be quite keen to meet this man, your Grace," he said and smiled. "Besides, he has been sent by your husband from France. It would be wise not to keep him waiting."

She was now intrigued by the figure she could see talking to the Earl of Surrey. He wore a black cloak and bore a red rose on his chest, and he sat atop a black horse, a beast the size of which she had never seen. "You had best send him over then, Pedro."

Pedro waved to the Earl who escorted Richard to her, and the closer he came, the more she thought she recognized him. He was devilishly handsome, but it was not his appearance that caught her eye, it was the way he carried himself, with such elegance and purpose. He smiled at her. She couldn't help but blush as she returned the smile. Richard bowed, never taking his eyes from hers. She felt like a child. He had a way about him that was almost intimidating, yet strangely comforting at the same time. She nodded and put out her hand.

"Her Royal Highness, Catherine of Aragón, Queen Regent of England," the Earl said.

"Catalina de Aragón," Richard replied, taking her hand and brushing his lips gently against it.

"You are Spanish, Señor?" Catherine asked in her native tongue.

"In part," Richard responded in equally fluent Spanish, leaving the Queen slightly surprised, but mightily impressed. "My father was an English knight, but I have lived in the Kingdom of Valencia for many years now, and my mother was Spanish."

"Do I know you?" she asked, looking closely into his face.

He smiled again, causing her a strange feeling in her stomach. "It has been twenty years since we last met, and you would have only been six or seven at the time. I served your father with the General Córdoba. You may know me as Ricardo de Guadalest."

"Señor Ricardo," she gasped. "I remember seeing you at the Alcazar in Córdoba, even you yourself, you could have been no more than-"

"Fifteen," he said.

"I was quite taken with you," she carried on. "I grew up hearing the great stories of your victories, my Lord, all the ladies at court used to talk of you. When I was of an age I begged my mother to allow me to marry you, but my father wanted a better suitor and shipped me off to England to marry Henry's older brother Arthur."

Richard laughed and then as if woken from a daze the Queen realised how childish she sounded; she was the Queen Regent of England, not some peasant girl with silly fantasies. She looked around at all the other men present. Fortunately most of them had puzzled expressions as they hadn't understood a word that was being said, except Pedro who was smiling at her. Quickly changing the subject she switched to English. "May I introduce you," she said, indicating to the man beside her. "To Sir Thomas Lovell, who was tasked with raising our army." He nodded in recognition. "And to Pedro de Ayala. He is a Spanish diplomat, who up until quite recently was an ambassador in Scotland with King James." The old man was still smiling as he waved in greeting. "And finally to Sir Thomas Howard, the Earl of Surrey, who will be leading the army into battle."

"Sir Richard, or is it El Cazador? Your reputation precedes you," the Earl said. "It is good to have you with us. I have heard of your involvement in the battle at Guinegate; the King wrote to me. He speaks highly of you."

"The Hunter?" the Queen asked.

But Richard just smiled at her before turning to the Earl. "He has asked me to assist you in any way that I can."

"You fought in France?" The Queen spoke again.

"I did, your Grace," Richard replied.

"Then I suppose you would be well acquainted with the Duc de Longueville. My husband thought it wise in sending him to me so I can hold him prisoner even though I suggested he be sent to the tower."

"Aye, he is King Louis' cousin. It was I that took him prisoner during the battle but I gave him to the King to ransom. But have no fear, my Lady, he will be of no trouble to you. He lacks the brain power. He fought foolishly during the battle and is one of many high ranking prisoners we took."

"I think you can expect the same from King James," Pedro cut in.

Richard turned to face the old man who started to splutter into his handkerchief. "Tell me Pedro, where do your loyalties lie? With England or Scotland?"

"My loyalties lie with Spain and what Spain requires is peace between Scotland and England. Yet I will not deny that my time in Scotland was pleasant, nor that I was quite taken with the King. I consider him a close friend and I do have his best interests at heart. However, I have no ties with Scotland but I do have ties in England. The Queen is the daughter of my King and Henry has an alliance with him. Although I am a man of peace and if it were down to me this battle would not be fought, I have spent many years persuading James from pursuing it and up until now I have succeeded. But if a battle is to be fought then it is in Spain's best interest if England wins and though it is regrettable if the Queen asks me for any information about the King of Scotland that may assist then I provide it willingly."

"Pedro is trustworthy, Sir Richard," the Queen said. "He is an honest man and I wrote to my father on several occasions to send Pedro to England to be the ambassador here, but my wishes were never adhered to. His initial deployment to Scotland was to deceive James into believing that I would marry him all the while knowing I was promised to Arthur. The idea was to neutralise the threat that was posed by Perkin Warbeck who was claiming the English throne during my father in law's reign, which would have led to a Scottish invasion. If my father in law lost the throne, my marriage to Arthur would have been rendered useless and Spanish interests in England diminished."

"Who is Perkin Warbeck?" Richard asked.

"He was a Fleming from Tournai, but he claimed to be Richard of Shrewsbury, the younger of the two princes in the tower,"

Lovell interjected.

Richard looked somewhat taken aback. "Was he?"

"Of course not," he said. "The remains of both their bodies were found under a staircase."

"I know the story. It was my father that saw them put there."

"Your father?" the Queen asked, surprised.

"You, you-" the Earl stammered. "You are the son of Robert Longsword? I had no idea he had had a son. I thought your name was merely adopted from the sheer size of the weapon you carry."

* * *

Richard saw a flash of anger flare in the Earl's eye and his hand shook as he pointed it at Richard.

"Have I offended you, Sir Thomas?" Richard asked.

"I lost everything after the Battle of Bosworth Field. My lands and titles were stripped from me and I spent three years in the Tower of London and all because of your damned father!"

Richard felt anger surge through him at these words.

"Careful now, Howard," Lovell intervened. "You chose the wrong side to support, remember that. Richard III was a usurper, and besides, were your lands and titles not restored to you by Henry's father? If I am not mistaken, you were made Lord High Treasurer after you switched your allegiance, so you are better off now than you were before."

"Apologise," the Queen demanded of the Earl.

Sir Thomas Howard had to bite back his pride. "I am sorry, Sir Richard, old wounds linger. I lost my father at that battle and I myself was severely wounded. The aftermath was a difficult time for my family. You must understand we fought and died for a man we loved, a man who admitted me into the Order of the Garter, who despite the claims of what he had done we still stood by because we believed them untrue, impossible even. I was shocked when I found out the truth of what he had done to those two little boys, and he lied to us when we confronted him about it. Your father may have been the man that brought about the downfall of my King, but it was he who was an unworthy King, and my true anger lies with him."

"Thomas is a loyal subject to my husband, as he was to his father before him. He has served us well, have you not?" the Queen said. Richard looked into the ageing face of the Earl of Surrey who must have been in his late sixties. He could see tears form in the man's eyes, then trickle down his wrinkled cheeks. He had lived a long and prosperous life but there were still events from his past that plagued his thoughts even to this day.

"You are kind to say so, your Grace," he replied.

"Sir Howard had the opportunity to escape the Tower and join the rebellion with the Earl of Lincoln in 1487 but he refused, convincing Henry's father of his loyalty," Lovell added.

The Earl smiled and he wiped his eyes on the back of his hand. "That was a tough decision. But you see, the Tower changes a man. I had three years to dwell on the events that had taken place. I realised that I am just a pawn in a big game, and my place is to fight and serve the king, whoever that may be. I wasn't going to make the mistake of being on the wrong side again."

"Very admirable, Sir Howard," Richard said and held out his hand. The two men gazed at each other for a moment and then the Earl returned the courtesy. He gripped Richard's hand with surprising strength for a man of his age. "I am honoured to fight alongside you."

"Likewise, Sir Richard, likewise."

"May I ask you a question, Sir Howard?" Richard asked, relieving his grasp.

"You may."

"While you were in service to Richard III, did you know a man by the name of Grenwick Ashbourne?"

"Grenwick, that foul creature? Aye, I knew him, he was a

blood thirsty killer. He may have been on my side at the time but that didn't stop him making me feel uncomfortable. He was amongst Richard's inner circle. My father and I fought and died for Richard's cause and he still held others in higher esteem. There was his second in command, Henry Stafford, Duke of Buckingham; he was the first to turn after the disappearances of the Princes. He was raving about Richard's involvement but we just thought he was going mad. Richard quelled his little rebellion and had him executed before he could convince anyone. If only we'd have listened to him we could have avoided so many deaths, my father included. Then there was James Tyrell, always clinging on to Richard like a leech wherever he went, he couldn't do enough to please him. After the war he admitted under torture to killing the two princes and was beheaded. Then of course, there was Grenwick his enforcer; he was the quiet one but the one you most wanted to avoid. He disappeared after the Battle of Bosworth and no one has seen him since."

"That's not entirely true," Lovell interjected. "Grenwick, like Sir Howard, lost everything after the battle; lands, titles, and his fortune. But the rumour is, rather than switch his allegiance, he decided to flee to France, which leads us to believe his role in the death of the princes may be more than what we know. If I am not mistaken he joined with King Louis and has been his man ever since."

"He did. I saw them in France."

"Am I right in believing there was some animosity between your two families?"

"That is correct. Grenwick held my father responsible for all he lost, but the feud between our two families runs deeper than that and has done so for many years. He has sworn to kill all of my kin."

"No!" the Queen gasped.

"That bastard!" cried the Earl.

"Where is he now?" Lovell asked. "Still in France?"

Richard smiled. "No, my Lords, what if I told you after all these years he has returned home? He is leading the small French force that is aiding the Scots in their invasion."

"Then we shall have his head on a spike!" the Earl promised. "I never liked that man, never."

"I hope so," Richard agreed. "But first and foremost we must win the battle. Pedro, what can you tell me of your friend King James? How will he fight on the battlefield?"

"Well, he is extremely courageous, that is unquestionable, probably more so than a king should be. I have seen him fight in several battles and he always puts himself in the most dangerous of positions, not taking the least bit of interest in his own personal safety. I suppose it has to be said that although he is a very good king he is not a very good captain. He often rides into the battle before he has given his orders. But he commands the respect of his men and he only asks of them that they follow him into battle, and for their loyalty he does not think it right to participate in any confrontation without being the first in line. I can honestly say his deeds are as good as his words."

"He is foolhardy, then," replied the Earl.

"So you think he will lead them across the field himself?"

"I am certain of it. You have to understand James is a man of value and of honour, and despite us moving into a new age he stands by the medieval way of things and adheres to the values of chivalry. All his lords and earls will be at the head of their men."

"So if we cut the head from the snake, the rest will be left in disarray. We must hit them hard and fast, if we take out their commanders, so there will be no one left to lead them."

"Our infantry men are all equipped with bills so that is entirely possible," said Lovell.

"Forgive me. I have not heard of a bill. What is it exactly?"

"It is a pole weapon, not as long as a pike, about five to six feet in length and slightly thicker, with a hooked blade on the end. It has the stopping power of a spear and the strength of an axe and with the addition of the blade it is equally useful against both horse and infantry. If the power from the swing does not take down horse or rider the blade has a useful knack for finding the gaps in the armour and will drag them from the saddle. It can be used in the same way against the infantry dragging them into the fray."

"What is the Scots' weapon of choice?"

"They tend to prefer the pike," Pedro replied.

"Most pikes range from ten to sixteen feet," Richard mused. "They will pierce our infantry before our bills come within range, will they not?"

Howard smiled. "The pikes may be longer but they do not have the strength of the bill. The blades would have chopped their pikes in half before they can even touch us. Do not fret, Sir Richard, they may have a superior force but no matter how many waves they send upon us they will be broken down. They underestimate us!"

"How so?"

"James is so confident of victory," Lovell intervened, "That he sent word of his invasion to us a month ago. He believes most of our forces to be in France with the King. He could have swept through the country by now but he wants to meet some form of resistance so he can say he beat us fairly. What he does not realize is that Henry foresaw this and so the army he took abroad was only made up from the southern counties. What you see before you today is a mix of the midlands and the northern counties."

"How many men do you have?"

"The current count is twenty six thousand."

"And James has no idea of your numbers?"

The Earl cut in. "He does not. Five days ago I sent our Herald Thomas Hawley, the Rouge Croix Pursuivant, to appoint a place for battle, suggesting we meet on the ninth between midday and mid-afternoon on the plains near Milfield. I gave Thomas strict instructions that any Scottish heralds that were sent to me would be met out of sight from our army."

"What was their response to that?"

"They detained Hawley and sent their Islay Herald, who informed me that James agreed to the terms and said that if he had such a pitiful force he would not want me to see them either."

Richard smiled. "Well, that will certainly be a shock when they arrive on the battlefield. They are over confident and when they see us it will strike fear and doubt into them."

"Aye, that it will," the Earl responded.

That brought about a temporary reprieve in the conversation while everyone pictured the upcoming battle, but was suddenly bought to a halt when Pedro burst into a fit of coughs.

"Excuse me," he murmured into his rag.

"My dear Pedro, you must rest if you are to make the long journey back to Spain," the Queen said, looking at him with a hint of concern. "Gentlemen." She turned to the group. "Shall we retire?" There was a general mutter of agreement and everyone made to move. "Richard?" she called before he could head off. "It has been many years since I have been to my homeland. Would you join me in my tent so we may speak of it?"

"I would be honoured, your Grace," he replied.

* * *

The Queen sat at a table. Her robe and crown had been removed and her hair was let down to loosely fall about her neck and shoulders. She had also taken off her jewellery and changed into a plain green dress; it suited her. Richard had always thought Catherine relatively pretty from what he remembered of her from his youth, but had never realised that under all the layers of what it took to be a queen that she was undeniably beautiful. It was as if the Queen whom he'd heard so much about over the years, who was forced to do a king's job while the King was away, was not this hardened woman with the will and determination to stand up equal amongst men, to bear the weight of royalty and reign supreme with the love of the English people. But was a beautiful young woman of twenty seven years forced to wear a mask.

"Please join me," she said, pointing to the seat opposite. She had silky smooth, red brown hair and equally compelling brown eyes, which caught Richard's as he sat. He smiled awkwardly which again caused her to blush, and she looked away.

"Thank you, your Grace."

She collected herself and turned back to face him. "So, Sir Richard, word has reached me that you are a wanted man in Spain, are you not? My brother Alonso is seething that you got away. If what the ambassador says is true, it is his son in law the Duke of Gandia who hunts you down, is it not? Tell me why I should not hand you over."

"Alonso has hated my mentor General Córdoba his whole life and he believes I had something to do with what happened at the Duke's fortress in Guadalest. The Duke was no doubt taken by Alonso's claim because he has held a grudge against me since first I met him. They accuse me of killing my brothers and burning down the castle in retribution for past animosity between Alonso and Córdoba, but it is a lie, I tell you. I loved my brothers and I served the Duke loyally. It was Grenwick, my enemy, that did these things and framed me for it."

"Have no fear, Sir Richard, I only tease. Alonso is only my half-brother, if that. In truth I hate him, I always have. My father doted on him, his illegitimate son. I was never held in such high esteem. My mother hated him, I can assure you. He has risen above his station. He is the Archbishop of Valencia, the Viceroy of Naples and last year he commanded the troops that conquered Tudela in the Kingdom of Navarre." She shook her head. "As for that runt Borgia, I had no idea my niece would stoop so low as to marry such a thing. But Alonso pushed it. I suppose he is always seeking more power."

"Aye, your father no longer had need of Córdoba when he had his precious Alonso."

"Is that why you stopped serving the Spanish crown?"

"No, that is a long story, your Grace, but in essence I fell in love with a woman who made me swear to give up the sword."

"You are married?" she asked.

"I was, but my wife was taken from me."

"By who?"

"Grenwick."

"What happened to her?"

"After interrogating one of his men, I am led to believe that she was raped. Overcome with grief she killed herself."

Catherine was mortified. "I had no idea, Richard I am so sorry-"

"Think nothing of it," he cut across her. "What happened has happened and there is nothing I can do to change that, but I can hunt down the man who is responsible."

"The Hunter?" she smiled.

He nodded. "Exactly, your Grace."

"And so now you fight for my husband."

"And now I fight for your husband," he agreed. "It has given me the chance to face my enemies and for that at least I am grateful."

"Well, you have my full support, Richard. If there is anything I can do to help you I will."

Richard thought for a moment. "There is one thing your Grace could do," he replied.

"Ask and it is yours."

"My father fought for your father in law before me. I know little of him and his ancestors. I would like to know more, if this is at all possible."

"I will have my historians look into it right away."

"Thank you, your Grace."

They sat silently for a moment both in their own thoughts before the Queen spoke again. "I had thought," she said, "that perhaps you had left my father's army to join Henry's because of him. He can be a very stubborn man, my father, and he does not appreciate all that his loyal subjects do for him."

"Aye, General Córdoba, Christopher Columbus and my friend Alexandre Jiménez will all contest to that," he said.

"How is the General? It has been many years since I saw him last."

"He is as well as can be expected, but dare I say it, he misses your mother."

Catherine smiled. "She often spoke highly of him. My father hated it of course but I was just pleased to see that there was a man at court who could make my mother smile, because my father certainly couldn't."

"He is a good man."

"Aye, he was," the Queen replied. "As are you, Sir Richard. You have learned from your mentor well."

"You honour me, your Grace but-"

"Please," she said, continuing. "My father sent me off at an early age against my will to marry a man just like him. Dominating, overpowering and extremely unpleasant and little did I know a few years later I would have to marry his brother who was even worse. I am the woman I am today because I have to be. I am forced to be strong because of the torments only a woman can be put through. My husband does not love me, of this I am certain. He loved me once in his own manner I am sure, and I him, but that has long since dwindled out. I envy your wife, Richard, despite being cruelly and unfairly taken from you, I envy the time she spent with you. I wish, that for just one moment in my life, I could smile the way my mother did all those years ago."

Richard was surprised by the Queen's words, and he was touched by them. She had spoken from the heart about feelings he was sure she had never confessed to another living soul. For a moment he felt a strange feeling inside that he had not felt for many months. It was not love. Richard was not sure that he could ever love another as he had loved his wife. It was more an understanding and for the briefest of moments all he wanted to do was hold her in his arms. Then she stood and roused him from the moment and realising the conversation was over he followed suit.

"My lady," he said bowing his head.

The Queen did not reply, but she walked around the table to him, placed her hands gently on his shoulders and kissed him.

Chapter Fifteen

Flodden Hill
Flodden, Kingdom of England.
September, 1513.

"Let not England forget her precedence of teaching other nations how to live."
John Milton

September 6th at Ford Castle.

King James seemed pleased at how easily Norham Castle had fallen to the Earl of Lennox and with only minimum casualties to boot. It had not taken long before Ford Castle was captured as well, from the Lady Heron, who decided she would rather surrender than have her castle partly demolished as Norham had been. So far the invasion had been a success and everything was going to plan. The army was camped on Flodden Hill, the high ground was secure and now they waited for the Earl of Surrey to arrive with whatever army he had managed to muster. For the time being, however, James was happy to enjoy the company of Elizabeth and her daughter, much to the annoyance of his nobles.

"Your Grace." The Earl of Angus spoke out at the King's war council in the hall at Ford Castle. "The men grow restless in your absence. While you spend time here with the Lady Heron they wait for the news of battle. Perhaps if you came to the camp it would put their thoughts at ease?"

"What I do in my own time, Sir Douglas, is no concern of yours," the King replied with a harsh tone in his voice. "You forget we are but humbled guests in the Lady Heron's household."

"Begging your pardon, your Grace, but the castle is yours to do with as you will."

"Enough. We will speak no more of this," the King said defiantly. "If the men are restless then march to Berwick and take the town. That should put their minds at ease."

"Berwick, your Grace? Have we not done enough for the French already?" Angus retorted, giving Grenwick an evil glare, something that did not go unnoticed by the King.

"You forget yourself, Sir Douglas. Grenwick is our guest and the French our allies. Besides, what we do here in England is as much for us, for the people of Scotland, as much as anyone else."

There had been no love lost between Angus and Grenwick ever since the Earl had arrived to join the King's forces at Ellemford. Indeed most of the earls gained little confidence from the presence of the French commander, who after all was English. That, along with his intimidating manner, had filled most of the Scottish nobles with unease. But still, Grenwick had to side with Sir Douglas despite his distaste for the man. "If I may, your Grace?"

The King nodded. "You may."

"Your army is well positioned and provisioned and the hill at Flodden has been well fortified. I think perhaps it would be unwise to stray too far from such a strategic advantage when we know that Surrey expects to fight on the plain at Milfield in two days' time."

Angus could not hide the shock in his face, at least not as well as Grenwick's face concealed his lie. His only interest was Richard Longsword and if he was marching against him then he wanted to be here to meet him, not traipsing half way around the north of England. "We do not have long to prepare and at least from our vantage point on the hill we will see them coming."

"No doubt you are right, Grenwick," the King said with a sigh. "If we are to meet them in open battle in a couple of days' time then it would be best if the men are rested and ready, but it is my intention to send some of them home."

There was a murmur of discussion that broke out amongst the

earls at this news, but it was the Lord Home who spoke first. "How many do you intend to send home, your Grace?"

"Twenty five thousand."

"But that is absurd!" the Earl of Angus blurted out. "You would send home nearly half our force two eves before the battle?"

"That is the last time you question my authority, Sir Douglas, and it is for that reason that it will be you who leads them home." The look on Angus' face was one of horror. It was as if he'd seen a ghost. "Our Islay Herald confirms my suspicions. When he met Surrey to accept his terms, he informs me that the Earl was asking several questions about the size of our force, nervously unwilling to mention anything of his own."

"What if it's all just an act?" Angus cut in. "Your Grace, he is playing you for a fool!"

"Silence, Angus!" The King rose to his feet trembling with anger, cutting Angus with a ferocious stare. "I am no fool!" He addressed his earls. "It is bad enough already that we invade while the English King and his army are abroad, I will not have it said of me that I was only victorious in this fight because we had a far superior force. Thirty five thousand men is more than enough to see off this pathetic rabble they send against us. The rest I send home with you." He said the last part tearing his gaze back to the Earl of Angus who now showed signs of tears in his eyes.

"Your - your Grace," he stammered. "I- I- I- beg of you, p-please do not send me from your side."

"You have your orders," the King replied coldly. "I will not leave the realm unprotected. You will lead them home. Minus those that will be assigned to garrison duty, here and at Etal, do you understand?" The Earl nodded, silent tears cascading down his ageing cheeks. "Then leave."

The Earl walked from the room but not before Grenwick caught him with a mocking smile.

"Gentlemen, we move out. Tomorrow I will join you on Flodden Hill but tonight I spend with Lady Heron. I will not be so rude as to deny her hospitality without so much as a thank you. But before you go, one of you have the Rouge Croix released and sent back to the English. We have nothing to fear from letting him go. You are dismissed."

* * *

September 7th at Wooler.

"It is good to see you back, Thomas. I hope the Scots treated you admirably?" the Earl of Surrey asked. The barons had all been called together in the Queen's pavilion the moment the Rouge Croix Pursuivant had returned. "Tell me. What have you learnt from your visit?"

Richard looked around the pavilion, noticing everyone's eyes were focused upon Hawley. Hawley nodded with recognition at all of their faces except one. The man clearly had no idea who Richard was and gave him a searching glance, Richard remained blank. Hawley returned his gaze to the Earl. "They have no intention of meeting you on the plain at Milfield. They wait for you to come to them at the top of Flodden Hill. They have fortified it, and it is nigh on impregnable; we would be fools to attack it but I fear you will be hard put to persuade King James to come out."

The Earl nodded. "I expected as much. I will write to him asking him to honour our agreement."

Richard spoke, drawing Hawley's gaze. "My Lord, you will find it most likely that he will refuse."

"I believe he will, Sir Richard," Howard replied. "But it will keep him occupied for a while. In the mean time we will out flank them. They expect us to approach from the south, I suggest we circle round them and cut off their route to the north. They will be forced to face us and their defences will be considerably lighter."

"An excellent suggestion, Sir Howard," the Queen said and smiled. Richard looked up at her but she avoided his gaze. They had spoken little since the events that took place the night he arrived and he hadn't expected anything less. War was approaching and there were things that needed to be done. The Queen once again donned her king's mask and Richard couldn't help but think that what he had experienced that evening was a one off. The Queen, for the briefest of moments, had wanted to feel like a woman again, but now it was back to work.

"Thank you, your Grace." The Earl nodded in her direction.

"Thomas Hawley?" Richard asked the Rouge Croix, taking his eyes from the Queen.

"Yes, Sir Richard, is it?"

The Earl turned from the Queen to join the conversation. "Hawley, this is Sir Richard Longsword, Baron of Portchester."

Richard winced. It was a title that would take some getting used to. "Tell me Thomas, do you know how many men King James has at his command?"

The Rouge Croix smiled.

"What's so funny, man?" Howard asked.

"He has sixty thousand men."

"Dear God," gasped Thomas Dacre, another baron with whom Richard had come to friendly terms with over the last couple of days. "How can we hope to defeat so many?"

"You think that is funny, Hawley?" Surrey asked in annoyance.

"No, my Lord, not at all," he replied. "What is funny is that he is so adamant that you have such a small force at your command that he has ordered nearly half of them to return to Scotland."

"He's done what?" the Earl asked, flabbergasted.

"He has sent home nearly twenty five thousand troops. The army that now awaits you is thirty five thousand strong. It is still a considerable force but one I would happily pit an army of twenty six thousand Englishmen against. The odds are turning in our favour."

"You have played your part well, Sir Howard. King James has no knowledge of our numbers whatsoever," the Queen confessed. "He genuinely believes we are no match for them."

"We shall match them and more," replied the Earl, banging his right fist into the palm of his left hand.

"Of that I have the utmost confidence you will, and if my lord husband was here he would tell you that himself," the Queen said to Sir Howard before turning to the group. "He could not have chosen better men to defend his realm in his absence, and you have my thanks, gentlemen. What you do for king and country is worthy of the highest praise. I am proud of you all and it is an honour to be here with you. Go now and do what needs must be done." There was a general murmur of approval from amongst the barons, most of whom muttered their thanks. The Queen bowed her head in recognition, but when she raised it her eyes found Richard. He looked into her eyes and they were telling him one thing; survive.

"So what are your orders, father?" asked the Earl's eldest son, who was named after his father but more commonly referred to as the Lord High Admiral. A title he had recently acquired from his brother Edward, who had died during a naval battle with the French. He had fallen from his ship wearing full body armour and drowned. The Admiral had arrived, along with another of his brothers Edmund Howard, to bolster their forces a few days ago bringing with them extra provisions. At the sound of his voice, despite his desire not to do so, Richard was forced to withdraw himself from the Queen's gaze to listen to what the Earl had to say.

"For now we march to Braxton. It is the nearest town north of Flodden Hill but we will not be heading there directly. We will reach it via Duddo and Twizel. I do not want the Scots catching wind of our movements," he replied to his son. "Gentlemen, ready your men; it is time to move. We will reconvene in Braxton when we've had time to assess the enemy's position, whereupon we will decide what our next course of action is."

* * *

The sun was doing battle with the clouds, an ominous sign, thought the King. Every so often its rays would penetrate to shine and glimmer off the lush green grass that ran down the hill and across the Milfield Plain, only to disappear again back behind the mass of grey, casting the Scottish army into an unpleasant gloom. *At least it's not raining anymore*, he thought. Despite being a relatively warm day there was a cool wind that licked at the King's face through the visor of his helmet and he watched his banner billow in the breeze, the red rampant lion of Scotland rippling on its sea of gold. He drew his gaze to the distance and still there was no sign of their foe. *Surely they should have been here by now; something wasn't right.*

"Where the hell are they?" the King leaned in to ask Sir William Graham, the Earl of Montrose. "If he wishes to commence battle between midday and mid-afternoon as appointed he had better hurry, had he not?"

"Indeed, your Grace," replied the Earl. "But the English have never been known for their punctuality."

"No, this is not like the Surrey I know. He's up to something, I can feel it in my bones." The King clenched his fists inside his mailed gloves. "That damned English dog!" James tore his gaze from the field to pick out the Earl of Bothwell whom he'd placed in command of the reserves. "Sir Hepburn, the scouts I had you send out, have they still not seen anything?"

"No, your Grace," he replied.

"Well, they couldn't have just up and vanished. Somebody find out where they are and do it now!" the King shouted at no one in particular, but Bothwell nodded nonetheless and removed himself from the King's presence. "Where is Grenwick?" the King asked Montrose.

"In his tent most like, your Grace."

"Aye, he spends more time with that bloody daughter of his than he does preparing his men for battle. Send one of your squires to fetch him, will you? He might be an odd bastard but he's a damned clever one."

* * *

Maria had spent so many nights tied to a post in Grenwick's tent that she had lost count of the days, but the strange thing was that the longer she spent there, the more she felt comforted by it. She hated it; that was never in question. She hated it even more when Grenwick was there, taunting her about what was to come or questioning her about things she didn't know. Yet at least there for the time being she was safe. As long as Grenwick had need of her and she was tied to that wretched lump of wood, she was safe.

The thing that Maria really hated, even more so than the long uncomfortable nights she spent crumpled on the floor with her hands bound and the bonds cutting bloody lines into her wrists, were the long days spent travelling, walking from one place to another until her feet were blistered and sore. Or being forced to ride at Grenwick's back, having to put her arms around him and take in his rancid smell. That, and the menacing looks she drew from his men, all of them looking at her lustfully. She knew what they wanted and she guessed it was only a matter of time before they got it. Any of them she felt she could take or at least brace herself for, but not Grenwick. *Please not Grenwick.*

She sat on the floor wearily resting her head against the post. It was one of those uncomfortable moments when Grenwick spent a long period of time just staring at her. The only way to pass through these horrible experiences were if she closed her eyes and thought back to a time in her life when she was happy, a time when she was with her mother and father. But today, despite her best efforts, she could not. She could not see her mother anymore. It was as if she was gone from the world. Her father, however, if Grenwick could be believed, would soon be dead and no matter how hard she tried she could not picture his face.

"My Lord." A new voice had entered the tent, and she recognized it. It was Philip, one of Grenwick's loyal body guards.

She lifted her head to see a burning gaze on her.

"What is it?" Grenwick asked.

"It's one of Montrose's squires to see you, Sir."

"I told you. No one is to come in here, so get rid of him."

"Begging your pardon, Sir, but he said it is urgent."

"Shit!" Grenwick glanced at Maria who met his gaze defiantly. "Keep him out there. I will come out to him."

"Right, you," he said, pointing at Maria menacingly. "You stay quiet—"

She screamed.

There was the sound of raised voices and muffled footsteps coming from outside. Then suddenly a young man pushed his way into the tent. He could have been no more than twenty with brown hair and bristle on his chin but he was built like an ox with broad shoulders and strong arms. He wore a haubergeon and was equipped with a sword at his belt. *Finally*, thought Maria, *someone has come to save me from this prison*. He looked at Maria, her clothes filthy, her face bloodied and bruised. Even so, his face seemed to register approval.

He turned his stare to Grenwick. "Is this how a man treats his daughter?" he asked.

"My daughter," Grenwick replied angrily. "She has tried to run off and get married on several occasions with one of your rabble. I will not have my daughter seen in the arms of a barbarian! What I do is for her own protection, and though she may not thank me now, she will one day. Besides, how I discipline my daughter is none of your concern, squire!"

"I am not his daughter-" Maria tried to blurt out, but the moment the words left her mouth she regretted them. Grenwick lost his temper and in a sudden burst of fury punched her in the face. She felt her nose break and warm blood trickled down into her mouth. It was blinding pain like she'd never experienced before. For a moment, she felt dazed but she was able to collect herself for a moment to see the young squire draw his sword. *He was going to save her, and he will be my hero.* But he never got the chance. Philip grabbed him from behind and before he even had the chance to swing his sword Grenwick paced up to him, pulled his dagger from his belt and rammed it up under the squire's chin. "No!" she sobbed.

"Do you know what he came for?" Grenwick asked Philip.

"He said the King wished to see you."

"Hide the body. It must not be found," he commanded before rounding on Maria. "And you, Miss Longsword, you dirty little whore, you will learn your place! You are mine now, and you damn well get used to it!"

* * *

Grenwick was still wiping the blood from his arm when he approached the King, who he noticed looked extremely restless atop his courser. He was eager for battle Grenwick knew, as were they all. It was the calm before the storm.

"Grenwick. How good of you to join us," the King said as Grenwick approached. "Is all well?" He glanced at the remainder of the blood on his arm.

"Yes, your Grace," he replied. "My men caught a deer."

"Ah yes, very common in these parts," he said. "But enough of hunting. War is approaching and we must be vigilant. Tell me, you know the English, where are they? Why have they not appeared before us?"

Grenwick cast his gaze to the south and saw nothing. "It is possible, your Grace, that they will not come from the south."

"Why not? They've marched all this way and it was Surrey's idea to meet on Milfield Plain."

"If I may, your Grace, you did not honour that agreement so what makes you think he will? The Rouge Croix by now would have told him of our position and our fortifications. Surrey would be stupid to attack us from the south. No, if I was him, I would attack from the north."

"Is it possible? Could he attack from the north?"

"Well, your Grace, we have spent many days in England, most of which has been spent sitting idle or taking castles of a lesser nature and in this time our scouts have only been watching the southern approach. It is entirely possible, yes, in truth he could be upon us at any moment."

"Then take some of your men and ride out north, to see if you can see them, Grenwick."

"Your Grace," came a gasping voice from behind them. It was the Earl of Bothwell, panting heavily from running. "That will not be necessary." He placed his hands on his knees.

"Why not?" the King demanded.

"They are coming, your Grace, my scouts spotted them coming from the north east. They are approaching the River Till near Crookham, and I believe they are headed for Branxton."

"How many are they, Adam?"

"Well over twenty thousand, your Grace!"

"Dear God," the King whispered under his breath.

"Your Grace," said the Earl of Montrose. "We are well positioned for an assault from the south, but the hill here levels out to the north, and we will have no advantage if they should attack us from the rear."

"What do you suggest, William?"

"If what Sir Hepburn says is true, then the English have not yet crossed the Twissell Bridge. If we hurry, your Grace, we can get to Branxton Hill before they arrive. We will not have the fortifications in place that we have here and our artillery will need to be moved but we will have the all-important advantage of the higher ground."

"Then so be it, we move to Branxton Hill." The King spoke loudly and confidently. "Gentlemen, ready yourselves, the battle is about to begin. To arms!"

* * *

Richard and the other English barons watched as the Scots army positioned itself on Branxton Hill. From across the River Till just outside the town of Crookham they could see the whole Scottish army arraying itself in the distance, and it was the largest that Richard had ever seen. They had formed themselves into five battles, a technique adopted Richard knew from the Holy Roman Empire. It was commonly used by them in the past. Four of their battles were spread across the tip of the hill with a further battle group in reserve. Richard was pleased to see that Pedro was right. The Scottish nobles were clearly visible at the head of their forces. But none stood out more than King James, his crown glinting every now and again when it caught a ray of sunlight. He had command of the largest battle in the centre, his royal banner raised high.

"He knows his tactics, I'll give him that, even if they are somewhat old fashioned," the Earl said, causing a ripple of laughter amongst the barons. "But he is stupid if he really intends to lead them himself. We have agreed no quarter, and there are to be no prisoners."

"Then he will die," piped in the Lord Admiral. "Along with all his nobles."

"That may be, but first we need to cross the Twissell Bridge. I will send Hawley back to James and request that his artillery do not fire upon us while we manoeuvre our forces. We will form up south of Branxton on the ridge there. They may have the hill but the terrain should suit us. Can you see that dip at the base of the hill?"

"Aye," replied a few of the barons in unison, while the others raised themselves in their saddles to gain a better view.

"That will not be visible to the Scots from their vantage point. If we can lure them down into that boggy ground we can crush them in the centre."

"Father?" came the voice of Edmund Howard, the Earl's youngest son. "May I have a command?"

"Aye, you will all get your chance to prove yourself today. What we must do, my Lords, is nullify their numbers, and to do this we are better off not splitting our forces too thinly. We will form up three large battles. Edmund, you will have command of the right, Thomas, you will have command of the centre and I will have command of the left. Sir Stanley, I wish for you to approach from the east, so take your archers, wait until they have descended the hill and attack their right flank."

Edward Stanley nodded to show he understood. "It would be an honour, Sir."

"Thomas will lead the greatest force in the centre followed by my own, and this is where the fighting will be most fierce, in that stretch of boggy ground." The Lord Admiral smiled. He was up for the challenge. "The hill, as I am sure you have observed, gentlemen, is steepest to the right, so this is where the fighting will break out. Edmund, as our right flank you will be first in line. The ground there is firm and so they will hit you hard but you must hold strong, and give your brother a chance to crush them in the centre."

"Yes, father."

"Sir Dacre, you will wait in reserve, but if for any moment it looks like our right flank may break, then aid my son with your horsemen. Our right flank must hold if we do not want to be overrun. If the right wing holds, it will give our left wing a chance to out flank them. Gentlemen, they will sweep down the hill like a closing door from the right to left. Hold steady and we shall see what happens when wood slams on stone!"

"Where do you want me, my Lord?" Richard asked, feeling as though the Earl had forgotten him.

The Earl of Surrey turned to face him. "Sir Richard, I have not forgotten you, have no fear. You will join your Cazadores with Sir Stanley's archers. This is the most likely place to over run them. King James leads the greater part of their force forming their right centre and will come on to me. If you can break the small contingent forming their right flank it will allow you to attack James from the rear. The French are in the King's command as well so this may be your best opportunity to meet our dear friend Grenwick and cut off any hopes he has of escape. You also have my leave, if and only if the battle is in our favour and Sir Stanley has no need of you, to take your men and find your daughter."

"Thank you, my Lord," Richard replied. *So this was it, this was his moment to avenge his father, to find his wife's tormentor and to free his daughter from her captivity*. It was to be the biggest battle fought on the borders between England and Scotland and Richard would have his name go down in memory as playing his part.

Chapter Sixteen

Battle of Flodden Field
Branxton, Kingdom of England.
September, 1513.

"12,000 at the least of the best gentlemen and flower of Scotland"
Edward Hall

"My Lord asks that you refrain from taking fire while his men cross the bridge," the Rouge Croix said to the King.

"Tell me Hawley, why should I do that? Was it not you who tried to play me false, asking that I honour the agreement to meet at Milfield while all the while you were planning to march around us to Branxton?"

"I am only the messenger, your Grace, but if I am not mistaken you never intended to move from Flodden Hill in the first place, so I would call you and the Earl of Surrey even, wouldn't you agree?"

"Be that as it may, this is war and I am by no means obliged to grant your request. However there are some things of old that I feel should be adhered to and chivalry is one of them. You have my word that your army will not be fired upon until you have crossed the bridge."

"Thank you, your Grace."

"But tell your Lord I will only wait until noon, and if he has not crossed before then, I will blow up the bridge and march my army south!"

* * *

Grenwick sat atop his spirited courser. He was fully armoured with plate mail, helmet, shield and sword. He was surrounded by his personal guard, most of which wore hauberks and gambesons. Some even had plate mail that they had retrieved from previous battles, but all of them wore jupons bearing the green leaf of house Ashbourne, which was also present fluttering in the breeze on black silk carried by his standard bearer. Behind them were five thousand French soldiers all wearing the blue livery of their country complete with the fleur-de-lis and together they would form the rear of King James' battle.

The King commanded the largest of the Scottish battles, the smallest of which was to their right, led by Argyll and Lennox. Grenwick hoped they would hold firm otherwise they risked being out flanked. But with the sheer size of King James' force supporting them, battering the English into submission, he reckoned that situation highly unlikely. The centre was made up of another large force under the Earls of Montrose, Errol and Crawford and bringing up their left flank was the Lord Home and the Earl of Huntly. All in all, it was a massive army and despite the English surprising them with a relatively large one of their own, it should easily sweep down the hill and annihilate them. Grenwick was confident of victory but what he wanted most of all was to take Richard Longsword as his prisoner; but there was to be no quarter given today. *So you survive, Richard, until I get my damned hands on you.*

To the north east near the town of Crookham, the English vanguard led by the Lord High Admiral along with their light artillery could be seen crossing the Twissell Bridge. They were an easy target for the Scottish artillery which consisted of several heavy guns including great culverins. They had originally been dug in on the hill at Flodden before hastily being removed and dragged to Branxton Hill. They were hauled hurriedly by teams of oxen, which was made difficult due to the muddy ground caused by the early autumn rain. But despite the difficulties the artillery had faced, they had been repositioned and Grenwick wondered why they had yet to start firing. He spurred his horse on to the front of the battle and pulled up alongside the King. He himself wore chain mail over a gambeson with a mailed hood on top of which he wore his golden crown. He was also sporting fine metal plated spaulders to cover his shoulders and vambraces on his arms. He did not see Grenwick approach. He had eyes only for the enemy. "Do you not plan to wear a cuirasse, your Grace?"

"That damned metal plate on my chest and back? All it does is weigh me down. I like to be able to swing my sword when I charge into battle. Once you're in the thick of things, Grenwick, it's not having the most armour on that will keep you alive, it's about moving the quickest!"

No, but it definitely helps, thought Grenwick but he wasn't going to argue with the King. If he'd learnt one thing from James since he'd been here it was that he would do what he wanted. He would, by all means, listen to others' advice like he would listen to Grenwick now but in the end he would still follow his own judgment. "Your Grace, the English are vulnerable crossing the bridge. Would it not be wise to use your artillery? We can cause them serious damage before we even have to confront them."

"No. I have given them my word that they will not be fired upon until they have reached Branxton."

"But your Grace—"

"It is not up for discussion, Grenwick. As I have said before, I will not have it said of me that I won this battle unfairly. We will meet them on the field and it is there that we will take the glory!"

* * *

When the English had formed into three battles at the bottom of the hill, the Scottish artillery were finally given the go ahead to take fire. The view of the Scots army that was spread above them taking up the skyline proved a daunting sight; their cannon fire however did not. The guns that had been moved with such priority were having as much effect hitting their target as a knight would if he replaced his lance with a flower. The higher ground did not suit them and the majority of their shots flew over the English heads to land harmlessly in the field behind them, much to the delight of the men-at-arms. They jeered at the Scotsmen who waited silently on the hill, emotionless and undeterred. Things changed, though, when the English artillery fired in response. Cannon after cannon found its mark and the first screams of the battle rent the air. This escalated when the English archers using their famed longbows, self-made from yew, put arrow to stave before drawing back the string to their chins and releasing. The sky darkened with the flight of arrows and they came crashing down into the Scottish ranks. Hundreds fell in the first hour alone.

With their artillery underperforming, and the majority of their force made up of infantry equipped with pike, the Scots knew their best chance lay in meeting the enemy head on. The first advancement came from the battle under the command of Home and Huntly who descended upon Edmund Howard. Their force, a little larger than Howard's own, drove into his division hard. The pike relied on the group staying close together and the battle under the command of Home and Huntly was tight knit and well organized. Here on the firm ground their pikes were put to good use, driving Edmund's force back. With the pikes so close together, the English were unable to swing their bills, meaning they were unable to break them, let alone get near the Scots who were ploughing over the English with devastating effect. Edmund tried to rally his men, get them to hold and push forward but he himself was struck a deadly blow and had to be dragged from the fray. Howard's division was in disarray; it had almost been shattered by that of Home and Huntly's and was close to routing, when Thomas Dacre rode to its aid. The Scots, knowing they had defeated the English right flank, chose not to risk any men against Dacre's heavy armoured horse. Home commanded them to withdraw. The Scots had been victorious in the first engagement of the battle, but Edmund's division despite heavy losses and with the help of Dacre had done what the Earl of Surrey had asked; it had held.

Buoyed by the success of their comrades the battle under the command of Errol, Montrose and Crawford began to advance, followed by the force under King James. As the infantry made its way down the sodden hill, the ground under foot became slippery and softer. Several of the Scots struggling for balance chose to kick off their worn boots to try and get a better grip. By the time they had reached the boggy dip below, the tight formations that had descended the hill were now breaking apart, gaps were forming and the closeness of the infantrymen on which the pikes relied had gone. The strength of the pike lay entirely when the enemy was kept at bay. But now, struggling in the mud and separated from one another, the English were allowed to surge in amongst them. The Lord Admiral's men charged into the fray and here in close combat the bills were put to good use. The Scots, unable to wield their pikes, hardly stood a chance as the English thrust, cut and stabbed with devastating effect. Beneath their feet the boggy ground was churned up like butter, and mud mixed with the blood of the dead and dying. James gazed on in horror as the centre under the command of the earls was hacked apart, but there was no turning back now. He raised his sword and bellowing his war cry spurred his destrier on towards Surrey's men and into the midst of battle.

* * *

The last Scottish battle to advance was that of Argyll's and Lennox's, but before they could reach the fight and aid their King against Surrey's division they were taken completely unawares. As they marched down the hill they were hit by a volley of arrows from the east, most of which found their targets, piercing through gambeson and mail. Several went down and the rest tried to line up to form some sort of defence, but they were hit with another volley and then another. Unable to do anything to withstand the barrage of fire, the Scots started to break. Pouncing on their misfortune, Richard led his Cazadores and charged into their ranks, followed by Sir Stanley and his archers who discarded their bows and took out short swords and daggers to join in the onslaught. With the arrows not firing, those that remained of the Scottish battle tried to make a stand, but they were disjointed and unprepared. Richard easily swept aside a pike that lunged at him before taking the man's arm off. He screamed that horrid scream that can only be heard in battle, but it was one of many that went unnoticed by the English, who howling at the scent of blood tore into the Scots. The men-at-arms under Richard's command fought with some discipline, but the archers sensing the Scots' vulnerability washed over them like a rogue wave, pulling them to the ground, stabbing and hacking, their bloodlust a horror to behold. The Scots that were still alive ran for their lives.

* * *

The initial onslaught from the King's centre proved difficult for Surrey's division, having the momentum coming down the hill and with the sheer size of his force the English were pushed back. But as the fighting continued and the first men died and thousands of feet sunk and stuck in the slippery mud, the tide began to turn. The Scottish pikemen under the King's command soon fell into the same difficulty the rest of the Scottish centre had found against the Lord Admiral. The terrain and their weapon of choice, of no use in such close proximity, were proving to be their downfall and as the English pushed back hundreds of Scots were slain, taken by the brute force of the bill. However, the King leading by example atop his horse, swung his sword and cut through the English ranks, and despite several losses the Scots held on. They were supported by the French of course, who unlike the Scots were all carrying swords and shields. With their help they were able to counteract the English bills and make a fight of it. It was a savage contest and the dip at the bottom of Branxton Hill turned into a blood bath. English, French and Scotsmen fell alike and yet both sides pushed on, unwilling to concede defeat, and all the while King James cut his way through the English towards the Earl of Surrey.

* * *

Argyll and Lennox were dead. Their command had been routed but more importantly the English had outflanked the Scots. Sir Stanley's archers had regrouped and retrieved their bows and now looked to attack the King's division from the rear. Unleashing their arrows with devastating effect they attacked Grenwick's French contingent from behind.

"Pick your targets now, lads," Sir Stanley called. "Don't want you hitting any of our own now, do we?"

Richard glanced into the fray for a sign of his enemy, for a glimmer of the green leaf of House Ashbourne. But it was in that moment that he spotted the King of Scotland as he barrelled his way through the English line towards Surrey.

"Sir Stanley, the Earl is in dire need of our assistance."

"What are you talking about? We have them on the-" then he spotted what Richard was pointing at. "Dear God, Martin, Martin!"

"Yes, milord," came the squeaky voice of a youth, one of Sir Stanley's archers.

"Never seen a better shot," Sir Stanley told Richard as he patted Martin on the shoulder. "Right now, lad, this will be the most important shot of your life so make it count, you hear?"

"Yes, Sir Stanley, milord," Martin replied.

"You see that gentleman there on his horse?" Sir Stanley pointed. "I need you to take him down."

The youth gasped a heavy intake of breath when he realised who his target was, but it did not deter him. His hand clasped around the wooden shaft of one of his arrows and he took it from his quiver. He placed it on his stave and pulled the string back to his chin and followed his target.

"Allow for the wind now, boy."

Richard watched closely as James descended upon Surrey. The King raised his sword primed for the assault; he was within metres now. "Hurry, hurry!"

"Take the shot, God damn you!" Sir Stanley cried.

Martin loosed and the arrow flew through the air with extraordinary speed and found its mark. The King poised to strike was taken unawares as the arrow hit him just below the armpit, piercing through mail, flesh and bone. His fingers, that clasped the hilt of his sword, loosened and the blade tumbled from his grip. He gazed at Surrey through darkened sight. He was so close yet so far. The King, sensing the inevitability of death, closed his eyes as he was caught in the side by a bill and dragged from his horse.

* * *

Grenwick saw the King fall with his own eyes and knew at once all was doomed. Since abandoning his country he had put his faith in the two peoples he had hated the most, the French and now the bloody Scots and where had it left him? Other than to bring him closer to his enemy who had the advantage of an English army at his back, while he stood surrounded by the dead and dying; *well, to Hell with them all.* The Scottish army had been felled by a bog, an obstacle they had not foreseen and now Scots lay dead in their thousands. The French, however, had put up a reasonable defence for a time and now Grenwick planned to use them to make good his escape. "Call my men, have them retreat," he called to Philip, the captain of his guard.

"Men of House Ashbourne to me, to me!" Philip cried.

There were thirteen of them left and all of them ready to flee the field, but as they did so they were spotted by one of the French captains. "Monsieur Grenwick!" he called, speaking English with a strong accent. "Do we retreat, my Lord? Shall I inform the men?"

"No, you must carry on the fight. I have more urgent business to attend to!"

"But my Lord, my men, they are dying."

"Then I pray they die well!" and as he said it, the young French captain took an arrow in the neck, crumpled to his knees with blood gurgling from his mouth, and died. "Stupid fool!" muttered Grenwick.

He led his men through the French lines across the hill to the east, as the English now had them penned in on both sides and it was therefore the only possible way out. It was a difficult manoeuvre as the ground was relentless and unforgiving. One of the men's foot sank so deep into the mud his boot stuck, so when he went to take his next step his foot came free of the shoe, but the tug was enough to send him sprawling face first into the mud. He rolled over only to witness in horror as an English bill took his bare foot clean off. His squeal was enough to cause even a veteran like Grenwick to wince. As the bodies thinned out, the air became cleaner and the ground firmer.

* * *

"Where do they think they are going, eh?" Edward Stanley asked Richard, pointing at Grenwick and his men as they emerged from the side of the fray. "Archers!"

"No, wait," Richard replied, squinting his eyes to get a closer look. "That's him!"

"That's him? Then what the bloody hell are you still doing here? Get the bastard!"

"Santiago! Señor Jiménez! Follow me!"

* * *

Grenwick and his men surged up the hill and away from the field of battle but they were not alone. It was two miles back to the camp on Flodden Hill where Maria was waiting, still tied to a post inside his tent. He knew that with Richard and his men in pursuit they would never make it. Two men guarded Maria and Grenwick knew they would be more than enough to help him escort her away. It was time to make a sacrifice. He had twelve men at his command while the small force that was following them up the hill numbered nearly double that, but his men were seasoned veterans who would do as he bid and they would fight to the death.

"Men," he called as he watched Richard make the climb from the top of Branxton Hill. He could see the different colours his men were adorned with. He really had formed a formidable band of brothers. But none of them caught his eye quite like Richard. He alone wore black with the red rose of the Longsword house. Grenwick had seen it before on Richard's father and now it had come back to haunt him.

"It has been an honour to serve with you. But the honour of your house requires you to make one final stand. Before you is our enemy and I will not have it said of us that we ran like cowards, I would pit anyone of you Ashbournes against two Longswords any day." His men banged their swords on their shields. *Brave fools*. "Brace yourselves, for the end is near." Grenwick's men turned to face their enemy and locked their shields.

"Steady now, lads," Philip called along the line. "It's time to finish these dogs once and for all."

Grenwick was pleased by their defiance. *I must see this through.* With a heavy heart he turned and left his men to die.

* * *

Richard charged towards his quarry and thudded into the wall of shields that stood firm. A sword poked through from between two of them and slashed at his arm. With a cry, he lifted his own sword and with savage strength slammed it against the shield in front of him, trying to force a way through. The rest of his men crashed into the wall and as the Scottish army at the bottom of the hill tried to retreat heavily defeated, at the top the battle fought on. Three of Santé's men were killed before they could be outflanked and the wall started to break. Richard forced his way through and found himself in combat with their captain, who took it upon himself to see off his master's enemy. Philip swung wildly at Richard who parried the blow, then braced himself for the next attack but it never came. A sword emerged from Philip's chest as Santé thrust his sword through the captain's back. "That's for my men, you son of a bitch!" he cried. "Ricardo, I will see to these bastards, now go and get your daughter before it is too late!"

"Good luck Cazador," Señor Jiménez said, patting Richard on the shoulder before a man surged towards them. Alexandre embraced him. "Go!"

"Paulo, Gringo, with me!" he cried and the three of them headed off in pursuit of Grenwick.

* * *

Maria worked at her bonds. Her wrists were bloody and raw but after hours of pain she was nearly free. She could hear the voices of the guards outside the tent, and she knew she could not escape that way but there was a sword on Grenwick's table and if she could just free herself she could possible carve her way through the canvas and escape out the back. Finally, and with excruciating effort, she freed her hands. She tried to stand and fell; it had been a long time since she had stood and her legs were weak. Picking herself up she stumbled to the table and grabbed the sword, but as she did so she heard the voice she had not hoped to hear again.

"My Lord, what has happened? Is the battle won?"

"Never mind that," Grenwick growled, panting. "Saddle three horses. It's time to get out of here!"

Grenwick burst into the tent. He had expected to find Maria sprawled on the floor but instead he found her standing and with a sword tip pointed at his throat.

"So you're not so stupid after all," he said.

"You can thank my mother for that," she replied defiantly. "She's dead, isn't she?"

"Aye, she's dead all right and so will you be if you don't lower that sword."

"No, I don't think I will and you can thank my father for that!"

"Your father is dead!" he shouted.

Horrible images ran through Louisa's mind. "No, that cannot be, I don't believe you. You lie!"

"I killed him myself." She lowered the sword, and Grenwick smiled.

I thought he'd come for me, I thought he'd save me.

"Maria!" came the cry. She woke from her trance, and she knew that voice; it was her father's. She brought the sword back to Grenwick's throat. She saw the anger flash across his face.

"Outside," she said. "Now!"

Grenwick obeyed. When he walked into the daylight it was to find that his two guards were dead and Richard and two of those wretched members of the Guardians of Guadalest were waiting for him. Maria poked Grenwick in the back with the sword and forced him forwards.

"Sir Richard Longsword, it is an honour to finally meet you," Grenwick said.

Richard ignored him. "Maria, are you hurt?"

"I am fine, father."

He turned back to Grenwick. "Where is Simon?"

Grenwick laughed, and it was clearly not the answer Richard was looking for so he approached him and rammed his father's sword into Grenwick's gut. He fell to his knees, his hands fumbling at the wound.

"For my father, for my wife!" Richard roared.

Grenwick tried to laugh again but it was more of a husky wheeze, as blood trickled from his mouth. "He is not here, if that's what you were hoping," he replied with difficulty.

"I am El Cazador! I am in no mood to be trifled with. I asked you a question. Where is Simon?"

"He followed you in London."

"James," Richard breathed.

"Is dead and the location of the gold revealed; with any luck he's found it already."

"What use is gold to a dead man?" Richard asked.

"My death does not matter, as long as honour is restored to my family, and my son will see it done."

"Your son?" Richard demanded, but they all knew the answer before he had even asked it. The truth was there to see in Grenwick's green eyes and he just looked at Richard and smiled that evil smile, one last time.

Chapter Seventeen

Woburn Abbey
Woburn, Kingdom of England.
September, 1513.

"They love me worst of any Englishman living, by reason that I found the body of the King of Scots."
Thomas Dacre

After the battle, the captured Scottish guns were transported to Etal Castle which was passed back into English hands after the Scots' retreat. The body of King James was escorted by the Earl of Surrey to Berwick-upon-Tweed where it could be identified by Scottish officials. The Earl would remain with his son Edmund and a small force as the King's Lieutenant in the North in case the Scots dared to launch another assault with what remaining men they had. Richard would head south with his men back to Portchester but would first escort Sir Thomas Lovell and the Rouge Croix Pursuivant, Thomas Hawley, who carried the blood-stained coat of the late King James to prove the result of their victory to the Queen. Thomas Dacre too was chosen to accompany them along with Sir Edward Stanley and the Lord High Admiral.

Catherine of Aragón, Queen Regent of England, was waiting for them at Woburn Abbey in Bedfordshire. It was a grand stately home that had been secured by her husband a few years previously. Catherine herself was quite taken with the place which was situated to the north of London, making it easy for the barons to reach her after their long journey south. She was eager to hear for herself the events that had taken place. A letter had already arrived with the result but she was desperate to hear a full account and more importantly to see the faces of her barons, to see who was still alive. There had been no mention of Richard in the letter and she hoped that nothing awful had befell him. *God please let him be alive.*

The barons arrived at Woburn and were greeted by the Queen's household and those of her court with a warm welcome. They were all aware that these gentlemen had, although outnumbered, defended the realm from an invading army. One of the Queen's heralds was there to greet them and have their horses taken and cared for. "The Queen is waiting for you in the drawing room. She is greatly anticipating your council."

"Thank you," replied Thomas Hawley. "We, too, are eager to see our Queen."

The herald led them into a grand entrance hall, before peeling off to head down a corridor to a room at the very end. They entered the room which was large and well decorated with paintings and vases. There was a grand table in the centre at the head of which sat the Queen who stood the moment they entered, a smile beaming on her face.

"Your Majesty, Thomas Hawley, Rouge Croix Pursuivant, Sir Thomas Lovell, Thomas Dacre, second Baron Dacre of Gilsland, Sir Edward Stanley and Sir Richard Longsword, first Baron of Portchester."

"I know who they are, Sam," she said, not looking at the herald. "Gentlemen, what an honour and a pleasure to have you here. I trust your journey went untroubled?"

"We return victorious, and nothing could have spoiled the journey home," Lovell responded.

"The realm thanks you, and the King wishes to reward you for your efforts. I only wish Sir Howard was here so I might thank him also."

"The Earl wishes to take no risks, your Grace. He stays to secure the north with his youngest son."

"Very admirable," she said. "So tell me of the battle. Is it true that King James is dead?"

Thomas Hawley stepped forward. "I have his blood stained surcoat, your Grace." He placed it on the table for the Queen to see for herself. "He led his men in a foolish assault. He gave up his position on the higher ground, putting faith in victory through numbers. But the boggy ground was ill equipped for their pikes and we annihilated them. Most of the Scottish nobles were killed, along with twelve thousand infantrymen. The King, however, was not deterred and cut through our ranks and was within yards of the Earl before one of Sir Stanley's archers put an arrow in his side."

"Who found him?"

"It was I, your Majesty," Dacre replied with a bow. "I found his body. I think for that reason the Scots hate me more than any other Englishman living."

"Let them," she said. "It was a complete victory. This is an historic day. My husband will be pleased to hear of the events himself. Thomas, after you are rested, you will leave for France and deliver this coat to my husband. Sir Stanley, you are to be made a companion of the Order of the Garter, for your decisive part in the battle."

Thomas Howard, the Lord High Admiral, had a broad grin on his face. He was already a companion of the order and had been since the King's accession to the throne in 1510. The Order of the Garter was the highest order of chivalry in England, set up by King Edward III two hundred years previously for his most loyal knights which included, of course, his son the legendary Black Prince. Sir Stanley was flattered, Richard could tell by his face.

"What say you?" the Queen asked.

"Your Grace, you honour me truly, but I feel perhaps I am not worthy of such an honour," Sir Stanley replied.

Thomas Howard, who was still grinning, shook his head in annoyance as he heard Sir Stanley's words. He clearly thought he was worthy of such recognition and would never have dreamed to decline such an invitation. But unlike Howard, Sir Stanley was a man of modesty and to show such personal ambition in the Queen's presence was not in his nature.

"Nonsense," intervened Sir Thomas Lovell, who like the Earl of Surrey was already a knight in the Order of the Garter. "If it were not for your archers, the battle would have been lost. It is an honour to have you join us, brother. Very well deserved indeed." He held his hands out and smiled.

"As for you, Sir Dacre, Sir Richard," she said with a smile. "I think had the order not been restricted to twenty four companions, you yourselves may have been raised. As it is I am afraid you will just have to wait. However, Sir Richard, it is the King's wish that you are to be re-knighted. You will join your friend Sir Dacre here as a Knight of the Bath. If you are to become one of the King's barons, it is only fitting that he should knight you himself."

Richard had heard of the Knights of the Bath. Knighting ceremonies were quite elaborate, particularly in England and it was pretty common place if the knight-to-be was bathed, as a symbol of purification before being knighted. They were not an order like the Garter but it was still a prestigious honour to be knighted by the King. In truth it was an honour Richard felt he did not deserve. All he had done was set out to retrieve his wife and daughter, and it just so happened that serving the King of England had helped him to achieve those goals. But it was not his place to question the King and he would gracefully accept it nonetheless.

"May I ask when my installation will take place?" Sir Stanley asked, still somewhat exalted.

"On the feast day of Saint George along with the Duke of Nemours, in Saint George's Chapel at Windsor Castle," the Queen said. "The King will be present, as will all knights companion of the order and your wives."

"You shall receive your ceremonial habits before the date which you will wear to the ceremony," Sir Lovell intervened.

"You will also be awarded several items of insignia including the garter on the day of installation which will be placed upon you during the ceremony and you will be asked to swear the oath required by all new knights of the order."

Sir Stanley nodded to show he understood.

"Well then, gentlemen, I say this calls for a celebration. Will you dine with me tonight?" the Queen asked.

"It would be an honour, your Grace," Sir Stanley replied, and the others bowed their heads in acknowledgement.

Sir Thomas Lovell walked over to congratulate Sir Stanley and shook his hand vigorously. "I could not have asked for a better companion," he said. After Lovell congratulated him he shared a handshake with Richard. Howard was once again smiling, the fact that Richard had not been raised into the order pleased him greatly. He was not overly keen on this new Spanish baron that was rising through the ranks quicker than he had done. Sir Stanley patted Richard on the shoulder, acknowledging their joint efforts together at the battle of Flodden Field. Dacre, however, pulled him aside and asked him if he could have a quick word. "Sir Richard, what an honour to be a Knight of the Bath alongside you."

"And you," Richard replied, wondering where the conversation was leading.

"As a fellow baron, I wondered if you might do me the greatest of honours. I notice you have quite a reputation with the King and Queen and you are a fearsome knight but most of all you follow order and discipline; I like that in a man. You have accomplished so much at such a young age. Your career is something that I admire and wish to see for my own son. He's a good lad, eager to learn and a bloody good swordsman but I feel it's time he got out and experienced some of the world away from home. I would be honoured if you would consider taking him on as a squire. I assure you he is a capable man-at-arms and perhaps there will be a knighthood in it in due course?"

"Sir Dacre, you have been good to me since my arrival in England, and I would be happy to take on your son as a squire. As long as he is willing to learn and work hard, I will make a knight of him for you to be proud of. But tell me, is he comely? Perhaps he would be a good match for my daughter?"

That did make Sir Dacre laugh. "It is an interesting proposition. Perhaps we should talk more of this tonight?"

In truth Richard had only been joking but Sir Dacre was a good man and his son if made from the same cloth would no doubt be a decent match. It would not hurt to marry into such a family and provide himself with some decent allies. God knew, he needed all the friends he could get. He wasn't entirely sure what his daughter would make of this, mind.

The barons made their way from the room and were shown to their lodgings where they could rest and prepare for the evening's activities. As Richard made to leave, Sir Thomas Hawley tapped him on the shoulder. "Sir Richard, the Queen would like a word with you in private." Then he smiled and left the room behind the others.

"Shut the door if you would be so kind, Sir Richard." He did as he was ordered before facing the Queen alone. She was as lovely as he remembered. She bore that warm smile that he had experienced that night in Wooler. He had wondered if he would ever get the chance to meet her again in such fashion and was unsure if she wanted to, but here they were again.

"You survived the battle, then?"

"I did, your Grace. The hope that I might one day see your face again was what kept me going."

She blushed at that, seeming strangely vulnerable in his presence, which oddly she appeared to enjoy.

"Thanks be to God," she stammered. "We have been victorious and I thank you for your part. My husband is quite taken with you. As am I," she added. "He was impressed by your exploits in Guinegate and now you have served him well at

Flodden. I think if your carry on this way you can expect an earldom!"

"My Lady?"

"The King rewards his loyal subjects. Anyway, pray tell me. I am eager to hear news of your daughter."

"She is well, your Grace. Before the battle was through I caught the men that were holding her prisoner, who were trying to escape. We were able to apprehend them and free my daughter. She is safely being escorted back to Portchester with my men."

"And this Grenwick, what of him?"

"He is dead, your Grace."

"Then he received his just rewards, praise be to God. I am happy for you, Sir Richard, that this heartache has finally come to an end. If you wish it, I will happily accept your daughter as a woman of my court."

"It honours me, your Grace, but after recent events I wish to keep my daughter by my side. I fear also that she has her father's strength; she wishes to take up the sword." Richard smiled.

"Maybe that is for the best, but the offer is there should you change your mind."

"Thank you, your Grace, you are too kind."

"Please," she said. "Enough of the pleasantries. Call me Catherine."

"As you wish then, Lady Catherine." He looked at her and for a moment they stared into each other's eyes. It was safe to say that they liked one another, perhaps more so than they should. But the Queen knew her place and Richard understood that he had the King's favour and he would do nothing to disrespect that.

"You asked me a question before you went into battle about information on your family," she said. "As promised I had my historians look into it and I believe I have some interesting news for you."

Richard looked up. She had made him curious. "Please tell me what you know."

"You will probably not believe me when I tell you that you are descended from royal blood."

"How is this possible?"

"Your ancestor, William Longespée a Norman, was the first of your name and so named because of his great size and the huge weapon he used to carry. He was the illegitimate son of King Henry II of England and his mother was Ida de Tosny, a royal ward and mistress of the King. She was, however, the great grand daughter of Robert de Beaumont, first Earl of Leicester, a powerful nobleman remembered as one of the wisest men of that age. Beaumont accompanied William the Conqueror on his invasion into England from Normandy, who was crowned William I after the battle of Hastings in 1066 and he was the great grandfather of Henry II. So as you can see you derive from strong Norman stock, an indirect decedent of William the Conqueror himself."

"It is a lot to take in, I don't really understand."

"Well, let me try to explain. William Longespée, jure uxoris, which is Latin for by right of his wife, became the third Earl of Salisbury after marrying Ela of Salisbury, who was the third countess of Salisbury, by order of his half-brother and legitimate son of Henry II, Richard I who succeeded their father to the throne, who you may know of as Richard the Lionheart. Together they had several children, but what many people do not know is that he had a secret lover whom he was secretly betrothed to before he was forced to marry Ela. Nobody knows who she was, as she was probably of low birth but he had two illegitimate sons with her. The eldest was named William after himself and the youngest Henry after his grandfather. Obviously William and Henry were not welcomed in Salisbury by the countess who was angered by their presence and this drove a wedge between Longespée and his eldest son. Longespée was known for his loyalty to his other half brother, John, who tried to steal the throne from King Richard while he was away on crusade. William, however, said they should be loyal to the crown despite his father's feelings of animosity to the King. For this, he was expelled from his father's household and to dissociate himself from his father. William disregarded his Norman roots and translated his name into English and thus went by the name of Longsword."

"What became of him?"

"He took up the call to crusade and joined the Holy Order of the Knights Templar, which is where I believe he made enemies with the Ashbournes. There were old documented accounts, which we believe were written by the younger brother Henry, which speak loosely of the events that took place there. So obviously he must have joined his older brother at a later date. Unfortunately, these documents are decaying and do not paint a vivid picture, so I am unable to tell you more. From then on, I am afraid that your family name only flitted in and out of the pages of history briefly. Other than your father, the only other account we can find was a journal written by a Sir Stephen Longsword whose father was the Earl of Hertford. He speaks with admiration of his ancestors who fought in the crusades, and we can only assume it was of William and Henry he spoke. He decided to emulate them by crusading against the Muslims in Spain. He also mentions the continuing feud between the two families and that another reason for venturing to Spain was to escape it, along with his lover who so conveniently happened to be an Ashbourne. I don't suppose her father was best pleased about that."

"He fell in love with an Ashbourne?" Richard asked, shocked, almost feeling disgusted until he remembered that he too had enjoyed the company of an Ashbourne; Simon. "Did he go after them?"

"Again I do not know. Most of the pages after that were burnt."

"May I see these documents for myself, your Grace?"

"I will have them sent to Portchester for you," the Queen replied.

"Is there any history of where the Ashbournes come from?" he asked, compelled.

"There is nothing. Only their name is mentioned in these brief accounts. It is my belief that they were a lowly family and have been around for years and have no doubt provided soldiers for their liege lord for as long as they go back, but there is no knowledge of how they came into existence. But I have a suspicion that they may have been amongst a few Saxon families that did not submit after the Normans invaded and took charge. After then, they were cast into shadow, and perhaps this is why they have been disliked by so many. It is only in recent years that their name became of note. When Humphrey Ashbourne, a notorious archer, led his own band of men at the Battle of Agincourt, so did James Longsword, your grandfather I believe. They allied themselves and stopped the feud for a few years until Humphrey died and his son Grenwick held James responsible. James mysteriously disappeared and Grenwick turned his attentions to your father, Robert."

"And then my father saw the princes murdered in the tower."

"That is how the story goes."

"I do not know much of my father's life before then. I know he went to Spain where he met my mother and before that he was a knight and fought in the Wars of the Roses but other than that..."

"Yes, he was present at the First Battle of St Albans. Unfortunately, he was on the losing side in that fight but he managed to escape."

"You know of the battle? Please tell me."

"I know much of the Wars of the Roses. As Queen of England I took the liberty of looking into the background of my adopted country and into the family that I married into, and it was interesting to gain knowledge on how my father in law secured the throne for the Tudor family, and how it came at the end of a war that lasted thirty years. The first battle took place in St Albans and your father was present. He served the Duke of Somerset whom he'd previously served at the Battle of Castillon. The Duke led the Lancastrian army for the mad King Henry VI. The Yorkists were led by Richard the Duke of York who was attempting to seize the throne. The dukes were arch rivals and hated each other passionately. Richard Neville, the Earl of Warwick, was the most powerful noble at that time and the Duke of York found him a worthy ally."

St Albans, Hertfordshire. May 1455.

Robert had arrived at the town of St Albans the previous day. The journey had not taken him long, for he had lived in Hertfordshire his entire life. He was steward, in his father's absence, of a village called Watford, an hour's ride away. He had been summoned by the Duke of Somerset, to whom he owed his allegiance since being knighted by him for his part in the Battle of Castillon two years earlier when he was just sixteen. Robert brought with him his small retinue of archers and men-at-arms. Since the battle, he had acquired ten men-at-arms and twelve archers.

The rumour was that the Duke of York who had fallen from power had returned north to raise a private army along with his ally Richard Neville, the Earl of Warwick. The King, sensing that Richard was up to something, had summoned the Duke to London to the King's council. The Duke, however, sensed a trap and so answered by marching his army south, all three thousand of them. This had greatly angered the King who was desperate to not let the Duke's army reach the capital, so he rallied forth with his own army numbering two and half thousand under the leadership of the Duke of Somerset.

They marched north until they reached the fortified town of St Albans. Upon arrival, the Duke sent out scouts to find the enemy's position. They returned within the hour to inform the Duke and the

King that the Yorkists' army was camped close by at Keyfield to the east of the town. Surprised by the sudden appearance of the rebel army, the King bade the Duke hurriedly occupy the town. They did so and put up stout defences by blockading the streets on Sopwell and Shropshire lane. Robert, whom the Duke was quite taken with, was tasked with manning the barricade on Shropshire lane. The rest of the army was to make camp in the town square.

Several hours of negotiations ensued between Richard of York and King Henry with Richard trying his best to convince the King that his intentions were totally honourable. Most of the Lancastrian army expected a peaceful solution as had happened at the previous encounter at Blackheath in 1452. But then, without warning, the Yorkists attacked and attempted to overrun the blockades on Sopwell and Shropshire lane.

Robert had spread his twelve archers out along the barricade and in between them he had placed his ten men-at-arms including himself in the middle. He intended that if the Yorkists came up the narrow street his archers would cause the most damage with their longbows, so it was necessary to have his men-at-arms protect them. If the enemy managed to get close enough to the barricade they could stab and jab over the top and be just as effective.

"Do you think they will come?" one of Robert's men-at-arms asked. He was two years Robert's senior and his name was James Clifford. "Or will they negotiate?"

"I do not know. Negotiations are on-going but I cannot help but think it a ruse. Richard did not come all this way to sit idle," Robert replied. "All we can do is be ready in case they do."

"Did you hear that?" an archer called.

"Hear what?" James replied.

"Shush; listen."

Robert craned his neck to listen closer. "They're coming," he said.

"Are you sure, Robert? We've had no word from the Duke."

"They're coming," he repeated. Two minutes later, the muffled noise Robert had heard some way off had multiplied and there was no

mistaking the roar that several hundred men made as they came into view, charging down the street with their cries echoing off the walls. Some of Robert's men shifted uncomfortably but none of them fled; they were here to fight.

"Archers at the ready." The archers took arrows from their quivers and raised their bows and took aim at the hoard coming towards them. When they were within one hundred paces, Robert gave the order. "Fire!"

Twelve arrows soared down the street and tore into the advancing troops, thudding into mail and flesh. Several of them were hit with such force they were thrown backwards. But before they could even hit the floor the next set of arrows were unleashed. The men at the front who were no more abreast than Robert and his men were like lambs to the slaughter. They were unable to withstand the barrage sent upon them and with men pushing from the back they had nowhere to run.

"Fire at will!" Robert called.

The bowmen needed no encouragement. One after another they loosed and despite coming close the enemy could not reach the barricade and the streets ran red with the first of the Yorkists' blood. "Fall back!" came the call. "Fall back!"

The Yorkists' retreat was slow and as they turned and fled, the archers could not resist taking a few more of them down as they ran. Robert's men-at-arms let out a cheer as they went. "Don't get carried away, boys, they'll be back."

He was not wrong. A while later the Yorkists tried to storm the street again, and this time they made it to the barricade but not before many more were felled by Robert's archers. When they reached the barricade, the men-at-arms hacked and stabbed as Robert had planned and soon Yorkists' bodies began to pile up against the barricade while all the while the archers continued to shoot arrows into the crowded street. After a time it was clear they were not going to make any headway and the twenty three Lancastrians held of the Yorkists' advance once again.

Robert and his men braced themselves in case the Yorkists came again but they never did. "All right lads, take a rest." The men were *tired, and they had fought well.*

"What's the rest of the army doing while we are here fighting our balls off? Shouldn't they send reinforcements?" asked Clifford.

Before Robert could even answer there were cries of terror that rent the air coming from the direction of the town square. What the hell is happening? he thought, but then with no time to react the roar from the other side of the barricade returned as the Yorkists' troops marched down the street for one final assault.

"Robert, they have outflanked us. We will be trapped if we stay here."

"We cannot be certain of that," he replied. "It is our job to defend this post. I will not abandon it without cause."

All of a sudden men burst onto the road, coming from a side street. They were the soldiers who had been manning Sopwell Lane. "You there, what is going on?" he called to them.

One of them turned as the others hurriedly carried on, heading off down another side street. "It's the Earl of Warwick," he cried. "He's led the Yorkists' reserves into the back lanes and through the town's gardens. They charged into the square and took the King completely by surprise."

"Why do you flee your post?" Robert replied. "Do you go to assist the King?"

"Bugger that!" he said. "There are hundreds of them trying to climb over that barricade and I'm not defending it only to be attacked in the rear. We're paid but we're not paid that much. The town is lost. You had best do the same unless you want to be overrun." And with that he was off.

"Shit!" Robert turned to see the Yorkists nearing the barricade.

"Sir, do we fire?" one of the archers called.

"No," he replied. "To the King!"

"But that man just said-"

"I do not care what that man said; we will not abandon our King or the Duke!"

Robert and his men abandoned their post and as they ran down the street there was no mistaking the sound of the Yorkists climbing over the barricade. As they cut deeper into the town they were greeted by the sound of battle, men's screams, horses whinnying and the unmistakable clash of steel on steel. As they approached the square there were men fleeing up the street, Lancastrians that had escaped the carnage, some running and others carrying their wounded friends. Robert could not fail to notice that most of them were not wearing helmets; the man was right, they had been taken completely unawares.

They burst into the square and were greeted by an unpleasant sight. The Lancastrians had been routed, and those trying to flee were being hacked down by the Yorkists soldiers. Only the King and some of his most loyal men carried on the fight in the centre of the square. The Duke of Somerset, Roberts's liege lord, had holed up inside the entrance to the Castle Inn and there were men trying to break in. "We must save the Duke," Robert cried. "Archers over there," he pointed. The archers loosed at the men attempting to reach the Duke and they were killed. "We must get to him before they do!"

As Robert tried to lead his men towards the inn they were beset upon and his men-at-arms leapt into action. One man attempted to stab Robert with his spear but he casually flicked it away with his sword. Before the man could bring it back, Robert was close enough to slash at the man's legs. He fell to his knees and Robert swung his sword which cracked into the man's jaw and embedded in his skull. Robert kicked the man free, his sword red and dripping, and looked towards the inn. The Duke had noticed him. Robert waved to suggest the Duke come to them. He nodded to show he understood. He burst from the inn and made a dash for it. He was only a few paces from Robert when an arrow took him in the back. Robert looked up to see Grenwick, his family's enemy, bow in hand. "No!" he cried, but it was too late, the Duke was dead.

Robert had no choice but to turn his attentions to the King, but at that moment the Earl of Warwick commanded his archers to send a heavy volley fire towards him. Several of the King's nobles were killed including Lord Clifford and the Earl of Northumberland. The Duke of Buckingham was severely injured as was the King himself. Although

*the dead only lay in the hundreds it was a complete Yorkist victory,
with the Lancastrian leaders all either dead or captured. There was
nothing left that Robert could do.*

*"We must get out of here, Robert." James grabbed him by the arm
and pulled him back.*

*Robert, however, only had eyes for Grenwick who just looked back at
him and smiled. There was nothing else for it. With his men he turned
and fled the town.*

* * *

Richard was starting to gain an understanding of the type of man
his father had been and he was extremely proud of him. "So, he
was forced to leave the King at the hands of his enemies?"

"What more could he do?" the Queen asked.

"Nothing," he replied. "He was helpless."

The Queen smiled and she took Richard's hand in her own.
"As were you the day the Ashbournes came for you in
Guadalest," she said. "There is nothing more you could have
done to save your wife so do not blame yourself, it cuts me to see
you so. If you'd have given them your life they still would not
have spared her. Sometimes, Richard, it is better to live and fight
another day."

Chapter Eighteen

Siege of Chinchilla
Chinchilla, Crown of Castile. October, 1513.

*"You have sat too long here for any good you have been doing.
Depart. I say, and let us have done with you. In the name of God,
go!"*
Oliver Cromwell

A month after the Battle of Flodden Field, Richard and his
Cazadores found themselves bracing to storm Chinchilla. It had
been six long years since Alexandre had lost his wife, his
daughter and the town of Albacete to the monster he knew as
brother. But finally he had returned home to reclaim it. The
neighbouring town of Chinchilla had fallen just days after
Albacete had been sacked. The town had a castle which Delmar
Jiménez claimed as his seat. From there, he would rule and
terrorise the surrounding land. *But tonight his reign will come to an
end.*

Richard was pleased to see the determination in Alexandre's
eyes. He was driven by a fierce hunger for revenge. Yet despite
that, he was undeniably calm. Richard had worried that the
emotion of such a personal occasion might get the better of
Alexandre. But despite his urgency to see the job done, he was
blessed with a cool focus. Richard was proud of his friend. He
was ready to fight and die for him, and so were his Cazadores.

After returning to Portchester, Richard had not rested but
instantly set about mustering the greatest force he possibly could.
Señor Jiménez had proved himself a worthy ally but it was his
friendship that Richard cherished the most. For that alone
Richard would honour his promise. After two weeks of
recruiting, Richard gave the order to depart. They set off for

Spain with two hundred men at his command. As Baron of Portchester he was entitled to fly his own banner, something he did with pride. He chose the sigil of his house, the red rose on a sea of black. *Finally the House of Longsword will return to its former glory.*

Richard had five knights sworn to him. These were; Joseph, Paulo, Gringo and the recently dubbed Santiago and Alexandre. Santé, despite being captain of General Córdoba's personal guard, was honour bound to help Richard and for his loyalty Richard rewarded him with the only thing he could, a knighthood. Señor Jiménez, by right, was a lord. But he lost his title along with everything else. He swore his allegiance to Richard and he would proudly call himself one of his knights.

Along with his knights, Richard also had a young squire named William Dacre, the son of his ally, Sir Thomas Dacre. The boy was young and ambitious and followed Richard's every word. Sir Thomas had long had visions of William becoming a knight in his own right before replacing him as Baron of Gilsland. Richard had promised to help in any way that he could. So far William had proved his ability with a sword in training. Perhaps tonight he would prove he had what it took to become a knight.

Richard's Cazadores now numbered in the region of fifty, thanks to some excellent recruitment on Joseph's behalf. The garrison at Portchester now totalled twenty five and when it was bolstered by the return of Santé's and Alexandre's men, it made a very formidable force. They were all dressed in the red and black livery of Richard's house, proudly wearing its sigil on their chests. The women of Portchester had worked night and day to have their jupons ready in time. Despite their new attire, Richard allowed them to carry pennons displaying the colours of their own houses. Santé carried a maroon one emblazoned with the lion of Córdoba. Gringo and Paulo, having relinquished their roles as Guardians of Guadalest had officially pledged their allegiance to the Baron of Portchester. But in honour of Richard's barony in Spain they carried a red and gold one emblazoned with the Tower of Alcalalí. Young William's bore his family's coat of arms, three yellow shells on a sea of red. As for Señor Jiménez, Richard allowed him to wear his own livery. The last time he had done so had been on that unforgettable night six years ago. He and his four companions were clad in grey, emblazoned with the three golden towers and bat of the Jiménez house.

The other hundred and fifty men were all volunteers. They wore no livery only plain gambesons or chain mail. King Henry had granted Richard special permission to see to his Spanish estates and to take whatever men he could gather. Of course he meant those who were not yet assigned to retinues of other lords and knights banneret. But to Richard's surprise restless stable boys and grown men-at-arms from all over the county and even as far afield as Salisbury had flocked to his call. They all wished to prove their worth to El Cazador. This provided Richard with a hundred men-at-arms and fifty archers. He had no doubt that on his return, the King would expect him to house them, train them and make them available to fight whenever he had need of them.

Richard split the volunteers into three separate forces. The men-at-arms, who carried a multitude of weapons including sword and spear, he split in two. Seventy five of them formed his infantry and were under the command of Paulo and Gringo. The other twenty five formed his horsemen and acted as his personal guard. The archers were assigned to Señor Jiménez and his men.

"Is he home?" Richard whispered to Alexandre.

"Aye, he's in there all right, I can see his banner above the castle," he whispered, black eyes glaring at the town that Delmar had fortified. "The bastard has taken the bat from ours and made his own." Richard could see it over the palisade flapping in the town's firelight. He had taken the bat but had replaced the towers with a human heart from which the bat was apparently taking blood. It was very crudely done. Richard supposed its purpose was to instil fear into anyone who saw it but this was not the effect that it was having on Señor Jiménez.

"Then we must draw him out. We will never defeat twice our number while they hide behind their palisade. What we need is a distraction, but first let's take out their sentries." Delmar had sent out two man teams to patrol the outer perimeter but fortunately the town had never been assaulted, other than the night they took it six years ago. The men were not expecting anything and the Cazadores were able to take them unawares.

"Take your archers and deal with them." Alexandre nodded and made to move but Richard grabbed hold of his arm. "The men of Albacete, would they be glad to see you return?"

"My brother is a tyrant. He has the love of no one, the people loved my father. Aye, if I was to avenge him and reclaim these towns, I believe they would."

Richard watched as Alexandre and the archers ran from the shelter of the trees, seeing their pale outline in the moonlight as they darted across the field that surrounded the fort before taking out the sentries one by one.

"Joseph, Santé," he called and the men hurried to his side. "I have an idea that could help us in this fight."

"What is it, Richard?" Joseph asked. They listened as he explained what he intended for them to do. A smile appeared on Santé's face but Joseph seemed a little less optimistic. "You think this will work?"

"We won't know unless we try, will we? Take your men and go, but you must hurry!" The two men, understanding what it was they needed to do, bade their men follow and disappeared into the trees. By this point Alexandre was reappearing with his own men.

"Where are they going?" he asked.

"Running an errand," Richard replied. "Right, now listen, I have a plan. Gringo, take half the infantry and set fire to the palisade. They will send out a small force to deal with you, but avoid a skirmish and let them chase you, and lead them to us. But take off your jupons and leave your shields here, we do not want him to recognise us just yet." Gringo and his men set off. "Take out as many as you can from the trees," he said to Alexandre. "My horsemen will take out the rest!"

"They will only send out a few, Richard, there are hundreds more in there that will follow out the gate when they see what we have done, by which point there will be no element of surprise."

"No, but we'd have hurt them and put some bloody fear into the bastards, that's what the Cazadores do. How long do you think they've been in there, sitting on their arses and drinking wine? They may outnumber us, friend, but every one of us is worth five of them!" Richard said, looking Alexandre in the eyes. "Besides, we can't sit here all night. Let's meet them in open battle and see what your brother is made of."

Alexandre nodded. He would kill his brother or die trying. "Let's meet them."

Gringo had made it to the palisade and his men set about lighting a fire. It was a while before they were successful and longer still before the wooden wall whooshed up in flames. The blaze caught the town by surprise and women's screams were heard coming from inside the town. The field became alight with an orange glow sent forth from the flames and Gringo and his thirty seven men cheered and danced, causing a scene, while the men inside tried to come to terms with what was going on.

* * *

There was a sudden banging on the chamber door. *For the love of God who dares to disturb me now? I'll have their head on a platter!* Delmar clambered off the wench who was crushed and suffocating beneath him. She meant nothing to him, but she was his favourite of all the young girls from the town. Most had stopped even trying to put up a fight, but this bitch? No, she still kicked and squealed like a pig and that's just how Delmar liked it. They never stood a chance. He was a brute of a man, all but seven foot, a strong muscular frame with hands like shields and legs like tree trunks. He began to put on his clothes and as he did so the banging came quicker and louder.

"I'm coming, you useless cunt! Your mother was a whore and I shit on her grave! This better be worth disturbing me, you hear? Otherwise I'll cut off your genitals and stick them up your own arse!"

"Señor," came the muffled cry of one of Fajardo's men. "The palisade has been set on fire."

Delmar growled. "Then put it out, you stupid dog, and hang the son of a bitch who did it!"

"No, Señor, you misunderstand. It was set alight from the outside; there are men out there."

Delmar burst forth from the room only half dressed, slamming the door into the face of the man who had disturbed him, breaking his nose and knocking him to the floor. The man instantly put his hand to his face as blood cascaded down onto his gambeson. "Get up, you fucking useless turd, get up. Go get my armour and bring it to me!"

The man scampered off in a hurry and Delmar made his way to the castle courtyard. "Fetch my fucking horse!" he screamed at the first guard that he approached. Finally armoured and atop his horse he made his way from the castle, through the town to the gate on the fort's easternmost side.

"Señor Delmar," the captain of his garrison called as he approached. "They have set fire to the palisade but I have men trying to put it out as we speak."

"Who has done this?"

"I am not sure, my Lord, most likely boys from the local villages who have had too much to drink and wish to avenge the death of their fathers."

"How many are there?"

"No more than thirty, I'd say."

"I'd say isn't good enough!" Delmar shouted. "What of our sentries?"

"We do not know."

Delmar let out a roar and leapt from his horse. *I will see these bastards for myself.* He made his way up on to the ramparts that he'd had built over the gate and he gazed down into the field below. As he appeared above the palisade it caused the men below to jeer and make rude gestures in his direction; there were thirty seven of them. They were too well armoured to be mere peasants, but they had no banner or colours to speak of. *Brigands most likely, filthy breed!* "Get some bloody archers up here!" Within minutes there were two crossbowmen above the gate loosing bolts at the men below but none were hitting their mark. The brigands had taken to running around wildly and were proving difficult targets to hit. "Captain," he cried down to his man. "Have the men readied to fight."

"How many, Señor?"

"Fifty ought to suffice to see off this rabble, but take a hundred to make sure. Do not stop until every last one is dead, you hear? Show no mercy, kill them all!"

A hundred armoured men bearing shield and sword under the command of the garrison captain marched forth through the gates of Chinchilla. Their prey, however, was thirty seven men only lightly armoured with no shields who were only brandishing swords. At the sight of the captain's force the brigands began to edge away towards the trees. One or two chose to stand their ground and fight but were swiftly cut down, and the rest fled in haste.

"Charge!" the captain cried and his men stormed across the field after the brigands. One of them fell and as he tried to push himself up the captain rammed his blade through the man's back, twisting it and severing his spine.

"Are we to follow them into the woods, captain?" one of the men called, looking uncertainly into the dark.

"Aye, his lordship will be displeased if we do not bring back all their heads." The captain was not concerned, with no casualties yet to speak of, and so the armed guard approached the tree line. Then all of a sudden there was a low whistling sound followed by a thud and one of the captain's men fell to the floor with a muffled cry as he took an arrow to the chest. The captain looked at the man crumpled on the floor. *That is no crossbow bolt; that is an arrow from a longbow.* The captain gazed into the darkness of the trees, realising he had no idea who was in there or how many there actually were. Fear suddenly crept across his face.

"Run!" he cried. Panic engulfed the group of armed soldiers and they scattered in all directions, but one after another they fell as more and more were pierced with arrow heads and the night was rent with the screams of men.

* * *

Meanwhile...

...a few miles north, Joseph and Santé and their men infiltrated the town of Albacete. There were only a few soldiers manning the streets, most of whom were dealt with swiftly, having their throats cut or necks broken.

"We must be quiet. We do not want to alert whatever garrison might be here. Go door to door, wake people from their beds and tell them what's happening but for God's sake, keep them quiet."

They scattered into the streets of Albacete. It was a town asleep but for how much longer? Joseph asked himself. He hoped they would react how Richard said they would; that they still had heart and would wake up to find that they were strong. Too long have they been butchered and tormented by their oppressor, and tonight was the night to rise up against him and fight.

"Joseph, there is an inn over there." Santé pointed to a white building, a dim glow coming from its windows. "We should see if there are men inside."

Joseph nodded, and led the way to the inn so called La Brújula. He could hear voices inside and men laughing; by the sounds of it they were gambling. Joseph eased the door open with a creak. This alerted the men inside who all stood up in fright, knocking the table causing the dice they were playing to roll onto the floor. They grabbed whatever was in reach to use as weapons. One man grabbed a chair and another took a dagger from his belt. There were four young men at the table, all as uncertain as each other as to who the two men in the doorway were, and a further older man standing behind the bar. Joseph edged his way in and Santé followed.

"Sorry we disturbed you, gentlemen. We do not want any trouble." Joseph spoke in Spanish.

The men looked from one to another, before one of them spoke, eyeing Joseph suspiciously. "Aye, that's what the last lot of soldiers who came in here said, except they beat and killed our friend and left me with this token," he said, pointing to a scar beneath his eye.

"I am sorry for your friend, truly," Joseph replied. "But we are not those soldiers."

"Who are you?" the innkeeper asked, cutting in.

"My name is Joseph and this is Santé. We are friends of Alexandre Jiménez, the rightful Lord of Albacete."

"Alexandre? He died six years ago, killed by his own damned brother."

"That's not true," one of the other men piped up. "I was only a boy but I saw him that night, walking off into the woods all battered and broken. I thought he wouldn't live long, mind you, but he was alive when he left."

"He is alive and he travels with my company. We have come

to exact revenge on his brother and free you all from the shackles of his tyranny."

"How do you intend to do that?" the innkeep asked. "He has a small army at his command. What are you but a few men?"

"We are two hundred men and we are laying siege to Chinchilla as we speak. But we will not overcome them without help. We need more men; we need the townspeople of Albacete to join us."

"You will find few here who will be willing, because people have become accustomed to keeping their noses down and avoiding trouble. If this went wrong then the people would be made to suffer. The last time someone stood up to Delmar he rode through here and raped and pillaged everything, and the town has only just recovered."

"It will not go wrong, you have my word. Together we can accomplish this."

"How can you say that? How do you know?"

Joseph smiled. "Because our commander is the fearless El Cazador, Señor Ricardo de Guadalest and he has made it his mission to help Alexandre and expel Delmar from this land."

The innkeep gasped. "Dear God."

"Who?" the man with the scar asked, looking round at his friends. They mirrored his confused expression, shrugging their shoulders. The scarred man turned back to face Joseph.

"General Córdoba's protégé, the famous knight that single-handedly won the Battle of Cerignola, you fool!" the innkeep answered, before Joseph could.

"Battle of where?"

"Do you know nothing of our history, Victor?"

"Evidently not," the man retorted.

Ignoring this last remark the innkeep turned to Joseph. "Is this really true? Has Sir Richard come to help us?"

"He has," Joseph replied. "I swear it on my honour as a knight, you have my word."

The innkeep nodded. "Then so be it." He left the room and within moments had returned with an axe. It had only ever been used to cleave wood before, but tonight it had another purpose. "Let's end this."

"Thank you," Joseph replied.

"You can't be serious? Are you really going along with this?" Victor said to the innkeep.

"Aye, I bloody well am and so will you. Or do you want to see your girl in the arms of another man again? All of you, you come here and you gamble and drink and forget it all but it's your women that bear the real pain. They are the ones the soldiers take, they're the ones who can't forget, they're the ones who suffer, while we sit here and do nothing, nothing! I lost my wife the night they came the first time and every day since I wished I'd done something. Well, tonight we've got that chance. Tonight we take back what is ours!"

The words hit home like a knife to the belly and all the men felt like cowards. "Fine," Victor replied, "What do we do?"

The innkeep looked at Joseph, who spoke again. "Rouse your neighbours and friends. Get whatever weapons together you can. Then-" He was cut short by a commotion coming from outside. He could hear the sound of raised voices. *What the hell is going on?* There was a sudden banging on the door as one of Santé's men entered.

He was smiling. "Begging your pardon, Señores, about the noise I mean, I know you said to keep it quiet and all but this has worked out better than we thought. The townsfolk are riled up something crazy out there, and they're assembling in the streets."

Joseph headed out onto the street and he saw for his own eyes what was happening. There were at least a hundred of them on this street alone. All of them were carrying whatever they could use as a weapon. Some had pitch forks, others had axes and clubs and a few even had swords. But it wasn't just men; there were women and boys too. The town was coming out in full force. *Oh to hell with it!* "Innkeeper," he called to the old man standing in the doorway of his inn, hefting his great axe. "Do you have any pots and pans?"

"Of course I do," he replied. "Why?"

"Get as many as you can and start banging the wretched things together. Make as much noise as you can. I don't want a single person left in their beds!"

"Yes, sir."

"Victor?" Joseph called to the young man who had followed him on to the street along with his friends. "The garrison. Where are they?"

"You will find they are drinking and whoring, most likely at El Zafiro, Señor, it's in the town square."

Joseph drew his sword from his scabbard and raised it into the air. This was his moment to shine, his turn to lead. Tonight he would show Richard his worth. He waved his sword and cried "To the square!"

"To the square! To the square!" The shout went up amongst the towns folk and together knight, man-at-arm and peasant formed a mob and to the centre of the town they marched, their numbers growing by the second as more joined them from every passing street; but when they approached the square they found the garrison was already waiting for them.

* * *

Delmar watched in horror. After the bombardment of arrows had dwindled to a halt, horsemen burst forth from the trees like riders from Hell, their very blades appearing awash with flame as they reflected the orange glare that shone forth from the fort palisade. Their shrill cries tormented their opponents as they descended upon them, savagely cutting and stabbing, killing all in their wake. Metal cracked bone as blades sliced and thrust through skin and muscle, limbs were hacked clean off, blood spurted from open wounds and men died.

All one hundred men he had sent out to see off this small rabble of brigands lay dead or dying. His captain, who had come within metres of the gate, had taken a sword through the back of his neck, slicing through his windpipe before piercing out the other side. He lay dead below the gate, his cold eyes looking up at Delmar, accusation written all over them. Delmar felt a shiver go through his spine. *How can this be? Who are these bastards?* The horsemen by now had dismounted and they were soon joined by more infantrymen carrying spears, most of whom bore red roses on their chest. *That is the sigil of El Cazador?* Delmar had heard much of him and his Cazadores. It was said that they fought like the very demons of Hell. *The Hunter and his Huntsmen, do they come for me?* The archers, who had so devastatingly killed many of Delmar's men, came rushing from the trees to join their compatriots outside his gates, led by a shadowy figure. *No, it cannot possibly be...*

But it was. Delmar would recognise that banner anywhere, as it was the banner of his house, of his father, of his brother. It flapped in the breeze as it edged closer towards the fort, the three towers evident loomed over by the bat that he had stolen to form his own banner. Beneath it he saw the man he despised. He recognised the red hair and matching red beard, the way he walked, his stout posture and his broad shoulders. *There is only one man in the world that looks like that and he is my brother, Alexandre Jiménez.* Delmar scratched his bald head that had started to sweat, before running his finger through his pointy brown beard. He looked down at the pitiful force that assembled against him, all caution and worry draining from him in an instant to be filled with anger and rage. "Elija!" he screamed down to the man whose nose he broke. "Take three hundred men and deal with these insolent bastards! Kill them all but not my brother, he's mine!"

"Yes - yes Sir!" Elija stammered in response.

"And do not fail me or your nose will not be the only thing I break!"

So my brother has made friends with English dogs. They have travelled a long way to be sent straight back to Hell! These were evidently not mere brigands lining up outside the fort; these were trained soldiers and some of them were knights. There were one hundred men-at-arms holding their shields in one hand bearing the three lions of the English King, and their spears in the other. They were flanked on both sides by twenty five archers and together they were a hundred and fifty strong. Delmar's forces would outnumber them two to one, but he had to admit the English were clever. They had come equipped with spears which would make it difficult for his men to get to them and this also protected the archers, keeping the enemy at bay while they loosed arrow after arrow after arrow. *It is no matter, we will cut through their spears with Spanish steel and before long we will outflank them. Soon they will be surrounded and they'll be nowhere for them to run.*

The English stood together, ready in a tight unit, shields barred together and spears held aloft. They were waiting for the enemy advance. Elija led them, all three hundred men down the slope of the street that led to the gate before which the English stood. There was an eerie silence except for the crackling of wood as it was licked by flame and the stomping of feet from the Spanish men-at-arms as their heavy boots shook the earth and their greaves rattled, but no man uttered a word. They approached the gate, only wide enough to allow them to pass through ten abreast, and the English knew this. All of a sudden there was an explosion of noise as the English men-at-arms surged forth, with the bowmen falling in behind screaming their war cries as they came. Delmar realised he was about to become an easy target for an English arrow and hastily withdrew himself from the gate's ramparts, while below in a horrendous clash of steel and splintering wood the two sides met.

* * *

Using the narrow gateway to even the playing field the English kept the Spanish at bay, preventing them from leaving the fort, making their numbers count for nothing. In this close proximity their spears had a devastating effect. Several Spanish men-at-arms went down in the first moment of impact as the spears found gaps in their armour, piercing arm pits and throats alike. With a grunt, Richard hefted his own, which slid straight into the eye socket of the newly-appointed Spanish captain before he even had the chance to close his visor.

"Hold them boys, hold them," Richard demanded of his men. Spurred on by the sound of his voice, they stabbed and jabbed and more Spaniards fell under the English barrage, only to be trampled on by their comrades from behind. The men at the front were walking targets but the men behind were just as vulnerable as the English archers were shooting arrows over the top causing them to hold their shields aloft. Some arrows thudded into wood but others sank deep into Spanish flesh.

Delmar watched on in horror as the small English force made light work of his own. He could see his brother's face in his mind and it was laughing at him. Fury surged through him. "Their spears, you stupid cunts, cut their bloody spears!"

One of his men heard the command, despite the cries of men and the deafening clash of iron and steel. As an Englishman lunged at him with a spear, he managed to dodge to the side, the point of the spear deflecting off his vambrace harmlessly and as it did so he slammed down his sword and cleaved the flimsy spear in two. The Englishman who had attacked with such confidence now looked at the broken shard of wood in his hand in dismay. Due to the effectiveness of the spears, most of the English men-at-arms had taken to throwing down their shields, using two hands to get a better thrust. Before the Englishman even had time to retrieve his sword from his scabbard the Spanish man-at

-arms rammed forth his own, the point of the blade piercing through gambeson and chain mail before crushing through several ribs and puncturing a lung.

Once one man went down, more followed when the Spanish realised how easy it was to counteract the threat the spears had become. They were nothing but fragile sticks of wood and one clean cut of the sword was enough to render them useless. All across the front of the English line, spears were broken, allowing the Spanish men-at-arms to come within sword distance of their opponents. They took full advantage of their numbers which still outweighed the English by more than a hundred men. Sword met sword in a savagely fierce contest but it was the Spanish who were on the charge using their shields to press the English and force them back from the gate.

"We must hold them here, we must!" came Richard's cry. The Englishmen dug their feet into the ground and tried desperately to stem the Spanish tide that would soon wash over them, but it was to no avail. The Spanish momentum was too great and anything that stood in its path was cast aside.

The Spanish, with an almighty final push, forced the English from within the confines of the gate and back out into the open field. Spanish men-at-arms spilt from the fort and outflanked the English men-at-arms. The archers were now vulnerable targets and with little or no armour they didn't stand a chance. Nevertheless, they threw down their bows and unsheathed their short swords at Alexandre's command.

"To the death, to the death!" he shouted, taking the sword that was granted to him by his father, the true Lord of Albacete. He surged forth in defiance of death and met his brother's men head on. The English were now surrounded on all sides, and it would not be long before they were overwhelmed yet they fought on with a brutal passion that Richard thought never possible.

* * *

Delmar knew the end was in sight. He smiled his evil smile and basked in the ambiance of this small but wonderfully satisfying victory. He thought of his brother. *This time, dear brother, you will not be let off so easily, this time you will die and I will do the honour myself.* Suddenly there was a low rumble in the distance, and though it was probably of no significant importance it wiped the smile from Delmar's face nonetheless. *Was that thunder?* He heard it again. This time it was louder and it sounded closer. *What in God's name was that?* He heard it again, and this time he recognised it as chanting, but who or what they were saying he could not make out. Then out of nowhere they appeared from the trees, hundreds of them, townspeople and villagers alike, peasants of all sorts, butchers, blacksmiths and even women. Their chant rent the air and the unmistakable, undeniable sound reached Delmar's ears. "Jim-én-ez! Jim-én-ez! Jim-én-ez!" It was his family name, but it was not to him that they referred; he lost that right the day he was banished by his father. The true Señor Jiménez of Albacete had returned and the people had risen in rebellion to join his cause.

"Close the gates!" he called to one of his men. "Close the goddamned gates!"

"But my Lord, we have men out there!" he replied in horror.

"Do not disobey me or by God I swear I'll cut your fucking head off!"

The soldier mustered a few companions and together they hurried down to the gate. Already a few of those closest to the fort, sensing the early threat, had run back through, and they were the lucky ones. The wooden gate was shut with an almighty thud and the men inside went about barricading it. Realising what was going on, the Spanish men-at-arms caught on the outside turned from the fight and huddled outside the gate, banging the hilts of their swords on it demanding to be let in, their screams of terror almost unbearable to be heard. The soldier tasked with closing the gate was on the brink of tears and had to walk away, unable to witness the inevitable onslaught. Already those at the back were forced to defend themselves against the Englishmen who until moments ago they had defeated. The blaring chant that had been taken up by the newcomers came to a shattering halt, to be replaced by a deafening roar, followed by the thunderous sound of hundreds of feet as they came tearing across the field. Now the retribution began.

Richard turned at the call of his name.

"Ricardo?" Paulo called. "Shall we build a ram, to break down the gate?"

Richard turned to assess the fort. Half the palisade was up in flames and it was spreading. "I doubt that will be necessary, Paulo. It will have burnt down before too long. Delmar isn't going anywhere so for now we just wait, reserve our strength."

"Richard! Richard!" he heard someone else cry. It was Joseph.

"I am here, Joseph," he replied, spotting him amongst the thousand people now assembled outside Chinchilla. They embraced. "I knew you could do it, I knew it."

Joseph smiled. "You'll be surprised, it was relatively easy. How were you faring without us?"

Richard returned the smile. "We were bloody struggling! Could you not have come sooner?"

"Ah we had a little trouble with the town's garrison. They put up a blockade in the town square. But unfortunately for them I don't think they quite grasped the intensity of the uprising. Within an hour of arriving we had accumulated a mob of over seven hundred, while they had less than one. In the end most of them barricaded themselves inside an inn which we burnt to the ground."

"I see more than seven hundred here," Richard replied, glancing around at the huge gathering, not entirely able to believe it.

"Aye, near one thousand you see before you. Every farm and village we passed, more and more wished to join us. If only you could have been there to see it."

"What on earth did you say to get them so riled?"

Joseph thought back to that glorious moment in the square. They had successfully overcome the town's garrison, their inn was up in flames and the people of the town sang and danced in jubilation. But there was hushed silence the moment he took centre stage and raised himself up onto the well...

* * *

"Do you see?" Joseph had asked the people. "Do you see for yourselves the nature and the cowardice of the men who look to oppress you? Tonight they feared you and it is only fitting that they should. Too long have you lived in fear of these men, too long has it been since they came, defiled your woman and murdered your children. They should know by now, that if you treat the dog badly then it is only a matter of time before the dog bites back!" A wall of noise erupted from the townspeople which echoed in the square. "People of Albacete, my friends, tonight you have bitten back, tonight you have stood up in the face of tyranny and sent out a message to any who would look to enslave you, that you will not bow down to their wills and their ways, that you are not here to placate their pleasures and desires, but you are free!"

The roar intensified again. "You have done your town proud tonight, but I would ask one more thing of you. Alexandre Jiménez, your right and lawful Lord, has returned to you this night to free you from your tormentor and with the help of his great and powerful friend, one of your country's greatest heroes, Señor Ricardo de Guadalest who some of you may know as El Cazador, have attacked the fortress of Chinchilla. There as we speak, outnumbered, they fight and they die to see you get your freedom."

The roar of noise turned to gasps as the people of Albacete were told this news. "Will you stand with me, will you come to the aid of Alexandre, will you come to Chinchilla and there avenge the deaths of your family and friends and rid yourself of this tyrant once and for all? Will you fight?" A ripple of noise spread over the crowd as they turned to their neighbours and spoke to one another. But there was one voice that rang high above the rest.

"I fight!" cried the innkeeper of El Brújula.

"And me!" came the voice of Victor.

Several voices echoed the call and soon nearly all were dedicating their lives to the rebellion.

"You have our answer," said the innkeep. "We fight!"

The townsfolk took up the chant. "Fight! Fight! Fight!"

"You have done well, Joseph," Santé leaned in and whispered.

"Aye, that may be, but let's just hope we are not too late," he replied before raising his voice to the people. "To Chinchilla then, and may God bless us all!"

* * *

Delmar could not have foreseen this; his brother's return accompanied with English compatriots, the town of Albacete coming to his aid and now, after losing over three quarters of his force, he was forced to barricade the gate. But all he had done was effectively imprison the remainder of his men. From the moment the people of Albacete arrived, the people of Chinchilla rose against him too, and with his remaining men in disarray they were swatted down like flies by the locals and torn apart on the streets by the bare hands of those that could get close enough to touch them. The chaos and destruction was relentless and if Delmar wanted to live he had but one choice; to get back to the castle and hold up until his brother offered him terms. Racing through the streets on his destrier Delmar rode with frightening speed, trampling anyone unfortunate enough to get in his way.

The castle itself was higher up from the rest of the town,

nestled at the top of a hill. To enter it you needed to cross a raised causeway. At the top of the causeway under an archway protected either side by towers were thick wooden doors that led to the castle's courtyard. These had been closed and barricaded by those that remained in the castle. The two towers that loomed over the causeway were joined at the top and it was on these ramparts between his banner and that of the Governor of Murcia's that Delmar stood. He gazed down at the mob that had formed as it climbed up the causeway and attempted to break down the doors. It was not long before they were joined by Alexandre and the hundreds of others that had been waiting outside the fort until its walls were reduced to ash. Over a thousand stretched down the hill as far as Delmar could see and they all watched as the red head of Alexandre wove its way up the causeway between his people.

"Brother," Delmar called down. "What is it that I can do for you? Do you wish to come inside and discuss matters?"

"What I want," said Alexandre with unnatural venom, "is for you to come down here and answer for your crimes. We have unfinished business, you and I!"

"You will have to forgive me, brother, for I must decline."

"You should go down to him." A soft voice spoke from behind Delmar.

Delmar turned to see the girl who had been tormented by his hands on so many occasions. The last time had been that very evening. She was dressed now, Delmar observed, and she had that defiant look in her face that she so often possessed. *He would soon break it, as he always did.*

"Shut up, you stupid whore!" he shouted before back-handing her across the face. He hit her with incredible force but still she stood, blood trickling from her lip down her chin.

Delmar turned back at his brother's call but he could not make out the words that had been said. He was too overcome with incredible pain and his fingernails scratched deep into the stone on which they were set. He felt the dagger penetrate almost as if in slow motion. It cut first through the flesh in his lower back before slicing deep into his kidney. He tried to speak but no words would come out, his head spun and his vision blurred, he swayed on the spot for a moment unable to keep his balance, his hands slipping on the stone before he lurched forward and fell from the ramparts.

He landed on his back with a sickening, bone breaking thump. Those below had to hurriedly push each other out of the way to avoid being landed on. To everyone's astonishment the giant of a man known as Delmar was still alive. He coughed and blood spurted forth from his mouth; his breath, what was left of it, was rattling. He watched through blood-shot eyes as Alexandre approached him, sword in hand. Delmar spoke, with incredible pain as he rasped, "Have you come to watch me suffer?"

"No, brother, I am not like you," Alexandre replied before piercing his heart.

Chapter Nineteen

Order of the Rose
Guadalest, Crown of Aragón.
November, 1513.

"In all of us there is a hunger, marrow deep, to know our heritage - to know who we are and where we came from. Without this enriching knowledge, there is a hollow yearning."
Alex Haley

Twenty eight years earlier...
...It was a warm evening. Father Jacob found himself rolling down the dirt track that led into the village of Guadalest. It was a beautiful place, he thought. High in the Spanish hills set deep in a vast valley that wound down to the sea. The sea was visible in the far distance, yet even so it must be miles to the coast. Despite that, there was the vague taste of salt on the priest's tongue. The wind must have carried it all the way up here. He took his hat from his head and mopped his brow before taking a swig of water from his flask. God bless the Spanish weather, he thought, in England they would have been hit by the early autumn chill, but here? No, the summers were twice as long, swamping up most of the spring and autumn with blissful sun. Though thankfully not as hot as previous months at least, the weather had been kind to Father Jacob on his travels. He had travelled alone, as was his wish, but he had come in his wagon which had proved a welcome source of accommodation along the road and his horse who had provided a silent but welcome companion.

He entered the village along its main street and found himself in the village square. It was mostly deserted except for one elderly man helping himself to some water from the town's well. No doubt this was where the locals came to trade on market days, meat, fruits, furs and such. There were only a few buildings that comprised the village of

Guadalest, most built from stone but there were still some wooden structures, all with thatched roofs. Some of them were houses but most were mainly small shops. There was a blacksmith, Father Jacob observed, and a bakery but the biggest building to the right of the square was the village inn and there were two middle aged gentlemen sitting outside, swigging ale from their tankards, enjoying the evening glow.

"Excuse me, gentlemen?" Father Jacob asked as he pulled up outside the inn. "But do any of you speak English? Eng-lish?"

They looked up at him at least, but he couldn't have hoped for much more because they clearly hadn't understood a word he'd just said. Rather than try and respond, however, they just sat there, staring at him. One of them did kindly take the time to snort rather grotesquely before spitting on the floor in front of him.

"Right then, I suppose I'll just move on, sorry for your trouble."

Just as Father Jacob made to rap the reins on his horse he saw, out of the corner of his eye, one of the men raise his arm. He was pointing towards the street. There was a man approaching, older than the two gentlemen here, perhaps in his late sixties. Father Jacob had to put his hand above his eyes and squint in the low evening sunlight to see him, but as the man came closer Father Jacob recognised him as the man from the well he had passed on his way into the village. He was carrying a heavy wooden bucket full of water.

"My dear sir," said Father Jacob. "Do you speak English?"

The elderly man glanced up at him, somewhat surprised. "Aye, a little, my son in law taught me. What can I do for you, father?"

"May I offer you a ride home, Sir? Perhaps we could talk on the way?"

The man looked at the priest sceptically but the look faded. "I suppose that would be welcome, for these legs aren't what they once used to be." He passed up his bucket of water to Father Jacob before climbing on board. Father Jacob clasped it and lifted it into the wagon with surprising ease for a man of the church, but the man took no notice.

"Do you live near?" Father Jacob asked.

"Not far," he replied. "Just down the road there a little ways." He pointed to the road leading out the other side of the village.

They set off and as the wagon trundled off down the street it left a trail of dust in its wake, much to the annoyance of the two men sitting outside the inn. For a while they sat in silence but when they were a little way from the town, the old man spoke. "So what brings an English priest this far into Spanish countryside?"

"I am looking for someone," Father Jacob replied casually. "An English knight who may have frequented these parts."

"Do you know his name? A name always helps."

"His name is Robert Longsword."

"Why do you seek this man?"

"I made a promise to him."

The elderly man thought for a moment. "I may know of this man that you speak, but it has been many years since I have seen him."

"Were you close to him?" asked Father Jacob.

"You could say that, I suppose," he replied. "I had hoped you might be able to bring me news of him, but if you say you are searching for him yourself, then we are both at a loss. I am afraid you will not find anything of him here. He went back to England a long time ago."

Father Jacob sighed. "I have not been frank, and for that I apologise, but one can never be too careful. You say your son in law taught you to speak English. Tell me, was that Sir Robert himself?"

The elderly man looked at the priest. "I saw how easily you hefted my bucket back there, and only a working man could have lifted it so easily. You are no priest, are you?"

Father Jacob smiled. "Ah, you have keen eyes, my friend. No, I am not. I am of all things an innkeep. My true name is James Clifford. I was, I am sad to say, a friend of Robert's."

"He is dead, then?"

"He is dead. He died two years ago."

"I had feared as much, James, I had feared as much. It had been so long since I had seen or heard from him. You are right in your assumption. My name is Mario Dellatorre. Robert was married to my daughter, my beautiful daughter. She died of fever nine years ago, not long after the boy was born. He was a good man, Robert, a very good man. He treated my daughter well and he kept his promises."

"Well, I come to honour one."

"Then we have much to discuss. Please, you are welcome in my home. But first tell me, why a priest?" He laughed.

"Ah, it was the only way to travel alone without fear of being robbed. Who attacks a priest, after all? If there's one thing even men of the sword fear, it's God's wrath. Robert had bitter enemies and I carry precious cargo," he said, patting the wooden seat between himself and Mario.

The wagon rolled on and they reached a bend that passed a small woodland on the right and a hill to the left. As they emerged around the hill, it opened up into farmland. But strikingly evident in the background atop a particularly high hill was a castle, its keep looming tall above the rest. "Who lives there?" James asked.

"No one. For a while it was abandoned but it belongs to Giovanni Borgia now, the Duke of Gandia. The title along with the castle and this land was bought for his brother by his father Pope Alexander but it passed to him. But of course, they live at the Papal Palace in Rome. Who knows? Maybe one day when he is not in Italy he will return to claim it. But for now, it lies empty."

They trundled on down the road and reached a crossroads where upon they turned right and made their way along a wooded path, coming out the other end to cross a stream that ran across the road. They crossed through the ford, the horses' hooves splashing as they went, and followed the open road that ran alongside a field.

"That's my olive grove there," Mario said, pointing to a clump of trees at the far end of the field. "My house is at the top end there beyond the grove, you'll see it when we pass over the next hill."

And there it was, it was a very small house. Its structure had been made from timber and then the walls had been filled in with plain wooden panels, the gaps of which had been crammed in with mud. It had a thatched roof with slits for windows but it did have a large stone chimney. Just to the back of the house, the roof of a very small barn was visible which no doubt you could get to if you followed the road round a little ways, and beyond that was woodland. When they reached the end of the field they turned left. The road now ran between the house on the right and the olive grove on the left, where beneath a particularly massive olive tree was a boy sitting alone. They pulled to a halt by the gate, where there was a path that ran through a small garden to the front door of the house. The garden had a wooden fence around it.

"Come, boy! Get inside. What have I told you about being out after hours, huh?" The boy hurriedly scuffled passed but as he did so the old man gave him a boot up the backside sending the boy to the floor with a humph. "Get up, Ricardo! Get inside and get cleaned up!"

The boy stood up and brushed the dirt from his clothes. "Sí, Mario," he replied, before walking into the house.

"Is that him?" James asked. "He looks just like Robert."

"Aye, that he does."

"Why does he call you by name?"

Mario, who was now leading James towards the house, stopped in his tracks, took a deep breath before responding. "He does not know that I am his grandfather nor does he know his true name and he must never find out. We call him Ricardo."

"But why?"

"Robert told me of this feud between his family and his enemies. He said that if it was to end, it would end with him. In truth I knew the day Robert left that he would never return. I will not see Richard face that same fate. I would keep the boy safe from harm. I will not have him caught up in this and if that means I have to pretend he is an orphan that I picked up off the street then so be it. I cannot have the boy growing up asking questions. He is a curious boy, and he would seek his father out, of that I am sure. He would make it easy for Robert's enemies to find him. James, we cannot let this happen. I treat the boy something terrible and one day I will pay for this sin. Every day I see my daughter in him and every day it kills me to do the things I must. But he is all I *have left of her, and he must survive."*

"I must tell you the reason I am here."

"Let's not talk out here. Come inside. You must meet my wife. She will make us some supper."

James followed Mario into a large room that provided a combined living space and kitchen. Richard was in the corner of the room washing his dusty face in a wash basin. He looked up to see the stranger as he entered. James smiled at him but he quickly averted his gaze.

"You done, boy?" Mario asked Richard. The boy nodded in return. "Then get yourself to bed and be quick about it."

"I wish you wouldn't be so hard on him," a soft voice said as a woman entered the room. She was carrying vegetables in her apron.

"What would you have me do? We have spoken of this; you know the reasons."

"I just wish there was another way," she replied.

"As do I, my love, if only there were." He sighed. "Anyway, we have an unexpected guest."

"I had noticed," she retorted before smiling at James. "Will you be joining us for supper? It will only be soup and bread."

"It would be most welcome," James answered.

"Wonderful," she replied before turning on her husband. "Are you going to introduce us?"

"Sofia, this is James Clifford. He was a friend of Robert's."

"It is a pleasure, Señora," James said.

"We have been expecting you," she replied.

"You have?"

"Well, we weren't expecting Robert but we knew someone would come."

"So, what is it that brought you all this way, my friend?" Mario asked James while Sofia fetched a knife to start chopping the vegetables.

"It has not been easy, that I can assure you. I will make it as plain as I can. Robert found information that turned the English civil war on its head in favour of the Lancastrians, but it came at a price. He was killed by the Yorkists before the information could be placed in the right

hands. Before he died, sensing his death was imminent, he tasked me to deliver it. It was the last time we ever spoke. But I was successful, however, and I took Robert's place and fought in his honour in the subsequent battle at Bosworth Field two years later. I did this because I made him a promise. This promise was that whatever reward was given for his information, information that gifted Henry VII the English throne, that I would see it safely to his son, to you."

Sofia had stopped chopping by this point. "Dear God," she whispered.

"He always wanted a better life for his son than this," Mario told James.

"Well, now he can," James replied. "Outside there is a wagon full of gold, and it is yours to do with as you will."

Mario laughed. "That gold will be the end of us, it is too dangerous. It cannot be kept here."

"There I agree with you. Robert's enemies know the gold exists and they have eyes everywhere. I fear they will not rest until they find it."

"Then we must hide it and never speak of it until such a time that it is safe to do so," Sofia said.

"By right it is Richard's and it is his to do with as he wills. We will inform him of this, but only, only when the boy is of an age to understand. While the gold exists and he lives his life will always be in danger. So we must hide it," Mario demanded.

"Where?" asked his wife.

"Oh, I have an idea."

* * *

Richard strolled around the grounds of his old house. So many of his young years had been spent here and just looking at it filled him with unhappy memories, most of which he thought he had forgotten. Perhaps it would have been for the best; maybe it was a life better left forgotten. He remembered an elderly couple that never loved him, the long tiring days they forced him to work and look after the animals and the questions, so many questions he had wanted answers to about his parents but he never found them. What had there been for him here, other than misery and pain? But that wasn't entirely true. He remembered going to the village and playing with the other boys and girls there when the old man had let him, and then there was the day he met his beautiful wife Louisa in the market place. Most importantly of all, however, he remembered what James had said. He was not raised by some random couple that had never loved him, but his grandparents who only did what they did to protect him.

So they did love me after all. Even his wife had taken a liking to the place when they had come to visit nearly ten years ago and he had to admit he too felt some kind of connection to the place. He was drawn to it, perhaps that is why he ended up buying it from the Castellan. So maybe he was wrong, maybe it was not a painful and lonely place after all but a place for a loving family that had only lost its way, lost each other.

"Do you miss her?" Maria asked.

He was still getting used to the sound of his daughter's voice. She had after all spent some months as Grenwick's prisoner; she too had been lost but now she was found. She had also been sent to stay with the General Córdoba upon their return to Spain while Richard and Alexandre saw to the tyrant Delmar. He had recalled her for his visit back to this place, because he did not want to be alone. Alexandre had remained in Albacete while Santé had returned to the General. Paulo and Gringo, on the other hand, had taken the opportunity to visit Alcalalí while Joseph had accompanied his men back to Portchester. Richard's place was of course in England now as Baron of Portchester and his loyalty lay with King Henry. But there was one final thing that he had to do. "Aye, I miss her, I miss a lot of people. But that doesn't mean they are not here with us."

Maria was not the only person that had been lost to him. His grandfather had been lost as well. Richard had had no idea that the whole time he was posted up at the old fort that his grandfather had lived, but the question that haunted Richard was why he never showed himself. Richard's eyes wandered to the trees and his memory flashed to the moment he had followed his grandfather into the trees only to be frightened beyond belief. There was something in there that his grandfather visited regularly, something that he had not wanted Richard to see.

"Wait here," Richard told his daughter. "I won't be long."

Richard moved to the trees, following the tree line along a little way until he found the remnants of a familiar little path that ran into the trees, overgrown and invisible to the naked eye. He pushed back the long hanging branches that threatened to tear away at his clothes and for a moment just stared down the winding path. He took a deep breath before taking a step forward to be swallowed up into the green abyss. He waded through the knee length grass, pushing back the branches which scratched at him. He forced his way through for several minutes until he reached a small clearing. The grass here was not long and quite surprisingly it looked as though it had been attended to. In the centre of the clearing there was no mistaking the two gravestones. This was a private graveyard.

Richard approached the gravestones cautiously, unsure of what he was about to see. *So this is where my grandfather used to come all those years ago? This is what he did not wish for me to see.* He knelt down in front of the graves, which had recently cropped flowers, Richard did not fail to observe. He ran his eyes over the names to which were carved crudely into the stones. On the left hand stone was carved the name, Sofia Dellatorre, the old woman, and on the right one, Josephine Dellatorre.

"Your grandmother and your mother," a weary voice said behind him, a voice he had not heard for near thirty years. "I wondered when you would come back here, boy."

Richard stood and turned to look at the old man who so many years ago chased him from this place and made him swear never to come back here. He was cloaked and he lowered his hood to reveal a very old and worn looking face with several lines across his brow and down his cheeks. He leant on a stick but it did not stop him from moving closer to Richard. "You were always so obedient, I thought perhaps you might never come. I have wronged you, dear boy and I have forgiveness to ask of you."

"*Abuelo?*"

"*Sí,*" the old man replied, tears welling in his eyes.

"Grandfather," Richard gasped and rushed forward to hold him. He was the only living survivor of a family that Richard had never known he had and for a brief moment the two men embraced one another, silent tears falling down their cheeks. "Why did you never show yourself? I came back here and all along you were alive."

"After your grandmother died, I had nothing left. The people of the village said I went mad, but there is a difference between madness and acceptance. I accepted death willingly and so decided to live out my remaining days here in the woods close to my wife and daughter; except I did not die, I kept on living. God yet had a purpose for me and I knew, I knew what it was. It was so that I may see you again and put right the wrongs that were done to you. But when the day came, the day you came home, I just couldn't do it. You arrived with your wife and daughter and you were so happy, you had found a life worth living away from all this grief and despair and I could not bring myself to change all that."

"But it was not a good life. We were struggling to make ends meet, and we had no money."

"My dear boy, I wanted nothing more than to tell you where the gold was, but even after all these years it was still dangerous. I received letters from James saying that Grenwick and his men were abroad searching for it. I knew if I told you, even then, it would open up a world that was better left avoided. You had a wife and a young daughter. I would not have jeopardised that for all the gold in the world. I knew you needed money and that's why I wrote to the Duke the moment you had returned to Guadalest, so he might offer you a job at the fort."

"I thought it was the Castellan who recommended me?"

"The Castellan was my friend and between us we made sure the Duke could not refuse. We knew the day that James arrived with the gold that something had to be done and so we started a secret order, the sole purpose of which was the protection of the last living descendent of the Longsword House, and of course your inheritance. We named it the Order of the Rose in memory of your father. There were few members; your grandmother and I were two of them, the Castellan was another, there was James your father's friend of course, and finally the General Córdoba of whom you are so fond. Yet for all those years we kept our word and saw to your safety and kept the gold hidden. Then to my astonishment you returned to these lands unexpectedly, a man grown and with a family of your own. Yet even then I knew it was not yet time to reveal the truth of the gold to you, it would only have brought pain and misery upon your family. But I saw no reason why you could not protect it unknowingly."

"The gold is at the fort, isn't it?"

"Aye, that it is and it has been for twenty eight years. I made a deal with Giovanni Borgia many years ago. I would make small annual payments if he would allow for me to hide my family heirlooms in the fort and we would provide him with a garrison to man the fort. Therein lays the reasoning behind the Guardians of Guadalest."

"But I was captain for several years and in all of that time I have never seen the gold."

"You wouldn't. That is an old Moorish fort, and there is a secret chamber, a vault where the gold remains hidden. In the days of old it would have been a crypt, a place to bury the lords of the castle that would preserve them undamaged, so if ever the castle be taken they would remain hidden and unmolested. That is where the gold is hidden."

"If the gold is so well hidden, how did they know to come by Guadalest? How did they find me?"

"Giovanni Borgia died two years after I made the deal with him. His son took his place as Duke of Gandia and he honoured the arrangement I made with his father, but he showed a bigger interest in what was going on here than his father did. It was him that I wrote to and requested you be taken on as captain of the guard and I was surprised by how willing he was to have you. He said you and he had some unfinished business."

"Oh he did, did he?" Richard remembered the scrawny youth who tried to stop him from taking Louisa all those years ago. In truth Richard had forgotten all about him and he was no boy any more but a young man full grown, with money and power; he would make a difficult enemy.

"He led me to believe you were friends, but there was something in the words that spoke differently. Instantly he made me feel uncomfortable but what choice did I have but to trust him? How do you know him?"

"My wife Louisa," he said. "She was the boy's maid when I found her in Rome. He has been besotted by her his whole life and he hates me for taking her away. Little did I know when I arrived home that the little shit had inherited this land from his father."

"Then I think we have found our rat. Nothing cuts a man deeper than a woman's love. He must have informed Grenwick that you were here in Guadalest, but he didn't know that the gold was here. He couldn't, for even you did not know."

"Simon knows."

"Simon knows? But how is this possible?"

"James." Richard sighed with regret.

"James told him?"

"James is dead, grandfather. I did not know, but Simon followed me to London and after I met with James, Simon killed him, but not before he revealed the gold's location."

"Dear God, then we must hurry before he finds it."

"I know Simon, he will not take the gold and run. I killed his father, and he will want revenge."

"Then what will you do?"

"I will go to the fort alone. It's time to finish this."

Chapter Twenty

Castle of Guadalest
Guadalest, Crown of Aragón.
November, 1513.

"Be of good cheer about death and know this as a truth that no evil can happen to a good man, either in life or after death."
Socrates

Richard gazed upon the remains of the castle from within the fortress walls. It had been reduced to nothing more than blackened stone. Most of the walls remained other than what had crumbled down when the roof caved in. The remnants were now no more than blackened timber and ash. Everything else that had been inside the castle had been incinerated. The rest of the fort, however, had gone relatively unmolested other than the stables, which had been sealed by the same fate as the castle.

It was strange, the way that Richard felt. Once this place had felt like home, but now it was just a ruin and it meant nothing to him. He had no attachment to it anymore, yet still it clouded his mind with hatred and a sense of betrayal. He had been given up to his enemies by the Duke of Gandia, the boy who had loved his wife, and he had been befriended by Simon, who played his part so well that Richard would have done anything for him and what did he get in return for that trust, for that friendship? His daughter and wife were taken from him and although he had found his daughter he would never have the chance to speak to his wife again, to feel her in his arms, the warmth of her skin, her love. There was nothing left for him here in Guadalest.

There was one building inside the walls of the fort that had been completely untouched by the assault and the fire. In the north east corner of the fort, made entirely of stone, was an ancient Moorish mausoleum, a burial chamber or tomb as the Guardians used to call it. It looked eerily preserved amongst the rest of the fort. Richard had only ever entered the building once, a long time ago with Simon, who had seemed fascinated by its purpose. Now it was nothing more than a house of the dead. *How I was wrong.* Richard crossed the courtyard and approached the small stone building. It had been made with expert hands and had been designed with a heavy stone door. The door itself was difficult to force open after years of no use, but it was ajar when Richard came to it.

Someone had already been here.

Richard forced his way through the gap. It was dark inside so he lit a torch. It was a small rectangular room tiled underfoot by great stone slabs, most of which were covered in an inch of dust. At the far end, next to each other, were two sarcophagi that had contained the bodies of two Moorish lords; or so Richard had been led to believe. But the lids of both had been pushed to the floor, and the stone lay cracked and broken. Richard edged across the stone slabs towards them to peer inside and as he approached he knew that they were empty. They had always been empty. There was a noise underfoot as Richard trod on a loose slab. He lowered the torch to the ground and bent down to observe the slab. It was a slab that Richard had examined on his last visit to the tomb. It lay in the centre of the room and on it were etched words in Arabic.

تَ حت الـ حجر يـ قع عـلى جـ ثث الـ لوردات
عـلى الـ رغم من أن حـ يات هم قـ د دتَ مر عـ بر مداخل إلـ ى الـ سماء
أجـ سادهم لا تَ زال قـ ائ مة ويـ جب أن يـ كون هناك يـ سـ تريـ ج حـ تى
ذهايـ ة أيـ ام
تَ دذ يس لـ هم بـ عـ يدا عن أولـ ئك الـ ذيـ ن يـ سعون إلـ ى
الـ كـ نز الـ مخـ في اذ تظار إلـ ى الأيـ د لـ هؤلاء
جديـ ر الـ عـ ثور عـ لـ يهم

Richard could not speak Arabic but he ran his fingers over the words. He knew what they said all the same. He remembered his last visit and he heard a voice from behind him. *"Beneath the stone lie the bodies of great lords, though their souls may pass through the doorways of heaven, their bodies remain and there shall they rest until the end of days, far from those who would seek to desecrate them, a hidden treasure for all eternity waiting only for those worthy enough to find them."*

Richard turned to see Simon - except he was not there, yet the memory had seemed so vivid, so real.

* * *

"I did not know you could speak Arabic," Richard remembered asking.

"There are a lot of things you do not know about me," Simon had replied. "I speak Latin as well. Does that impress you?"

"Not really," Richard smiled.

"So what do you suppose that means, then?" Simon asked pointing to the slab.

"Well, obviously the bodies of the lords lie beneath the stone," he said, pointing to the sarcophagi. "It is as it says, I suppose."

"What about the bit about treasure?" Simon asked. "You don't think there is any here, do you?"

"Here? Are you mad? This fort has been in Spanish hands for hundreds of years. Do you think if there was ever anything here it would not have been found? Besides, the hidden treasure is not gold but the bodies of those that lie within the sarcophagi. Treasure means many different things to different people, Simon, and the Moors prized their leaders above wealth."

"So there is no gold hidden inside them?"

"What is it with you and your obsession with gold? No, of course there isn't. If I was going to hide gold I would think of somewhere a little less obvious then a coffin. The only things you'll find in there are two dead bodies." That seemed to satisfy Simon's thoughts because he

did not enquire anymore of gold. "Come on, let's get out of here. This place gives me the creeps."

"It's strange though, don't you think?"

"What is?" Richard asked.

"Well, it says the bodies will remain hidden for all eternity. Well, they're not exactly well hidden, are they, they're two great big bloody sarcophagi inside a burial vault. They're not exactly hard to find, are they?"

That was a strange thought. Richard could not deny Simon had a fair point. But he thought it unwise to encourage Simon and his desire to find buried treasure. "Perhaps we are just worthy," he said, taking one last look at the slab before closing the heavy stone door.

* * *

Richard ran his fingers over the writing and felt the slab move under the touch of his fingertips. *So perhaps there was another meaning after all.* Richard pressed his fingers into the cracks around the slab and gripped it. He lifted it with a grunt and placed it as gently as he could against the wall. Beneath where the slab had been, in place of what should have been earth, was a wooden panel with a handle attached to it. It was a trap door, and he lifted it to see a staircase winding down into the darkness.

So this was the crypt that Mario spoke of. Taking his torch, Richard carefully wound his way down the steps. The walls were damp and the air was stagnant down here. When he reached the bottom of the staircase he came out onto a corridor and on either side of the corridor, built into the walls, were on separate shelves the bodies of ancient Moors, the treasures that had been hidden. But it was not the same treasure that Richard was looking for. He only hoped that he was worthy to find what he was looking for, as the words on the slab said. The sound of Simon's voice was ringing in his ears.

He came to the end of the corridor and here there was another staircase leading down. Richard followed but there were not many steps. They led to a circular room and it was empty except for a single chest that lay open in the middle of the room. Richard approached it cautiously and inside he found only a letter that bore the seal of the Duke of Gandia. The seal had been broken and the letter already read but Richard picked it up and read the words.

As you took something precious from me, I shall take something precious from you.

Reading the words, he pictured the face of Juan Borgia, laughing at him. He had underestimated the slimy youth whom he had never thought of as a threat. He saw the anger in the young boy's face all those years ago, but never thought for a second that he would seek revenge; yet now he had it. Louisa was dead and the Duke had the gold. He felt a stab of pain in his chest and anger cut through him.

Then Richard remembered something, something he had said to Simon the last time he was here. "Treasure means many different things to different people, Simon." He had not been wrong, the gold had proved to be the downfall of two great families, the Longswords and the Ashbournes and all that remained of them both were two sons, Richard and Simon. The gold was cursed, Richard told himself, and the real treasure was in front of his eyes all along; his family. He had his daughter back and that was all that mattered to him in this world.

Richard left the tomb of the Moors and despite not having his father's gold in his possession, he left feeling lighter, like a weight had been lifted from his shoulders. He felt free. He pushed his way out of the tomb past the heavy stone door and out into the fresh air. The sunlight was hard on his eyes and he was forced to blink, but there was no mistaking the figure of the man who stood waiting for him.

"Hello, Simon."

"Richard Longsword," he replied. "I never thought to return to this place, least of all to find you. Yet here we stand."

"Yet here we stand," Richard repeated.

"It appears we have been betrayed by the same man," Simon carried on.

"How so?"

"The Duke told King Louis where we could find you. All he wanted was your wife and in return we would keep the gold."

"My wife lies dead and her blood is on your hands. The only traitor here is you. You betrayed your brothers, you betrayed your oath and you betrayed me."

"All I did, I did for my father, for my family. There is no shame in that."

"There is shame in the things you've done and more. I curse the day you walked into this fort."

"As do I brother, as do I."

Richard was seething. "Be gone from here, Simon, I never wish to see your face again. This ends today."

"You don't get it, do you? I have nowhere to go. I have nothing left. My family lost everything thanks to yours. That gold would have restored it all but now it's gone and you, you killed my father, you son of a bitch. There is only one thing left for me to do; to kill you!" Simon pulled his sword from its scabbard and pointed it at Richard. "You are right about one thing, though. It ends today. Let's see what El Cazador is made of!"

"So be it."

Richard knelt and grabbed a handful of dirt, rubbing it in the palms of his hands to improve his grip. He drew his sword and looked around the fort. So it had come to this, a three hundred year feud, the fate to be decided between the two remaining sons. They had once been the best of friends, they had once been brothers but now they would fight to the death and only the victor's name would live on in memory.

They edged closer together, swords raised, circling. Their breath was heavy and sweat dripped from their brows. Simon lunged with a roar and brought his sword down with ferocious force. Richard parried but the vibration tore up the nerves in his arm causing him to wince. But he had no time to dwell on it. Simon was not in a forgiving mood. He came at Richard again and again with brutal attacks, first high then low. There was no time to think, only to react. The years of training and experience on the battlefield were telling him what do.

Neither were particularly well armoured, which although making both more vulnerable to the steel they carried, did allow for easier manoeuvrability. They moved with pace and efficiency, neither backing down but pressing with determination. Simon, in his anger, led the charge in the early exchanges, forcing Richard to defend. There was no denying that Simon was a great swordsman but he was rash, too eager to attack and perhaps that would allow Richard a chance. Simon forced a low swinging blow towards Richard's legs and slamming down his sword Richard managed to pin Simon's sword to the floor. From this position, Richard was unable to get much force into the swing but he was able to cut his sword upward with enough power to slice a deep gash in Simon's arm, who grunted in pain.

Simon stumbled back and raised his other hand to his cut arm. When he pulled the hand away it was bathed in his own blood. He looked at it in anger before bringing his gaze back to Richard, his eyes bursting with fury. He came in with another scathing attack, and despite tiring he came in harder and faster than before, driven by the insanity and blood lust for his foe. Richard defended, parrying as he did before, he too was tiring but Simon's attack was relentless.

Simon's next blow came with such force that Richard, who temporarily had his sword in one hand, was knocked off balance and his defences were left open. Simon swung his sword round in an attempt to slash Richard's throat but Richard ducked back in time only for the tip of the blade to slit his cheek. Richard felt the warm rush of blood cascade down his cheek and onto his tunic. *This was it,* he realised, *life or death and Simon was up for the challenge.* Richard needed to change the game. He feigned to attack high and Simon fell for it, bringing his sword up to meet steel with steel that did not appear. Richard was already plunging his sword downwards which tore a gash in Simon's thigh, causing him to cry out in pain. Temporarily disorientated by the searing pain, Simon swung his sword back and forth blindly as he stumbled backwards. Richard rushed forward and grabbed Simon's sword arm as he attempted to swing it in Richard's direction. Using the hilt of his sword, Richard slammed it into Simon's face, again and again until Simon tripped over his own feet and crashed to the floor.

His nose was broken and blood poured into his mouth, and he spat a mixture of blood and tooth onto the ground. He heaved himself up and staggered into a standing position but not before he grabbed a handful of dirt from the floor. The two men stood apart, eyeing one another. Both were sporting injuries but it was Simon that looked the worse for wear. Richard approached him and as he did so he received a face full of dirt blinding him. Simon limped forward on his injured leg and attempted to finish Richard off. Richard wildly tried to fend off Simon's blows but with a certain amount of difficulty. He could only just make Simon out through his dirt gritted eyes that were uncomfortably sore as the sand grazed against his eyes every time he blinked.

The best Richard could do was back away, knowing Simon was finding it difficult to manoeuvre on his injured leg. His blood was seeping down into the sand and the dusty floor was turning red. Knowing this was his best chance, Simon put all his remaining energy into one final assault but Richard continued to defend valiantly.

Simon aimed a blow at Richard's head which came mightily close but Richard managed to fend the blow. Again Simon's blade made contact with Richard's face and raked a line across his forehead. Simon, mustering all his strength, hit Richard with a stinging blow. Richard blocked it but it forced his sword wide. Taking full advantage, Simon plunged his sword towards Richard's chest. Richard was able to dodge the worst of the blow but the blade slid past his side slicing into flesh and into the muscle between his rib cage.

Richard knew it was a serious wound and he would not be able to fight on for long, so he did the only thing he could. He brought down his arm and trapped Simon's blade between his ribs and arm. Simon tried wildly to free the blade, causing it to cut deeper into Richard's side and into his arm. But still Richard held on and grabbed the blade with his hand, which soon too began to bleed and pour blood onto the floor. With his free hand, Richard grabbed for his dagger, the jewel encrusted blade that had been given to him by his friend Alexandre. Simon, sensing what was about to happen, tried in vain to free the sword from Richard's grip but nearly all strength had left him. Horror spread across his face and the blood drained from his cheeks as his mouth opened and stammered, "No, no, no."

Richard raised the blade. He looked into Simon's terrified face and despite the overwhelming pain in his side took pleasure in what was about to happen.

"This," he said, "Is entirely for me." He ploughed the dagger into Simon's throat and felt the warm gush of blood pour down his arm. Simon's hand loosened its grip on his sword which fell from between Richard's arm and landed on the floor with a clatter. In the heat of the moment, pushing the pain aside, Richard took his other hand and grabbed Simon by the hair and forced the blade deeper into his neck. Simon crumpled to his knees and Richard went with him. Simon lifted his arm and rested it upon Richard's arm that grabbed the blade as blood frothed and splattered from his mouth. Despite everything that had happened, everything he had been through, Richard felt tears well up in his eyes and they flowed silently down his cheeks. Never in a thousand years did he ever think this day would come.

"I loved you!" he cried. "You were my brother. Between us we could have ended this stupid feud. We could have been friends. It didn't need to come to this."

"I know," Simon rasped as the light started to leave his eyes. "I'm sorry."

Simon died in Richard's arms and in doing so ended the Longsword feud with the Ashbournes that had ravaged on for over three hundred years. Three centuries of twisted bitter hatred that had spawned from generation to generation had passed down and endured through the Crusades, the Reconquista, the Hundred Years War and the Italian War until its remaining two survivors, who for a time had been sworn brothers and best of friends, now ended it like this.

Richard was distraught. Tears cascaded down his cheeks. All his life he had wanted to be loved, to be a part of something, a family. He finally thought he had found it, but then in the cruellest of circumstances he had lost the love of his life and now his best friend was dead. Simon's blood was on his hands. Painful memories started to pulse through Richard's head. He had wished that there could have been a peaceful resolution to this long ago, but men's hearts bleed anger and hate and war and death and this was, Richard knew, the only outcome. Only one family could live on in memory and today that was secured by Richard Longsword and he did it in the memory of his father who had died for him all those years ago.

Richard tore himself away from the body. He could no longer look at the man he had killed. His wound was sore and needed tending to but he would not leave until he had seen Simon properly buried. It took him a long time to dig the grave but he placed Simon's body in the hole next to his brothers who had been killed in the night of the assault. He may have played a part in their deaths but he had once been their friend and he had paid for his mistake with his own life. He would have Simon remembered in these parts as a proud member of the Guardians of Guadalest who died in service to the cause, not as some traitor that betrayed his friends.

Richard went to his horse and there retrieved the sword and shield Joseph had made for Simon, proudly embellished with the Guardian's sigil. Richard laid them on his grave.

When it was done, Richard collected his own sword and stumbled from the old fort and as he left, with a saddened heart, took one last look at the grave, the Moorish tomb and the ruined castle. He made himself a promise to never return to this place unless it meant putting the Duke of Gandia's head on a spike. But Richard had felt enough hate, pain and grief to last him a lifetime. Now it was a time to live and to enjoy the days that were left to him and what was left of his family. Wiping the crusted blood and sweat that had mingled and trickled from his face and run down his forehead and into his eyes on the back of his hand, he breathed a heavy sigh and turned from the fort and stumbled into the hills.

* * *

Richard staggered into the clearing to be greeted by an unpleasant sight. His grandfather was lying on the floor and his daughter was crouched over him. "What's wrong with him?" he asked her hurriedly.

"Father," she gasped. "You're hurt?" She rushed over to him to survey his wound. "We must get into the village and have someone look at that, father!"

"What's wrong with him?" Richard repeated.

Defeated, Maria returned to her great grandfather's side. "He just collapsed while you were gone," she said. "He has been clinging on to life in the hope that he might see you again, but I think in his heart he just wants to be reunited with his loved ones." She gazed to the headstones set in the centre of the clearing beneath which rested her great grandmother and grand-mother. There was a mumble from the floor.

"What did he say?" Richard asked, wincing as he clutched his chest.

"Did you get him?" Mario asked his grandson. "Did we win?"

Richard knelt down next to his daughter and grasped his grandfather's hand. "Aye, he is dead," he said, gripping it firmly. "We won."

"Good," he said. "Very good. I will tell your mother what I have seen you become."

Maria began to sob and even Richard had to fight back the tears.

"Are the tales true? About Granada and Cerignola?"

"Yes," Richard croaked.

"You remind me of El Cid." That made Richard smile. It was not the first time that had been said of him. "My ancestor fought alongside him, did I tell you?" Richard shook his head. "Yes, it was not just your father's side that has a proud history. I was a soldier myself, you know," he stammered. "I might not look it now but I was once strong and I could fight. I was there at the fall of Constantinople."

"Truly?"

"Aye, I fought alongside your father at the Battle of Castillon as well, that was before I returned to Eastern Europe and met Vlad III Dracula."

"The Impaler?" Richard asked.

"The very same. I was a mercenary, like you. I am proud of who I was and you should be proud of who you are. You truly did become the man you were born to be. Your father would be proud, I am only sorry I was not there to be part of it."

"You did what you had to and if it was not for what you did, I would probably not be here speaking to you today."

"Well I'm glad to see you are, although you won't be much longer if you don't get that seen to," he said, noticing the blood seeping from Richard's side. "I have lived my life, now you go and live yours."

"I will," Richard promised.

* * *

On the 15th October 1513 I buried my grandfather alongside my grandmother and my mother. I could not thank them enough for the sacrifices they had made for me. On that very same day I was made to bury my best friend who betrayed me and was a member of the house that has been at war with my own for over three hundred years and with his death it finally came to an end. I had avenged the death of my father and my wife who were so cruelly taken from me. Those integral to the monstrosities that befell me have been apprehended but there are still those who need to face justice. I am a knight and a mercenary. I fought for the Great Captain, General Córdoba and was victorious in the final battles of the Reconquista and the Italian war. I am "El Cazador" and my name is Sir Richard Longsword. I am Baron of Portchester and Alcalalí and a Knight of the Bath and this has been my story, but it is far from over.

Epilogue

Hôtel Tournelles
Paris, France. January, 1515.

"They come! Ships call! The hooves of night, the horses of the sea, come on below their manes of darkness. And forever the river runs. Deep as the tides of time and memory, deep as the tides of sleep, the river runs."
Thomas Wolfe

The Santa Maria carved her way through the waves of the English Channel. Maria stood on the deck, her face just visible in the moonlight. Her eyes were closed as she listened to the sound of the waves. Her heart was racing; she could feel it beating in her chest. She took a deep breath.

"Can you not sleep?" a comforting voice called.

Maria opened her eyes and smiled. "No, I'm afraid I cannot, yet it seems neither can you."

"Me?" Gonzalo mused. "I am old and frail, and there will be enough time for me to sleep in the afterlife. You however, you need your strength."

"Yes, you are right, as always. But never fear, my father's strength runs through my veins. There is no doubt in my mind. I will do what must be done."

"You truly are your father's daughter," the Great Captain replied, bringing a tear to his eye. He had watched Maria transform into a woman over the past year whilst in his care and he saw Richard in her now more than ever. *How I miss my apprentice.*

"I am glad to have you with me, Señor," she replied, placing a hand on his shoulder. "I could not have done this without you."

"Your father asked me to look after you and I have tried my

best to do so. Although I fear this mission is more dangerous that you can comprehend. But if I can protect you by my life or death then I will. There is a long life ahead of you, Maria, please, make it so."

Maria gazed out across the sea. Dawn was approaching and the coast of France was visible in the distance.

"We should have brought the Mary Rose. Then we could have blown them all to Hell," she said.

Gonzalo laughed. "The Mary Rose? There is peace now between England and France or had you failed to notice? King Louis himself married Henry's daughter."

"He is more than forty years her senior! That man is an animal. There can never be forgiveness for what he has done, never! Oh, there may be peace between England and France but there will never be peace between me and him."

The captain nodded and said, "So what do you intend to do about it?"

"I intend to drive a knife straight through his vile heart!"

"It is true, he deserves to die, but we must be wise in our pursuit. The Mary Rose is a distinguishable English carrack. To be seen would only prompt a declaration of war. Despite her ability in battle she would be an easy target so far into enemy territory. What we require is stealth, and the Santa Maria is more than capable of the task, and besides, the Rose is too large to sail into the Seine."

Maria was taken by surprise. She turned and looked into the ageing face of the General Córdoba. "You mean to sail straight into the heart of Paris?"

"I do. The best plans are often the most rash. It is the last thing the French will suspect. Anyhow, you share the name of this ship, do you not? A good omen." Gonzalo smiled at her.

It was only at that moment looking into his eyes that she realised it; *he does not think to return.* She diverted her eyes from his and gazed up at the ship's colours flapping in the breeze.

Upon it she saw the royal coat of arms of the Crown of Castile.
"You do know Spain is still at war with France?" she asked.

That made the captain chuckle. "You do not miss a thing,
Maria, as it happens I know everything there is to know about my
fellow countrymen," he replied. "But what do you suggest we do
about that?"

"A disguise."

The captain nodded, before raising two fingers to his mouth
and whistling. Two of his men came from the cabin, both clad in
French uniform. "We are nearing France, so change the colours
and ready the men."

Maria watched as the men lowered the red and white of
Castile to be replaced by the royal standard of the Kingdom of
France, golden fleur-de-lis on a sea of white. For the first time
that evening she smiled. *This may just work.* "I wonder, what will
King Ferdinand make of your expedition?"

"I have spent the last six years stuck in my family estate. One
small journey should not hurt. However the King, for want of a
politer phrase, can go fuck himself." Maria couldn't help but
laugh. Even at times like this Gonzalo only saw the bright side.
"Besides," he carried on. "The King is ill and my only consolation
in life is in the knowledge that he won't long out live me."

"He deserves all he gets. It's horrendous how you have been
treated by the King. You only ever served him well. You were his
greatest General, for God's sake!"

"Aye, I was. But it was only the love of Isabella that kept me in
his service. Ferdinand was jealous of my exploits and Alonso was
always poisoning his ears. Isabella was never warm towards his
bastard born son and why would she be? He was not hers but his
mistress's and she was the Queen. His presence at court was an
insult upon her. Alonso hated the fact that she favoured me.
Nothing he could ever do would appease her, not like I could. It
was no surprise after her death that Ferdinand had him replace
me as Viceroy of Naples. I was condemned by my King and

despised by his evil bastard son."

"Does Alonso still hold you responsible for the destruction of the Duke's fortress at Guadalest?"

"He is adamant that I persuaded your father to burn his son in law's castle in retribution. He knew your father was my man."

"But how could he think such? My father would never betray someone he served, and you would never ask him too."

"I'm afraid hatred runs deep, Maria and clouds most men's judgment. Alonso sees only what he wants to see. Banishment by his father to the confines of my family home was not enough for Alonso, it seems. I fear it is my life he seeks. "

The Santa Maria sailed towards the mouth of the Seine River where it opened out and poured into the Atlantic Sea, and with it came an icy breeze that brought on a thick fog, a bad omen. As they neared the coastal town of Le Havre the sound of French voices could be heard in the air as the early morning fisherman took to the water. Within hours the water would be swarming with them and the busy port laden with trading galleys. *We must hurry ourselves,* thought Maria.

"We will anchor the ship in the port," Gonzalo called to her. "From here we will sail the small boat."

"Are you coming with me?" she asked.

"To the end, as will four of my men," he replied. "Henrique?" the captain called to one of his guards. A smallish man with greasy curly brown hair and a goatee came to join them. Maria had only spoken to him on one or two occasions and both times he had made her feel uncomfortable. "Have the men lower the small boat, and then anchor the ship in port. I leave her in your capable hands, await our return."

* * *

As they lowered the boat into the water, the sound of raised voices drew ever closer. Out of the early morning mist came a small vessel heading straight towards them. Instantly the captain knew something was awry.

"Maria," he spoke softly. "Get into the boat." She had always been obedient, just as Richard had promised him she would be. She had never yet questioned his judgement, but this time there was a hesitant pause before she responded. He could feel her eyes at his back; *she can see straight through me.* Never had he felt as vulnerable as he did in that moment. Yet before long he heard the sound of her footsteps as she retreated to the small boat. The captain sighed in relief. He was glad that she hadn't chosen this as a first time to argue.

"Who are you and what is your business here?" a voice called in French. The men on the boat were soldiers.

"They want to know who we are, Señor," Henrique called to the captain. "What shall I tell them?"

"To bugger off!" he replied. "Can't they see we're French soldiers too?"

Henrique responded to them in their native tongue. Gonzalo had no idea what he had told them, but whatever it was they didn't seem too impressed. He watched the soldiers gathered at the bow of the vessel exchange awkward glances. They began to talk to one another hurriedly in French. "Ready the gun."

"Sir?" Henrique responded.

"You heard me. Do it now and do it discreetly."

"You heard the Captain, ready the gun larboard side," he whispered.

The Santa Maria had not come prepared for battle. Indeed she was no more than a merchant vessel if truth be told. A medium sized carrack, never designed for exploration, but already she had sailed the world and back. She only had two guns, one on the larboard side and one on the starboard side. They were not big guns as was usual with a military vessel such as the Mary Rose; they were more a precautionary measure if anything. *But they'll blow these bloody bastards to smithereens,* the captain thought.

"We know who you are!" the French voice called again, this time in English. "Surrender now and you will not be harmed. Refuse and you will all die!"

"I am afraid we will have to gracefully decline," the captain replied, causing laughter amongst his men.

"I am warning you, this is your last chance!"

"Turn the gun," Gonzalo commanded.

As the larboard gun was swivelled to face them, fear showed on the Frenchman's face. He started screaming at his men. Some of them let of shots into the air from their arquebuses but most attempted to escape into the sea.

"Fire!" the captain roared.

One minute the vessel was there, and the next it was on its way down to the water's depths. It was hit on the bow of the ship just below the water line. It was soon taking on huge amounts of water and within seconds was sinking front end first. Before long it was gone, the only evidence of its existence a few planks of woods and the bodies of the dead French soldiers as they bobbed on the water's surface.

"Maria," the captain called. "You must go. There will be more of them and they won't be far. I am sorry I cannot be with you till the end, but I will hold them off for as long as I can."

"Gonzalo no, please you can't," Maria cried in despair.

"Do not be afraid, child. You will see me again. My men will see you safe to the Hôtel Tournelles but you must hurry."

There was a dull thud that sounded off from somewhere in the distance followed by a small orange glow coming from the town of Le Havre, then came a low whistling that gradually got louder and louder until the sea erupted. Water splashed onto the deck and the ship started to rock. The town had opened fire and on the first attempt had only just missed.

"Take her and go!" the captain screamed at his four men who accompanied Maria in the small boat. They lowered their oars into the water and attempted to put some distance between themselves and the Santa Maria. Gonzalo could see the tears in Maria's eyes as she slowly moved away, disappearing into the fog. It was gut-wrenching watching her sail away and for a moment Gonzalo was lost.

Then there was a sudden glow of orange to the starboard side followed by a deafening explosion and the screaming started. The centre mast was struck and it came crashing down in spectacular fashion. Splinters of wood flew through the air, and men had to dive to the deck to avoid being hit as the sails went up in flames. *Where the hell did that come from?*

Then he saw her bow emerge from the fog; she was unmistakeable, and he would recognise that hull anywhere. She was the second biggest warship in Europe, the whole one thousand tons of her, with twenty four guns broadside. "My God," the captain stammered. "The Great Michael."

Maria was right, we should have brought the Rose. Naïve fool. Did you really think we would go unnoticed, you knew this would happen, you knew...

Sudden searing pain stabbed at Gonzalo's back. He gasped. Wincing, he lowered his hand to feel the hilt of the knife that had struck home. With severe agony he pulled the blade out and crumpled to his knees in a pool of his own blood. He looked at the blade in his hands. *I know this blade.*

"Compliments of Alonso," a voice behind him growled menacingly.

Henrique? Henrique, is that you?

"You will die alone, old man." The voice came closer now, clearer, whispering in his ear. He could feel the man's breath on his neck.

Mustering all the remaining strength he had left in him, Gonzalo grabbed the knife with two hands and drove it up hard over his shoulder. The blade plunged towards Henrique's face, who saw it coming. He was just able to raise himself enough in time to avoid a deadly blow, but could not stop the blade from tearing into his lower thigh just above the knee. There was a sickening crack as the tip of the blade penetrated the bone. Listening, Gonzalo could hear his grunts of pain and his stumbling footsteps as he tried to pull the blade free from his leg. It was short lived. Henrique crashed into the side rail of the ship which gave way and he fell into the sea below with a splash.

The Great Captain Córdoba watched as the Michael drew level with the Santa Maria. He raised both of his hands into the air and welcomed death. Looking up towards the sky his thoughts were only of one person, the only person he truly ever loved, his Queen... *Isabella... Isabella.*

* * *

The Hôtel des Tournelles, so named for the many small towers that adorned it, was a collection of buildings in Paris covering a mighty twenty acres. It was owned by the Kings of France and at present that honour belonged to King Louis XII. Deep in the confines of the Hôtel Tournelles, Mary Tudor lay in the King's bed. It was where she seemed to spend most of her days since her marriage to Louis. She was naked, as was his preference, and her young supple skin glinted in the candle light. She had been oiled and perfumed by her maids, though she didn't see the point. The King did not care. Sex was not joyous for them anymore; it had become nothing more than a chore. He had lusted for her once, of that she was certain, she had seen it in his hungry eyes, felt it in the way he had squeezed her breasts. But now they rarely even talked. He would climb on top of her, have his way and then he would leave. The King wanted one thing and one thing only and that was a male heir.

Despite two previous marriages, the King had no living sons and Mary knew she was his last hope. But as of yet she had been unable to provide him with a possible legitimate heir to the throne and she couldn't help but think the King held her entirely responsible. After all, they had only been married for three months, what did he expect? There would be plenty of time for her to conceive. Yet she couldn't help but notice how tiresome he had become of late, particularly how worn out he would be after their exertions in the bedchamber.

Tonight, however, she would try to please him, try to make him happy again. She would pleasure him in the ways her maids had taught her, allowing him to relax. She would show the King that she could love him and be the wife that he wanted her to be. Maybe tonight she would conceive him a son and spare herself his wrath. She waited for him to arrive. Her red hair flowed down past her shoulders, her breasts were visible above the silk sheet that covered her abdomen and her legs hung out from below. She felt pretty, and she hoped the King would think so too.

Louis arrived, slamming the door behind him. He stumbled across the room, muttering to himself as he went. Mary could not make out his words as they were slurred. *He's drunk again.* He didn't so much as even glance at his wife when he entered, let alone speak to her. She watched him as he tried to undress himself, keeping his back to her.

"Would you like some help, your Grace?" Mary asked the King.

His only response was a grunt. She slipped from the sheet and rolled out of bed. Taking her time, she walked around in front of the King. She took off his sword belt first and then helped him remove his shirt before lowering his hose. He was looking at her, she could tell. *What is he thinking?*

"Will you ever give me a son?" he asked. Mary could smell the wine on his breath.

"If it please your Grace, I would like to try tonight."

She took Louis by the hand and walked him to the bed, and there she gently pushed him down onto his back. When he was comfortable, she got onto the bed and put one leg over him and with her hand she began to stroke his manhood. When he was hard she lowered herself onto him and felt him enter her. Slowly she started to raise herself up and down. She closed her eyes and let out a moan but when she looked back down into the King's face all she saw was anger.

"Do you think you can sway my mind with such games!" he growled. "All I require from you is a son and nothing more!"

The King grabbed her wrist and pulled hard, forcing her down onto her front. She lay face down on the bed. With his left arm, Louis held her down by her neck, while with his right he helped himself inside her. He took her then from behind in brutal fashion while she sobbed into her pillow.

* * *

There was movement in the shadows. *So this is what my mother was put through, pain and humiliation.* Maria witnessed all from the corner of the room as the man she despised above all others tormented another woman. But it would all be over soon, she knew. She watched the King roll off his victim to lie alongside her. He was panting fiercely.

"Get me water!" he demanded of his wife.

Still sobbing, Mary obeyed. She slipped out of bed, put on her robe and left the room. *Now is the time to act.* Maria stepped out of the shadows, clad in black, her hood raised and made her way towards the King. He lay on the bed, beads of sweat glistening on his chest, his breath heavy. He never heard her approach. Maria looked down upon him, gazed into the face of the wretched creature, a foul beast and scum of the earth. She raised her blade high into the air. *For mother!*

The door to the King's bedchamber opened. Mary entered, carrying a jug of water. She gasped when she saw the assassin stood over her lord husband. She let go of the jug and it went hurtling to the floor where it smashed into pieces and water trickled across the stone floor. The King's eyes opened. Although ageing, he was quick, and he rolled to avoid Maria's thrust, causing her blade to sink deep into the mattress releasing a sudden bombardment of feathers into the air. Louis had time to react. He flung himself from the bed and made for his sword. Maria drew her own. *So this is how you choose to die, so be it.*

They met head on in a clash of steel high in the King's tower in the Hôtel Tournelles, the robed assailant and the naked King. From the far side of the room, Mary watched on in horror, scared and frightened. She wanted to scream for help but no words came out, she wanted to run but she couldn't move. The King came at Maria in a flurried attack, and his blows were heavy. Maria parried them with difficulty but she could sense he was tiring and soon would be unable to swing no more and she would have her vengeance.

But the King did not stop coming, his blows came more frequent and heavier still. Soon Maria's hands started to ache, and her feeling of anger and hatred soon turned to fear. She could not hold on to her sword any longer. With a grunt, the King gave one final cut and drove Maria's sword from her hands, to go clattering across the floor. She fell to her knees.

"Who are you?" the King demanded as he ripped the hood back over her head. "You!"

Maria had tears in her eyes. She had failed. *My mother, my father and now Gonzalo, all of their deaths have been in vain, I have failed them.*

"I remember you," Louis said. "I remember your mother too, I watched her die but not before I fucked her tight cunt! But you," the King went on. "I'm going to do you the other way round. I'm going to stick you with my sword then I'm going to fuck your dead corpse!"

"Louis," Mary said.

He turned his head. She smiled; she had obviously done all she needed to.

Maria was shaking with fury. She only had eyes for the King, but someone else had drawn his attention. Mary stood there defiantly. She had the same pain in her eyes this night that Maria felt herself every day. They had both suffered at the King's hands, but no more. She pounced. Taking the dagger from her belt, the same blade her father had used to kill Simon, the last thing he had bestowed upon her before he disappeared. She wasted no time in driving it high and hard, crunching into the King's chest. She heard ribs crack and heard the King's muffled groan before he fell to the floor, dead.

Maria put her head in her hands. *Mother, I have avenged you, mother.*

"Who are you?" Mary asked.

Maria raised her head to look at Mary Tudor, the Queen Consort of France. "My name is Maria Rois of Llauri."

"I know you. Your father served my brother Henry, and it was your mother that died at the Battle of the Spurs."

Is that what they were calling it now? Maria nodded.

"God, I am so sorry. I never wanted to marry him, my brother made me, he wanted peace with France. You must believe me."

"Did you ever love him?"

"No, I tried to, but I couldn't. I have only ever loved one man."

"Who?"

"Charles Brandon, the Duke of Suffolk." Mary sighed.

"Then I suggest, my lady, that you find this Charles and you reconcile."

Footsteps could be heard on the staircase.

"You must go," Mary replied. "I will give you as much time as I can but I must cry out for help otherwise they will think I played a part."

Maria stood up, bowed to the Queen and made her way towards the window.

But before she could leave, Mary spoke again. "How old are you?" she asked.

"Thirteen," Maria responded, her back still turned.

"Such a brave young soul, you are."

"No less than is expected of me."

"But, why?"

This time Maria turned and she smiled. "Because, your Grace, I am a Longsword."

Author's Note

For me history is everything. Without it we would not exist, with it we have purpose, integrity and inspiration. To look into our past is to unlock a door of mystery, a world of discoverable truth long forgotten. What makes it potent however is when it is accompanied by a good story. After all, history over the years has provided us with some of the most memorable of tales. Robin Hood and King Arthur are two such notable figures that spring to mind. Whether or not these characters were real or fictional is debatable but often it is necessary to distort the truth in order to tell a good story. What matters is that history is preserved and if this means romanticizing it somewhat then so be it; we all learnt, did we not, from the story of William Wallace, having witnessed his exaggerated portrayal in Braveheart? Who cares if it wasn't 100% historically accurate, it was a good story, right?

I read something that one of my favourite authors once wrote in an article to aspiring HF writers and he said in essence that we are not historians but story tellers. It is easy to become bogged down with historical detail but what is more important is that we tell a good story, the history will follow. I felt I had a good story and one worth telling and so where better to set it then in a real time period, a fictional plot twisted with real and exciting events that actual took place. I have a fondness for all things medieval and it is there at the end of the medieval age, during the early Renaissance that I chose to set my novel. I have, as you can imagine, made several tweaks in order to let the story flow but I have to the best of my ability tried to make the story as historically accurate as possible.

The first thing to note is in the second prologue, Richard Longsword is of course a fictional character but his exploits at the Battle of Illora were based on real events experienced by the Duke Infantado. For this I must acknowledge the text by

Washington Irving titled; Conquest of Granada: From the Manuscript of Fray Antonio Aqapida. When I was researching into the Conquest, I stumbled upon this book completely by chance and I was so intrigued by Aqapida's account of the Duke's story that I felt compelled to include it. The Duke, as you know, I did not replace entirely but included still so that he may share in the adventure.

In the first chapter Richard introduces himself as the Baron of Alcalalí, however the barony of Alcalalí was not created until a hundred years later in 1616, for the first Baron Ximen Pérez Rois of Liori. Note that Liori is the official term, though I once read it referred to as Llaurí which is of course the way in which I chose to portray it in the story. The reason for this was that there was a village called Llaurí in that part of Spain that I wanted to use as the birth place for Richard's love interest Louisa, so as you can imagine it fitted together quite nicely.

Descriptions of some of the locations namely Guadalest were somewhat imaginary. All of them have been researched thoroughly but not all locations were visited and not all have substantial enough evidence in books for me to draw my own conclusions. I have visited the castle at Guadalest but little remains from the era in which I have written and therefore I have described it both how I picture it and how I visualise my characters in it. The emblem of the Guardians bears an uncanny resemblance to that of the Crown of Castile, that's because it is, all be it with two bulls instead of lions and a slight change in colour.

For those of you that know your history I am sure you will already have cursed me for the inclusion of Christopher Columbus' ship the Santa Maria which did indeed run aground on his first voyage to the Americas in 1492. I did this purely because I felt it proved a nice touch particularly in the epilogue where it guided Maria on her final quest. That said, if rumour can be believed, Columbus' flag ship on his final voyage he renamed after the first, so the Santa Maria's inclusion is potentially realistic.

The Battle of Guinegate, more commonly referred to as the Battle of the Spurs, I did exaggerate somewhat. It is true that an army under the leadership of King Henry VIII routed a body of French cavalry under the leadership of Jacques de la Palice. However King Louis himself was never present and the courageous defence of the bridge by the Chevalier de Bayard though true, actually took place at the Battle of Garigliano.

Other inclusions include the Priory Inn which was the first location I ever conceived when planning the novel and is not knowingly based on any real establishment. The character Alexander Jiménez and his story are completely fictitious though both Albacete and Chinchilla are real locations. The murder of the princes in the tower, though widely regarded as accurate, has never been proved. Bodies thought to be theirs were found beneath the chapel staircase but there was no way to determine if they were in fact those of the princes. Richard III is a name thrown in the mix as a potential killer because he gained to profit the most from their deaths but it was James Tyrell who actually admitted to killing them under torture. The exact truth will probably never be known but I have come to my own conclusion after consulting the facts.

King Louis' death was somewhat dramatized. He did die at the Hôtel Tournelles in January 1515 but not because he was murdered. The General Córdoba too did not die as described but died a month earlier at his home in December 1514. There is no evidence to suggest my claim that the General's love with Queen Isabella was real, however, I am pleased to inform you that his prediction of not long being out lived by King Ferdinand proved true. He died a very bitter man in January 1516.

Any other historical inaccuracies that occur are completely my own doing but were not done so intentionally.

Acknowledgements

First and foremost I would like to congratulate my fellow course mates from Southampton Solent University, Davie Toothill and Sam Kearns, whose novels *Armed* and *The Darkness Under the Rainbow* were published in May and December 2013 respectively. I must mention Sandra Cain my tutor, without whom quite simply I would never have persevered. I must also say a special thank you to Darrell Foley whose insight proved both helpful and inspiring. My appreciation goes to my proof readers, chiefly among them Stephen and Ross Cavinder whose time and energy was most encouraging. I am grateful also to my family and friends for all their support, in particular my mother and father for both their confidence and their guidance and to Sam for all things but most importantly for putting up with me. Lastly I must add thanks to Autumn Barlow and the rest of the team at Top Hat for realising my potential. My gratitude to all goes beyond mere words.

TOP HAT BOOKS

Historical fiction that lives.

We publish fiction that captures the contrasts, the achievements, the optimism and the radicalism of ordinary and extraordinary times across the world.

We're open to all time periods and we strive to go beyond the narrow, foggy slums of Victorian London. Where are the tales of the people of fifteenth century Australasia? The stories of eighth century India? The voices from Africa, Arabia, cities and forests, deserts and towns? Our books thrill, excite, delight and inspire.

The genres will be broad but clear. Whether we're publishing romance, thrillers, crime, or something else entirely, the unifying themes are timescale and enthusiasm. These books will be a celebration of the chaotic power of the human spirit in difficult times. The reader, when they finish, will snap the book closed with a satisfied smile.